THE PERFECT HOME

NATASHA BOYDELL

Boldwood

First published in Great Britain in 2024 by Boldwood Books Ltd.

Cover Design by Head Design Ltd

Cover Imagery: Shutterstock

The moral right of Natasha Boydell to be identified as the author of this work has been asserted in accordance with the Copyright, Designs and Patents Act 1988.

A CIP catalogue record for this book is available from the British Library.

Paperback ISBN 978-1-83533-310-5

Large Print ISBN 978-1-83533-311-2

Hardback ISBN 978-1-83533-309-9

Ebook ISBN 978-1-83533-312-9

Kindle ISBN 978-1-83533-313-6

Audio CD ISBN 978-1-83533-304-4

MP3 CD ISBN 978-1-83533-305-1

Digital audio download ISBN 978-1-83533-307-5

Boldwood Books Ltd
23 Bowerdean Street
London SW6 3TN
www.boldwoodbooks.com

The Westford Star

23 July 2024

Police are investigating the disappearance of a sixteen-year-old girl from Westford.

Poppy Sanderson was last seen by her friends at 11 p.m. on Saturday in the grounds of the Westford Park housing development where she lives. She didn't return home that night.

Poppy is described as tall, with long, dark brown hair. She was wearing blue jeans and a cropped white T-shirt. Officers are appealing for anyone with information to get in touch.

Westford Park is a new, luxury development on the land of the former Westford Golf Club, which was sold five years ago. The one hundred acres of grounds boast a country club, swimming pool and lake. Building of the 240 homes was completed in 2023.

One resident, who asked not to be named, said: 'Everyone is in shock. I can't believe that something like this could happen here. Westford Park is usually a friendly, close-knit community but people seem to be turning on each other and tensions are really high. Yesterday I actually saw two middle-aged women fighting in the street. There are all sorts of rumours flying about.'

The resident added: 'The parents here seem to let their children roam around the grounds at all hours without any supervision. I just pray they find Poppy soon.'

Since Poppy disappeared, the hashtag #findpoppy has gone viral on social media, and police have urged people not to speculate about her disappearance. Chief Inspector Jane Summers of Westford Police said: 'Our priority is to ensure that Poppy returns home safely to her family and I would urge anyone with information that may help our enquiries to contact us.'

1

A YEAR EARLIER

Evil. Avril Jones recoiled as the word appeared in her mind. Once, it would have had no effect on her, it would have been as innocuous as the next word in the dictionary. *Evince. Eviscerate.* But now it was loaded with meaning, a haunting and relentless reminder that no matter how hard she tried to escape, evil was determined to follow. Even up the M1.

Profoundly immoral and wicked (4). Avril reread the crossword clue and gripped her pen tightly as she wrote the answer down. Then she turned the newspaper over so she couldn't see it any more. She had lost her appetite for finishing the crossword and it was making her feel carsick anyway.

There were four of them crammed into a small, silver Mini Cooper and yet the silence was deafening. Avril glanced anxiously at her children in the rearview mirror. Tom had his headphones on and was playing a game on his iPad and Bethany was staring out of the window, her expression vacant like someone had reached inside her and ripped out her soul.

Avril looked away and fanned her face with the glossy brochure she was clutching in her left hand. The brochure promised buyers an exciting new lifestyle in a unique, luxurious setting. If anyone needed a new lifestyle right now, it was them. Or a new life, come to think of it.

Stuart was driving seven miles per hour under the speed limit, his hands in the ten and two position he'd been taught during driving lessons and had adhered to rigidly for the next three decades, as though someone might snatch his licence away if he deviated for even a second. Avril wondered if his hands might one day become permanently stuck in the position. She imagined him getting older and balder, his arms outstretched in front of him and his fingers curled around an imaginary steering wheel, long after he had stopped driving. Sometimes she looked at him and wondered what she'd ever seen in him, if she'd ever truly loved him. She thought that she had but somewhere along the way, the love had eroded, perhaps around the time they had stopped laughing. Or listening. Or considering one another.

She hadn't considered him when she had spontaneously part-exchanged their sturdy, reliable Honda for the Silver Bullet, as she liked to call it. Stuart loathed the Mini Cooper. He thought it was overpriced and impractical, and he complained that he felt like he was driving a go-kart. Avril adored it because it was new and exciting. When she bought it, he had asked her if she was having a midlife crisis. She had responded, through gritted teeth, that if it was a midlife crisis she was having, she'd have left him for a hot young man and bought a Ferrari.

Not that they could afford a Ferrari. They'd just spent all their savings and taken out an eye-watering mortgage on a three-storey townhouse so that they could enjoy an 'exciting new lifestyle in a unique, luxurious setting'. They may be living off air for the fore-seeable future, but, as far as Avril was concerned, it was a price worth paying.

Stuart was worried that they had borrowed too much money.

He fretted about leaving their home in Hampshire, which was closer to his parents, and his job in IT. He thought their new neighbours would be snobs. He said the service charge was extortionate and the country club an unnecessary extravagance. Avril disagreed with him on all counts.

What was wrong with wanting to better their lives? To live among the wealthy, to swim in a beautiful pool every morning and then stroll down by the lake, watching kayakers bobbing about on the water. For their children to have more opportunities and the glorious freedom to explore that they could never have in the city. To breathe in fresh air every day. But these weren't the real reasons why they were moving, nor were they the reason why Stuart had reluctantly agreed to it.

The real reason. It was unspoken between them, just like the four-letter word that tormented her. *Evil.* Avril glanced in the mirror again and then, uncharacteristically, stretched out a hand and placed it on top of Stuart's. It was hot and clammy. He didn't enjoy long drives and he loathed motorways. But she was grateful to the M1 because it was taking them away from the past, towards a better life. It was their chance to start again, to wipe the slate clean. Rebuild their family and repair the damage that had been caused. She just hoped they weren't too late.

She had to stay positive because she was the only one of them who was, so it was her job to buoy them all up. She had initiated this life-changing move, and she was determined to prove that it was the right decision. She closed her eyes and imagined having coffee with her new friends while the kids played with the neighbour's children. Starting work in a new school, where people didn't stare and whisper behind her back. She thought of Tom joining a local football team and making new buddies who knew him only for him, and not for what his family had unwittingly become notorious for. Of Bethany smiling, her beautiful face lighting up just like it used to, her daughter coming back to her again. And of laughing with Stuart and him turning to her to say, 'You were right, Avril, this was the best bloody decision we ever made.'

Not that Stuart ever said 'bloody', but that wasn't the point. Things were going to be different at Westford Park. Avril was going to make bloody sure of it.

* * *

'Grab that box over there, will you, Micky?'

Sandy Delahaye swept her hand across her sweaty brow and wiped it on her shorts as she watched her sixteen-year-old son lean down to pick up the box.

'Where do you want it, Mum?'

'In the kitchen, sweetheart.'

Micky obediently carried the box inside and Sandy paused for a moment to take in the house, its gleaming windows and white wooden porch. Inside it smelled of paint and varnish and it was so spotlessly clean that they'd been able to start putting their crockery straight into the cupboards without even wiping them. Sandy sighed with pleasure.

Clare emerged, holding their four-year-old daughter Isla's hand. Isla's brown eyes were as wide as saucers, and she was bursting with excitement. Sandy wished that her son felt the same way but that was just how it was with teenagers. He'd get over it. Eventually.

'Isla and I are going to explore the grounds,' Clare said. 'Want to come?'

'Mummy, I want to go swimming,' Isla said, hopping from foot to foot impatiently.

Sandy smiled fondly at her daughter. 'There'll be plenty of time for that, sweetheart. But I don't even know where your swimming costume is. You two go off adventuring and I'll get stuck into the unpacking.'

She watched Clare and Isla disappear down the gravel path, heading towards the lake. She should go inside and check on Micky, start tackling the endless piles of boxes, but she couldn't resist standing a while longer, with the sun beating down on her face.

It felt like they were on holiday, and she couldn't quite believe that this was their life now. That they would be coming home to this house every day, barbecuing in the garden, swimming in the heated outdoor pool, and having dinner on the clubhouse terrace. Isla would start at the local primary school after the holidays and when they went to see it, Sandy had fallen in love with the colourful displays and happy, smiling teachers. It was all perfect.

Their friends had said they were mad when they told them they were selling their beautiful house in Northampton and moving eight miles away to Westford Park.

'What on earth are you going to do there, out of the thick of it all?' one of them had asked.

'Relax,' Sandy had replied with a beatific smile. 'Be free. Be with nature.'

And their friends had rolled their eyes and said they'd be selling up again within a year. But Sandy was perfectly happy to prove them wrong. This, here, was paradise. She was going to walk every morning, listening to the birds' dawn chorus, and search for rabbits and hedgehogs in the fields and woodland. She was going to paint every day; she could feel her fingers itching, inspiration already building inside her.

But first, unpacking. She walked through the open front door and located Micky, riffling around in some boxes in the kitchen.

'Where's the food, Mum? I'm starving.'

'There's some milk in the fridge and some cereal in that box over there. It'll have to do for now until we've unpacked a bit more.'

Micky walked over to the fridge, his long limbs making the journey in a fraction of time. He was a handsome boy, and popular too. He looked so much like his father that sometimes Sandy had to look away and catch her breath, reminding herself that the likeness was in appearance only. Micky was not his father; he was kind, thoughtful and good-natured.

Today, though, he was sulking. He didn't want to move. But it was only a few miles away, nothing needed to change for him. He'd still go to the same school, have the same girlfriend. Sandy thought about the other kids who would be living at Westford Park. She imagined tall, confident, privately educated girls, and wondered if Micky's head would turn. And so what if it did? He was only sixteen and he had the rest of his life ahead of him. Lucky Micky.

Micky devoured his cereal in seconds and threw his bowl carelessly into the sink. Sandy tried not to flinch at the clatter it made.

'I'm going for a walk,' he said, already pulling out his phone.

'Okay, enjoy yourself.'

With Micky gone, the house was quiet and still. Sandy could faintly hear children laughing and shouting in the distance. She peered at the cereal bowl in the sink and remembered Micky as a young boy, before the adolescent years set in. In those days he'd wanted sugary cereal, Coco Pops and Frosties, not the plain Weetabix he favoured now.

Other mothers might have become nostalgic in that moment, remembering the innocence of their child's early years. And Micky had been such a fun, energetic little lad, always busy looking for something to climb up or hurtle down. They should have been happy memories, but they weren't. They were tarnished and Sandy shook her head, trying to rid them from her mind. She was safe now, she reminded herself. They were all safe.

Perhaps it was the upheaval of moving that had brought the past to the forefront of her mind again. She was exhausted from the last few days, overwhelmed by the prospect of all the unpacking they had to do. That was it, nothing more, and it would pass again soon. This was their new start, a place where history didn't belong and wasn't welcome.

Sandy smiled as she heard Clare and Isla's voices and moments later, they appeared in the kitchen. Isla was clutching a lollipop.

'They have free lollipops!' she exclaimed ecstatically. 'This is the best day ever!'

Sandy looked quizzically at Clare, who grinned. 'We went to the boathouse and the man who works there very kindly gave Isla a lolly.'

'Ah, I see. And did you enjoy exploring?'

The question was aimed at Clare, but Isla interjected. 'I loved it, Mummy! I love Westfield Park!'

'Westford Park, darling. Your new home.' Sandy turned to Clare. 'And you?'

'It's great. It's really great.' Clare came over and put her arm around Sandy. 'I think we're going to be extremely happy here.'

'Tell that to Micky.'

'Micky will be fine.'

'I know. I know he will.'

'Right.' Clare was rolling up her sleeves. 'How about we put on a film for Isla so we can carry on unpacking? Where on earth is the box with the remote control?'

Sandy watched her wife rummage around in a couple of boxes before pulling out the remote control and waving it victoriously in the air. She was so lucky to have Clare. To have Micky and Isla. To be able to afford to live here, in the glorious grounds of Westford Park.

Their friends were wrong, she thought determinedly. This was where they were meant to be, she could feel it in her bones. This would be the last time they moved. They would finally settle down here and build the happy life that they all deserved. She'd said it before, but this time she really meant it and nothing, or no one, was going to stand in their way.

She glanced over at the patio doors and felt the immediate urge to make sure they were locked. *Just once. I'll check them just once.* She frowned, yearning and frustration growing inside her. This wasn't meant to happen here, things were supposed to be different. She stayed rooted to the spot, a statue frozen in a storm of indecision, an internal battle raging.

'You okay, love?'

Sandy tore her eyes away from the doors and looked at Clare, who was watching her curiously. Shame began to creep up inside her. She owed it to Clare to make things work at Westford Park, and Micky and Isla too. Most of all, she owed it to herself.

She clenched her fists and smiled. 'I'm great. Where shall we start?'

* * *

Lily Sanderson was hot and more than a little bothered. The removal men were supposed to have followed them to the new house but, after half an hour, she hadn't seen hide nor hair of them. The sods had probably gone to McDonald's, or the pub. She wished she was at the pub.

Eric was outside, talking on his phone. His tanned legs were muscular from his after-work golf and squash sessions, and Lily cocked her head to the side and admired the way his salmon polo shirt fitted tightly over his broad shoulders. Seventeen years of marriage and she still fancied the pants off her husband. How many people could say that? Not many, she bet.

But where the hell were the removal men? Lily peered up the road looking for any signs of them. She started when she heard a noise behind her and turned to see her daughter, Poppy.

'Poppy, you made me jump,' she said, putting one hand over her chest.

Poppy didn't reply. With a huff, she lifted herself up onto the kitchen island and crossed one long leg over the other. She had inherited her father's beautiful skin and dark hair, and his stubbornness to boot. But her eyes were definitely Lily's. At least she could lay claim to the eyes.

'I'm bored,' Poppy declared, rolling said eyes up to the sky.

'You're always bored. Go and find something to do.'

'And how am I expected to do that when none of our things have arrived yet? Or when you've moved us into the arse-end of nowhere, come to that.'

'Language, Poppy!'

'Arse isn't a swear word, Mother.'

Lily appraised her daughter. 'Why don't you go for a walk? See if you can find some friends.'

'Because I'm not six years old, Mother.'

Lily tried not to wince at Poppy's use of the word Mother. She wasn't fussy, she'd take Mum, Mummy or even Ma, but it had been quite some time since she had been blessed with one of these terms of endearment from her daughter. Or any, come to think of it.

To cheer Poppy up, she said, 'As we were driving in, I saw a boy about your age walking towards the lake. He was quite handsome.'

'Oh, God.' Poppy slapped her hand against her forehead. 'You are *so* embarrassing.'

Lily's patience, already tested after days of organising and packing, threw in the towel. 'For goodness' sake, Poppy, stop complaining. We've just bought the most expensive house in this development, you'll have the best facilities in the area on your doorstep and you'll be the envy of all your friends. What more, exactly, do you want?'

'And you think that's what matters in life, do you? A posh house and a posh pool. That's the key to happiness. Throw money at it and it will all be fine. As long as everything looks shiny on the outside, who gives a shit what's going on inside?'

'*Language*, Poppy!'

Lily wanted to empathise, but she couldn't really see what Poppy had to complain about. She was young, beautiful, popular and clever. She came from a stable, loving home. Lily had done everything she could to ensure that her daughter had the perfect life, one far better than she'd had growing up. She had shielded her from life's cruelties so that she could have an innocent, happy childhood. Poppy didn't know about the sacrifice that Lily had made for her, and she didn't need to know, but an occasional acknowledgement of her privilege might be nice.

She was a teenage girl, though, ready to take on the world, to fight convention, to argue every little point. Lily had to admire her daughter's passion, if not her temper.

She turned to the window again. 'These removal men better get here soon.'

'Speaking of handsome, one of the removal men was quite fit.'

'Very droll, Poppy.'

'I'm serious. I might ask him out.'

Lily hid her wry smile. When she'd been a teenager, she'd fancied older men too, but that was another thing Poppy wouldn't be hearing about. 'Knock yourself out. Even better, do it in front of Daddy because I'd really like to see his reaction to *that*.'

'Father knows better than to say anything.'

Lily's head swivelled away from the window. 'And what's that supposed to mean?'

Poppy looked away. 'Nothing. Maybe I will go for that walk.'

Lily scrutinised her daughter. Poppy had once adored her father but now she had a bee in her bonnet about everyone, him included, and Lily wasn't sure what he'd done this time to earn her disapproval. Most likely refused to give her the money for a new handbag.

Poppy hopped elegantly down from the kitchen island and flicked her long hair behind her shoulders. 'Call me when my stuff arrives.'

Lily watched her leave with a sinking heart. She fretted about Poppy going out alone. She worried about stalkers and serial killers. Most weekends she stayed up late so that she could go and pick her daughter up from evenings out and Poppy complained that she was too controlling, that her friends were allowed out later and they all took Ubers home. Lily didn't care what Poppy's friends did, she cared about Poppy. But here, things would be different. This was a safe, secure community. Poppy could enjoy a bit more freedom without Lily breathing down her neck. And maybe that would help to mend the rift that had formed between them when Poppy turned thirteen and decided that her parents, once her heroes, were her mortal enemies.

But now she was nearly sixteen and she wanted to rebel. Lily could hardly blame her; she had been a tearaway at that age herself and sometimes she marvelled at how she'd survived those years given the risks she'd taken. But her experience meant she also knew that life was full of danger and she couldn't bear the thought of Poppy facing such peril. That was one of the reasons why they had moved to Westford Park. She craved the golden days, when children played out on the street without fear of abduction or being squashed by a speeding car, and neighbours looked out for each other. It was the life she had always dreamed of: white picket fences and the smell of apple pie. The heated pool and country club certainly helped.

Speaking of neighbours, there was a car pulling up outside the house opposite. Lily gazed out of the window curiously as a woman emerged from a Mini Cooper and stretched her back before pulling the front seat forward. A minute later two gangly children climbed out. Christ, how on earth did they all manage to fit inside that little car? Lily's eyes wandered gratefully to her Range Rover parked in the driveway and then back to the new arrivals.

The husband had appeared and was standing by the car, cleaning his glasses. The woman went to talk to him, gesturing at the boot. She was wearing a pretty Boden dress and Lily made a mental note of it, storing it up as a conversation starter for when they met. Perhaps they might share clothing catalogues or go shopping together once they got to know each other. Lily glowed at the prospect of making new friends at Westford Park. Then she felt the familiar twinge of anxiety and wondered if the woman would like her, or if she would see straight through her.

Next, she appraised the two children. The boy was around eleven or twelve, she guessed, but the girl looked a similar age to Poppy. Although she was tall, she was a slip of a thing, all pale skin and dark, baggy clothes. She looked miserable too and Lily guessed that, just like Poppy, this girl was sulking about being forced to move house and be separated from all her friends. Maybe she and Poppy could pal up. It would be nice for Poppy to have someone the same age living nearby. Perhaps they'd go to the same school and could get the bus home together. Poppy could even give the girl a makeover, get her out of those dowdy clothes. Like in her favourite film, *Clueless*.

Lily heard the rumbling of an engine and craned her neck to look down the street. Here was the lorry at last. She glanced at Eric, who was still on the phone, and felt a sudden urge to cry. This was not the new start she had planned, the one where Eric was finally present, came home on time every evening and spent the weekend with his family. He couldn't even switch off his phone on moving day. Any second now, her husband would slink over with a remorseful expression and say that there was some work emergency or that a coveted last-minute slot had become available at the golf club. He'd probably return with a present for her, some flowers or an expensive bottle of wine that he'd picked up on the way home. And she would smile, and kiss him, and thank him for the thoughtful gesture. It was how they'd always done things, but she'd hoped it would be different here.

Still, it was only day one. There was plenty of time for things to change. Lily would go shopping to get some sexy new underwear and maybe even send a naughty photo to Eric. That would get him off the golf course and into her arms. It was all she wanted, her husband in her arms. She pushed aside her habitual feeling of dread and went out to greet the removal men.

2

Avril took a deep breath and dived into the pool, relishing the shock as her body hit the cool water. She resurfaced and started doing a front crawl, swimming ten lengths before stopping to catch her breath. Resting her arms on the side of the pool, she looked around.

The poolside was quiet. They had been one of the first families to move into Westford Park but, by next summer, it would probably be rammed from dawn until dusk. By then, they would have been here a year, and it would really feel like home. Avril wondered how they would be. Would she and Stuart have healed the rift between them? Would Bethany be Bethany again? The prospect felt like a mirage, floating tantalisingly on the horizon, teasing her with its allure. But maybe it would happen. The sun and the swim had made her hopeful.

She spotted a woman lying on a sun lounger, reading a glossy magazine. She was wearing oversized sunglasses and a large sunhat, and her pink toenails gleamed in the sun. She was preened, polished and beautiful, and Avril couldn't tear her eyes away. The woman looked up and saw Avril watching her, and Avril smiled shyly, embarrassed at having been caught staring.

But the woman didn't seem offended by the attention. She got up elegantly and walked over, sitting down near Avril and dangling her legs in the turquoise water.

'Christ, it's hot,' she remarked.

'Yes,' Avril said.

'I'm Lily.' The woman extended a hand.

Avril took it, smiling apologetically at her wet fingers. 'Avril.'

'When did you move?'

'Three days ago, you?'

'Same. Actually, I think you might live opposite us.'

They exchanged addresses, confirming that Lily was right, before moving on to other perfunctory topics, like where they had moved from and how many children they had.

'Will your daughter be going to Weston Abbey?' Lily asked.

'Oh no,' Avril replied, almost apologetic about the fact that their children wouldn't be attending the popular nearby private school. 'Both kids are going to Westford High.'

Lily seemed disappointed. 'That's a shame.'

'Yes.'

Avril's eyes drifted over Lily's perfect outfit, her highlighted hair and gleaming nail polish. She looked like she belonged at Westford Park and, for a moment, Avril panicked. Had Stuart been right all along? Were they going to be the outsiders among the other residents who played tennis and golf and drank gin and tonics with breakfast? She was terrible at tennis, but she was willing to try the gins if that's what it took. But what about the kids? Had she taken them to a place where they'd be even more like fish out of water than they had been previously? All she wanted was for them to be happy, to make friends and to live a normal life but suddenly she began to wonder if she'd made a terrible mistake by moving to Westford Park.

She was surprised when Lily said, 'Do you fancy a coffee?'

'Oh, yes, I'd love that.' Avril thought about the unpacking she still had to do, and the fact that Bethany and Tom were at home alone, and then climbed out of the pool and wrapped herself in a towel. 'Just give me five minutes to change.'

'Take your time.'

Lily drifted back to her sunbed and picked up her magazine again, and Avril hurried towards the changing rooms, peeling off her costume and slipping her underwear and sundress on. After quickly towel-drying her hair and then stuffing her damp things into a bag, she dashed outside, not wanting to keep her potential new friend waiting.

She waved at Lily and they walked to the clubhouse together. They chose a seat inside, away from the glare of the sun, and ordered their drinks. Avril felt like a child on the first day of school, but Lily seemed perfectly at ease as she leaned back in her chair and smiled.

'I love your sundress. Boden?'

Avril beamed. 'Yes. I got it in the sale last year.'

'We should introduce Poppy and your daughter. Bethany, is it?'

'Yes, that's right, Bethany. She's at home at the moment, with her brother.'

'Poppy's an only child. And before you ask, yes she acts like one, the spoiled little madam.'

Avril's eyes widened in surprise at how openly Lily had criticised her own daughter. She'd never said a bad word about Bethany to anyone, even after all the vile rumours and gossip. But then she saw the wry look on Lily's face and realised that she was teasing.

'Takes after her father, of course,' Lily continued proudly.

'Beautiful, stubborn and strong-willed. No interest in studying for her GCSEs, even though she's perfectly capable. Just wants to shop, go out with her friends and flirt with boys. I bet Bethany's the same, right?'

Bethany couldn't be any further from the same. Avril laughed nervously. 'Bethany's very studious, actually. And she prefers staying in to going out.'

Lily raised her perfectly threaded eyebrows. 'Really? Lucky you.'

'Tom, my twelve-year-old, is very sociable,' Avril added quickly, in case Lily thought they were oddballs. 'He's sporty too so he's looking forward to joining the school football team. Hopefully, there will be some boys here at Westford Park for him to play with.'

'I've seen a teenage boy hanging around a few times, but he's more Bethany and Poppy's age. Other than that, it seems to be younger children so far, but there are plenty more families still to move in. I think all the properties are sold now.'

'We were so lucky to get one,' Avril gushed.

'Yes. When I saw the house, I said to Eric, "This is the one, I can just feel it."'

Avril got the distinct impression that Lily and Eric hadn't had to take out a hefty mortgage to buy their home. Or perhaps any mortgage at all.

'Do you work?' she asked Lily.

Lily shook her head. 'No, not any more. How about you?'

'I'm a teacher, part-time. I'll be starting at Bethany and Tom's school in September.'

Lily snorted. 'I bet they're delighted about that.'

Avril grinned. 'Tom's not bothered. I don't think Bethany's impressed at all.'

'So why did you decide to move so far away?'

Avril was immediately on high alert, beads of sweat beginning to form, despite the air conditioning in the clubhouse. She had known that she would be asked this question and she had rehearsed her answer enough times, but saying the words in her head was different to saying them out loud. She silently counted to three and forced a smile.

'I was targeted on Facebook, would you believe it? An ad came up on my feed about Westford Park and when I clicked on the link and downloaded the brochure, I was completely seduced. It's just such a unique setting, isn't it?'

It wasn't a lie, but it wasn't the truth either. Lily didn't need to know that, though. No one needed to know because that was the whole point of fresh starts. Avril waited nervously for her reaction, fearing that Lily might see straight through her.

'Oh, that's *so* funny. It's terrifying isn't it, how well social media knows us all?'

Avril exhaled. 'Tell me about it. Anyway, I made Stuart come and have a look at it and we were both completely bowled over.'

Another fib but she was on a roll now.

'Same here,' Lily said emphatically. 'It's exactly what Eric and I were looking for. By the way, did you know that Weston Abbey offers bursaries? It's a tremendous school and if Bethany is as studious as you say, perhaps it's worth looking into.'

'Oh, thank you, I will.'

'Where are our coffees?' Lily was looking around. 'This isn't a good start, is it? There's no point having a lovely clubhouse if the service is subpar.'

Avril had forgotten all about the coffees. She watched as Lily caught the eye of a terrified-looking girl and beckoned her over.

'We're still waiting for our coffees,' Lily told the girl with an encouraging smile.

The girl scuttled off and Lily turned to Avril. 'Teething problems, I expect, with everything being so new. I'm sure they'll get everything ship-shape in no time. Tell me, Avril, do you enjoy tennis?'

'Oh, no, I'm terrible at tennis. Sorry.' Avril wasn't sure why she was apologising.

'It's easy once you get the hang of it. We should have lessons together.'

'Oh, I'd love that, but you'd get fed up with me. I'll be nowhere near as good as you.'

Lily waved a hand dismissively. 'We're not training for Wimbledon, darling. It's just a social thing. It's so much more fun when you have company.'

'Well in that case, yes, please. I work Monday to Wednesday though.'

'I'll speak to the coach and see if I can book us in for weekly lessons on Friday mornings.'

'That would be lovely!'

Avril beamed. It seemed that Lily was as keen to make friends as she was. And she had a daughter the same age as Bethany too. Bethany needed some friends, it wasn't healthy for her to be on her own all the time and if Poppy was as outgoing as her mother, she might even bring Bethany out of her shell again. Avril dreamed of the day when that happened. Already her earlier anxiety was beginning to ebb away, the mirage getting closer. What a great start to their new life. She couldn't wait to tell Stuart about it as soon as he got home. With a start, she realised that for the first time in months, she was looking forward to seeing her husband.

The waitress arrived with their drinks and Avril took a sip of her latte and smiled with satisfaction. When she looked at Lily, her new friend's eyes were staring across the room.

'You know, I think I recognise that couple over there. They're the Barringtons, I believe. What a coincidence. I wonder if they've bought a place too or if they're just visiting. Will you excuse me a moment?'

Avril watched as Lily stood up and went over to greet the older couple, kissing them both on each cheek. Lily seemed so comfortable and at ease, like she didn't have a care in the world. Avril already had a mental image of Lily's husband and daughter before she'd even met them. She bet they looked like the families who appeared in the clothing catalogues she pored over whenever they came through the letterbox. Boating types. Yet Lily had been warm and friendly, and Avril usually had a knack for sizing people up quickly. She sensed a comrade.

After a few minutes, Lily came back over. 'They've bought one of the houses on the other side of the development. Apparently, their son, who Eric plays golf with, told them about it. Well, it's just like a reunion here, isn't it!'

Avril was certain that there was no chance of bumping into anyone she knew at Westford Park, thank God, but she nodded in agreement. They continued making polite chit-chat until they had finished their coffees and then Lily signed for the drinks and stood up to leave.

'Give me your number,' she said to Avril, pulling out her phone. 'I'll call you about the tennis lessons.'

Feeling like a schoolgirl again, who'd been asked to join a playground game, Avril read out her number and followed Lily out of the clubhouse. She immediately collided with a young child.

'Goodness, I'm sorry,' she said, looking around for the girl's parents.

A moment later, a woman with long, wild curly hair appeared, breathless. 'Isla, what have I told you about running off like that?' The woman smiled apologetically at Avril. 'Sorry about that.'

'Don't worry.' Avril stretched out a hand. 'I'm Avril, we've just moved into Regal Close.'

The woman gripped Avril's hand tightly. 'Sandy. We're a couple of roads away from you. This is Isla.' The little girl stared up at them with huge, dark eyes.

'Well, Isla is just gorgeous!' Lily beamed at the girl. 'Where are you two off to?'

'We're on our way to the pool. Isla is desperate to have her first swim.'

'Oh, the pool's fabulous. Avril here just took a dip! Enjoy yourselves.'

As she walked home with Lily, Avril was wistful. 'I kind of wish we'd moved when the children were younger,' she confessed. 'They would have loved this so much at Isla's age.'

'Oh, I know, but wasn't it hard work? Toddlers and tantrums and all that? Although grumpy teenagers aren't much better, are they?'

Avril wished that grumpy teenagers were the only thing she had to contend with when it came to Bethany. 'We really should introduce our girls,' she told Lily. *And please let Bethany like Poppy,* she thought silently. *Or, more to the point, let Poppy like Bethany.*

'We must. And think about that bursary for the private school too. It might be too late but you just never know. Anyway, bye for now.'

Lily kissed Avril on both cheeks and strode off, and Avril drifted dreamily into the house to find Tom on the sofa, playing on his iPad.

'Have you moved at all since I left?' she asked him and received a grunt in response. 'Where's Bethany?'

'Dunno.'

'Five more minutes on the screen, okay?'

Tom grunted again and Avril went upstairs to check on Bethany. But when she got there, she looked around her daughter's empty bedroom with surprise. Bethany never went out, not any more. Avril hurriedly took her phone from her pocket to call her daughter, but it rang out. With rising panic, she dashed back downstairs again.

'Tom, when did Bethany go out?'

'Dunno.'

Avril snatched the iPad from her son. 'This is serious, Tom. When did she go out?'

'I didn't even know she'd gone out, Mum! She never tells me anything.'

Avril tossed the iPad back onto the sofa and called Bethany again but there was still no reply. Trying not to show her fear in front of Tom, she ran for the door.

'I'm going to go and look for her. If she comes back, call me.'

She raced back out of the house again and set off towards the lake, her heart banging against her chest. She shouldn't have left Bethany alone, not when she was so down. What had she been thinking? What if Bethany had run away? Or done something even worse? Visions of finding her daughter's lifeless body flooded her mind and they were so unbearable that it made her dizzy. And then another unwelcome thought seeped into her mind. *What if she's hurt someone?*

She started to jog and then to run, reaching the lake and following the path around it, calling Bethany's name over and over again. People were staring at her and one or two asked if she needed help, but she ignored them. She was too frantic to explain what had happened, too worried to voice her fears aloud or call the police, just in case. Even after everything that had happened, her instinct was to protect her daughter. Tears began to stream down her face as the realisation set in that something very bad had happened. But who had it happened to?

Who did she think she was, going for a leisurely dip and having coffee with a potential new chum when her daughter was vulnerable? She was selfish, that's what she was, and she was filled with self-loathing. Resentment was flooding back too, though, at Bethany for making her feel this way in the first place. Their new life was already unravelling after just three days. This was not how she had imagined Westford Park. This was supposed to be a new start, a place where bad things didn't happen. Where there was no place for evil.

But now she was fearing the worst, the very, very worst.

3

Sandy beamed as she watched her daughter dipping her toe in the water. She felt like she was living in a dream that she never wanted to wake up from. How could Westford Park be so perfect? Surely there was a catch? But if there was, she hadn't found it yet. Maybe in winter, when the pool was closed and the sun wasn't warming her skin, she might feel differently but she doubted it. She imagined a Christmas tree in the clubhouse, lights twinkling along the paths, and felt suddenly festive despite the heat.

She heard footsteps and looked up to see Clare jogging towards her. 'Good run?'

Clare stopped in front of her and started stretching. 'Fabulous. I did five miles through the woods and round the lake a couple of times. I thought I might find you two here.'

'Isla was desperate for a swim. We were waiting for you so she could go in properly.'

Clare looked down at her. 'You're not going in with her?'

'No, not today. Maybe another time.'

Clare's eyes narrowed and Sandy knew what she was thinking. She couldn't hide anything from Clare. They had no secrets between them and that was just how Sandy liked it. Clare knew exactly why Sandy didn't want to go in the pool and Sandy knew that her wife would gently bring it up later when the time was right. No pressure, no judgement. *Think about it, love, you have nothing to be ashamed of.* That was Clare and that was why Sandy loved her.

'I'll go and get my costume in a second.' Clare sat down by the side of the pool next to Sandy. 'I can't believe I've got to go back to work tomorrow. I feel like we're on holiday.'

Sandy smiled. 'I know what you mean. But we live here now. You can jog in the morning, or swim in the evening. And we'll have the pool every weekend.'

'I know, I still can't believe it.'

'I've been thinking about my work too. Isla will be at school soon and I really can't wait to start painting more regularly again. This place is so inspiring.'

Sandy sold prints and greeting cards of her work online. It didn't make a fortune – certainly not enough to pay the mortgage at a place like Westford Park – but she had slogged away for years and earned a nest-egg before quitting her job in finance soon after Isla was born. And Clare was successful and supported Sandy's desire to work freelance around the children. Sandy had wanted to be around for her daughter, to be a better parent this time after she'd got it so wrong with Micky when he was little. With Clare's support, she had set up her online shop, enrolled on a social media marketing course, and painted at weekends or whenever Isla napped. Over the years, she had built up a decent following and had some loyal customers.

Clare was looking around, shielding her eyes from the sun. 'It's the perfect place to paint.'

'I'm going to go down to the lake, I think I want to try some landscapes.'

'Speaking of the lake, something very peculiar happened when I was out jogging.'

He's found us. Fear hit Sandy with the full force of a train and her body was instantly on edge, ready to flee. Terror never really left her, even after all this time. It lay dormant, sometimes for months on end, but it was ready to activate at any second and at any given moment. *Did you check the doors? The windows?* She clenched her fists and looked at Clare. 'What do you mean?'

'A woman was running around in tears, shouting. I thought maybe she'd lost her dog. But when I tried to help her, she completely ignored me.'

Sandy closed her eyes and exhaled as her fear began to ebb away again. It wasn't him, it was nothing to do with them. She felt foolish now for overreacting because Clare would never have been so flippant about something that serious. She opened her eyes again and watched Isla sitting on the pool step, absorbing her innocence. 'What was she shouting?'

'She kept screaming "Bethany" over and over again.'

Sandy frowned. Bethany didn't sound very much like a pet's name to her. 'What if it wasn't her dog? What if Bethany's a child?'

Clare's face paled. 'I didn't think of that. I tried to help her, Sands, I really did.'

Sandy's heart was already racing again, adrenaline beginning to course through her body. Clare didn't know what it felt like to have lost a child. The terror that gripped at your throat and made it impossible to breathe. Numbing shock competing with unbearable pain.

She stood up. 'I'm going to see if I can help. Stay with Isla.'

'Sandy, wait,' Clare called but Sandy was already running down the path, away from the pool. She ran until she got a stitch and eventually, she had to stop, winded, to catch her breath. She looked around for any sign of an emergency, but everything was as peaceful and serene as it had been the day before when she had taken Isla for a scoot around the lake. Spotting the little wooden boathouse in the distance, she hurried towards it.

Inside, a man was sitting behind the desk with his feet up, watching something on his phone. Sandy spied the bowl of sweets on the table and realised that this was probably where Isla had got the free lollipop from. The man looked up and smiled when he saw Sandy.

'Morning. What can I do for you?'

'I heard there was a woman in distress and I came to see if I could help.'

The man frowned. 'What kind of distress?'

'Apparently, she was calling for someone. I thought maybe she'd lost her child.'

The man pocketed his phone and sprang up from his seat. He had longish hair and wore scruffy jeans, and Sandy guessed that he was probably in his late thirties. Something about him was familiar but, in her panic, she couldn't put her finger on what. Had they met before? She didn't socialise in wide circles, so it seemed unlikely. But she didn't have time to figure it out because the man had raced around the desk and was making his way for the door.

'Where was this lady last seen?' he called behind him.

'I don't know,' Sandy called back. 'My wife told me about it a few minutes ago. She was out jogging and she saw this woman near the lake looking very upset.'

The man stopped as they reached the water. 'All right, you go that way and I'll go this way. That'll give us a better chance of finding her. We'll meet round the other side.'

'Okay.' Sandy set off at a jog, scanning the path for any sign of the woman and wishing that Clare was with her. She'd know what to do; she was always calm in an emergency. Part of Sandy was annoyed with her wife for not doing more to help the woman, but she knew it was unfair. Clare had assumed it was nothing serious, most likely a boisterous dog who had run off chasing squirrels and would be back again in minutes. Clare was the sort of person who always saw the best in life. Sandy, however, usually saw the worst.

She slowed down as she spotted a figure in the distance, crouched down and sobbing. As she got closer, she recognised her as the friendly, cheerful woman who had introduced herself outside the clubhouse less than an hour earlier. Taking a few deep breaths, Sandy approached the woman slowly, as one might do a terrified animal, and called out so as not to startle her.

'Hi there, are you okay?'

The woman looked up at Sandy with a tear-streaked face but didn't reply.

'Can I help you? I want to help.'

'It's Bethany, it's my daughter…'

Sandy's heart constricted. She'd guessed correctly but she took no pleasure in it. 'It's Avril, isn't it? We met earlier, by the clubhouse. I'm Sandy. When did you last see Bethany?'

'I don't know.' Avril was distraught, confused. 'A couple of hours ago.'

'Okay,' Sandy said calmly. 'And how old is Bethany?'

'She's fifteen.' Avril dissolved into tears again.

'Could she be out for a walk? Perhaps she's gone to meet her friends?'

'She doesn't have any friends. This is all my fault, I should never have left her.'

Sandy crouched down and rubbed Avril's back. 'We're going to find her, okay?'

'It's all my fault,' Avril repeated.

Sandy stood up again. 'I'm going to search for her. What does she look like?'

'She's…' But Avril didn't finish her sentence. Both women heard footsteps and looked up to see the man from the boathouse running towards them from the other direction.

'I hear your child is missing?' he called.

'Yes, Bethany. She's fifteen. She's not answering her phone and I can't find her anywhere.'

The man pointed behind him. 'I just saw two teenagers on the fishing platform over there. It's not visible from the path. Maybe one of them is your daughter?'

Avril scrambled to her feet. 'Where?'

'Follow me.'

Sandy and Avril ran after the man as he tore back up the main path and then guided them down a narrow dirt track towards the water. 'There.' He pointed.

Sandy followed his gaze and saw two girls sitting at the end of a rickety wooden platform, their legs dangling over the edge. They were throwing pebbles into the lake and Sandy heard the splash as the stones hit the water. It all looked very peaceful. She turned to Avril and knew from the woman's relieved expression that one of them was Bethany.

'Is it her?' the man asked.

'Yes.' Avril's voice was barely above a whisper. 'It's her.'

The man puffed his cheeks and blew out air. 'Thank God for that. Everything okay, then?'

'Yes.' Avril was staring at her daughter, her eyes fixed on Bethany's back.

The man seemed to be waiting to be dismissed and Sandy stepped in. 'Thank you so much for your help. I don't know if we'd have found her if it wasn't for you.'

He grinned. 'I know all the secret hiding places around here.'

Sandy felt another stirring of recognition and she studied the man intently, trying to work out where she knew him from. But her mind was blank. Maybe he just had one of those faces that looked familiar or perhaps she'd seen him around Westford Park without even registering him properly. 'You're a star, erm... Sorry, what's your name?'

The man extended a hand. 'Steve.'

Sandy clasped his hand tightly. 'Well, thank you again, Steve.'

'No problem. I'd best get back the boathouse.'

He began to pick his way through the overgrown bushes back towards the main path and Sandy turned to Avril. 'Are you okay?'

'Yes.' Avril seemed to finally register that she had company. 'I'm so sorry for all the fuss.'

'Not at all. You have nothing to apologise for.'

'You must think I'm crazy for getting into such a state.'

Sandy smiled. 'I don't think that at all. I have children, I know what it's like.'

Avril gazed at Bethany. 'She used to be such a happy child. I don't know what happened.'

'Puberty,' Sandy said knowingly. 'It happens to them all. She'll come back to you.'

'I don't think she will.'

Avril sounded so bleak, and Sandy looked again at the two girls, who were still unaware of their presence, and wondered what had happened to rip this poor family apart. 'All we can do is love them and let them know we're here for them.'

'But I wasn't there for her, that's the problem. I wasn't.'

'What do you mean?'

Avril shook her head, as though realising she'd said too much to a stranger. 'Forget it, it doesn't matter. Thank you for your help, it's very kind of you.'

'Are you okay? Shall I stay with you?'

'No, I'm fine now. Thank you.'

'Okay.' Sandy was reluctant to leave, but she sensed that Avril wanted her to. 'Let me know if there's anything I can do. Or if you ever want to talk. I'm Sandy.'

'Sandy, yes. I remember.'

'Bye, then.'

With a last look at Avril, Sandy turned away. In the panic, she'd stayed calm and collected but now that it was over, her mind was already hurtling back through the years, to a time she wished she could forget. She could feel her fear as if it was yesterday, even though more than ten years had passed since it happened. Waking up with bleary eyes and staggering into Micky's room to find it empty. The first stirrings of dread as she ran from room to room calling his name and then the cruel, undeniable realisation that he was gone. No parent should ever have to feel that pain, it was more acute and horrific than any physical injury, and she had known that if anything had happened to him, she would not survive it either.

She had been one of the fortunate ones, thank God. She had got Micky back within twenty-four hours and then she had moved them far, far away, where no one could ever hurt them again. So much had happened since then, so many happy memories had buried that dark time. But for a few minutes, fear took over her body again, running through her veins and reminding her that no matter where they went, they would never be completely free.

Suddenly Westford Park didn't seem like a holiday resort any more, it felt sinister. The woods were full of danger, the pool a tragedy waiting to happen, and the boathouse a convenient place for someone to hide. They were isolated here, away from the comforting light, sounds and crowds of the city. How long would it take for the police to come, if she had to call them in an emergency? Sandy crumpled as she saw her vision of the perfect life shatter around her, each shard of glass piercing her dream. How had she not learned by now that a new address couldn't fix old problems? She had moved five times and yet Sandy still didn't feel settled. She had promised Clare that Westford Park was their final destination, and she had fervently wanted to believe it herself, but now she was no longer sure that this was the place for them.

Glancing anxiously over her shoulder at the sound of a twig snapping, she reached the main path and saw Clare and Isla walking towards her hand in hand. Isla had put a summer dress on over her swimming costume and it was Sandy's favourite, pink with yellow lemons dotted over it. Sandy could hear the clip-clap of her daughter's sandals.

'There you are,' Clare called. 'We came to see if we could help.'

Sandy looked at her family and, slowly, her adrenaline began to recede. She stepped out of the shade of the trees into the sunlight and Westford Park was once again glistening.

'False alarm,' she called back, trying to keep her voice steady. 'A woman's teenage daughter went AWOL but we found her.'

'Oh, thank goodness. I'm so sorry I didn't do more to help at the time.'

'It's okay.' Sandy reached them and leaned down to cuddle Isla, craving the comfort of her daughter's warm body, wanting to feel her close.

'I'm such an idiot.' Clare looked distraught. 'I should have known this might trigger you.'

Sandy released Isla. 'It did a bit,' she admitted. 'But I'm okay now. I'm good.'

'And the teenager. They're okay?'

'Fine. She was hanging out by the lake with another girl. You know what teenagers are like, wandering off with no regard for the fact that their parents might fret about them. The mum, Avril, was in a right state, though. I got the sense that there's more to the story.'

'Mummies,' Isla looked up at them both accusingly. 'I'm hungry. And you said I could go in the pool.'

Sandy smiled and tousled her daughter's hair, feeling safe again surrounded by her beautiful, happy family. 'Shall we go and check out the menu at the clubhouse? We might as well make the most of Mum's last day of holiday before she's back at work tomorrow. And then after we've digested our lunch, I promise you can go in the pool all afternoon.'

'Do they do pizza?' Isla was hopeful. 'And milkshakes?'

'I'm not sure, sweetheart, but there's only one way to find out.'

Sandy and Clare took one of Isla's hands each and the three of them began to make their way back around the lake. Sandy's mood got lighter with each step. She glanced at the boathouse and all she saw was a welcoming cabin, with kayaks resting against the walls. The birds were singing in the trees and the water dazzled on the lake. What had happened to her today was a one-off. They were here to stay because she refused to let old demons drive them away. She smiled, satisfied, and her mouth watered at the prospect of lunch. Little things, like the simple pleasure of eating with her family, made her happy. She didn't need anything else, she wanted nothing more.

'Shall we see if Micky wants to join us?' Clare asked.

'Yes, I'll text him now.'

As she messaged her son, she thought of Avril again and the haunted expression on her face even after they had found Bethany safe and sound. 'It's my fault,' she had said. Was that mother's guilt talking, her shame at not knowing where her daughter was, or something more? Sandy knew guilt better than anyone, and she also knew the pure joy she had felt when she had been reunited with Micky. She had expected to see the same joy mirrored on Avril's face, along with a healthy dose of fury at Bethany for wandering off without telling her.

But Avril hadn't seemed joyful or angry at all. She had seemed afraid.

4

'Amanda, darling? It's Lily. Listen, I have something to ask you.'

Lily leaned back into the sofa and told the schools admissions manager all about the gifted and talented girl called Bethany she'd met, who would simply thrive on a bursary at a school like Weston Abbey. Given that her only encounter with Bethany was a fleeting glance across the road, she had no idea if she was either gifted or talented. But she wanted to help her new friend Avril.

Friend. It had a nice ring to it. She'd only met Avril briefly, but she already knew that they were going to get along. It wasn't that Lily didn't have any friends – she had plenty – but they were fair-weather friends, as fickle as the British sunshine. They enjoyed sharing tittle-tattle on lunch dates or moaning about their husbands over a large glass of wine, but they were nowhere to be found in times of need and Lily had no doubt that they'd stab her in the back to protect their own interests. They were not people she could truly be herself around, there was no one she could rely on, or even trust. Like Amanda, on the other end of the phone, whose husband played golf with Eric and whose favourite pastime was gossiping about anything with a pulse. But Lily had worked hard to keep people like Amanda on side because you never knew when it might come in handy. Like now.

Lily was good at keeping people on side. She'd had to learn quickly, but she'd been an eager student. She had been thrust into an unfamiliar world of power and wealth when she first locked eyes on Eric in her twenties and she had adapted not just to survive but to thrive. She had learned how to dress correctly, which fork to use, where to buy furniture. And she had slotted in seamlessly, as though she had always been there. It had never been about money, even though she knew that there had been whispers at the time. She had loved him with all her heart, and her youthful naivety had made her feel like she was living in a fairy tale. Even after the bubble had burst, she had continued to pretend that she was a Disney princess, refusing to see any other narrative. Because by then, they had Poppy and Lily's focus had shifted to her daughter.

It wasn't always easy, playing the part. Lily worked hard to maintain her youth and beauty, and to keep her husband satisfied. She was a good wife. She entertained Eric's pals with wit and charm, she shone at every social engagement (but not too much that she overshadowed Eric), she made sure the house always looked like a show home. And she did it gratefully because she knew how lucky she was. She didn't take her life for granted, not like the other wives who acted so entitled that Lily sometimes fantasised about sticking a pin into their lip-fillers and watching their perfect mouths shrivel up like prunes.

No, the difference between those women and Lily was that they expected nothing less from their lives, but Lily knew how privileged she was. She lived a seemingly idyllic life and had been able to give her daughter a wonderful upbringing. Poppy was the reason why she still continued to play the part. Why she got up every day, blow-dried her hair, applied her make-up and plastered on a smile even when, sometimes, she wanted to hide under the duvet and cry because she was so lonely, and so very sad. She would do anything for Poppy. *Anything.*

Anyway, it wasn't all doom and gloom. Sometimes things with her and Eric were so perfect that she felt like Cinderella again and she clung on to those moments, cherishing them, hoping that this time it would be happy ever after. And she had a beautiful house and plenty of money. She went on five-star holidays. Nothing to complain about, really.

Unlike Poppy, Lily hadn't been born into money. She had grown up with an unemployed father who preferred the company of a bottle of cheap whisky to his own family and had delighted in telling her that she would never amount to anything. Her mother had learned the hard way to turn a blind eye to what went on in her house and on the few occasions that Lily had challenged her father, she had paid the price with a black eye or a belt to her bottom, and she too had learned, just like her mother, to stay silent.

As a child she had spent hours hidden away in her bedroom dreaming of another life. One where she was part of a happy family who sat around the dinner table together and talked about their days. Who went on walks together and held hands. Who told jokes and laughed. Lily had drawn dozens of pictures of this family, the one she belonged to in her dreams. They were always stick people, standing together with smiles on their slightly wonky faces outside a picture-perfect home with a little porch and a white picket fence, not dissimilar to the homes at Westford Park. There was one picture that Lily had been particularly proud of because she'd managed to colour inside all the lines and she had pinned it up on her bedroom wall so that she could look at it every day. When her father found it, he had pulled it off the wall and ripped it into pieces. That was when she had finally understood, at a young age, that under her father's roof she was not even allowed to dream of a better life let alone pursue one. After that, she had kept the drawings hidden under her bed until, at last, she stopped drawing altogether.

At sixteen, she had packed a bag and left home. She hadn't studied A levels or gone to university like the people she socialised with. She had educated herself in the school of life and she had learned the vital skills of survival, determination and tenacity. She had used her looks to get modelling jobs, working in restaurants and, later, bars to top up her meagre earnings, and she made enough to get by. Plenty of people had tried to take advantage of her but one thing she'd learned from her father was to trust no one. She was streetwise before her years, and it served her well. And she bided her time, waiting for her big break.

In the end, the break didn't come from modelling, it came from love. When she was in her early twenties she got a job in a bar in London, the type of establishment where rich bankers gathered at the end of the day to spend their bonuses on expensive champagne, and that was where she first saw Eric. Tall, dark, and almost intimidatingly handsome, he was holding court in the centre of a crowd. He oozed charisma and charm, and she vowed there and then to make him hers. She craved him, not his money but *him*. She wanted to be the one he chose, above all the other women who fawned over him. To prove to everyone, and especially to her father, that she was good enough for a man like Eric.

It had been easier than she thought it would be. She had made eyes at him, flirted a little when he came over to order drinks and ended her shift with his number in her pocket. He had wanted to take her home with him that night, but she had turned him down, just like she had thrown his number into the bin on her way home. She was not going to be a one-night stand, she was going to be more to him. It was all or nothing and she was prepared to take the risk.

He had come back a couple of nights later and when he headed straight for her, she knew that she had played it right. She made him chase her for weeks, waiting until he didn't just want to sleep with her, he wanted to be with her, before she finally agreed to a date.

When she tasted life with Eric, it was as good as she had imagined it would be. He was intoxicating, as addictive as the bitter liquor was to her father. The affection he bestowed upon her, the way he treated her like a queen and made her feel worthy. How he adored her and told her that she could be anything she wanted to be. At first, she had wondered if he would be embarrassed of her, if he would keep their relationship a secret from his banker friends and his rich family but he had done the opposite. He had taken her everywhere with him, introducing her to the world she now lived in, and that was when she had known that, for the first time in her life, she was in love. With Eric, yes wholeheartedly, but also with the woman he promised her she could be. They had got engaged after eighteen months.

Lily had felt obliged to tell her parents she was getting married, and as soon as her father had found out that Lily's husband-to-be had money, he'd been all sweetness and smiles, behaving as though his daughter was, and always had been, the apple of his eye. He had slung his arm around Eric, chewing gum to mask the scent of alcohol on his breath, and tried to persuade his son-in-law-to-be to invest in his useless new business venture. It hadn't taken long for him to reveal his true colours when Eric had politely declined. Lily had watched, cringing with shame, as her father raved, ranted and threatened, and she had vowed to do whatever it took to get her father out of her life for good. 'Whatever it took' turned out to be a cheque for an undisclosed sum and she hadn't heard from him since. She didn't know exactly what Eric had said to her father when he handed over the money, or how much he had paid, and she didn't need to know. He was gone and never coming back.

Despite that, Lily had tried to keep in touch with her mother, driven in equal parts by a sense of duty as well as a growing empathy. Her mother had not been there for her as a child, she had not protected her from her father, but over the years, Lily's resentment towards her had softened, her anger turning to pity as she became an adult and understood more about the complexities of life. She had invited her to visit, as well as to the wedding, but her invitations were never accepted. Lily didn't know whether this was on the strict orders of her father, or whether it was her mother's choice, and in the end, she had buried her hurt deep down where it wouldn't trouble her too much and vowed to be a better mother to her own child.

And so, thanks to Eric, her childhood drawings became a reality, of a fashion at least. Poppy arrived two years after they were married and Lily immersed herself in motherhood, showering her child with love and affection. While the other mums hired expensive nannies, even though they themselves didn't work, Lily refused offers from Eric to pay for help. She had wanted to do it all herself. For years, she and Poppy had been the best of friends. They had held hands when they walked down the road, they had told each other about their days at the dinner table. Perhaps Eric was often missing from the scene but what did it matter? He was working, that was the reality of everyday life, but Lily still believed that their life was almost perfect.

Then Poppy started going up to her bedroom and closing the door. She wanted to hang out with her friends or watch films on her iPad rather than coming downstairs to be with Lily. And then came the petulance and the emotional withdrawal. Lily had known that it was a natural part of growing up, but it had made her realise for the first time that perhaps she needed Poppy more than Poppy needed her. She was surrounded by people – she could find someone to meet for lunch in a heartbeat – but the one thing she was lacking was a true friend. Someone she could talk to in confidence and know that her secrets wouldn't be the talk of society the next day. Someone who didn't want to judge or compete with her. Someone who she could just be herself around. Eric thought that money could buy anything, but he was wrong. It couldn't buy friends.

But that wasn't why she was trying to get Bethany into Weston Abbey, she assured herself. No, this wasn't about paying for Avril's affections, it was about using her family's privilege to help others. She had been given a chance in life and she wanted to pass that on.

But the news wasn't good. 'Darling, we've allocated all our bursaries for the next academic year,' Amanda told her. 'Perhaps she could try again for the following year?'

'You couldn't squeeze her in?'

'Afraid not. We only have a limited number of places. But we can't wait to see Poppy at school again next term. She's such a talented young lady.'

'Yes.' Lily's heart sank as her best laid plans flew out of the window. But she quickly rallied. Avril was a neighbour, their children didn't need to go to the same school for them to be friends. Instinctively, she looked out of the window at the house opposite and frowned.

There was someone outside Avril's house. Despite the heat, the person had their hood up and something about them set Lily on edge. Was Avril being burgled? Without tearing her gaze away from the window, she said goodbye to Amanda and considered whether to call security, or the police, or both. Then the figure turned away from the house and Lily saw it was a man, clutching on to a handful of flyers. She relaxed.

She'd overreacted, but then she and Eric had been burgled

once, years ago, and it had made her paranoid. She wondered now how secure Westford Park really was. It boasted round-the-clock security but a development as huge as this couldn't be completely contained, could it? And it would be rich pickings for burglars. She made a mental note to speak to the security team about it and then remembered that she hadn't seen Poppy since breakfast. She quickly unlocked her phone to check her daughter's location. It had been a condition of Lily's that Poppy activated her location settings when she got her new phone. There was the little dot blinking on the screen, which showed that Poppy was down by the lake. Lily hoped that she was with friends and not just sitting about moping. Poppy had been complaining ever since they arrived at Westford Park and although Lily had suggested that she invite her friends round, she hadn't done so yet. She had even refused to go in the pool, as though having fun would be an admission of defeat.

But Lily had stuck to her promise and was trying to be more relaxed. She had let Poppy go off exploring on her own, no questions asked. Just yesterday, when she was on the way back from the clubhouse, she had seen Poppy talking to the teenage boy with floppy hair who seemed to be hanging about and she had watched, with a smile on her face, as she saw her daughter laughing about something. She wondered now if Poppy was with the boy at the lake and a familiar panic surged through her before she told herself to stop. She wanted Poppy to make new friends, didn't she? Anyway, she'd be back at school soon, so she should enjoy her last few moments of the summer holidays before GCSE preparations kicked in.

Still, she couldn't resist sending Poppy a text to tell her that lunch would be ready soon. She'd see what she could find out about the boy while they were eating, not that Poppy told her anything. But maybe things would be different here. Maybe they would become friends again. Lily dreamed of that. She headed to the kitchen to start preparing a salad, her mind already preoccupied with plans to call the tennis instructor that afternoon and book in lessons for her and Avril. She smiled to herself as she chopped the cucumber. She had already made a new friend and perhaps Poppy had too.

She thought about her childhood drawings. The happy family. The white picket fence. It was like she'd known about Westford Park before it even happened. Like it was written in the stars. She'd make an apple pie this afternoon, she decided, fill the house with the aroma of family and goodness. Eric would enjoy that with a splash of custard when he got home. Because that was the thing with Eric. Wherever he was, and whatever he did, he always came home. And that would have to be good enough for her.

It wasn't until much later, when Lily was sorting through the post, that she remembered the man outside Avril's house. And as she looked down at the envelopes in her hands, she wondered why, if he really was distributing flyers, she didn't have one.

5

Avril waited until she could no longer hear Sandy's retreating footsteps and then she let out a gasp and fell back onto the sturdy trunk of a tree. She had been on the edge of a panic attack and she knew the drill. It would take time to subside, for her body to stand down from its state of high alert. She just had to breathe and slowly, she would recover.

She couldn't believe how quickly she had fallen apart. How easy it was to unravel. She had padded herself with a layer of protection, but it had peeled off within minutes of her realising that Bethany was missing. She should be angry with her daughter for wandering off without telling her but, instead, she was angry with herself. For not trusting Bethany. For thinking the worst. For everything that had happened to make it this way.

Because, she realised now, as her breathing began to slow down, Bethany had done exactly what Avril had been hoping she would do for months. She had gone out. She had found a friend. Avril should be happy but yet she didn't feel any pleasure in that moment.

She watched Bethany from a distance. Her shoulders were hunched and her head was covered by the hood of her jumper, despite the summer heat. In contrast, the girl beside her was wearing a short crop top and cut-off jean shorts. They might have been a similar age but, sitting side by side, they couldn't have looked more different.

Bethany, finally alert to her gaze, turned her head and stared at her, and Avril forced herself to smile and wave as she walked towards the fishing platform. Hearing her footsteps, the other girl turned too before looking questioningly at Bethany. Avril saw her daughter mumble something but she was too far away to hear what she had said. The other girl nodded, turned back to the lake and threw another pebble into the water.

Avril called out, trying to sound casual. 'Bethany, hi! Didn't you hear me calling? I've been looking for you.'

Bethany kept her gaze fixed on Avril, but she didn't reply. Avril knew that she had to hide her emotion because she didn't want to embarrass Bethany in front of her new friend, and she didn't want her daughter to know how afraid she had been either.

She reached the girls and smiled. 'Nice to meet you. I'm Avril, Bethany's mum.'

The girl looked up at her. 'Hi, Avril, I'm Poppy. I live across the road from you.'

Ah, so she was Lily's daughter. Her hair and skin were darker than Lily's and Avril guessed that she took after her father, but there was something about her eyes that reminded her of Lily.

She smiled back. 'It's lovely to meet you, Poppy. I was just with your mum.'

'Let me guess, she's signed you up for tennis lessons.'

Avril laughed nervously. 'Um, yes, she has, actually.'

Bethany still hadn't said a word, and Avril felt awkward and unsure of what to do or say next. Eventually, she said, 'Bethany, it's nearly lunchtime. Perhaps start to make your way back soon?'

Bethany looked away but Poppy stood up and smoothed out her top. 'I've got to go too. It was nice to meet you, Avril.'

'You too, Poppy. I hope to see you again soon.'

Poppy walked away, her long, shiny, dark hair reflecting the sun and giving her an almost angelic glow. Just before she disappeared into the trees, she turned and waved.

'She seems nice,' Avril remarked.

More silence from Bethany.

Avril took a deep breath. 'Bethany, I'm glad you've made a friend, but I was really worried about you. You can't just wander off without telling me and ignore my calls.'

Bethany turned away, picked up a pebble and passed it from hand to hand, before lobbing it into the lake. 'You said things would be different here.'

'Yes, and they will be. But I still need to know where you are, love.'

'You don't trust me.'

That was the problem and they both knew it. Avril didn't trust her. She had tried so hard but there was a seed of doubt lodged in her mind and no matter how hard she fought to conceal it, she hadn't fooled her daughter. But this, like everything else, was unspoken between them so instead, she said, 'Of course I trust you, but you're only fifteen. Just leave me a note if you're going out. And answer your phone when I call. It's not too much to ask.'

'Fine.'

'Thank you. Are you coming back for lunch?'

Bethany stood up and followed her back along the platform. As they walked, Avril racked her brains to think of a conversation topic, as though she was on a blind date rather than in the company of her own child. How had it come to this? They used to be so close, the two of them. Bethany had been such a tactile, affectionate child, always wanting to be near Avril, to hold her hand or cuddle up on the sofa. And even when she had started to grow up, she had not distanced herself as other children did. Avril had listened to other mums complaining about their aloof teenagers and she had felt proud and happy that she and Bethany had a different relationship. They went shopping or to the cinema at weekends while Tom was at football practice. They watched films together. They talked and laughed and gossiped. She never had any concerns about her daughter other than the usual worries about whether she ate enough vegetables or brushed her teeth properly. But then everything had changed.

It was like she had lost her daughter overnight. Bethany became withdrawn and her smile, which she had flashed so frequently, disappeared. She spent hours in her room with the door closed and when Avril went in to see her, she hid whatever she was doing under her pillow. Bethany loved art, she always had, and Avril suspected that she was drawing but she was at a loss to know why her daughter was hiding it from her.

It had happened around the same time that she got friendly with a new crowd of girls at school, and at first, Avril worried that she was being bullied. But when she asked Bethany about it, her daughter insisted everything was fine. Avril called the school and they said that Bethany seemed perfectly happy, her grades were good and there was no evidence of bullying. Stuart told her to stop fretting and to give Bethany some space. And so Avril told herself that this was simply teenage hormones finally kicking in and that her daughter would come back to her in a few years, when she had navigated the tricky path of puberty.

But eight months ago, it had all come to a head. It started with a call from the head teacher requesting an urgent meeting, and when she pushed him on why, all he would tell her was that some serious allegations had been made against Bethany. Initially, Avril had been outraged and she had marched into his office ready to defend her innocent daughter. But instead, she had left a broken wreck. The evidence against Bethany had been irrefutable and Avril had been forced to consider the fact that the horrifying claims about her were true. *Evil*. That was the word she had heard in whispers around her, that she had read on social media, and it haunted her still.

She had tried to talk to Bethany so many times, desperate to hear her deny the allegations and provide an alternative explanation, but her daughter had clammed up. She wouldn't say a word and this had only fuelled Avril's fear and anxiety. Avril had begged her, pleaded with her, but she had been met with a wall of stony silence. It was like Bethany had given up and resigned herself to what she was, and always would be, known as. Evil.

Avril had not wanted to believe it. Her beautiful, kind and thoughtful Bethany would never do those things. This was a cruel witch hunt, and the truth would come out eventually, and Bethany would be cleared of any wrongdoing. But she was consumed with doubt and Bethany's withdrawal, her refusal to fight to prove her innocence, had made it so much worse. Avril had tried to talk to the other girls' parents, but she'd had doors slammed in her face, her phone number blocked. So, unable to do anything else, she had spent months tormenting herself, wondering who her daughter really was and what kind of a mother she was to not know.

There had been one silver lining. The school had not wanted to involve the police and the parents had agreed. Instead, they had expelled Bethany and wiped their hands of the whole business. Initially, Bethany had moved to the nearby secondary school where

Avril taught but that hadn't stopped the rumours in the playground or in the staffroom. Avril felt like a pariah and it must have been a thousand times worse for Bethany. She watched her daughter like a hawk and knew that she hadn't made any friends. She was always alone, head down, ignoring the taunts of the other pupils. Every day, Avril expected the headteacher to summon her and tell her that Bethany had done something terrible, but it never happened. She felt like a ticking time bomb, waiting for life to explode, and she wasn't sure they'd survive the fallout again.

Eventually, she had decided that they should move far away, to give Bethany, and all of them, a fresh start, in a place where whispers and stares didn't follow them. To remove Bethany from the toxic situation and give her a chance to make new friends who didn't know about her past. It wouldn't happen again, she told herself, and then she would finally know that the allegations were all lies and that Bethany, her darling Bethany, was innocent.

But the damage to their relationship was already done. Bethany knew that Avril had doubted her and the trust between them had been shattered. And how could Avril blame her? She had failed her daughter, she had been unable to infiltrate the fortress that Bethany had built around herself and so she had left her daughter to suffer alone.

Stuart had buried his head in the sand over the whole thing. He couldn't cope with it. He liked predictability, for the world to be as black and white as the computer code he worked with every day. He had said simply that Bethany would never have done those things and that was that. He was not willing to consider a grey area, a different version of the truth, and nor was he willing to spend hours discussing and dissecting it, something Avril had needed to do to process it all. So, they had not been there for each other, and this had ripped them apart, causing a tidal wave of resentment. She didn't know how to fix that either.

Then there was poor Tom who, by default, became an outcast and stopped being invited to play dates and birthday parties without fully understanding why. Avril had lost count of the times he had come home crying, saying that no one would play with him any more. They had moved as much for him as they had for Bethany and Avril had hoped that this new life would bring them all together again, to allow them to pick up the pieces of their broken family.

All she wanted was to see the people she loved smile again. To heal the cracks in her relationship with Bethany and go back to how it was before. To see Tom be the carefree boy he should be and to laugh with Stuart again, like they used to. But they could never go back, so instead, Avril had tried to move forward. Now she feared that she had made a big mistake. Westford Park was a sticking plaster which was already beginning to peel at the edges.

An involuntary sob escaped and she clasped her hand over her mouth, horrified. She always tried to hide her emotions in front of Bethany, to be the solid, reliable presence that she felt her daughter needed. Yet here she was, losing it because Bethany had wandered off for a few minutes without telling her. She tried to swallow her tears but they refused to play ball and rolled down her cheeks. Avril turned her head away, hoping Bethany hadn't seen.

And then, suddenly, Bethany reached out and took Avril's hand. It was the first time they had touched in months, and Avril needed every ounce of strength she had not to fall apart. Because this small, seemingly casual gesture, meant everything to her. It was like the first buds that appeared at the end of a long winter and brought with them a feeling of hope and new beginnings. This brief, physical contact told Avril something profound and wonderful. It told her that wasn't too late to get her daughter back. She had no idea what had triggered this peace offering from Bethany, whether it was the move to Westford Park, the new friend she'd made or simply the healing effect of time and space. She'd unpick it later but right then she didn't care.

'I love you, Bethany,' she said, her voice quivering.

Bethany didn't reply but she squeezed Avril's hand once.

I love you too. That's what she meant.

6

Sandy was in the middle of making dinner when Micky arrived home from school and threw himself down onto the sofa.

'Hey, love, how was the first day?'

Micky had just started sixth form at Westford High and Sandy didn't want to think about the fact that he was growing up and would be leaving home for university in no time. Life was moving so fast, every day a flash. At least she still had Isla, even though she would be full-time at primary school soon. She wasn't ready for a completely empty nest, not yet, not ever.

'Fine,' was Micky's considered response.

'Any problems with getting the bus?'

'Nah.'

'Were there any other kids from Westford Park on it?'

'Yeah. A girl and her little brother.'

'Oh, that's nice. Is the girl in your year?'

'Year below.'

Sandy smiled. 'Oh, Micky, I do love these scintillating conversations.'

'What's for dinner, Mum? I'm starving.'

Micky was always starving. 'Lasagne, it'll be ready at six.'

Micky grunted and started watching CBeebies with Isla. He was a good older brother. Sandy had worried about how he'd feel when she told him that she and Clare were having a baby, but he had taken it in his stride, just like he always took everything.

Clare had always longed for a baby. Sandy had been more uncertain because life was finally wonderful and she was worried about any change that might tip the balance. She fretted about how Micky would feel and remembered how afraid and isolated she had been as a new mother. But Clare had persuaded her that this time, things would be very different.

Sandy hadn't been in a good place when Clare started working at the same firm as her. But there was something about Clare that had energised her. Where Sandy saw a bleak world full of danger, Clare saw beauty and adventure, and her positivity radiated to those around her. She was always laughing, the person who brought fun to the most boring of meetings. Sandy used to watch her sometimes, across the table, and marvel at her. It was as though Clare held the secret to happiness, the key to a different world that Sandy wanted to inhabit.

When Clare started inviting her out for a drink after work, Sandy was flattered that someone so vivacious and fun-loving would want to socialise with her. She worried that Clare would think she was too nervy or uninteresting, a moth to her beautiful flame. But she soon realised that Clare didn't see her that way and, with a glorious sense of hope and new beginnings, Sandy decided that she no longer wanted to see herself in that way either.

Clare didn't hide her intentions from Sandy. She made it clear from the start that she was interested in her romantically, not platonically. Sandy, who had never been with a woman before, was curious, afraid and, she realised with mounting excitement, aroused. Her mother later speculated that she'd been turned off men by her past experience, but Sandy knew it wasn't that. It wasn't *women* she wanted, it was a woman. Clare.

Even then, it had still taken a long time for her to trust Clare enough to take the next step. And Clare had waited for her, patiently, for months.

Finally, she had said, gently but firmly, 'I need to know if you feel the same way.'

And Sandy had made her decision.

Looking at Isla and Micky now, curled up on the sofa, Sandy felt a warm glow as she remembered her early relationship with Clare, the discovery and the pure elation she'd felt at falling in love with someone unconditionally and knowing that they felt the same way. Even now, years later, Sandy still caught herself watching her wife and marvelling at her. She was so strong, so capable, that she made anything seem possible. Yet she was gentle too, ever patient and understanding. Sandy knew she wasn't always the easiest person to be with but Clare let her be her, she didn't try to change her or make her into something she wasn't. It was her acceptance, and her fierce loyalty, that meant the most to Sandy.

'It's quite good, this cartoon,' Micky remarked now, making Isla giggle.

'Got any homework to do, Micky?'

'Nah.'

The doorbell rang and Sandy wiped her hands on a tea-towel before walking over to answer it. Two girls stood on the porch, one pale and wearing an oversized hoodie that almost covered her entire body and the other looking like she'd just stepped off a private yacht after two weeks sailing around the Caribbean. They made an unlikely duo and Sandy had to stifle a giggle. She felt a jolt of recognition and remembered that they were the same two girls she'd seen on the fishing platform. Which meant that one of them was Bethany, the girl who had upset her mother so much when she wandered off. And she had a fair idea which one it was.

Sandy hadn't spoken to Avril since that day, although she had looked out for her, hoping to bump into her again. She had thought about her frequently and wondered if everything was okay. And now here was her daughter, right on Sandy's doorstep, looking like a ghost next to the other girl who exuded health with her bright eyes and crystal-clear skin.

'Hello,' the olive-skinned one smiled, showing perfect teeth as she extended a hand. 'I'm Poppy Sanderson. This is Bethany.'

Sandy shook the girl's hand, impressed with her manners and confidence. The other girl, now confirmed as the infamous Bethany, was staring at the floor.

'Hello, lovely to meet you. Are you here to see Micky?'

'Yes.' Poppy beamed. 'We're going to the clubhouse and wondered if he'd like to join us.'

'Oh, I'm sure he would. Hang on, let me get him. Come in, come in.'

Sandy ushered the girls into the house and they followed her into the living room. Hearing voices, Micky looked over his shoulder and sprang to his feet with such haste that Sandy immediately suspected that he was keen to impress. But which one? she wondered.

'Hi,' he said, tucking his hair behind his ears.

Poppy gazed at the television screen, amused. 'Still watch children's TV do you, Micky?'

'It's for my little sister.'

'Oh sure, blame it on your sister.'

Isla, thrilled at having visitors, ran over to the girls. 'Do you want to see my dolls?'

Poppy rolled her eyes but Bethany looked at Isla and her face morphed into something that might have been a smile. 'Sure,' she said.

Delighted, Isla took the girl's hand and dragged her over to the play area, handing her two dolls. Micky's eyes remained firmly on Poppy. *Oh no*, Sandy thought. *That's the one he wants to impress.* She didn't know why she was disappointed by this.

Poppy tapped a foot impatiently. 'When you're finished playing dolls and watching cartoons, shall we go to the clubhouse?'

'Can I come?' Isla asked hopefully.

'No,' Sandy, Poppy and Micky said in unison. Only Bethany remained quiet.

Sandy looked at Micky. 'Home for dinner, please.'

'Yeah.'

Micky followed the two girls out and Poppy turned and waved as they left. How nice that he'd made friends already, and they'd only been living at Westford Park for a couple of weeks. And Bethany had been very sweet with Isla. Perhaps she might even babysit so that Sandy and Clare could go out together once in a while? That would be a treat. Sandy thought about the three teenagers hanging out together at the clubhouse and smiled. She loved the fact that Micky could explore Westford Park, safe inside the community.

Isla was glum at having been left behind and Sandy went over to give her a cuddle. She could tell that her daughter was tired. She had gone to her new school for a settling-in session that morning and Sandy had taken the opportunity to do some painting. She had carried her easel and sketchbook down to the lake and had drawn a heron, sitting on its perch, waiting patiently to dive underwater for fish. Sandy's work was usually abstract, not landscapes, but at Westford Park, she felt a different pull and she was happy to go with it and see where it took her. It was all part of the change, the final reinvention of herself. The one that stuck.

She glanced over at the half-finished painting now and couldn't wait to show it to Clare later. Then she looked at the time and cursed. The lasagne was supposed to have gone in the oven ten minutes ago. Sandy picked up the dish with a tea-towel and placed it on the shelf. As she did, her eyes moved habitually to the scars on her bare arms.

She'd hidden the marks for years, wearing long sleeves even when it was hot. It was Clare who had given her the confidence to show her skin again although, even now, she rarely wore a swimming costume. The scars had faded over time, but they had never disappeared completely, a constant reminder of what had happened, and what might still happen. And that's why she ran.

Sandy never stayed in the same place for very long. At first, after each move, everything would be fine. But inevitably the fear would creep in again. It would start with checking the locks on the doors every evening. Soon she'd be scrutinising each window too. Then she'd get up in the night to check them a few more times before lying in bed, wide awake, wondering how she had ended up there again. She would start looking over her shoulder constantly every time she went out. She would persuade Micky not to go out with his friends, to stay at home instead. And, eventually, she would be so afraid and exhausted that she would tentatively suggest that it was time for a change. The city was too busy, the countryside too quiet. They needed to find a better secondary school for Micky, the right primary for Isla.

Of course, Clare saw right through her. But she didn't argue, she didn't try to talk Sandy out of it. Instead, she always nodded thoughtfully. *Yes, you're right, we should move into the catchment of a good primary school. Yes, the city is so chaotic, perhaps the kids would benefit from some fresh, clean air. Won't it be a fabulous new adventure!*

Anyone else would have had enough of her years ago but not

Clare. Patient, kind, wonderful Clare who had stood by Sandy time and time again.

This time, Sandy was more determined than she had ever been. Westford Park was the place where Isla would grow up, and she and Clare would grow old together. She was a different person now, a stronger one. But, just like the faded scars, the memories of her past never completely disappeared. They were always hiding in the background, ready to resurface and remind Sandy of what could have been. What might happen again, if he ever found them.

Little things triggered her. The smell of cigarette smoke or the sound of crockery smashing sent her hurtling back in time and suddenly she was in the cramped, dirty flat, cowering in the corner as glasses and plates crashed against the wall. Waiting for the moment when he got tired of throwing things and came for her instead. Wondering if this would be the last time he hurt her, not because she escaped but because he killed her.

She looked now at her fastidiously clean kitchen, the gleaming surfaces and the polished floor. Sandy liked everything to be neat and perfect. It was how she felt in control, how she kept order in her life. When she was in control, she felt safe. And if that meant checking the doors and windows, and moving house every few years, then that's what she had to do.

But the rest of her family didn't deserve to live like that. The skeletons from her own past shouldn't haunt them. Anyway, it had been ten years since she and Micky finally got away for good and if he was going to come for them, surely he would have done it by now? Logic told her she had nothing to fear and yet it stayed with her, a legacy that refused to die.

And then there was Micky. He was too young to remember that chapter in his life, thank God, but sometimes Sandy panicked that nature was stronger than nurture, that no matter what she did, Micky's character was decided by his DNA and not her parenting

And if that was true, then what did it mean for her son? What would he become?

Clare always reassured her. Micky was a sweet boy, she'd say, a gentle boy. Just like his mother. You've raised him well. You have nothing to worry about. But she did worry.

A sound startled her from her thoughts and a few moments later, Clare appeared.

'It smells amazing in here,' she said.

Sandy smiled. 'Lasagne.'

'Can't wait. Hey, sweetheart.' Clare blew a kiss at Isla. 'Where's Micky?'

'He's gone out with some new friends from the development. Two girls.'

'Two girls, eh? I bet they'll be fighting over him in no time. He's a catch is our Micky.'

Sandy lowered her voice so that Isla wouldn't hear her over the television. 'One of them was Bethany, the girl I was telling you about the other day.'

Clare raised her eyebrows. 'The one who went missing?'

'Well, not really missing. It was all a fuss about nothing in the end.'

'But didn't you get strange vibes? You thought something was off?'

'Yes, but maybe I overthought it in the heat of the moment.'

'Maybe.' Clare went to the fridge and reached for a bottle of wine. 'We've been lucky with Micky, though. He always tells us where he's going and checks in regularly.'

'He knows it's important to me. But I'm hoping to be a bit more easy breezy here.'

Clare laughed. 'Sandy, I love you, but I'm not sure you'll ever be easy breezy.'

Sandy pouted, but she was smiling. 'Are you saying I'm uptight?'

'Yep. And I love you for it.' Clare poured a glass of wine and took a sip. 'Ah, that's good. I've had a stinker of a day. But do you know what? As I drove through the gates of Westford Park, I instantly relaxed. I love this place, Sandy, I really do.'

It filled Sandy's heart with joy to hear those words. She knew that she'd been the instigator and that everyone else had agreed to it because of her. But Clare's contentment, Isla's joy when they went swimming, and the speed in which Micky had made friends proved that it had been the right decision. There was no danger here, only fresh air and happiness.

The phone rang and Clare went to answer it. 'Hello?' A few seconds passed and Sandy glanced over to see who it was. But Clare was frowning. 'Hello?' she repeated. Sandy watched, her breath catching in her throat, and waited for what she knew was coming.

Clare put the phone back down with a shrug. 'Just a few seconds of silence and then they hung up. Damn landline, all you ever get is nuisance callers. If we hadn't got it in our broadband package, I wouldn't have bothered having it installed.'

But it was too late. Clare's pragmatic words fell on deaf ears. Sandy dropped the spoon she was holding with a clatter and felt herself being dragged back into the tunnel again.

7

The hot, young tennis coach was giving Lily the eye. Dressed in her fitted white T-shirt and tennis skirt, with her hair tied up in a neat ponytail, Lily knew she looked good even after an hour of exercise. Next to her, Avril was sweating profusely. The summer weather was still in full swing, which was more than could be said for Avril's tennis playing.

'Good work, ladies,' the coach said. 'Same time next week?'

'Yes, please, Juan. See you then.' Lily cocked her head as Juan began to walk back towards the clubhouse and then whispered to Avril, 'He can restring my racquet any time.'

'Honestly, Lily, I'm too knackered to even notice.' Avril lay down on the floor of the tennis court and spread her arms and legs like a starfish. 'How did I get so unfit?'

'Nonsense, you did great.' In truth, Avril had been abysmal, but who cared? 'Coffee?'

Avril nodded and began to peel herself off the floor again. 'Absolutely. I need a caffeine boost after that. Will they let me in, though? I'm sweaty and horrible.'

'Of course they will. Come on, we can sit out on the terrace anyway.'

They walked the short distance to the clubhouse and Avril collapsed gratefully onto a chair. 'If you want to ditch me and have private tennis coaching, I won't be at all offended.'

'Don't be silly.' Lily panicked that Avril might give up the lessons. The past hour had been so much fun and she didn't want it to end already. It had been joyful to play with someone who didn't behave as though they were Martina Navratilova in a Grand Slam final, like the women from her old tennis club. Lily was already looking forward to the following week's lesson and the coffee afterwards, which she hoped would become a tradition.

'But you're so much better than me,' Avril insisted.

Lily held up a hand. 'I just want to have a bit of fun and get some exercise.' She glanced over at Juan, who was talking to one of the waitresses. 'And the view's rather attractive.'

Avril followed her gaze and giggled. 'You're terrible, Lily.'

'It never hurts to window-shop, darling.'

It was all bravado. Lily had never cheated on Eric and she had no intention of doing so. She was loyal to the core, and she would not do anything to jeopardise the life she had built for her and Poppy. She looked over at Juan's toned legs and grimaced. More fool her.

'Oh, I've been meaning to ask you,' she said suddenly. 'Did you get a flyer through your letterbox the other week?'

Avril frowned. 'What kind of flyer?'

'I don't know, I saw someone outside your house with a handful of them.'

'Oh yes, now you mention it I did get an ad for a car cleaning service.'

'I wonder why I didn't get one.'

'Probably because your car always looks spotlessly clean, whereas ours is a state.'

Lily smiled. 'It's just that I spoke to one of the security team who said they check everyone at the gate and they don't usually let people in to flyer.'

'Could he have got in another way?'

'There's only one vehicle entry and exit point and they regularly carry out patrols around the perimeter. The man I spoke to reckons it's the safest place in England.'

Avril was looking at her curiously. 'Perhaps he was already on-site cleaning another resident's car and he saw an opportunity? Are you worried about security?'

'Eric and I were burgled a few years ago so I'm more vigilant than I used to be,' Lily confessed. 'But you're right, I'm sure it was legit. I must say, it's reassuring to know we're safe at Westford Park. Anyway, how's the new teaching job going?'

'Great,' Avril enthused. 'The staff seem really nice and it's big enough that I'm not bumping into Bethany and Tom every five minutes.'

'And how are Tom and Bethany settling in?'

Avril's face clouded over, before abruptly clearing again. 'Yes, fine, thank you.'

Lily narrowed her eyes, sensing trouble. 'What is it?'

'It's nothing.'

But she was clearly fibbing. 'You can tell me, you know. I'm a good listener.'

Avril hesitated and then said, 'Tom's fine, he's slotted right in. It's Bethany.'

Lily nodded with understanding. 'Finding it hard to make friends?'

Avril fiddled with her baggy T-shirt. 'Yes.'

'Well, don't worry about that, she's only just started. These things can take time, especially when strong friendship groups are already established, but she'll get there.'

'Mmm.'

Lily scrutinised Avril. There was more to this than she was letting on. Perhaps she was worried about confiding because their friendship was so new, but Lily wanted to prove that she was trustworthy, not a gossip. She might even be able to help; she was good at giving advice. And if anyone knew what it was like to have a difficult teenager it was Lily.

She decided to change tack. 'Well, she seems to have palled up with Poppy anyway.'

Avril's face lit up. 'Oh, I know, I'm so pleased. They've been spending quite a bit of time together after school. There's a boy too – Micky, I think he's called.'

'Yes, that's right. He's the older brother of that little girl who crashed into you a couple of weeks ago, remember? Their mum's called Sandy.'

Avril looked alarmed at the mention of Sandy. 'Oh yes, I remember her.'

'Speaking of which, isn't that her over there?' Lily saw a woman walking up the path from the lake, holding what looked like an easel under one arm.

Avril followed her gaze. 'Yes, I think it is.'

Lily stood up and waved. 'What a coincidence! We should see if she'd like to join us.'

'Oh, um, yes.'

Avril seemed reluctant but before Lily could ask her why, Sandy saw them and made a beeline for their table. 'Hi there,' she called.

'Sandy, right?' Lily smiled. 'Our coffees have just arrived. Would you like one?'

'I'd love a cold drink.' Sandy placed her things on the floor and took the spare seat, pulling a hairband off her wrist and tying her long, curly hair up into a messy bun. 'I've been painting all morning down by the lake and it's so lovely and shady down there that I didn't realise how warm it was until I started walking back. What have you two been up to?'

'Tennis,' Lily said. 'Do you play?'

'A little when I was younger, but not for years.'

'You should join us, we have lessons every Friday morning. All abilities welcome. Avril here's a beginner, aren't you?'

Lily glanced at Avril, who still seemed uncomfortable. 'Oh, um, yes,' she stuttered.

If Sandy sensed Avril's discomfort, she didn't show it. 'That would be super. I'm keen to get fit again. My wife, Clare, is a runner and I'm always left behind, huffing and puffing.'

'That's decided, then.' Lily was delighted by this turn of events. Their duo had turned into a trio. 'And I hear our children have already formed a little gang too.'

'Oh, yes, that's right, you're Bethany and Poppy's mums.' Sandy leaned forward conspiratorially. 'I think my son Micky has a crush on Poppy.'

Lily laughed. 'You might want to warn him that she's high maintenance.'

'She's such a lovely girl, and so polite.'

Avril still hadn't said a word and Lily looked at her in concern. What on earth was up with her? A few minutes ago she'd been fine and now she looked like she wanted the ground to swallow her up. Had she and Sandy had a run-in that Lily didn't know about?

They sat in an uncomfortable silence and, in a desperate attempt to keep the faltering conversation going, Lily had an idea. 'Are you both free on Sunday afternoon? How about a barbecue at mine? We should make the most of this weather before it turns.'

'That would be lovely.' Sandy beamed. 'Thank you.'

They both looked at Avril. 'Oh, um, I'll have to check with Stuart, but I think we're free.'

'That settles it, then. Shall we say one o'clock?' Lily was already making a mental list of the food and drinks she'd need to buy that afternoon. Was there time to bake a cake? She'd have to tell Eric to be home from golf in time too, which he was bound to moan about. But she was keen to host her new friends, so he'd have to get over it.

Sandy's phone rang and she stood up. 'Sorry, ladies, I need to take this.'

Once she was out of earshot, Lily leaned forward and whispered to Avril, 'Everything okay?' On closer inspection, Avril looked like she was about to cry.

Avril hesitated before replying. 'I'm just a bit embarrassed. You see, I had a bit of a scare and, well, I got into rather a state.'

Lily was intrigued. 'What happened?'

'It was Bethany. She went off without telling me and I was worried about her. Sandy found me down by the lake and helped me to look for her. It all seems a bit silly now.'

Again, Lily got the distinct feeling that there was more to it than Avril was letting on.

'Is everything okay with Bethany?'

With shock, she saw Avril wipe away a tear. 'Oh gosh, I'm so sorry, Lily. You barely even know me and here I am, crying in front of you already. You must think I'm crazy.'

Lily reached out and put her hand over Avril's. 'I don't think that. You can talk to me in confidence about anything. In fact, let's make it official. I call to order the first meeting of the Westford Park Ladies Club. And what happens in our club, stays in our club.'

Avril laughed. 'Lily, you are funny.'

Lily wasn't sure she'd ever been called funny before. Beautiful, yes. An excellent host? Many times. But not funny. This was the new Lily though, she reminded herself, Lily 2.0, and she liked it. And maybe she needed the Westford Park Ladies Club just as much as Avril.

'So, what's happening with Bethany?' she asked.

Avril sighed heavily. 'She was such a happy girl. And then about a year ago she changed. She started hanging out with these new girls at school and after that she was different. She became withdrawn and non-communicative, which didn't make any sense because I thought having new friends should have the opposite effect.'

Sandy had returned and Avril glanced at her apologetically, but she didn't stop talking.

'I thought she was being bullied but there was no evidence of it. She would go for these sleepovers and when she came back, she was agitated and moody. I assumed she was just tired because they'd been up all night chatting but she refused to talk about it and when I suggested that she stopped going she became angry with me.'

It sounded pretty run-of-the-mill to Lily. They'd probably put on some God-awful horror film that had scared the daylights out of Bethany, who had been too afraid to say anything in case her new friends teased her. Poppy had watched something about a poltergeist once at a friend's house and had made Lily sleep in her room for two weeks afterwards.

But Avril wasn't finished. 'A few months ago, the school called me and said that Bethany had got into some trouble. I couldn't believe it, my Bethany had never even got a detention before and I said as much to the headteacher. But they expelled her.'

Lily's eyes widened. 'What kind of trouble?'

Avril looked distinctly uncomfortable. 'Bullying,' she admitted. 'But it was all lies, some sort of smear campaign against her by those horrible girls.'

There's no smoke without fire, though, Lily thought. And if Bethany was a troublemaker, should she let Poppy spend time with her? What if Bethany bullied Poppy too?

Maybe Avril sensed what was on Lily's mind because she immediately started to backtrack.

'Gosh, that sounds a lot worse than it was. It really was nothing and like I said, none of it was true anyway. Bethany is a good girl, and she's the victim in all this.'

But all Lily could think was, *The school wouldn't have expelled her if it was nothing.*

'Is that why you moved here?' Sandy was looking at Avril kindly, without a hint of judgement on her face. *That's how I should look*, Lily thought guiltily.

'Actually, I saw an ad for Westford Park on social media and it pulled me in, hook, line and sinker. I mean, it's just such a unique place, isn't it?'

Avril's reply, which Lily had thought nothing of the first time she heard it, now seemed rehearsed. They'd clearly moved away because of this whole business and she could hardly blame them. She'd probably have done the same thing. But it did make Lily wonder if, by sticking firmly to her script, Avril was hiding something. Something bad about Bethany.

She should be reassuring Avril, telling her that of course Bethany was a lovely girl, of course she was the victim. But the tiger mum inside her was starting to growl. She was fiercely protective of Poppy, ready to pounce on anyone who even looked at her the wrong way. In her mind, Bethany had already morphed from a sweet – if a little morose – girl into a potential threat.

But she couldn't say this to Avril, so instead she adopted her most reassuring smile and said, 'Well, this will be a fresh start for your family and a chance to put it all behind you.'

Avril smiled gratefully. 'Thanks, Lily. That's the plan.'

The conversation lingered in Lily's mind, however, long after she had said goodbye to Sandy and Avril and walked home. In her kitchen, as she wrote down her shopping list for the barbecue, Lily mulled it over. Should she warn Poppy off Bethany? Or tell her to be on her guard at least? And if she did that, would she be betraying her new friend? Avril seemed nice but how much did Lily really know about her and her family? They'd only met a couple of weeks ago. The more she thought about it, the more she realised that new friends were wonderful, but family came first. And that meant putting Poppy before anyone else.

* * *

Later, when Poppy got home from school, Lily was waiting for her.

'How was your day?'

'Fine. Can I have some money? I'm going shopping on Sunday.'

'Actually, you're not. Bethany and Micky's families are coming over for a barbecue.'

Lily braced herself for Poppy's wrath, so she was surprised when her daughter said, 'Okay.'

'You don't mind?'

'No. Bethany and Micky are cool.'

The opportunity had simply presented itself, Lily decided. She'd certainly not forced it. That was how she justified what she said next.

'This Bethany girl, what's she like?'

Poppy was scrolling on her phone and barely looked up. 'Yeah, she's all right.'

'Is she, you know, *kind*?'

Poppy raised her eyebrows. 'You mean does she share her Peppa Pig toys nicely?'

Lily ignored her daughter's sarcasm and sat down on the sofa beside her. 'I heard something today about Bethany and I just wanted to make sure everything's okay.'

Now she had Poppy's attention. 'What did you hear?'

'Apparently, she got expelled from her old school.'

Poppy looked delighted by this. 'Wow, that's so cool!'

'Poppy! That is not cool at all. It's terrible.'

'Whatever, Mother.'

'It seems that she was accused of bullying.'

At this, Poppy laughed. 'Bullying? Bethany? No way.'

'What makes you so sure?'

'I just know.'

'Look, Poppy, if she was expelled it must have been bad. Really bad. I just wonder if you should maybe stay away from her.'

'And that's why you've invited her over for a barbecue, is it?'

She had a point. 'Well, just be careful. Be on your guard. I don't want you to get hurt.'

'Don't worry about it.'

But Lily did worry about it. 'I take it Bethany hasn't mentioned anything to you about it?' she asked her daughter.

'No.'

'Well, if she does, tell me, okay?'

'Sure, whatever.' Poppy stood up again. 'I'm going out.'

'Where are you going?'

'I'm meeting Micky and Bethany at the clubhouse for a drink.'

'A *drink*?'

'Chill, Mother. A smoothie. Can I put it on your account?'

Lily narrowed her eyes. 'Yes. But tell me everything when you get back, okay?'

'Like that's going to happen.'

'Poppy, I'm serious.'

Poppy reached into her bag and smothered her lips with gloss

'Don't worry, I'll tell you if Bethany snatches my Peppa Pig toy and refuses to give it back. See you later.'

She was infuriating, that girl. But Lily knew she had to let her go, she couldn't wrap her up in cotton wool forever. And, she realised, she had already broken the rule that she'd made up herself just hours earlier. She had shared Avril's secret with someone else and defied the Westford Park Ladies Club code of conduct when it had only just been introduced. What if Poppy told Bethany about it and Avril was furious? Had she just ruined everything?

But she'd done it for the right reasons. Nothing was more important than Poppy. She would lie, cheat and kill to protect her and God help anyone who stood in her way.

8

Avril clutched the chilled bottle of white wine to her chest. The condensation was dampening her dress but the feeling of cold glass against her overheating body was soothing. It wasn't even hot any more, but she was still sweating. She wondered if she'd ever stop.

She'd been stressing ever since she'd spilled her guts to Lily and Sandy at the clubhouse. What on earth had possessed her to tell them about Bethany being expelled? They'd come here for a fresh start and she'd already blown their cover. She was absolutely furious with herself. And Lily had almost visibly recoiled from her when she'd heard, reminding Avril that although they had hit it off straight away, they didn't really know each other at all. Avril was now panicking that Lily would cut off contact and order Poppy to stay away from Bethany, the only friend her daughter seemed to have.

To top it all off, she kept hearing this God-awful noise in the middle of the night, which pierced through her dreams and set her heart thudding as she woke up with a start. Stuart, who wore earplugs and slept through it all, said it was probably foxes fighting. But to Avril, it sounded like children being tortured and it was beginning to torment her, as she wondered if it was real or she was finally going mad. The lack of sleep was making her even more paranoid, about her own state of mind and what other people thought of her.

If she somehow managed to scrape through this barbecue, she wouldn't make the same mistake again. She would leave the old baggage behind, where it belonged. From now on, Lily and Sandy would only know the new version of her, the one who had a perfectly normal, functional family, who enjoyed learning how to play tennis and chatting about the weather. Not the Avril who lay awake at night, sweating and panicking that there were ghosts of murdered children at Westford Park or that she was being haunted by her family's past.

Lily hadn't cancelled the barbecue at least, so that was a good sign. Avril was wearing a new dress and had blow-dried her light brown hair straight, although it was already starting to frizz in the heat. Stuart hadn't even bothered to change.

'We're only going across the road, what's the point?' he'd said as he put on his Crocs.

Avril was fretting. What if everyone thought they were the oddball family? What if Eric thought they were boring and told Lily not to invite them round again? What if Poppy ignored Bethany? She felt like they were going to a battle, not a barbecue.

And the worst thought of all, the one which seemed to be on a repeat loop, despite her trying to drown it out, was, *What if Bethany does something bad to Poppy?* Ever since Bethany had held her hand, Avril had been waiting for some sort of breakthrough. For her daughter to open up to her and for them to finally be able to put the past behind them. But Bethany had remained quiet and sullen and the intimate moment between them had not happened again, leaving Avril wondering if it had happened at all, if she had not imagined it.

At least there had been no drama at school. Avril kept waiting for the moment when the headteacher called her into his office to discuss Bethany, but it hadn't happened yet. And a few of the other teachers had praised Bethany in the staff room, telling Avril that she was such a bright young lady. Her art teacher said that she had a unique talent and Avril had glowed with pride. She had wanted to gush about it to Bethany after school but the chasm between them had kept the words lodged in her throat, unable to escape.

Seeing Bethany getting along so well with Poppy and knowing that she at least had one person to talk to was the only thing keeping Avril going. So, if she'd messed it up for her daughter by telling Lily about her past, then she would never forgive herself.

But Lily opened the door with a wide unreserved smile, as though the conversation they'd had two days previously had never happened.

'Hi, everyone, welcome! Do come in. Sandy and Clare are already here. Bethany, darling, Poppy's in her bedroom if you want to go up. You must be Stuart!'

Avril watched as Lily leaned forward and kissed Stuart on both cheeks like they were already the best of friends. Stuart looked a little taken aback as he proffered a dessert at Lily.

'Oh, a trifle, how lovely, thank you!'

Bethany plodded upstairs and Avril followed Lily out to the garden, where Clare and Sandy were sitting at a huge, round wooden table, with Isla sandwiched between them.

'Wow, Lily, your garden is stunning.' Avril looked around in awe. There was a pergola at the bottom, with an egg chair underneath, a rattan corner sofa on one end of the patio and the dining table on the other. Beautiful plants sat in expensive-looking pots.

How had Lily already managed to furnish their garden so beautifully? Avril had barely even glanced at hers.

Lily smiled modestly. 'Thank you. Would you like a glass of wine?'

'Yes, please.' Avril made a mental note to stick to one glass so she didn't become loose-lipped again.

'And Stuart? Wine? Beer? Soft drink for you, Tom?'

Lily took the drinks orders, looking completely at ease, as though she'd been born to host parties. Eric, who was over by the barbecue, came over to shake everyone's hands firmly, putting his arm around his wife as he did. What a handsome couple they made, Avril thought, and so much in love. Just look at how adoringly Lily looked at her husband, almost as though they were newly-weds. She felt a pang of envy, finding herself unable to look away. They were captivating.

She came back down to reality when she realised that Sandy was talking to her. 'Micky tells me that Bethany enjoys art. I'm happy to give her some tips, if she'd like that.'

Avril looked at Sandy gratefully. 'She'd love that, thank you. What kind of art do you do?'

'Well, funny you should ask because I've recently had a change of direction.'

As the wine kicked in and the conversation flowed, Avril began to relax and enjoy herself. Lily flitted about, switching seamlessly between joining the conversation and bringing out bowls of salads, while Eric hovered by the barbecue, drinking from a bottle of beer and occasionally throwing comments over. Sandy and Clare were great fun and by the time she'd finished her first glass, Avril decided to treat herself to a second one after all.

When she'd finished it, she stood up to go to the loo and realised that she was swaying. She made her way inside self-consciously, following Lily's directions to the downstairs toilet.

Christ, she was tipsy. As she passed the stairs, she heard a noise from above and stopped dead, immediately sobering up. Was that a cry or a laugh? The hairs on her arms stood on end as she listened intently, waiting for another sound, but none came. Bethany, Poppy and Micky were up there, alone and unsupervised, and all of a sudden Avril didn't like the idea of it.

Looking behind her to make sure that no one was watching, she slipped off her shoes and crept up the stairs, grateful for the soft carpet which cushioned her footsteps. Once she was on the landing she looked around until she saw a door ajar at the end. In the crack, she could see a pair of jeaned legs hanging off the side of the bed. Now that she was closer she could hear music playing and soft voices talking, although she couldn't make out what they were saying. She tiptoed along the landing until she was outside the door and then peered in, hoping that they wouldn't see her and already thinking of what to say if they did.

Bethany was on the bed, leaning up against the wall, her legs tucked underneath her and Micky was sitting beside her. Avril couldn't see Poppy but she could hear her and guessed that she was on the other side of the room. Unnoticed, Avril stared at her daughter in shock. Bethany's face was animated and she was smiling at something Poppy had said. As Avril watched, she threw her head back and laughed, wincing as she hit the wall, and then dissolving into giggles again. Beside her, Micky started laughing too. They looked like regular teenagers just hanging out and having a good time. Avril moved away from the door and began to creep back along the landing again. The scene had completely thrown her.

She hadn't seen her daughter laugh in months and the sight of Bethany having fun had been one of the most life-affirming things she'd ever witnessed. Relief flooded over her as she realised that the fresh start she had hoped for was working. Bethany was happy again and it was everything she had wished for. But there was something else too, something she couldn't shake off even though she wanted to. This wasn't about her, it was about Bethany and yet she couldn't let go of the feeling that had grabbed her by the heart and was squeezing it tightly.

If Bethany is so happy to be here, why is she still so withdrawn and uncommunicative with me? And the only thing Avril could think of, the thing that chilled her to the bone, was *Because she hates me.*

'Avril! What are you doing up there?'

The sound of Lily's voice gave Avril a fright and she peered down the stairs to see her host looking at her curiously. She padded back down the stairs, thinking on her feet.

'Sorry, Lily, I couldn't resist having a little snoop. Your home is just so lovely.'

Lily beamed with pride. 'Oh, thank you. Everything okay up there?'

'Yes, they're all in Poppy's room having a great time.'

'I was just about to go up myself,' Lily said before adding quickly, 'Lunch is nearly ready.'

Lily had been on her way to check up on them too, Avril realised. Because she didn't trust Bethany. The last drop of her earlier wine glow trickled away as paranoia replaced it.

'I'll tell them to come down now,' she told Lily.

She shouted up to the kids and then nipped into the downstairs loo. By the time she got outside, Bethany, Poppy and Micky had come downstairs and were lurking around the barbecue. As soon as their plates were full, they disappeared back upstairs.

'Bye, then,' Lily called before rolling her eyes. 'They don't leave you alone for ten years and then they don't want anything to do with you. You two are lucky you still have little Isla.'

'Tell me about it.' Sandy laughed, looking at Isla who had run off to sit on the egg chair. 'There's nothing like the unconditional love of a child to restore your faith in life.'

'Speaking of children, has anyone else been hearing strange noises in the night?' Avril asked suddenly, the words out of her mouth before she'd even thought them through.

Sandy dropped her fork with a clatter and everyone looked at her. 'Sorry,' she said. Avril noticed that Clare had reached out and put a hand on Sandy's leg.

'What kind of noises?' Lily asked.

'It's foxes,' Stuart said. 'I've told her already.'

Avril ignored him. 'It sounds awful. Like children being strangled.'

'I haven't heard it, but I sleep like a baby,' Lily said. 'Have you, Eric?'

'Now that you mention it, something did wake me up the other night.'

'Was it foxes?'

'I don't know. But it sounded ghastly.'

Avril smiled at Eric, relieved that she wasn't alone in hearing the noises. 'I know. Do you think the woods are haunted?' She made light of it, but she was only half joking.

'Perhaps,' Eric said with a grin, playing along with what he clearly thought was a game. 'It could be coming from the boathouse. It is rather creepy.'

'Oh, come off it,' Lily scoffed. 'It's charming.'

'I suppose so, in a terrifying, isolated log cabin in the woods kind of way.'

Lily slapped Eric's arm playfully. 'Stop it. Anyway, it's hardly isolated. It's only a few minutes' walk away. And the development's brand new so it can't be haunted.'

'The development is new, the boathouse isn't,' Eric corrected her. 'I played golf here a few times before the land was sold and I saw it then. I imagine it's been around for years.'

'Well, it's still not haunted.'

'You just never know,' Eric said with a sly wink.

Avril knew that Eric was joking, but she wasn't enjoying the conversation one bit. She glanced at Sandy and was shocked to see abject terror on her face.

'Are you okay, Sandy?' she asked.

'Yes,' Sandy replied quietly. She looked at Avril and then at Lily with a small smile. 'The food is delicious, thank you so much.' Avril frowned as she looked at Sandy's full plate and discarded fork. She hadn't taken a single bite yet.

'Can we talk about something other than the undead please?' Lily said with an eye roll, as she turned to Sandy. 'If you don't mind me asking, how were Micky and Isla conceived?'

'I don't mind at all,' Sandy replied. She seemed relieved by the change of subject too. 'I had Micky with my ex-partner. Isla was conceived using a sperm donor.' She looked at Clare quickly, who nodded. 'We decided I'd carry Isla as well but we shared maternity leave.'

'And does Micky still see his father?' Lily asked.

You could have heard a pin drop. Avril saw Sandy and Clare exchange looks before glancing at Isla, at the end of the garden.

'No,' Sandy said finally. 'He doesn't.'

Lily still seemed unaware of the tension. 'Oh, it's so sad when that happens. We had a friend – remember her, Eric? From Poppy's school? – whose husband left her and made no effort to see his children. It's just awful, there's simply no excuse for it.'

'Yes.' Sandy was staring at her plate. Clare began stroking her arm and it was only then that Avril noticed the scars. Quickly, she looked away, worried about being caught staring.

'Sandy's ex wasn't a good guy,' Clare said, finally breaking the silence. 'And Micky is much better off without him.'

The penny finally seemed to drop with Lily, and she looked mortified. 'Oh my goodness, I'm so sorry to pry. I'm such a bull in a china shop sometimes.'

Sandy shook her head. 'Please don't worry, it's fine.'

'It's not fine.' Lily seemed crushed. 'I really am sorry. It was insensitive of me.'

Avril glanced over at Stuart to see what he made of it all, but her husband was now reading a comic book over Tom's shoulder. Like father, like son, she thought with a surge of irritation. The two of them could lose themselves in a book or computer game for hours, oblivious to what was going on around them. Neither of them would have even registered the awkwardness. Sometimes she envied their ability to switch off from life when she was so acutely tuned into it. Other times it infuriated her. She risked a quick look at Sandy's scars again. Were they connected to Micky's father, who Sandy clearly didn't want to talk about? Her eyes moved up to Sandy's face and she blanched when she realised that Sandy was looking at her. But Sandy smiled at her, as if silently saying, *don't worry, I'm not offended*. Avril smiled back. Sandy had been so kind to her, so unjudgmental, and now Avril was beginning to realise why. She had her own secrets. Was that why she had so evidently blanched when Avril had mentioned the strange nocturnal noises? Maybe that was what separated them from Lily. Lily was lovely but she lived such an easy, uncomplicated life.

She didn't have time to mull it over, however, because then Lily said something that blew her theory out of the water. 'My father wasn't a good guy either, Sandy. He was an alcoholic and a bully and I'm far better off without him in my life. So, I do understand.'

Avril took another fortifying sip of wine and wondered how the conversation had become so serious so quickly. At least it wasn't her sharing her secrets this time; she was keeping her cards close to her chest again after her slip-up a couple of days ago. But she had just learned that Lily's life wasn't so perfect after all. She had misjudged her and that was unfair. They all had their demons – Lily, Sandy, her. Some hid their past better than others but there were skeletons in every closet. And suddenly, Avril didn't feel so alone any more.

'Well, it sounds like we need an emergency meeting of the Westford Park Ladies Club,' she said, and Sandy and Lily laughed.

'Avril, the first rule of the Westford Park Ladies Club is that you don't talk about the Westford Park Ladies Club,' Lily said with mock disapproval.

'What on earth are you talking about?' Eric was looking at his wife, bemused.

Lily leaned forward and whispered into her ear, 'Next meeting's on Friday morning.'

And despite her nerves and paranoia, Avril smiled and thought, *I can't wait.*

9

Sandy woke up in a cold sweat, her heart pounding. Her mind was screaming at her body to run but her limbs hadn't woken up yet and she was paralysed. Where was she? Who was sleeping beside her? She was trapped and fear had her in a headlock. But as she rapidly regained control of her body she recognised the shape of Clare, still fast asleep. She remembered that they were at Westford Park, in their new home, and that they were safe.

She hadn't had a nightmare that vivid in months, and she knew what had triggered it. First the anonymous phone call and then all that talk about strange noises in the night. Clare had reassured her, telling her that nuisance callers and local wildlife were to blame. Sandy knew that she was probably right. It was the 'probably' bit that scared her.

The call had been from a withheld number so it could have been anybody.

It could have been him.

Logic told her that it was unlikely. How on earth would he have got their landline number when they'd only just had it installed? And why would he come looking for them now, anyway? She hadn't heard from him in years and for all she knew, he might even be dead. Yet sometimes she still got the sensation that he was watching her, waiting for his moment. And no matter how many times she relocated, the feeling lingered. Perhaps she could dismiss the silent caller but ever since Avril had mentioned the noises, she'd been lying in wait, half wanting to hear them, half dreading them. *Like children being strangled.* That's what Avril had said. What if it was him, reminding her that he was there? Messing with her head. Watching. Waiting.

She was furious that this had happened at Westford Park because it had tainted their new beginning and blotted the blank canvas that Sandy had hoped for. It had made her fearful of what was out there in the dark, looking in. And the conversation about Micky's father at the barbecue hadn't helped in the slightest.

Clare had complained about Lily on the way home. 'Who does she think she is, asking all those personal questions when we barely know her?'

But Sandy had been philosophical. 'Lily's a nice person. She's just curious, that's all. But she was extremely apologetic afterwards and I really think she felt bad.'

'And so she should. Her husband's a funny one, isn't he? I mean, he's disgustingly handsome and he couldn't have been more charming, but he spent most of the time on his phone.'

'He has a demanding job. I imagine he never stops working, even at weekends.'

'Maybe. But anyway, enough about them. Are *you* okay?'

Sandy had thought she was okay, but the nightmare had proven otherwise. She had been back in the flat, breathing in the stale stench of his cigarette smoke as she waited for him to come for her. She had anticipated his grip around her neck, knowing that this was the last time he would hurt her. This time he would finish it. Except that it didn't happen. And it was then that she realised it wasn't her he was coming for. It was Micky. *Like children being strangled.*

Before Micky came along, she had not resisted Grant, not once. He had stolen her fight and he had done it so slowly, so stealthily, that she hadn't realised until it was too late. She was his plaything, his toy. At first, she had been his prized possession but then he had got bored of her and had started pulling her apart, bit by bit, until she was broken.

When they had met, he had been charming and she had fallen for his every line, his every promise. She had introduced him to her friends and they had liked him. She had taken him to meet her parents and they had approved. There were no red flags, no alarm bells ringing in her mind. She didn't come from a broken home, she didn't have an unloving, alcoholic father like Lily; she was surrounded by people who loved her and she was a confident, intelligent woman. All these things had made it even harder for people to understand what happened next.

It had started gradually. Urging her to stay in with him rather than go and meet her friends. Booking weekends away when he knew they were supposed to be going to a family event. Slowly, he isolated her from her support group and the worst thing was that she let him because she loved him and she wanted to please him.

The first time he hit her, he had been full of tears and remorse, promising that it would never happen again and she had wanted to believe him so much that she had accepted his apology. It was her own fault, she told herself, because she had got drunk and flirted with one of his friends. It had been harmless but she could understand why he had taken offence. The second time he did it, because she had gone out for lunch with a male colleague, his remorse, and her belief, had been less. By the time she had lost count of the times he attacked her, there was no point in pretending that it would be the last. This was what their life was now, their new normal.

She hardly understood it herself. He'd objectified her, as if he held the remote control to her mind and body so that she had no power over herself any more. But by then she was in too deep. She had quit her job, she was ashamed to go back to her family and friends and, worst of all, she was afraid of losing him. Even after everything he did to her, she was still afraid of losing him. She was a loyal pet, cowering away from a cruel owner but always going back to them, desperate to be loved. Because the truth was that, by then, he owned her.

When she fell pregnant with Micky, she was elated and terrified. Part of her hoped that this would be the end of his violence because she had finally given him what he wanted most in the world, a child. But another part of her knew that it just didn't work like that. And so she wasn't even surprised when the attacks continued, although he always aimed carefully so as not to damage his precious child. That's when he started on her arms. She had been absurdly grateful to him, pleased that he was being considerate of their baby and hopeful that when the child was born, it would be safe. She would take a thousand burns, a million punches, to protect it.

But when Micky arrived and was placed into her arms, it was like someone had flicked a switch and turned on the light. She had looked down at her beautiful, perfect baby boy and had known that he deserved a better life. She couldn't be the mother she wanted to be if she lived in fear and shame, and she couldn't be any mother if she was dead. And what if he started hurting Micky? It would be her fault for letting him, for not leaving when she had the chance. And so, as soon as she was alone in the hospital, she had picked up Micky, ignored the nurses' protests as she discharged herself and got a taxi to her parents' house. This was the end, she told herself joyfully, and the beginning.

But she had walked into the kitchen and found him, sitting at the table with a cup of tea, smiling at her as though this was a perfectly normal thing to be doing, even though they hadn't visited her parents in months. And that's when she knew that there was no escape, that he would always be one step ahead of her, predicting her every move.

She had cried then, and her mother had taken Micky from her and told her that she was exhausted and that baby blues were to be expected, and she had wanted to tell her parents everything but she could feel his eyes boring into her, silently warning her to stay quiet, and she knew then that it was over, that the light had been extinguished forever.

He moved them a hundred miles away so that she couldn't go running back to her parents and he cut off all contact with her family. And that was how she and Micky ended up in the cramped, dirty flat that became their home for the next three years. He took her phone so that she couldn't call anyone and he controlled her every move. She was not allowed to leave the flat without him. She was not allowed to take Micky to baby and toddler groups or to mix with other mums. And she accepted her fate because she was no longer a human being, she was a broken toy. But she still clung on to one thing – he had never laid a hand on Micky.

And then one day something happened which changed everything.

Micky had been playing with some trains, banging them together and pushing them along the floor while Sandy folded up some washing and kept an eye on him. Then, out of nowhere, he had picked up a train and thrown it at her. It had hit Sandy on the side of her head and she had cried out and turned to her son in shock to see both fear and confusion on his face. Fear of her reaction and the realisation that he had hurt her, and confusion as to what he had done wrong when he had seen his father throw things at her a hundred times.

She had put the washing down, picked him up and left the flat without packing a single item. She called her parents from a payphone and told them everything and when her mother broke down on the phone, sobbing with horror and guilt at what she had just learned, Sandy finally realised that she had not been alone, he had just made her think that she was.

Clare was stirring now and Sandy watched her for a while before getting up to check the windows and doors of the house. The curtains were closed and everything was as it should be, but she was too shaken to go back to bed, so she went over to the bookcase and picked up a photo of her, Clare, Isla and Micky, taken on holiday the previous year. They were all grinning at the camera and Isla's face was covered in chocolate ice cream. Sandy smiled at the memory.

Micky didn't remember his early years, but she sometimes wondered whether he remembered what had happened when he was five years old. It was two years after they had escaped from that flat. With her parents' help, they had moved to a new area, Micky had started school and Sandy had got a job in finance, steadily working her way up the ladder. She was putting in long hours to prove herself, but it meant that she could provide for her and Micky, so as far as she was concerned it was worth the sacrifice. She saw her parents infrequently because she was too afraid of them accidentally leading him to her and Micky, but they spoke a lot and she was beginning to make new friends. She hadn't told the police what had happened and she knew that he wouldn't call them either, even though she had taken his son from him, because if he did, she would tell them what he had done. She was careful to cover her tracks, to make sure he never found them, and for the first time she was starting to relax and believe their nightmare was finally over. She stopped looking over her shoulder. And so, inevitably, the moment she let her guard down, he seized his opportunity.

One Saturday afternoon, Micky was playing and Sandy had gone to lie down in her bedroom and read a book but she was exhausted from working fifty-hour weeks and she dozed off. When she woke up, she had sensed immediately that the flat was too quiet.

He had found them and taken Micky. She had understood that straight away. And, when she went downstairs and found the back door open, she knew how he'd got in too. She'd been out in the garden hanging up some washing and she'd forgotten to lock it when she came inside. She had got complacent and she was paying the worst possible price for it.

This time she hadn't hesitated to call the police and she had told them everything. She felt sick to the bone and she hated herself for making it so easy for him to take Micky. For not calling the police in the first place. For not realising that not only had he found them but that he must have been watching them for some time, waiting for the right moment.

They located him the next day. He was trying to board a ferry to France and he was arrested at the port. This time Sandy had testified against him because she needed to make sure that he never came near Micky again. She forced herself to go to court and she forced herself to confront him, even though it terrified her. The last time she saw him was the day he was sentenced and just like that he was out of their lives for good.

But she could never let herself relax completely again. She had made the mistake once and she wouldn't dare repeat it. Because she never knew if he was watching, waiting for the moment she let her guard down. Over the years she had felt his presence and she had never determined whether it was physical or psychological because she moved them before she found out. That was why Westford Park, with its twenty-four-hour security, was the perfect place for them. The place where Sandy could finally relax.

Except the illusion had now been shattered. Where Sandy had seen peace and tranquillity in the grounds of the development, she saw danger again. He could get in, if he really wanted to. He was clever and he was calculating. He could hide in the woods, he could even be there right now. She looked over at the patio doors again, the curtains drawn tightly shut, and shuddered. Micky was sixteen, not a child any more. He wanted to go out with his friends and she had to let him. But she was afraid. She was so damn afraid.

She forced herself to look at the photograph again. To absorb the innocence and happiness of it, and slowly, her resolve began to return. She had confronted him, she had faced her fears. She couldn't control her nightmares but she *could* control her waking life and she was not going to let her fear filter down to her family either. She stood up and made her way back to bed, climbing in next to Clare.

Tomorrow she would paint. She would go to the woods and see them for what they were, nature at its finest. And on Friday she would have her first tennis lesson with Lily and Avril, followed by a meeting of the Westford Park Ladies Club. It was silly and childish, but the idea still cheered her. Maybe she would even tell them some more about her past if it felt right because it was part of who she was and nothing to be ashamed of.

That was the problem, she realised. She'd been trying to run away from it. Perhaps if she confronted it instead, it would no longer haunt her. She had not known Avril and Lily for long but she liked them. With Lily's incessant talk of fashion and private schools and how hot the tennis coach was, she wasn't Sandy's usual type of friend, but she was an open book and it was refreshing. And

Avril had such a kind soul. They made an unlikely duo, just like their children, but it seemed to work and Sandy was flattered that they had so warmly welcomed her into their newly formed friendship. When she had first mentioned that she was married to a woman, she had waited for their reaction, curiously and almost a little challengingly, but they hadn't so much as raised an eyebrow. It made her think that it was finally time to let her guard down. Satisfied, she closed her eyes but after a few seconds, they sprang open again.

She'd just check the locks one more time. Then she'd go to sleep.

10

'No. Absolutely not.'

Lily muted the television and watched with mild amusement as her husband and her daughter went head-to-head. Eric disapproving, Poppy mutinous.

'Don't be so old fashioned, Father.'

'That's not a skirt, it's a belt.'

Lily stifled a smile. Poppy looked rather gorgeous in her miniskirt and tight T-shirt, although she had to agree with Eric that it was a bit much for a trip down to the lake. Not to mention cold. A few months ago, Lily might have sided with her husband but she was Lily 2.0 now, the more relaxed, tolerant version of herself, and if her daughter wanted to freeze her baps off in November just to impress her friends, then good luck to her.

'She's going for a walk with Bethany and Micky, darling,' Lily told Eric. 'Not to an illegal rave in a warehouse. She'll be fine.'

Eric scowled. 'Put a coat on at least.'

Poppy rolled her eyes. 'Obviously.'

Their daughter strutted off and Lily smiled at Eric. 'She's growing up.'

'What do we know about these kids she hangs out with, anyway? Are they okay?'

Lily considered the question. She still had her reservations about Bethany, but she had to admit that the girl had not put a foot wrong in the three months since they'd moved to Westford Park. Although she'd barely spoken a word to Lily. She was like a little church mouse and Lily was struggling to believe that she could bully an ant, let alone another human being.

And Micky was so sweet, just like his mother. It was painfully obvious that he had a stonking crush on Poppy, but Lily sensed that the feelings weren't reciprocated and perhaps that was a good thing. A romance could cause trouble between the three friends.

But there had been no trouble, not even a hint of it. The three of them, Poppy, Bethany and Micky, had slotted together as though they'd known each other all their lives and although Poppy still saw her schoolfriends from time to time, she seemed to prefer the company of the Westford Park gang. They spent most weekends together, either in one of their bedrooms, at the clubhouse or down by the lake. Whenever Poppy came home, Lily surreptitiously sniffed her for evidence of alcohol or cigarette smoke, but Poppy was as fresh as a daisy. She had wondered if Poppy would get bored at Westford Park, or feel imprisoned by the remoteness of the development, but she was happier than Lily had seen her in a while.

And the most astounding thing of all was that they even studied together. Bethany was bright and she'd been helping Poppy with her homework. The girl who Lily had once feared was turning out to be one of the best things that had ever happened to Poppy.

'They're lovely kids,' she told Eric. 'We've been extremely fortunate with our neighbours.'

It wasn't just the children. Friday morning tennis followed by coffee was now a weekly occurrence and it had quickly developed into other social engagements too. That evening, Lily was going out for dinner with Avril and Sandy at the clubhouse. She wondered, tentatively, if she had finally found the friends she had always hoped for. But she still hadn't let her guard down completely yet because some secrets were best left alone.

Poppy called out from the hallway. 'Bye, then.'

As the door slammed, Lily looked at Eric, but he was scrolling on his phone, his feud with Poppy already forgotten. She turned off the television and stood up.

'I'm going upstairs to get ready.'

'Okay, darling.' Eric didn't look up from his phone.

Upstairs Lily changed into smart jeans and a white silk shirt, and then started applying her make-up. She felt like a teenager again, the anticipation of a fun evening ahead building up inside her. Poppy was out having fun and soon she would be too.

By the time she was ready to leave, Eric had dozed off, his phone still in his hand. Lily let herself out, closing the front door softly. As she walked up the path towards the clubhouse, she looked up at the little string lights hanging above her and almost giggled with excitement.

Avril was already at the table when she arrived, and Lily kissed her on both cheeks before sitting down opposite her. 'How was your day?'

'Good.' Avril grinned. 'I took Tom kayaking on the lake. I'm making the most of him still wanting to spend time with me before he becomes a grumpy teenager. He loved it. The man who runs the boathouse – Steve, I think his name is – was so friendly and help-ful. And he's brilliant with kids. Tom's already talking about when he can do it again. How about you?'

Lily had met the wives of Eric's friends for lunch at the golf club. They had talked about tutors and floral arrangements and the latest gossip, and Lily had felt increasingly distant from them. She had nothing in common with these women, except for their husbands, but then she never had, so why was she only now finding it such a chore?

But she said none of this to Avril. 'I met some chums for lunch. It was delicious.'

Sandy appeared at their table. 'Sorry I'm late. Isla kept trying to distract me.'

'Avril was just telling me about how she went kayaking with Tom. Have you been yet?'

'No, Isla's a little young I think, and Micky doesn't seem interested.'

'Maybe we should all try it together. Westford Park Ladies Club in action.'

Sandy smiled. 'Why not? Now, are we drinking red or white? Or maybe cocktails? I do love a margarita.'

'I used to make the best margaritas,' Lily said nostalgically. 'I was famous for it. All the customers used to come to me when they wanted a cocktail.'

'Customers?' Avril looked confused.

'Yes, I used to work in a bar.'

Avril's eyebrows shot up. 'Really?'

'Don't look so surprised, darling. I wasn't always a housewife, you know. In fact, that's how I won Eric's heart. I mixed him such a good cocktail that he simply had to marry me.'

Sandy laughed. 'So, you met him when you were working at the bar?'

'That's right. I used to model but I never made it into the big time, so I worked evenings and weekends to pay the rent. I was in my twenties and working at this flashy bar in town when in walked Eric with his banking cronies. Oh, he was so gorgeous, ladies, I couldn't stop looking at him. I vowed there and then to make him mine.'

'Wow!' Avril was impressed. 'And you clearly succeeded.'

Lily smiled at the memory. 'Yes. It was love at first sight. Or lust at least.'

'Did you carry on modelling?'

'I stopped after I got engaged. To be honest I didn't miss it. It had its highs, but it also had its lows too. I was young and didn't have a support network before I met Eric. Some men tried to take advantage of that.'

'In what way?'

'Well, there was this one man, I was eighteen and he must have been in his fifties. He promised me a lucrative modelling job if I spent the night with him.'

Avril was wide-eyed. 'And did you?'

Lily smirked. 'I fluttered my eyelashes and agreed, and we checked into a hotel room. He took all his clothes off and then I grabbed them and ran from the room. Needless to say, I didn't get the job.'

'Lily, that's the best thing I've ever heard.'

Lily flushed with pride. 'Well, I'm not sure about that but it felt good at the time.'

Sandy, who had been listening in quietly, looked at Lily sympathetically. 'It must have been hard for you though, being out there alone without anyone looking out for you.'

'Oh well.' Lily waved her hand dismissively. 'I was thick-skinned. Or at least I was until I met Eric, and then he brought out the softer side in me. The rest, as they say, is history.'

'And you're still so much in love.' Avril was wistful. 'It's very romantic.'

'Yes.' Lily smiled sweetly. That was one part that she was still happy to play. She beckoned to a passing waiter to order their drinks and then turned to Avril. 'How did you meet Stuart?'

'At a friend's dinner party. I ended up sitting next to him and he made me laugh so much that I was hooked. Humour is definitely the way to my heart.' Her face dropped. 'Not that there's been much of that lately.'

'You have to find time for yourselves as a couple,' Lily said. 'When you have children it's easy to forget about each other. I'm always happy to babysit or keep an eye on the house if you're not comfortable leaving Tom and Bethany at home alone all evening yet.'

'Thanks, Lily. What about you and Clare, Sandy?'

Sandy smiled. 'We met through work. Clare made her feelings clear early on, but I was afraid. I hadn't been in a relationship for a while and the last one didn't end well.'

Lily assumed she was talking about Micky's dad, but she'd learned her lesson about asking too much, so she kept her mouth tightly shut and waited for Sandy to continue.

'I told her I needed to take things slowly, as in snail's pace slowly, and she said that she would wait. That's when I knew that I'd found the right person.'

Lily smiled wistfully. 'Now *that's* romantic.'

'It was rather. Clare was – is – unlike anyone I'd ever known. She taught me how to see the joy in life again. I don't know where I'd be if it wasn't for her.'

'How long have you been together?'

'About seven years. It was a while before I introduced her to Micky, but he took to her straight away. They're very close now.'

Their drinks arrived and they all clinked glasses before taking a sip.

'Now that's very good,' Lily remarked. 'But I think I can do better. You must come over for cocktails one evening.'

As the margaritas disappeared and were replaced by another round, and then the food arrived, the conversation moved on to the children, as it often did.

'You should have seen what Poppy was wearing when she went out this evening,' Lily confided. 'I thought Eric was going to have a coronary.'

'I wonder what they do down there by the lake,' Sandy mused.

'I think they just talk,' Lily replied. 'Honestly, this Generation Z or whatever they're called are so strait-laced. At Poppy's age, I was a tearaway, sneaking off to kiss boys or stealing cigarettes from my mother's pack. What about you, Avril?'

Avril blushed. 'I was quite well-behaved, to be honest. I do sometimes wonder what the kids get up to myself. It must be freezing down there by the lake.'

Feeling reckless from the alcohol and company, Lily leaned forward conspiratorially. 'I don't know about you ladies, but I wouldn't mind a walk after dinner to work off all this lovely food. How about a stroll around the lake?'

'Oh, I don't know,' Avril said. 'I'm trying to show Bethany that I trust her. It won't go down well if she catches me snooping.'

'Who's snooping?' Lily was all innocence. 'We're just having a post-dinner walk.'

She looked at Sandy whose cheeks were flushed from the cocktails. 'I wouldn't mind stretching my legs,' Sandy said with a wink.

They hurriedly paid the bill and put on their coats, giggling as they walked down the path towards the lake and shh-ing each other when they reached the water. Lily linked her arms through Avril's and Sandy's, feeling as high as a kite.

'Where shall we start?' she whispered.

'Let's walk around the main path,' Avril said, shivering. 'They may even have gone home by now because it's so cold.'

They circled the lake, trying unsuccessfully to suppress their laughs, as they scanned their surroundings, listening out for the children, but the only sound they heard was the gravel underfoot and the occasional rustle of an animal in the bushes. The lake was nowhere near as welcoming at night, and as their laughter faded away, the silence soon became deafening.

Suddenly an ear-splitting noise cut through the quiet and sent a shock of fear through Lily's entire body. 'What the hell was that?' she demanded.

Avril reached out and grabbed her arm. 'That's the noise I was telling you about.'

'That's not foxes. That sounds like children being tortured.'

'That's exactly what I said!'

Lily's heart was pounding. 'What if it's the kids? What if they're in trouble?'

They both turned to Sandy who had gone as white as a sheet. 'We need to find them,' she said urgently. 'We need to find Micky. Shit. I'm scared.'

Sandy's reaction sent chills running up Lily's spine and she started running along the lake path, calling out Poppy's name. What had started as a light-hearted caper was no longer funny and the idea of the kids being out there in the dark wilderness terrified her. What was that horrendous noise? Who was out there? What were they doing to the children? Unless, could it be one of the children hurting the other?

The warming effects of the alcohol seeped away as she imagined Poppy, freezing cold in her skimpy outfit. She shouldn't have let her go out dressed like that. What if Micky tried to take advantage of her? What if Bethany did nothing to stop him? Maybe she was even complicit. Avril hadn't divulged any more information about why Bethany had been expelled and now Lily was jumping to all sorts of terrible conclusions.

By the time they arrived back where they'd started, Lily was out of breath and very, very afraid. She pulled out her phone. 'I'll check Poppy's location.'

But Avril was staring into the distance. 'The light's on in the boathouse.'

Lily frowned. 'It's not open at this time of night, surely?'

'I wouldn't have thought so.'

The women looked at each other and rushed towards it. In the darkness of the November night, the old wooden cabin, which looked quaint during the day, loomed in front of them, sinister and creepy. Fear multiplied in the pit of Lily's stomach. She had been wrong to let Poppy wander around the grounds of Westford Park at all hours. It wasn't safe. She reached the door first and tried the handle, but it wouldn't budge.

'It's locked,' she called out to the others, unable to keep the fear from her voice.

'Give it a good push,' Avril called back. 'The door's sticky.'

Lily used her shoulder to push the door with all her might and almost fell into the boathouse.

The warmth hit her immediately as she took in the sight of the teenagers sitting on the sofa. Three pairs of eyes looked up at her in alarm.

'Mother! What are you doing here?' Poppy was not impressed.

Avril and Sandy piled in after her.

'What are *you* doing here?' Lily asked.

'Steve said we could hang out in the boathouse. He doesn't lock it at night.'

Lily, swaying slightly, felt a flood of relief wash her fear away.

'Did you hear that noise?' she asked Poppy.

'What noise?'

'The horrible noise, a few minutes ago.'

The three teenagers looked at each other. 'Mother, I have no idea what you're talking about. Are you *drunk*?'

'We may have had a few cocktails,' she confessed. 'And we decided to walk it off around the lake. Then we heard that noise and we were worried about you. When we saw the lights on, we thought we'd come and check everything was okay.'

But Poppy wasn't fooled. 'You were checking up on us, more like.'

Sandy stepped forward to address Poppy but her eyes were fixed firmly on Micky. 'No, love, we weren't. We didn't even know you were here.'

Only Avril remained silent, hanging back and refusing to meet anyone's eye.

Lily looked around the cabin, which now seemed perfectly safe again. With the electric heater on, music playing softly from Poppy's phone and a scattering of blankets on the sofa, it was cosy and welcoming. 'So, this is where you come, is it? To hang out?'

'When it's cold,' Micky replied.

Lily tried to decide how she felt about them being alone in the boathouse. But they were safe, they were warm, and they were only a hundred metres or so from their homes. A quick scan found no sign of any contraband. And she didn't believe all that silly talk about ghosts. Maybe Stuart had been right after all, and it was foxes they'd heard.

All in all, she couldn't find much to have a problem with.

'Well, we'll leave you to it then. It's nearly time for curfew though, mind. And stay away from the woods, I really didn't like that noise.'

Poppy rolled her eyes. 'Whatever. See you, then.'

Sandy was still staring at Micky. 'Come home now, Micky.'

Micky nodded and stood up to leave. 'See ya,' he said to Poppy and Bethany.

Sandy and Micky walked off with barely a backward glance

With one last look at Poppy and Bethany, Lily followed Avril out of the boathouse and pulled the door to.

'Well, that was awkward,' she whispered. 'Do you think Sandy is okay?'

Avril spoke so quietly that Lily barely heard her. 'Why did you want to check on the kids?'

'It was just meant to be a laugh. It was only that noise that set me on edge.'

'Were you worried about Poppy being alone with Bethany?'

Lily did not want to lie to her friend. But she couldn't tell the truth either, she couldn't admit what she had very briefly feared. 'Why would it be anything to do with Bethany?'

'Because of what I told you,' Avril's voice was shaking. 'You don't trust her.'

'Of course I trust her.'

'You don't. I knew at the barbecue when you said you were going to check on them.'

Lily's guilt made her defensive. 'It was *you* who was upstairs checking on them.'

'Bethany is a good girl. A *good* girl.' Avril was almost in tears now.

Horrified that their perfect evening was descending into an argument and desperate to fix it, Lily said, 'Bethany is a lovely girl. If anything, it's Poppy I don't trust. If anyone is going to lead that lot astray, it's my daughter. Please don't get the wrong end of the stick.'

Avril's face crumpled. 'I'm sorry. I don't know what's wrong with me.'

Lily took Avril's hand. 'We're a bit sloshed, that's all. Those cocktails were potent.'

Avril smiled. 'Sloshed. I haven't heard that word in a while. Forget I said anything.'

'It's already forgotten. But I see what you mean about the

noises. It probably is animals but I'm going to speak to security about it first thing.'

'It scared the bloody life out of me.'

'I'm sure it's foxes,' Lily said, to reassure herself as much as Avril.

'It does make you think, though. Those woods are huge. Anything could be out there.'

'Stop it, Avril, I'll never sleep again.'

'Sorry. I'm drunk and paranoid. Anyway, all's well that ends well. Shall we go home?'

They parted ways with hugs and kisses, the best of friends again. But as Lily walked across the road, she felt uneasy. Did Avril really believe her when she said she hadn't doubted Bethany? And what had upset Sandy so much that she had rushed Micky away without even saying goodbye? The noises had frightened Lily too, but Sandy's reaction had been different.

Sandy was terrified. And if she was, then maybe Lily should be too. After all, her daughter was hanging out with Micky. If Sandy knew something, Lily needed to know as well.

Lily glanced over her shoulder as she let herself into the house, craving the warm comfort of being inside. Maybe she should have insisted that Poppy come straight home too. She was trying so hard to be liberal but now she was nervy and restless. She hoped that Eric would be up so that they could talk about it. He would calm her down and make her see sense again. But the house was dark so he must have already gone to bed.

Lily poured herself a glass of water and sat down on the sofa to wait for Poppy. She felt deflated. It had been a stupid idea to go and spy on the kids, and in suggesting it, she'd ruined an otherwise perfect evening. She'd upset Avril, frightened Sandy, and scared herself too.

The house was warm and cosy and as she snuggled into the

sofa, a wave of exhaustion came over her, the alcohol sedating her despite the tense events that had unexpectedly unfolded. She awoke with a start to find her daughter watching her.

'Mother, you're such a floozy.'

'Hi, darling.' Lily sat up, rubbing her eyes. 'Did you have a good time?'

'Yeah, until the parental invasion.'

'Sorry about that. It was innocent, I assure you.'

'Yeah, yeah.'

'Did you stay at the boathouse all evening?'

'Yep.'

'You didn't go into the woods?'

'Nope.'

'And did you see anyone else at all?'

'No, Mother. Why are you acting so weird?'

'Never mind. We'd better go to bed.'

Lily clambered up from the sofa and followed her daughter upstairs. 'Goodnight,' she whispered softly and got a handwave from Poppy in response.

She opened the bedroom door quietly so she wouldn't disturb Eric but when her eyes adjusted to the darkness, she realised that the bed was empty. She already knew the drill. Eric would sneak in at some point during the early hours and slip into bed next to her and she would pretend to be asleep. In the morning, he would clutch his head and explain that his pals from the golf club had invited him over at short notice to sample an expensive bottle of wine, or a rare whisky, and they'd got carried away. She would cluck sympathetically and then go downstairs to make him a coffee. She would cry silently while she picked out his favourite mug, turned the coffee machine on and got the milk from the fridge. Then she'd wipe her eyes and go back upstairs to Eric with a smile on her face, and he would put his arm around her and tell her that he was cancelling golf to spend the entire day with his amazing wife and daughter. And the worst thing was that she would feel grateful to him for it.

They had been living the lie for so long that Lily no longer knew what was true any more. She hadn't wanted to know because it would shatter the narrative that she had painstakingly created. To the rest of the world, they were the dream couple and she had clung to that image because she liked it. She needed it. So she turned a blind eye and told herself that she had so much to be grateful for. She had a beautiful husband, a beautiful daughter and a beautiful home. Her life was perfect.

But she'd had a strange evening, and she didn't want to be alone. She felt like a small child again, afraid of what lurked under the bed. She wanted her husband to put his arms around her and make her feel safe. Instead, his absence was a cruel reminder that she could not rely on him to be there when she needed him. And, as she stood in the darkness, staring at the empty bed where Eric should be, her life felt anything but perfect.

11

Avril was glowing. She'd borrowed some of Stuart's earplugs and was sleeping soundly again. The weekly tennis lessons and long walks had made her look, and feel, better than she had in years. She walked with a new air of confidence, no longer afraid of whispers and stares. And she was making more of an effort with Stuart too because she knew she was just as much to blame for how distant they had become.

She was starting to remember how they used to be. When she first met Stuart, she had thought he was a geek. By the end of the evening, she had discovered that he was a brilliant and hilarious geek with beautiful eyes, a kind smile and a sense of humour which was almost in perfect sync with her own. She'd been thrilled when he shyly asked for her phone number and even more so when they naturally transitioned from dating into a relationship. It had been easy, without any drama or heartache, and their friends, delighted for them both, had said that they were the perfect match.

Stuart had always been able to make her laugh but over time, as they settled into married life, and the stresses and strains of family life took over, it seemed to happen less and less. She began to see Stuart as boring and old before his time. His unflappable steadiness, which she had once admired, became a negative trait as she craved excitement, a break from the mundanity of everyday life. They had responded differently to approaching their forties and Stuart's eagerness to embrace middle-age wasn't aligned with her desire to challenge it. He was the Honda and she was the Mini Cooper, neither willing to meet in the middle.

Still, they had muddled along, and Avril had never seriously questioned their marriage because she knew it was stereotypical of many couples. Who had time for passion and unpredictability when there was always a child who couldn't sleep or a work deadline that couldn't wait? Stuart was a good man and she had not regretted marrying him. She had assumed that they'd sort it out eventually, when they had more time and headspace, and she had simply added it to her already very long to-do list, along with finding a better football club for Tom, repainting the house, and calling her mother more often.

But their failure to address it had been their undoing when Bethany had got into trouble at school and the divide between them became an inaccessible chasm. While Avril had spiralled into a frenetic whirlwind of fear and anxiety, needing a strong and reassuring response from her husband, Stuart had chosen denial and refusal.

'She didn't do it,' he'd said. 'So there's nothing to talk about.'

But there was so much more to talk about and, feeling alone and unsupported, Avril's resentment towards Stuart began to fester. The magnetic force which had once pulled them together began to repel them until the aspects of his character that she had once found endearing – his unflappability, his ability to switch off from reality – became ugly.

She could see him more clearly again now, the man she had fallen in love with, like grey clouds lifting and exposing the blue sky underneath. It was little things. The way he brought her a cup of tea in bed every morning. How he stood and watched Tom play football every weekend, come rain or shine, without a single word of complaint. How he was the only one who could bring even a hint of a smile to Bethany's face. How he told Avril she was beautiful, even when she didn't feel it.

He was trying, she knew he was. And now she had to try too. Last night she'd cooked his favourite meal and they'd eaten at the table rather than in front of the television as they usually did. She'd asked him about his day, and he'd told her a story about something that happened at work, making her snort with laughter. Then Tom had walked in and helped himself to the leftovers and a few minutes after that, Bethany had appeared and sat down at the table. Avril's heart had nearly exploded at the sight of them all together, being a family. They were reconnecting and it seemed too good to be true. But it *was* true, and it was heaven.

Westford Park had changed her. And it had changed Bethany too.

But there had been bumps in the road. After the incident at the boathouse, Avril had arrived home a nervous wreck. She had been worried that Bethany would accuse her of not trusting her again. She had fretted that Lily didn't like Bethany. She had worried about Sandy and what had caused her to get into such a state. And when Stuart, who had waited up for her, asked her what was wrong, she had clammed up and refused to talk to him. It felt like they had stepped back in time and Avril feared that the damage was irreparable.

But then Bethany had arrived home in a good mood and said that she'd had a fun evening. The next day Lily had called round with a huge pair of sunglasses on and some takeout coffees from the clubhouse and declared herself to be disgustingly hungover, and no more had been said about the previous evening's almost row. Lily said she had spoken to security about the noise, and they had said it was probably wildlife but that they'd step up patrols to put her mind at ease. And life had carried on as though the incident had never happened until it soon became a distant, if unpleasant, memory.

The previous weekend Bethany had stayed over at Poppy's house and Avril had been nervous, remembering how morose Bethany used to be after her sleepovers with the girls from her old school. She had been unable to sleep, worrying about what was happening across the road and occasionally getting out of bed and looking at the darkened windows of the house opposite. But Bethany had come home in the morning with bright pink fingernails, a new top that Poppy had lent her and a smile. She'd told Avril about the midnight feast they'd had, and the pancakes that Lily had made them for breakfast. She'd gushed over Poppy's extensive wardrobe and all her coordinated outfits.

And, caught up in the moment, Avril had asked, 'Do you fancy going shopping today? I could buy you some new clothes.'

She had waited for Bethany to shake her head. To disappear up to her room and shut herself away from her family and the world. But instead, her daughter had said, 'Yes.'

Yes. That one small word was music to Avril's ears. Even when Bethany had asked if she could invite Poppy along, Avril's enthusiasm hadn't waned. So, it wouldn't be just the two of them but this was even better because Bethany finally had a friend to invite.

The three of them had piled into the Mini and headed to the shopping centre and Poppy had persuaded Bethany to buy some very un-Bethany outfits, including a new minidress. Bethany had smiled shyly as she looked at herself in the mirror and Avril had thought that she no longer looked like a ghost, she looked like a fifteen-year-old girl having fun.

She wondered if Bethany's sudden interest in clothes was

because of Poppy's influence or because she had a crush. Perhaps Micky, or a boy from school. Or a girl. She didn't care who it was, all she cared about was that Bethany was happy. She had taken them for burgers afterwards and the two girls had gossiped while Avril watched on, beaming from ear to ear.

When she had dropped Poppy home, she had gone inside to have a cup of tea with Lily. They met regularly now outside of the tennis lessons, often popping round to each other's house for a drink or some lunch on Avril's days off and their friendship was growing stronger every day. Avril now realised that she had been wrong to think that Lily didn't trust Bethany. It was her own paranoia getting the better of her. The problem was that all the people who she had considered friends in her old life had abandoned her when she needed them the most and that had made her insecure. But Lily wasn't like that and nor was Sandy.

It's because they don't know what happened. Avril couldn't prevent the intrusive thoughts, but she was getting better at pushing them away. And she was getting better at trusting Bethany again too. Now she could hardly believe that she had ever doubted her daughter, even for a second. It was those horrible, malicious girls' fault at her old school; they had victimised poor Bethany for their own pleasure. Stuart had been right to not even entertain the idea of Bethany doing anything wrong and she finally realised that. She saw her family again for what they were, and it was just like coming home.

It was December and Westford Park was sparkling. A huge tree had appeared in the clubhouse, adorned with lights, and Avril had dug their old artificial tree out of the loft and had a nostalgic hour looking through the baubles and remembering Bethany and Tom as young children, picking the most garish of decorations. She had hung on to every single one of them, wrapping them up carefully in tissue at the end of each festive season. Her parents were visiting for a few days over Christmas and it would be the first time that they'd had guests since they moved. Avril couldn't wait to show them around the development.

It was all so *normal*, with a sprinkling of Westford Park magic. Because there was something magical about the place, something so special that every morning when Avril woke up, she thanked her lucky stars that they lived there.

When she arrived at the Friday morning tennis lesson and saw Lily and Sandy waiting for her, she was in good spirits despite the cold, damp weather. But her happy mood quickly vanished when she looked at the tennis court and stopped dead. At first, she couldn't quite believe what she was seeing, her brain trying to make sense of it, her body rigid in shock. The usually pristine tennis court had been completely desecrated. The net had been slashed in several places, and there were deep red stains splashed all over the floor. It was like a crime scene from a grisly police drama.

Evil. That was how it looked, Avril thought, as she stared at it in horror.

'What the hell happened?' she asked, aghast.

'We don't know,' Lily said, staring morosely at the ruined floor of the court. 'The police are on their way.'

'Was...' Avril could barely say the words aloud. 'Was someone hurt?'

Lily looked at her curiously. 'It's paint, Avril. It's been vandalised.'

Avril blinked and, as the ominous red splashes slowly came into focus, she realised Lily was right. It was paint, she thought with relief. But who would do such a thing?

'I don't understand,' she said feebly.

'Juan thinks it was probably a gang of youths,' Lily explained.

'But how did they get into Westford Park?'

'Maybe they didn't get in. Maybe they live here.'

'You don't think...?' Avril looked at her, horrified. 'Not our kids?'

'Of course not,' Lily scoffed. 'But there are other teenagers here now.'

Avril glanced at Sandy, who hadn't spoken. The colour had drained from her face and her tennis racquet was hanging limply by her side. 'Are you okay, Sandy?'

'I don't think it's youths,' she said quietly.

'What's that?' Lily asked distractedly.

'I don't think it's youths,' Sandy repeated, her voice shaking.

Avril and Lily both stared at her. 'What are you talking about?' Lily asked.

'It's a message for me. He wants me to know that he's found me.'

For a moment, Avril had no idea who Sandy was talking about but then the penny dropped.

'You think this is your ex?' she asked.

'Yes. Grant. Micky's father.' Sandy's legs buckled and she began to sink to the floor. Avril and Lily lunged forward to support her.

'Come on,' Lily said to Avril. 'Let's get her home.'

They gripped on to Sandy's arms as they gently guided her towards the house. She went willingly, clinging on to Lily and Avril as though her life depended on it. As Avril found the keys in Sandy's bag and opened the door, she tried to make sense of it.

They hadn't talked about Sandy's ex-partner since the barbecue. All they really knew about him was that he wasn't a good man but if Sandy truly believed that he was capable of such mindless vandalism, then there had to be more to the story.

They sat her down on the sofa and Lily fussed around in the kitchen, making coffees. Sandy was silent as she stared at the patio doors, her fists clenching and unclenching.

Avril waited for Lily to return, before saying gently, 'Sandy, what's going on?'

'It started with an anonymous phone call,' she began shakily. 'And then it happened again the other day. Clare says it's nuisance callers, but I'm not convinced. Then when you told me about the noises you kept hearing, I began to wonder if it was someone playing a cruel game. And now this has happened. It's too much of a coincidence.'

'You think your ex could be behind it all? But why would he do that?'

'Because he wants to scare me. He wants me to know that he's still in control.'

Avril leaned forward. 'What happened between you, Sandy?'

Sandy didn't answer at first, perhaps weighing up how much she wanted to say. But then she began to speak. 'Grant and I were in an abusive relationship.'

Avril wasn't surprised but Sandy's words still upset her. 'I'm so sorry.'

'It went on for years and then, when Micky was three, I finally left him.'

'Good for you,' Lily said. 'The bastard.'

'I thought I'd escaped and I was finally rebuilding my life but then when Micky was five, Grant found us and abducted him. I've never gotten over it and I live in constant fear that it'll happen again, even though Micky's sixteen and no longer a little boy.'

Avril was appalled. The mere thought of losing a child gripped her with terror so she couldn't begin to imagine how Sandy must have felt. 'How long was Micky missing?'

'Only twenty-four hours, thank God, although it was the worst twenty-four hours of my life. After that I knew that I needed to make it stop so I told the police what Grant had done to me and I testified in court. He was sent to prison and I never heard from him again.'

'Until now.'

'Yes.' Sandy nodded. 'Until now.'

'You know,' Lily began tentatively, 'it might not be him.'

'It might be him, though.'

'But why now, after all this time?'

'He's out of prison, he's bored, he's angry. I don't know. He once told me that wherever I went, and whatever I did, he would find me. And Grant doesn't like to be wrong.'

Avril tried to process it all. Sandy's theory didn't quite add up to her. Why would a grown man, presumably in his thirties or forties, do something so juvenile? It seemed more like something young people messing about would do. Either way, the incident had upset her and the idea of Westford Park being infiltrated by such nasty people made her indignant with rage. What had happened to their safe sanctuary? Who had violated it and to what end?

And what did it mean for their children, who currently pretty much had the run of the place, unsupervised? Was it safe for them? Avril had loved the fact that Bethany and Tom could have a bit more freedom here but now she was wondering if she'd been too relaxed.

Whoever had done this, Westford Park didn't seem very safe to her any more.

To reassure herself as much as the others, she said, 'Stuart's convinced that the noise is coming from foxes. And the phone calls could well have been nuisance callers.'

'What about the tennis courts?'

'Vandals,' she said with more conviction than she felt. 'Senseless vandals.'

Lily nodded vehemently. 'I think Avril's right, Sandy. But listen, why don't you talk to the police just for some peace of mind? We could go and see if they've turned up yet.'

'And what do I tell them?'

'What you told us, darling.'

'They'll think I'm mad.'

'Of course they won't,' Avril interjected. Although even as she heard herself say it, she wondered if perhaps Sandy was over-reacting.

'Shall we call Clare for you?' Lily suggested.

'No, she's at work, I don't want to disturb her.'

'I'm sure she won't mind.'

'I know she won't, but I still don't want to.' Sandy forced a smile. 'I'm fine, really.'

Lily frowned. 'You're not fine. There's really no harm in speaking to the police.'

Sandy toyed with her curly hair, wrapping it around a finger and pulling at it. 'Let's see what they find out first. I'm sure there'll be CCTV and maybe you're right and it'll show some bored teenagers getting up to no good.'

'The noises could have been them too,' Avril said. 'It if wasn't foxes.'

'But why?' Lily asked. 'Why would anyone want to mess with us all?'

'Maybe they're bored. Or they're not from here and they're jealous?'

'But then how did they get in without being detected?'

'I don't know.' Avril threw her hands up in the air. 'It's just theories. We need to tell the kids to be careful though. I don't like the idea of them being out and about at night if there are trouble-makers hanging around.'

She looked at Sandy who was still playing with her hair,

pulling it so hard that Avril was sure it must hurt. 'Sandy, I'll stay with you until Clare gets home.'

'There's really no need.'

'I insist.'

Avril looked at Lily who nodded and pulled out her phone. 'I'm going to call security and see if they've found anything yet.'

As Lily stood up to make the call, Avril turned to Sandy. 'What can I do to help?'

Sandy smiled. 'You are helping. By being a friend. By not judging me.'

'Why on earth would we judge you?'

'I know I sound deranged. And I wouldn't blame you for doubting me. But he's found me before. He's watched me without me knowing. He could easily be watching again now.'

'Then why show himself in this way? If he was watching.'

'I don't know, Avril.'

'I still think we should call Clare.'

'I'll talk to her when she gets home. You know, I haven't spoken about Grant to anyone other than Clare before. I've always tried to pretend it didn't happen. But things like this, they bring it all back again and remind me that I can't forget.'

Tears pricked at Avril's eyes. 'I think you're incredibly brave.'

Sandy smiled. 'I don't feel very brave at the moment.'

'Well, you are.'

Lily returned. 'This is what we know so far. There were no unaccounted-for visitors last night and the patrol team didn't see anything untoward. They're checking the CCTV around the development. But the theory is that it was done by someone who lives on-site.'

'There you go, then.' Avril smiled brightly at Sandy, although a new theory was beginning to form in her mind, leaving a bitter taste in her mouth. They'd been quick to dismiss their own children, but Bethany had a history of causing trouble, didn't she?

No. Don't think like that. Don't get all up in your head again. Anyway, Bethany had been safely tucked up in bed every time Avril had heard those strange noises and she hadn't gone out last night. So, there was no way it could have been her.

Relieved, Avril added, 'I don't think you have anything to worry about, Sandy.'

'Maybe you're right.' Sandy smiled, but it didn't reach her eyes.

'Can I ask,' Lily began hesitatingly. 'Does Micky know much about his father?'

'No. I told him that his dad had left when he was little, which had hurt me a lot. I said I didn't know where he was but he was probably overseas. Clare thinks I should tell him now that he's older. To be honest, it's pretty much the only thing we argue about.'

'Why don't you want to tell him?'

'I just can't do it. Every time I think about having that conversation, I imagine the look on his face when he realises his father is a monster. It's almost worse that he's older because he's not naive any more and he'll understand exactly what I'm saying. There's nothing I can say, no careful wording I can use to sugar-coat what Grant did to me, and to Micky.'

'But don't you worry that Micky might try and find him?'

Sandy shook her head. 'Not really. He hasn't asked about him in a long time. I'm more worried that he'll try and find us. That's why we moved here. I liked the idea of a secure community. I wanted Micky to have more freedom because I was always so nervous about him going out on his own. It wasn't fair to keep him on such a tight leash. When we came to Westford Park it was like being in a bubble. But now it feels like the bubble has burst.'

Lily was thoughtful. 'I know you're not keen on talking to the police, but I know this private investigator. Eric used him to vet potentially dodgy clients. Don't tell anyone I told you that. We could get him to find out where Grant is if you like? It might give you some peace of mind if you know that he has nothing to do with all this.'

'Oh, I don't know.' Sandy looked unsure. 'Wouldn't that make things worse?'

'Not if he's dead or living in a rainforest in the Amazon. Then you'll know you're safe.'

'But what if he's not?'

'Then we'll have him watched, make sure that he's not behind all this.'

'That sounds expensive. I don't think we can afford it.'

'I'll put it on Eric's account. He won't even notice.'

'I'm not sure. Can I think about it? Speak to Clare?'

'Of course, just let me know.'

Avril listened to the exchange in disbelief. The idea of hiring a private investigator sounded so far-fetched it seemed impossible that they were genuinely discussing it.

Trying to lighten the mood, sensing that they all needed it, she said, 'Lily, I can't believe you know a private investigator. Is there anyone you don't know?'

'I don't think so, darling, no.'

Once again Avril was struck by what a charmed life Lily led. Here she was, taking control of this awful situation while Avril floundered, trying to work out what she could do to help Sandy and coming up with nothing other than sitting with her. But Lily was all action, finding practical solutions. She even had a private investigator in her contacts. She was also blissfully married, beautiful, wealthy and she had a stunning daughter who oozed sass and confidence. Avril couldn't help but feel a small pang of both awe and jealousy.

But what was she doing, becoming a green-eyed monster about

Lily when poor Sandy was in such a state? She couldn't imagine what it must feel like to be constantly looking over your shoulder, to fear for yourself and your child. She'd experienced only a small taste of it when her family had become public enemy number one and it had almost destroyed her.

'I don't want to talk about this any more,' Sandy said abruptly, removing her hand from her now knotted hair. 'Let's discuss the New Year's party. I hope you're both going?'

'Of course,' Lily enthused. 'I wouldn't miss it for the world.'

It was the event of the season and everyone was going. But as they talked about their outfits, as well as the guest list, Avril couldn't stop thinking about what Sandy had told them about her ex and the fear she must have felt when she realised Micky had been abducted.

When she was walking back home with Lily, she brought it up again. 'What do you think of this vandalism? Do you reckon it's Sandy's ex?'

'I don't know. It could be but I'm not convinced, especially about the noises. I don't think he'd get away with sneaking in so many times.'

'Even if it's not him, I can't believe what he did to her and Micky.'

'I know. I'd like to kill him with my bare hands.'

'I was thinking about what you said, about the private investigator. Maybe we should do it? I know Sandy wasn't sure but it might just give her that peace of mind she needs.'

'But we can't do it, not without Sandy. We don't even know what his surname is.'

'True.' Avril mulled this over. 'But if he went to prison, we might find something about it online. And if we have his name then we can get the ball rolling.'

'I'm not sure. Won't Sandy be upset with us?'

'We're doing this *for* Sandy.'

'I suppose so. It wouldn't harm to do a little googling.'

'I'm not working today so I'll have a look when I get home.'

'Fine, let me know what you find out.'

'Do you think we should be worried?'

'About Sandy's ex?'

'About whoever is doing this.'

'I still think they're isolated incidents. I don't think we have anything to fear.'

But as Avril let herself into the house, she couldn't shake off a feeling of dread. Her mind was consumed with thoughts of Sandy, of Bethany, and of whoever was responsible for what had happened at the courts. She kept thinking about the noises and about the anonymous phone calls to Sandy. She had no idea what was going on but whatever it was, she didn't like it one bit. Were they linked, as Sandy thought they were? Or were they isolated incidents, as Lily believed? And which one was worse?

She thought of the kids, hanging around at the boathouse after dark. Tom was too young to go out on his own at night but soon he'd want to do the same thing. And she'd thought that Westford Park was the perfect place for them to do that, away from the crime that often plagued towns and cities. But now the crime had come here, to this beautiful development, and the realisation sunk in that, just as Sandy had said, Westford Park wasn't a bubble. It often felt like one but now the darker side of life had infiltrated it.

To distract herself from her increasingly morose thoughts, she made herself a cup of tea and settled down at her laptop to do some research into Sandy's ex. She felt guilty about what she was about to do but she told herself it was to help her friend. She wanted to be more like Lily, to offer practical support to Sandy, to try and find a solution for her. Where was it Sandy had said that she used to live years ago? She was pretty sure it was Devon. She started googling Devon, along with the name 'Grant' and terms like 'assault' and 'abducted' but nothing relevant came up in the time-line that she had worked out from Sandy's story.

But Sandy had moved around a lot. Hadn't she mentioned a brief stint in Cambridge? Avril started searching in that area until, eventually, she found an archived article in the local newspaper, dated ten years previously. She scanned the copy, her eyes widening.

A man who tried to abduct his son in Cambridge has been jailed for six years.

The man, who cannot be named for legal reasons, spied on his ex-partner before entering her home and taking their five-year-old child when she was sleeping.

Officers intercepted him at Dover, trying to board a ferry to Calais, and he was arrested. He was found guilty of kidnapping a child, engaging in coercive and controlling behaviour, causing actual bodily harm and assault by beating.

Police said the man had been planning the kidnap for weeks. They found false documents in his car as well as a disguise.

During the trial, the court heard that he repeatedly assaulted his ex-partner over the five-year period that they were together, including burning her with cigarettes and beating her. She was left with permanent scars as a result of his attacks.

The man, who had a successful career and earned more than £40,000 a year, kept his partner and child locked up in a flat, deleted her social media accounts and took her mobile phone. He prohibited her from talking to other people, including members of her own family.

After the trial, Angela Michael, of Cambridgeshire Police, said: 'This man subjected his partner to years of abuse, which culminated in him attempting to kidnap their child and flee the country. The account she shared in her victim statement shows the devastating impact domestic violence has on the lives of victims and their families.'

She added: 'I would like to thank this woman for her immense bravery in supporting our investigation and giving evidence in court, which led to this successful conviction.'

Avril slammed the lid of the laptop down, appalled. It had to be Sandy but the names had been withheld, presumably to protect Micky's identity. She felt wretched for snooping. What that poor woman had been through was unthinkable. And they'd sat there talking about sparkly dresses and New Year's parties. It seemed so shallow and insignificant.

She didn't want to share this information with Lily, or anyone. She opened her laptop again and deleted her browsing history, not wanting there to even be a footprint of that terrible story on her computer, or in her life. Then she closed the lid again and stood up.

She was restless, agitated and angry. This man was a monster. She was now starting to think that maybe Sandy was right about the incidents at Westford Park being down to Grant. Clearly, he was capable of anything. And what did that mean for Bethany, if she was hanging out with Micky? What if Grant approached them?

She couldn't ban Bethany from going out with her friends at night, but she was going to be more vigilant from now on. They needed to keep an eye on the teenagers and make sure that they always knew where they were. Even if this wasn't down to Grant, then there were some other troublemakers hanging around on-site. Perhaps the boathouse wasn't the best place for them. She felt awful for thinking, even for a second, that the vandalism might have been down to Bethany. No, this was the work of someone nasty and vicious. Someone like Grant.

Something else was on her mind too. Sandy had been so brave for confiding in them about her past. It must have been difficult for her to tell them, but she'd faced her fears and done it. Maybe it was time for Avril to be brave too. Full disclosure. She would tell them the truth about Bethany, she decided. Let them judge the story and make their own decisions about it. That's when she would know if they were true friends.

She was afraid, but she was exhilarated by the idea too, imagining the feeling of that weight off her chest. The knowledge that the Westford Park Ladies Club was genuine. She reached for her phone and opened the WhatsApp group between her, Lily and Sandy and, before she could change her mind, suggested dinner the following Friday evening.

One week to go. It would be the day of reckoning. And she just hoped that she'd made the right decision in trusting her friends.

12

Sandy was looking for the perfect spot to do some painting by the lake when she heard someone behind her. She spun around in fright and exhaled when she realised it was Bethany.

She had been on edge for weeks now and she couldn't shake it off. Every noise in the night was a threat, every footstep she heard behind her was danger. The only time she felt at ease was during the day when she was painting, and with Isla at school, she found herself down by the lake more and more, despite the chilly temperature.

She smiled at the teenager. 'Hi, Bethany, how are you?'

'Fine.' Bethany looked so much healthier than when Sandy had first met her, her pallor almost gone, but she was still a girl of few words, around Sandy at least.

'Are you out for a walk?'

Bethany looked behind her shoulder. 'Actually, I was meeting someone but I'm not sure they're coming.'

'If it's Micky, he's gone to the cinema with a schoolfriend.'

Bethany shrugged. 'It doesn't matter. What are you doing?'

'I'm drawing the kayakers.' Sandy pointed to the small boats on the lake. 'Would you like to join me?'

'Oh, I don't have any art stuff with me.'

'That's okay, you can borrow mine. I have a spare easel at home, shall I go and get it?'

She was expecting Bethany to say no, so she was surprised when the girl said, 'Yes. Okay.'

'Stay right there.'

Sandy jogged to the house, located her spare easel and walked back to the lake, wondering if Bethany would still be there. She was delighted when she saw that she was. Bethany was standing in front of the easel, her right arm moving quickly and Sandy called out so as not to frighten her and then went to stand beside her.

'Sorry,' Bethany said quickly, backing away like a frightened mouse.

Sandy observed the easel. Bethany had taken some paper from Sandy's pad and started sketching the old boathouse. Sandy must have only been gone ten minutes but already Bethany had begun to capture the cabin perfectly.

'Oh, Bethany, that's beautiful,' she said admiringly.

Bethany blushed. 'I didn't mean to use your things without permission.'

'It's fine, don't worry. It's nice to have some company.'

Sandy set the easel up for her and moved her drawing over to it. Then she fished around in her bag and pulled out some pens. 'These would be perfect for your drawing. See how you can change the thickness of the lines by slightly adjusting the angle.' She demonstrated on the edge of her own paper. 'And you can create some depth by doing this.'

Bethany watched her like a hawk and then wordlessly took the pen from Sandy's hand and started using it on her own picture. Sandy watched with approval.

'You're a natural, Bethany. Use these when you're ready to add some colour.'

'Thank you.'

They worked in companionable silence and Sandy was so lost in her work that she was startled when Bethany suddenly spoke.

'When I'm drawing, I feel better.'

Sandy smiled. 'I know exactly what you mean. It's very therapeutic.'

'It's like I can put my feelings on paper, you know? When I can't say them.'

'I understand.'

Sandy stole a glance at Bethany's picture and her eyes widened in surprise. She had drawn the boathouse at night, with light coming from the windows and a dark sky above. There was something haunting about the picture, something beautiful but also frightening.

'That's really good, Bethany,' she said. 'It almost looks like it's haunted.'

'Apparently, it is.'

Sandy turned to the girl. 'Where did you hear that?'

'It's a rumour going around.'

Sandy smiled inwardly. Teenagers loved scary rumours and it probably gave them a thrill to think the place had ghosts. 'Is that why you go there? Are you ghost-hunting?'

Bethany smiled. 'We haven't seen any. Although sometimes the lights flicker on and off. It's freaky.'

'Do you believe in all that stuff?'

'I don't know. Do you?'

'No, definitely not. There's always a rational explanation for everything and the lights are most likely the product of patchy electrics. But if it freaks you out, you shouldn't go.'

Bethany shrugged and continued painting in silence.

'Have you always enjoyed art?' Sandy asked, keen to keep the conversation going. It was the most Bethany had ever spoken to her.

'Yes. I used to draw all the time when I was younger. I made comic books and stuff. Then when I went to high school, I loved my art teacher. She was amazing.'

'She inspired you?'

'Yes.'

'You must have been sad when you had to move schools.'

Sandy regretted her comment as soon as she'd said it, remembering that Bethany had been expelled. The last thing she wanted to do was drag up Bethany's past.

Bethany stopped painting for a moment, her hand hovering in the air. Then she put it to the paper again. 'Yes,' she said simply.

'Are you happy you moved here, though? To Westford Park.'

Bethany smiled shyly. 'Yes.'

'Micky too. He sulked about it at first but now he seems very happy. I think I have you and Poppy to thank for that. It's lovely how friendly you've all become.'

Bethany didn't answer and Sandy continued. 'You're welcome to join me any time you'd like. It's probably too dark for you after school now but I'm down here most Saturday mornings if the weather is nice enough. And you can keep that easel if you like.'

'Wow, thank you, Sandy.'

'Oh, you're welcome, Bethany. Like I said before, it's good to have company.'

'You said that art was therapeutic. Did you find that too?'

'Yes. I went through a bad time, a long time ago now, and art helped with the healing process. It still does now, if I'm being honest.'

'I went through a bad time too.'

Bethany's words surprised Sandy. She hadn't expected the

usually quiet teenager to be so candid and she considered what to say next. 'Life is complicated and messy, Bethany. We all go through dark times. But there's a lot of light in the world too. A lot of happiness.'

'Yeah, maybe.'

'How are you feeling now?'

'Okay.'

'Do you want to talk about it?'

Bethany didn't answer at first, and Sandy thought she was going to ignore the question, but then she said, 'Do *you* talk about it?'

'Yes, I do. To Clare, and to some close friends too. Sometimes it helps to talk.'

Bethany considered this. 'What happened to you?'

Sandy wanted to be honest, but she had to be tactful too. For a start, Bethany was only fifteen, and she had Micky to think of. Anything she told Bethany might get back to him. 'I knew a man once, a very long time ago. He wasn't very kind to me. I was afraid of him.'

'I was afraid too.'

'Who were you afraid of?'

'Them.'

'People from school?'

Bethany nodded.

'Girls?'

Another nod.

'Did they hurt you, Bethany?'

'They said they would. If I didn't do what they wanted.'

'What did they want you to do?'

But Bethany had reached her limit. She turned to Sandy and her expression was stricken. 'Promise me you won't say anything. Promise me you won't tell Mum.'

It was a difficult position to be in, but Sandy sensed that Bethany had, for some reason, chosen her as the person to confide in and she couldn't break that trust, not unless she felt there was a compelling reason to do so. And Bethany hadn't told her anything yet that made her want to speak to Avril about it. 'I promise,' she said.

Bethany put her paintbrush down. 'I've got to go.'

'Okay, Bethany, it was good to talk to you. See you next week?'

The girl shrugged and began to walk off. But then she turned around. 'Thank you.'

'You're very welcome.'

It was only after Bethany had disappeared into the distance that Sandy realised she'd left her picture of the boathouse behind. It really was tremendously skilled work for a girl of Bethany's age. Then her eyes homed in on a dark figure in the window. It hadn't been there when she had last looked at the picture. It was a silhouette of a girl, with long flowing hair and her hands were splayed up against the window. Even with no facial expressions drawn on, Sandy instinctively knew that the girl was afraid. And, she realised, as she stared uneasily at the picture and saw the padlock on the cabin door, she knew why.

The girl was trapped inside.

13

Lily was harried as she made her way towards the clubhouse. Poppy wanted some new trending handbag for Christmas, but it was sold out everywhere and Lily had spent hours scouring the shops and the internet to no avail. On top of that, Eric's parents were ill and had told them not to travel up for Christmas, which had sent Lily into a spiral of panic as she hadn't done any food shopping. There were only a few days left to get everything prepared and perfect, and she was beginning to wonder if it was beyond even her capabilities.

When she entered the restaurant and saw Avril and Sandy waiting for her, she tried to put her own stress to the side and adopt her winning smile.

'Hi, darlings, happy nearly Christmas!' she said, kissing them both before sitting down. 'We've had a dis-as-ster. Eric's parents have got the lurgy so we're staying put and now I have to create the perfect Christmas spread in just four days.'

'You're welcome to join us,' Sandy suggested. 'Clare's parents are coming down but there's plenty of room for everyone.'

'You're very sweet,' Lily replied. 'But I've promised Poppy

Christmas at home now. Perhaps we can all meet for a drink in the afternoon, though. I can host!'

Why on earth had she suggested that? Now she had to organise a drinks party on top of a lunch. But already she could feel herself getting excited about the idea.

'That would be lovely,' Sandy enthused. 'Are you in, Avril?'

'Sure, yes.'

Avril seemed distracted. Maybe she was stressed about Christmas. She'd complained the other day that she'd forgotten to book her festive food delivery slot and she was dreading the supermarket crowds. Lily wondered if she should offer to pick some things up for her.

'We've ordered some wine,' Sandy said. 'We thought we'd better stay off the margaritas.'

Sandy was joking but Lily still felt bad. It was water under the bridge now though. Since then, the families had been getting along well and any lingering doubts Lily had about Bethany were gone. And the girl was really coming out of her shell too. She even chatted easily with Lily, something that would have been unthinkable a few months ago.

They had all become nervous about the kids going out at night, but any suggestion that they meet at home had gone down like a lead balloon, especially now the boathouse had become a popular meeting spot. A few other teenagers had moved into the development and word had got out, turning the boathouse into an unofficial youth club. So, naturally, Poppy, Bethany and Micky wanted to go. After much discussion, the three women had decided that they could, as long as they stuck together at all times and did not go into the woods.

Poppy dressed up to the nines whenever she went, even though it was just a shabby log cabin, and Lily had thought, more than once, that she was trying to impress someone. Maybe it was one o the new boys who had moved into the development. But whenever she tried to bring it up with Poppy, she was rewarded with an eye-roll and a change of subject.

It was natural for teenagers to be private, so Lily didn't take it personally. But ever since the courts had been vandalised, she'd been on edge. She knew she couldn't keep Poppy under lock and key, and she'd seen the Westford Park security out on patrol in the evenings, but she wanted to know who her daughter was social-ising with and where she went. Inevitably, though, the more she probed, the more reticent Poppy became. It was a fine line between giving her daughter freedom and keeping her safe, and Lily was struggling to navigate it. She knew that Avril felt the same way about Bethany.

'How was Bethany's end-of-year report?' She asked Avril now.

'Oh, it was good,' Avril said. 'They said she was shy but slowly starting to contribute more in class. And her art teacher couldn't have been more complimentary. It must be those extra sessions she's having with you, Sandy.'

Lily looked at them quizzically and Avril explained. 'Sandy has been giving Bethany some tips. They've been down to the lake painting a few times too.'

'Oh, how lovely.'

'Speaking of Bethany,' Avril began, but was interrupted by their wine arriving. By the time the waiter had opened the bottle, poured them each a glass and taken their food order, Sandy was enthusing about Bethany's natural talent as an artist.

'She drew this beautiful sketch of the lake the other day,' Sandy was saying. 'It was so ethereal and magical. I was really impressed.'

'Oh, I haven't seen it,' Avril said. 'I must ask her to show me.'

'Does she show you her work?'

Lily thought she detected more than a hint of curiosity in

Sandy's voice, but Avril didn't seem to notice. 'Not really. She's quite secretive but then aren't all teenagers?'

'I'm still a bit funny about them going to the boathouse at night,' Lily said.

'I know,' Avril agreed. 'But it's warm and we know where they are. It's very good of Steve to let them use it.'

'That reminds me,' Sandy interjected. 'I keep getting this strange feeling that I know him from somewhere, but I can't for the life of me work out from where.'

'Have you asked him?'

'No, I've barely spoken to him. How about you?'

'We've chatted a few times,' Avril said. 'Tom's got into kayaking so we're down there most weekends. He's a nice guy and very friendly with the kids. They all love him. Speaking of the kids, there's something I wanted to talk to you both about Bethany...'

'Oh look.' Lily glanced at the entrance to the restaurant. 'There's that new family who have just moved into the end of Regal Close.' She waved at them and flashed a smile. 'They've got a gorgeous little puppy, it's making me dog-broody. I keep thinking about getting one myself.'

'I love dogs,' Sandy said. 'But Clare's allergic so it's a no-go for us.'

'Eric's not keen either. Sorry, Avril, what was it you were going to say about Bethany?'

But Avril simply gave a small smile. 'Oh, never mind, it doesn't matter. How are you doing, Sandy?'

'I'm okay,' Sandy said hesitatingly. 'Better.'

'Have you had any more anonymous calls?'

'No. Clare's been wonderful about it, and we've talked it all through. Perhaps I jumped to the wrong conclusions about every-thing. And I've been thinking about what you suggested too, Lily, about getting a private investigator on the case. I'm grateful to you for wanting to help but I've decided not to do it. I just feel like it might be opening a can of worms.'

Lily nodded, avoiding Avril's eye. They hadn't mentioned their previous conversation about hiring the investigator without Sandy's consent and she was relieved. It would be wrong of them to do it. Normally she couldn't resist meddling if she thought it was for the greater good, but these friendships were too precious to risk.

'But thank you both,' Sandy continued. 'I appreciate your support more than you'll ever know. Westford Park's really become a community, hasn't it?'

Lily felt the same. 'It has. I can't believe we've only known each other for a few months, it feels like forever.'

She looked at Avril, waiting for her to murmur her agreement, but she still seemed distracted. Keen to draw her back into conversation, she said, 'Remind me what your plans are for Christmas again, Avril?'

Avril smiled, almost gratefully, and told them about her parents visiting, and how she was looking forward to welcoming them. The conversation flowed easily and when Sandy asked for the bill, Lily was disappointed that the night had come to an end. But she needed to get to bed because she had an early start in the morning, raiding the supermarkets to see what was left on the shelves and now planning a drinks party on Christmas Day too.

She walked home with Avril and let herself into the house, calling out to Eric and Poppy but the house was dark and silent. It was only ten o'clock, too early for curfew, so Poppy was probably out with her friends, but Eric had said that he was too tired to go out that evening. Already she could feel disappointment kicking in, the realisation that she didn't know where he was, or what he was doing, but that she had a pretty good idea.

It was the same script, and she was fed up with it. It had always hurt her, but she had grown accomplished at covering up her pain, telling herself that she was lucky, that her deliberate ignorance was for the greater good. For years she had reasoned that it was for Poppy but who was she really protecting – her daughter, or herself? And who else was getting hurt in the process? She had never allowed herself to think about that.

She poured a nightcap and slumped onto one of the bar stools, the glow from her lovely evening already ebbing away. She had convinced herself that when they moved to Westford Park it would stop. Once they had the white picket fence and she baked apple pies, Eric would forget about his other life, as she had come to know it, and commit fully to his family. It would be perfect, she had thought. But she had always known deep down that she was lying to herself.

It would never stop. She knew it really, even though it killed her to admit it. Eric, the perfect man, the perfect husband, was not so perfect, but Lily was the only one who knew it. And she had kept his secret. Why? Because she loved him, even after everything. She didn't want to rip their family apart. She didn't want Poppy to come from a broken home.

But she was tired, so tired of it all. The thing that kept her going was knowing that she was providing Poppy with a happy, stable family environment. That, and the impression that everyone else had of her and her marriage, which she clung on to with all her might.

Lily liked being admired by other people. She liked how they were envious of her and Eric's marriage. It gave her a reason to keep going, it softened the blow of Eric's lies and deception. But sometimes she thought of her mother. She had loathed her for her passiveness, her refusal to acknowledge what was going on in their home. She had even resented her mother for being afraid of her father. Occasionally, she wondered if she was any better.

But she *was* better. She did what she did for Poppy. To protect her daughter, to make sure she had an easy, carefree childhood. Her mother had done the opposite. Lily was not afraid of Eric and she never had been. He adored her, and Poppy too and when he was at home, he treated them with nothing but love and kindness. But she knew that it was more than that for her. She didn't want to shatter the picture-perfect life she had created. She was the lead character in her own movie and it was a blockbuster.

Yet the facade was beginning to rankle her.

Poppy had no idea about her father's other life and that was how it would stay. So tomorrow she would make him a full English breakfast and kiss the top of his head. Then she would go shopping so that she could create a Christmas spread worthy of a glossy magazine cover. And she would find that damn handbag if it was the last thing she did.

These things made her happy. Poppy made her happy. Even Eric made her happy, sometimes anyway.

She heard the front door and for a moment her heart soared as she imagined Eric strolling in, telling her he'd been for a quick walk around the block. But it was Poppy who entered and threw herself dramatically onto the sofa.

'Hello, darling, did you have a good evening?'

'Fine. Where's Father?'

'He's gone out with some friends.'

'You two have a busier social life than me. How was dinner with the ladies? Any gossip?'

'I'm afraid not. Oh, but I did invite them all round for Christmas Day drinks. I thought you might like to see Bethany and Micky.'

'I'm not friends with them any more.'

Lily thought she'd misheard at first. 'What did you say?'

'I'm not friends with them any more.'

'What on earth happened?'

But Poppy stood up and started heading towards the stairs. 'I'm going to bed.'

'Poppy, wait...'

It was too late. Poppy was flying up the stairs and Lily heard her bedroom door slam. This was just what she needed right now, teenage drama. And it scuppered her drinks party plans. She just had to hope that whatever had happened, they all made up before then. Poppy was always falling out with her friends and it usually blew over after a good night's sleep.

The house was silent again and Lily gazed at the twinkling lights on the tree. Eric was out God knew where and Poppy was sulking in her bedroom with the door closed. Christmas was meant to be a time for family, for togetherness, but she was lonely.

Thank goodness for the Westford Park Ladies Club. For Avril and Sandy. She yearned to tell them the truth, to finally admit that her and Eric's marriage wasn't as rosy as they thought. What a relief it would be to get that confession off her chest. And yet she hadn't done it and she wasn't sure she ever would. She couldn't bear to see the sympathetic looks on their faces and wonder if they were secretly relieved that Lily wasn't as perfect as they thought. It would eat her up inside and erode her last shred of dignity. And what if one of them told their children and it got back to Poppy? All these years of hard work would be destroyed.

No, she decided. This was a secret she'd take to her grave.

14

———

The clubhouse had never looked more impressive. Self-conscious in her new black, glittery number, Avril looked around at the crowds and the expensive decorations and felt at once horribly out of her depth and absolutely thrilled that she was part of this community.

Bethany was wearing her new dress too and she looked lovely. Avril couldn't believe that she would be turning sixteen in a few weeks' time. And Tom was growing up too, awkwardly handsome in his smart shirt, jeans and trainers as he waved at some boys he'd made friends with. She turned to Stuart, who was appraising the buffet.

'Lobster?' he said, scrunching up his nose.

'There's plenty of other food too, Stuart. You don't have to eat the lobster.'

Stuart still moaned about the extortionate service charge and the expensive food in the clubhouse, but he was finally embracing life at Westford Park. He had started kayaking with Tom and walking with Avril. And things between them were so much better. It was as though their happiness was inextricably linked to

Bethany's and as she began to bloom again, so did their relationship. They were beginning to feel like a partnership again.

'Bethany, Poppy's over there,' she said, spotting Poppy on the other side of the room looking effortlessly stunning in a red strapless dress which made her look about five years older than she was. God help her parents, Avril thought. Poppy was a boy-magnet.

'I'll talk to her later.'

Avril frowned. 'Is everything okay between you two?'

Lily had cancelled the Christmas Day drinks at the last minute, explaining that Eric's parents had recovered and so they were going to visit them after all. With them being away and Avril's parents visiting, she hadn't seen Lily since their dinner a few days before Christmas and Bethany hadn't seen Poppy either. Bethany had been sullen over Christmas, but Avril had thought she was just overwhelmed by having such a busy house, with grandparents who loved her but were full on, and hadn't put two and two together, until now.

Bethany was looking at the floor.

'Bethany, what is it?'

Avril's heart sank as she realised that the two girls had fallen out. What did that mean for Bethany's happiness? Or for her and Lily's friendship? She stood awkwardly on the side of the room, unsure whether to go over to Lily or not. What if Bethany had done something to upset Poppy and Lily was furious? The old anxiety immediately began to creep in.

'You and Poppy are such good friends,' she told her daughter quietly. 'Don't let a row ruin that, darling.'

'She started it.'

It was petulant for a girl of Bethany's age and Avril relaxed a fraction. Whatever had happened sounded like a tiff, rather than anything sinister. And it also seemed like Poppy had been the instigator. Yet again, she had jumped to the wrong conclusions, feared the worst. Yet again, she had failed to trust her daughter. She wondered if it was over a boy, but it could just as easily have been an item of clothing one had borrowed and lost or refused to give back. It could be any number of reasons why teenage girls fell out every day.

Luckily Lily took the decision out of her hands. She came striding over, looking as beautiful as her daughter in a slim-fitting cocktail dress and leaned in to kiss her.

'Our girls are in some sort of feud,' she whispered into Avril's ear.

'I've just heard about it this second.'

'Shall we get them together? See if they can't sort it out?'

'Oh, I don't know, shouldn't we leave them to it?'

'It'll all be a storm in a teacup. The sooner they sort it out the better.'

Eric came over to shake Stuart's hand and Avril marvelled again at his good looks. He looked like a Hollywood star, and with Lily by his side, they were the golden couple.

'The lobster's excellent,' he told Stuart, who had the good grace to smile and nod.

'Poppy, over here.' Lily beckoned to Poppy, who scowled at her mother but came over. 'Doesn't Bethany look gorgeous in her dress?'

'I suppose.'

'Why don't you two go and order a soft drink at the bar? Go on, off you go.'

Lily ushered the two reluctant teenagers away and then turned to Avril with a knowing smile. 'Hopefully, they'll make amends over a Diet Coke.'

Looking at the two sets of hunched shoulders heading towards the bar, Avril wasn't so sure. But she was distracted by Sandy and Clare, who arrived with Micky and Isla in tow. Micky greeted them before making his way over to Poppy and Bethany, who were standing a considerable distance apart, the tension palpable even from across the room.

'I hope Micky will knock our two girls' heads together,' Lily said. 'They've had a tiff.'

'Oh dear.' Sandy was sympathetic. 'Micky didn't mention anything.'

'You look lovely, Sandy.'

She really did, Avril thought. Sometimes it was hard to believe that Sandy had been through what she had because she always seemed so warm and open, so positive about life. But maybe she was like that because of what had happened, not in spite of it. Sometimes you had to experience the dark to appreciate the light. Avril was beginning to feel like that herself. They had been through dark times but now they were heading towards the light again. And that was why this row between Bethany and Poppy was worrying her.

'Don't worry about it, Avril,' Lily said, reading her thoughts. 'They'll be fine.'

'I hope so.'

'Oh look, Juan is over there.' Lily smiled indulgently. 'Well, he certainly wears a suit well, not that I'm surprised. Isn't that Steve from the boathouse with him? He scrubs up rather nicely, I've never noticed before.'

'I know what you mean,' Avril agreed, glancing at Eric to see if he minded his wife eyeballing other men, but he was talking to poor Stuart about golf. Stuart did not care for golf.

Avril's eyes drifted over to Bethany and Poppy to see if they were talking to each other yet but, to her surprise, their eyes were fixed firmly on Juan and Steve. Suddenly it all started to make sense. They had a crush on Juan. It wasn't surprising; he was in his twenties and he was hot. She wondered if that was what they had fallen out about. If so, it was a terrible shame because Juan was too old for them and would never be interested in fifteen-year-old girls. Anyway, after months of tennis lessons with him, she already knew that he had a girlfriend back in Spain, who was hoping to move to the UK to be with him soon.

She looked at Juan and then back at the girls, who were whispering quietly. Then she looked at Micky, who was scowling, and suppressed a smile. It was so obvious it was almost comical. Micky fancied Poppy, Poppy fancied Juan and so did Bethany. It wasn't so much a love triangle as a love square. Oh, the trials and tribulations of being a teenager. But, in a strange way, it made her happy that Bethany's problems were so typical of girls of her age. So normal.

'See,' Lily was triumphant. 'They've already made up. I told you!'

Avril had to admit that Lily was right. The girls had their heads together, talking quickly and she couldn't help but feel sorry for Micky, who was hovering next to them, on his own. But then, as she watched with relief, the girls pulled apart and started talking to him. Yes, everything was back to normal, everything was as it should be. And now she could finally relax and enjoy the evening.

Within a couple of hours, most of the adults were several glasses of champagne down and the youngsters were grouped together in the corner, alternating between staring at their phones and chatting with each other. Lily and Eric were dancing and Avril watched them, captivated yet again, at their elegance and adoration for each other. She considered asking Stuart if he fancied a spin around the dance floor but next to Lily and Eric, they'd look like elephants. Sandy and Clare had no such qualms and were dancing together, each holding one of Isla's hands.

When Bethany wandered over, Avril put her arm around her in

a moment of joy and was even more thrilled when her daughter didn't recoil.

'Mum, we're going to go to the boathouse.'

'What? Now? But the party's just getting started.'

Poppy appeared by Bethany's side. 'Yeah and it's fun for you oldies, but it's boring for us.'

Avril frowned. 'Who's going?'

'Us and Micky.'

Avril looked to Stuart who shrugged. 'Let them go, Avril. It is a bit boring for them. What teenager wants to eat lobster?'

Poppy probably does, Avril thought. And would Stuart ever let the lobster thing go? But she was in a good mood and she was happy that the girls were friends again, so she relented. 'Okay, go and have fun. But come back for midnight.'

'Okay. See you.'

They were gone in a flash, with Micky hot on their heels and Avril smiled and turned back to the dance floor. It was getting rowdy now, with lots of people up on their feet, and when Stuart took her hand and beckoned her to follow, she decided to let her hair down.

Twenty minutes later, Avril was sweating, again, and she went to sit down for a break, her eyes drifting around the room. She spotted Juan being cornered by a group of middle-aged ladies and stifled a smile. Lily sat down beside her.

'Well, isn't this so much fun!'

'It's wonderful,' Avril agreed.

'Where are the girls? I haven't seen them for a while.'

'They went to the boathouse with Micky.'

Lily rolled her eyes. 'Free-flowing champagne and a spread of food and they'd still rather hang out in a gloomy log cabin.'

'Do you let Poppy drink?'

'Not usually but I said she could have a little glass tonight. It is New Year's Eve, after all.'

'Well, they don't know what they're missing.'

'Maybe they've stolen a bottle of champagne and run off with it.'

Avril was alarmed. 'Should we go and check?'

'Oh, let them have some fun, darling. It's a special evening.'

Avril tried to put her unease about Bethany, Poppy and Micky drinking alcohol out of her mind. Lily was right, it *was* a special evening, and they were good, responsible kids. If rebelling meant having a few sips of champagne, then it could be worse.

By the time the clock reached ten to twelve, Avril had almost forgotten about the children. It was only as it got closer to midnight that she remembered they should be back by now.

'Where's Bethany?' she asked Stuart. 'She said she'd come back for New Year.'

'They've probably lost track of time, don't worry about it.'

'But what if something's happened?'

'Avril.' Stuart gave her a stern look. 'Stop. Nothing's happened.'

'Will you go and get her, Stuart?'

Stuart looked reluctant, but then he nodded. 'Fine. Keep an eye on Tom.'

Avril glanced at Tom, who was slumped over a chair, playing a game on his iPad. He wasn't used to late nights, and he looked exhausted. She'd take him home straight after the bells chimed, she decided, Bethany too. But what a fun evening it had been.

She walked over to Lily and was about to ask if she wanted a drink when she saw Micky running into the clubhouse, his eyes wild and his face pale as he frantically scanned the room. He was searching for someone and when Avril caught his eye and he dashed towards her, her heart started pounding. *It's me he's looking for. Something's happened.*

'Call an ambulance,' Micky screamed and his voice carried over the music, making some of the partygoers stop and stare. Stuart, who hadn't even put his coat on yet, hurried back over to see what the commotion was and Avril felt Lily tense by her side.

'What is it?' Avril shouted over the music, hysteria rising inside her. When Stuart reached her, she gripped his hand. *Please don't let this be happening again.*

Micky reached them, his hands shaking as he fought back tears. 'It's Poppy,' he said and it was only then that Avril realised he was looking at Lily, not her. 'Please, you have to help her!'

15

Sandy had never run so fast in her life. She ran until she could hardly breathe and even then she kept going, fuelled by raw adrenaline. But Clare, who had discarded her heels and was barefoot, despite the frosty, uneven ground, was still faster and so were several others.

By the time she reached the lake, a small crowd had formed and Sandy pushed in and gasped when she saw a body on the ground. Her heart constricted when she realised it was Poppy. Poppy's hair and clothes were soaking wet and a puddle of water was forming around her on the gravel footpath. A man was on his knees beside her and it took Avril a second to realise that he was performing chest compressions. Sandy watched in horror as Lily arrived, gasping for breath, and saw her daughter's body. Lily screamed and fell to her knees beside Poppy. Eric stood behind her, frozen in shock, his body as immobile as his lifeless daughter's.

Sandy ran towards Lily and put her arm around her. The man was pushing down on Poppy's chest, counting under his breath. She felt someone standing behind her and looked up to see Micky, his face as white as Eric's.

'What happened, Micky?' she demanded.

'She fell in the lake.' He looked like a terrified little boy.

'How long was she in there for?'

'I don't know. I went for help as soon as she went in.'

But Poppy was a strong swimmer; Sandy had seen her diving into the pool at Westford Park many times. If they'd been drinking, though, perhaps she got into trouble in the lake. And the water must be ice cold. This was a nightmare, a horror story unfolding in front of them. The man was still doing compressions and as Sandy watched him, transfixed, she realised that it was Steve. This couldn't be real, this couldn't be happening. But it *was* happening, right in front of her, and she couldn't watch it. She squeezed Lily even tighter, closed her eyes and prayed.

A spluttering sound made her snap her eyes open again and she saw Poppy coughing, water spilling out of her open mouth. Steve turned her onto her side and someone draped a coat over her. Before long, all the men had taken off their jackets and draped them over Poppy's cold, shivering body. Sandy exhaled and her cold hands, still gripping on to Lily, trembled.

'Thank God. Oh Poppy!' Lily was inconsolable as she reached down and embraced her soaking-wet daughter. 'Poppy, you're freezing.'

Someone else appeared, towering over them and Sandy recognised him as the manager of the clubhouse. 'The ambulance is on the way. Is she okay?'

Lily didn't answer, so Sandy said, 'I think so. She's breathing. But she's very cold.'

The man nodded. 'I'll go back up and wait for the paramedics.'

The crowd began to disperse, as onlookers became conscious of gawking and the family's need for privacy. Sandy looked at Clare. 'You need to go back and find Isla. We left her in the clubhouse in the panic and she'll be scared.'

'She was with our neighbours, she was fine.'

'Still, you should go.'

Clare nodded and began to follow the others back to the club-house. A few minutes later, Sandy saw the blue lights of the ambulance.

'Stand back,' she ordered to the last few remaining people. 'Paramedics are here.'

She stood up to give them some space and looked around. There was Micky, fidgeting nervously, and a few metres away Avril and Stuart were talking quietly to Bethany, who looked just as shaken. Sandy walked over to Micky, took his arm gently and guided him towards Avril.

'We should take the kids home,' she said. 'Give them something sweet for the shock and warm them up again. There's nothing we can do for Lily and Poppy right now.'

'What happened?' Avril was distraught.

'We'll find out in due course. But right now, being here isn't helping.'

Stuart nodded. 'She's right, let's get Bethany home.'

'I want to stay,' Bethany insisted. 'I want to make sure she's okay.'

'I'm staying too,' Micky said, his voice firm.

But Sandy was firmer. 'You're both going home. *Now*. I'll follow in a minute.'

Avril and Stuart managed to manhandle the two distressed teenagers away, despite their protesting, and Sandy went over to Lily and Eric, who were huddled together, watching the paramedics attend to Poppy. Steve was the only other person still left.

Sandy turned to him. 'You saved her life.'

'It was nothing,' he said, pulling at his wet shirt collar. 'It's what anyone would have done.'

'Not everyone would have known what to do. Thank God you were here.'

'I'm just glad I could help.'

Impulsively, Sandy embraced him in a tight hug, feeling his sodden clothes against her body, and then, with one last look at Lily, she started following everyone else back up the path. When she glanced at her watch, she realised that midnight had been and gone. What a horrendous start to the New Year. She just hoped that they'd got the poor girl out of the lake before hypothermia set in.

They. Sandy's head was swimming with questions. Who had pulled her out of the water? It couldn't have been Micky because he'd run for help as soon as she fell in. And he wouldn't have left her there alone, at risk of drowning. Which meant that someone else had been there, someone else had got Poppy out. But Bethany had been bone-dry, she was sure of it. If she'd gone in after Poppy or even if she'd dragged her out of the water, she'd be wet.

Steve had been wet, she remembered. So perhaps he was the one who had got Poppy out. Come to think of it, it was the second time he had come to the rescue because he'd also helped to find Bethany all those months ago when she went out without telling Avril. Either he was a superhero, or he was exceptionally good at being in the right place at the right time.

But what had he been doing there in the first place when he should have been at the New Year's party? Sandy had seen him chatting with Juan earlier on in the evening. Had he gone for a walk? Maybe to check up on the boathouse in case any drunken revellers had foolishly decided to go for a late-night kayak? And more to the point, how on earth had Poppy ended up in the water? There had been no sign of any stolen boats and if they'd stupidly gone for a late-night swim, they would all have been wet, not just Poppy.

Something had happened down by the lake and, as always,

Sandy feared the worst. Was this simply an accident, kids fooling about after a glass of champagne, or was some darker force at hand? Had Poppy fallen in or had someone pushed her? Was it Grant, she thought with horror? But no, why would it be Grant? It didn't make any sense.

Her mind was whirring at a million miles per hour, and it kept coming back to the same thing. Steve. Only moments earlier she had hailed him a hero. There was nothing at all to suggest that he was anything other than a good Samaritan who had come to the aid of a girl in need, and yet Sandy had her doubts. Perhaps it was the persistent feeling that she recognised him or maybe it was just a deep-rooted cynicism about humans, and men in particular. Poppy was only fifteen, but she acted, and looked, a lot older than her years and she was undeniably beautiful. Had she been alone with Steve, having some sort of tryst by the lake? Would he dare try something on with a girl more than half his age? Had they gone swimming together, a romantic gesture gone wrong? But no, that couldn't be right because Micky and Bethany had been there.

Another thought came to her. Had Poppy entered the lake of her own accord? She came across as the most confident, together teenager that Sandy had ever met and although there had been an argument with Bethany, it seemed to have quickly resolved itself.

No. It was something else. Sandy passed the ambulance, its lights still flashing and was grateful to see the glowing windows of the houses in the distance. She wanted to get home, to feel safe and warm again. She wanted to check the windows and doors and make sure that Micky was okay. And she wanted to find out exactly what had happened at the lake.

Because Sandy smelled a rat. She couldn't help it; it was in her nature after the hand that life had dealt her. And she needed to sniff it out before anyone else got hurt.

16

Lily stroked her daughter's ice-cold hand. The paramedic was talking, possibly to her, but his voice was muffled, and she felt like she was underwater. The sound of blue sirens above her head seemed miles away. The only presence Lily felt, the sole focus of her concentration, was her child. Poppy's face was hidden under an oxygen mask and her hair was wet and tangled. She looked so fragile, as though she could break at any second.

Lily had never been so afraid in her life. She couldn't lose Poppy, she just couldn't. She didn't know how she could live without her; there was no way forward without her daughter.

Logic told her that everything was going to be okay. They had found Poppy in time, Steve had saved her and she was breathing. But terrifying and hideous thoughts tried to persuade her otherwise. She would die of hypothermia or secondary drowning. She would suffer a cardiac arrest from the cold. She would fall asleep and never wake up.

She didn't know what had happened that evening and she didn't care. As long as Poppy was okay, nothing else mattered. It was a horrible accident, she had already decided, and if Poppy had drunk too much and fallen in the lake, she wouldn't be angry or judgemental. She wouldn't punish or scold her because that was the deal she had made with whatever higher power existed out there. As long as Poppy survived, she would forgive everything.

But Poppy wasn't in any condition to tell her what had happened. Her eyes were closed, her usually radiant face wan. Lily kept her eyes fixed on her daughter, praying for her to fight, to make it through. *You've got this*, she silently urged her child. *Just stay strong.*

Eventually, the ambulance slowed and then stopped. There was a flurry of activity, the doors opening, Poppy being wheeled out and taken into the hospital, medics rushing to meet them, and all Lily could do was watch helplessly as they took her daughter away from her.

She tried to follow but a nurse put her hand on Lily's shoulder and told her that she'd show her to the family room. She would come and find her as soon as she had any news, she promised. Lily was too numb to object, so she followed the nurse meekly, semi-aware of Eric, who had got a lift from someone sober, appearing beside her, as they were escorted into a room with rows of metal seats and a television on the wall. Lily glanced at it and saw the televised New Year's celebration in London, still in full swing. How could the party still be going, she wondered, after what had happened? Didn't they know? Hadn't the entire world stood still?

Eric was saying something to her, and she turned to face him, trying to make out his words. Something about tea. She shook her head and he turned and left.

She began to pace, striding up and down the room, occasionally glancing at the television but not registering what was on the screen. She couldn't sit, she couldn't rest, she just had to keep walking. After a few minutes, Eric returned and handed her the tea she'd refused and she took it because she didn't know what else to do.

Neither spoke to the other. Five minutes turned into ten, and then twenty, and then thirty. Lily could hear her phone beeping, but she made no move to check her messages. She was trapped in a halfway house between life and death, removed from reality and the existence of other people, fearing what lay ahead. She wondered if this was what purgatory was, a faceless hospital waiting room, an eternal wait. A loved one hanging in the balance.

When the doctor finally appeared, Lily no longer had any idea how long they'd been there. It could have been minutes or it could have been days. But the moment she saw him in the doorway, she came crashing back down to reality and she ran to him, studying his face desperately and trying to decipher what he was going to tell them from his expression. The second it took for him to speak felt like a hundred eternities.

'Poppy is fine,' he said and with his words, the greyscale world flooded with colour again. Lily threw herself at him, her body pulsating with relief.

'Thank you, oh thank you.'

'We're going to keep her in overnight for observation, but all her vitals are steady and she has no signs of hypothermia. She's awake and asking for you.'

'Take me to her, please.'

Lily hurried down the corridor on the doctor's heels. When she saw Poppy, lying in bed, she crumpled. 'Oh, Poppy, thank goodness you're okay.'

Eric hovered behind her. 'You gave us quite a shock, Popsicle.'

He hadn't called her Popsicle for years, but somehow it seemed fitting because, in her hospital bed, Poppy seemed like a little girl again. Lily finally acknowledged her husband with a smile, remembering that he was there, that he had been scared too.

She pulled up a chair and sat beside her daughter, taking her hand. 'How are you feeling?'

'Fine.' Poppy's voice was hoarse.

'What happened, darling?'

'I don't remember.'

'Okay, well, don't worry about that for now. The main thing is that you're okay. The doctor said you should be able to come home tomorrow.'

'I don't want to stay here by myself.'

'I'll stay with you all night.' Lily wasn't sure if this was permitted but her fight was back now and no one was stopping her from staying with her daughter. They'd have to manhandle her out kicking and screaming, and even then, she'd find a way back in.

'Shall I go home and get some pyjamas and slippers? Clean clothes?' Eric was restless, wanting to be put to use, desperate for a practical purpose.

Lily gave him what he needed. 'That's a good idea. Thanks, Eric.'

He nodded, kissed Poppy on the forehead and left, his hand already reaching into his pocket for his mobile phone.

Alone with Poppy, Lily decided to try again. 'It's just you and me now, darling, Daddy has gone. Do you want to tell me what happened? I won't be angry.'

'I told you, I don't remember.'

'If you were drunk, I—'

'Stop it, Mum. Just stop it.'

'Okay, I'm sorry.'

She was pushing too much when Poppy was tired and shaken. She should let her sleep and she'd try again in the morning. But now that she knew Poppy was okay, now that the nightmare was over, Lily's focus had moved elsewhere, her deal with the higher power already forgotten. She wanted answers. She needed them.

Something had happened down at that lake and if there was someone to blame, Lily needed to know who it was. If someone had deliberately hurt her daughter, then they would pay for it. Her fear was already morphing into rage, and, in a fever of impatience, she couldn't resist probing again.

'Did someone hurt you?' Poppy started crying quietly and Lily puffed up her chest as adrenaline coursed through her body. She'd kill them. 'Who hurt you, Poppy?'

But then Poppy said in a voice so low it was almost a whisper, 'No one hurt me. It was my fault. Leave me alone.'

And then she turned her head to the side and closed her eyes, leaving Lily alone with her horrible thoughts, desperate for a fight but unsure who her opponent was. Already she was running through a potential list. There was Bethany, of course, with her track record of bullying. What if she'd been fooling Lily for all these months with her sweet shyness? What if she'd been plotting to hurt Poppy the entire time, to lure her in with friendship and then damage her?

Her mind frantic, she switched to Micky. He seemed like a gentle boy but his father was violent. And hadn't he hurt his own mother once? He had form. What had she been doing, letting her child go out with these kids?

It didn't feel right, though. It felt unfair and a betrayal of Avril and Sandy. But she was running out of other ideas. Sandy's ex? Sandy had been convinced that he was lurking around Westford Park, trying to scare her. Could he have been involved? But why did that have anything to do with Poppy? Or maybe it was the people who'd vandalised the courts. Could it have been an animal, even? The same beast in the woods that was responsible for the ghastly noises they'd heard? No, she was being irrational now.

Unless, she realised with a start, the perpetrator was right here in this hospital ward? Was this her fault? She had moved them to

Westford Park, she had let Poppy go out on her own at night, she had even given her a glass of champagne. In her attempts to gain Poppy's affection again, she had been too liberal and now she was paying the price.

Poppy's breathing began to steady, and Lily watched the rise and fall of her chest. She was asleep now and Lily should try to get some shut-eye too. Tomorrow was going to be a long day. But she was too wired, too tense. Instead, she rested her arms on the edge of her daughter's bed and watched her sleep, vowing that she would do whatever it took to protect Poppy and to make sure that nothing bad ever happened to her again. The long night stretched ahead, with plenty of time to linger over her own failures. But Lily was not one to drown in self-pity and soon she found herself planning instead, working out the ways that she was going to be a better mother. She would get things right from now on, she decided. She would be stricter with Poppy and the evenings at the boathouse would come to an end, starting right now. She would find out exactly what had happened at the lake and make sure that if someone had hurt Poppy, they paid the price. She would do whatever it took to protect her daughter. There were no limits.

* * *

Nurses came in and out all night, checking Poppy's vitals, fussing around her. Poppy slept through it all, dead to the world. No one told Lily to go home and someone even brought her a blanket, which she draped over herself as she watched her daughter, a one-woman vigil. When dawn appeared, Lily was grateful for the comforting morning light.

Eric appeared just after seven, clutching a holdall of belongings and looking fresh-faced from a shower and change of clothes. Poppy was still out for the count.

'How is she?'

'Fine, she slept all night.'

Eric lowered his tone. 'Has she told you what happened?'

'No, only that it wasn't anyone else's fault.'

'Do you think she went for a midnight swim?'

'Maybe, I don't know. She was fully clothed, though, so I doubt it.'

'Well, the main thing is that she's okay.'

'Yes. But she's never going out again. Never.'

Eric smiled slightly. 'Good luck with that.'

'I'm serious, Eric.'

'You can't do that, Lily. She's a teenage girl.'

'I can do what I like, I'm her mother.'

'She'll hate you, it'll only make things worse.'

'What could be worse than this, Eric?'

But they both knew the answer to that. Poppy could have died and so Lily's insistence that she stay at home didn't seem unreasonable to her.

Poppy stirred and they abruptly stopped talking and assumed their best smiles. She looked at them, rubbing her eyes drowsily.

'Mother. Father.'

Lily exhaled. She was feeling better, then.

'Hey there, Popsicle,' Eric said. 'How are you feeling?'

'Like I nearly drowned in a lake.'

'Sounds about right. You hungry?'

'No.'

'Thirsty?'

'No.'

Poppy looked at Lily and, even from her hospital bed, her eyes were challenging. They were saying, *Don't ask me questions. Let this one go.* But it wasn't in Lily's nature to let things go, especially after she'd spent all night stewing on it.

'Last night you said you couldn't remember what happened,' Lily began tentatively but Poppy interrupted her.

'I remember what happened.'

Oh, thank goodness, Lily thought. 'Go on.'

'We were fooling around by the lake and I fell in. It was freezing and I got my legs tangled up in some weeds. Next thing I know, I'm in an ambulance.'

Lily frowned. Was it possible Poppy was telling the truth? Was it really that simple?

'Who was there with you?'

Poppy frowned as if trying to remember. 'Bethany and Micky I think.'

'Anyone else?'

'No.'

'And there was no argument? No fighting?'

'No, Mother, I told you. It was an accident.'

'It's just that you'd had this row with Bethany and I wondered...'

'This wasn't Bethany's fault, Mother. Stop harassing me.'

Lily was poised to continue her questioning, but Eric stopped her. 'These things happen. All's well that ends well. Hopefully, you can come home as soon as the doctor's been to see you.'

Poppy looked around. 'Where's my phone?'

Lily frowned, trying to remember seeing it. 'I don't know, darling. Was it in your pocket? It might have fallen in the lake too.'

'I *need* my phone.'

Eric took her hand. 'We'll get you a new one, darling.'

'But I need it now.'

Eric was already reaching for his coat. 'I'll go to the shops now and buy you one.'

Lily looked up at him, frowning. Eric threw money at things, especially in a crisis, but that wasn't always the answer. 'It's New

Year's Day, Eric. The shops won't be open. Anyway, Poppy needs to rest. Perhaps a couple of days without a phone is a good thing.'

'I need a phone!' Poppy was becoming distressed, her panic visible. Lily felt her temper rising, the long night making her agitated. It was ridiculous how dependent teenagers were on their screens and Poppy was starting to sound like a spoiled brat. Eric wasn't helping, with his insistence on solving the problem with an instant replacement.

'Poppy, we'll get you a phone, okay?' she said. 'Just not today.'

'You don't understand.'

'What don't I understand?'

Poppy fell back against the pillow. 'Forget it.'

Lily pulled out her own phone. 'You can borrow mine, darling, if you want to speak to your friends. Is it Bethany and Micky...'

'I said forget it!'

The force of Poppy's anger shocked Lily. But, she reasoned, everything would be okay as soon as they got home. She'd make Poppy a hot chocolate, her favourite, and they would lounge on the sofa and watch films together all day. And the next day too. She was almost looking forward to it.

'When you're feeling better, we should go and thank the boatman guy,' she said.

'His name is Steve.'

'Yes, Steve. He saved your life, you know. He performed CPR on you. He's a hero.'

Was it Lily or did Poppy seem upset about this? But she hadn't slept all night, she was tired and confused. Her phone beeped and she pulled it out and saw a message from Avril.

'Everyone's asking about you,' she said. 'They're so relieved you're okay.'

But Poppy had closed her eyes again.

Eric peered at her. 'Is she asleep?'

'I don't know. We should let her rest.'

'Have you eaten? I could go and see if the canteen is open and get you some breakfast.'

Lily winced. She had no appetite at all, especially not for hospital canteen food. 'I'm not hungry but I'd love a coffee.'

Eric nodded. 'I'll go and see what I can find.'

Alone again with her daughter, Lily rubbed her eyes and hoped that the doctor wouldn't keep them waiting too long. It was time to get Poppy home, where Lily could look after her.

Home. They had only lived at Westford Park for a few months, but it felt like much longer and that was because of the friends she'd made. Avril and Sandy had been there for her last night and they had been in touch constantly to find out how Poppy was. They were good people and she was lucky to have them. She felt bad now for thinking the worst of Bethany and Micky but she had been afraid and paranoid. In the light of day, she was beginning to accept that it might have been an accident after all, teenagers fooling around. But now Westford Park was, and always would be, the place where her daughter had almost died.

This was far from what she had dreamed of. She thought of Eric, resentment rising inside her. Even as he walked to the canteen, she knew he would be on his phone and she wanted to chase after him and snatch it out of his hands. She wanted to scream and shout and tell him that his daughter was lying in a hospital bed and all he cared about was his stupid phone. All he cared about was texting and plotting and lying. It sickened her. No wonder Poppy had kicked off the way she had when she realised that her own phone was missing; she had learned from her father. What else had she learned from him?

But she was being unfair. Eric had been just as frightened as she was last night. Even now he was thinking of Lily, checking if she'd eaten and fetching her some coffee. When he came back he would sit beside her and take her hand. He would watch Poppy sleep. He would order her the best new phone on the market and pay a ridiculous amount for it to be delivered the next day, and Poppy's face would light up with joy at the sight of it. And he would put his arm around his daughter and tell her that she was worth it. Whatever else he was, he loved Poppy, and he was a doting father.

As for whether he was a good husband, now was not the time to go down that road.

17

Avril read Lily's text with relief. 'Poppy's fine,' she told Stuart. 'They're coming home today.'

'Thank goodness. Do you want a coffee?'

'Yes please.'

Stuart headed into the kitchen and Avril looked at Bethany, who was slumped on the sofa, her face pale. They had sent her straight to bed the previous night with a hot water bottle, knowing that she was too shaken and exhausted to tell them what had happened. But now it was time to talk and Avril was dreading it.

Things were only just starting to improve between her and Bethany and a difficult conversation like this could send them hurtling backwards again. She had to tread carefully, make sure that Bethany knew she wasn't accusing her of anything, she simply wanted to know what had happened. Because she wasn't accusing her. Was she?

No, she wasn't. There was no reason to think that this incident had anything to do with Bethany, other than the fact that she had been there at the time. But then so had Micky.

Bethany was gripping on to a glass of orange juice, but she

hadn't touched a drop. Her pale pink fleece pyjamas made her look childlike, a stark contrast to the mature young lady in the dress she'd worn to the New Year's Eve party. It all seemed a long time ago now.

Avril sat down next to her. 'Did you hear? Poppy's doing well and she's coming home.'

Bethany nodded and stared at her orange juice.

'What happened, love?'

Bethany didn't respond and Avril tried again. 'I won't be angry.'

Bethany's eyes fixed on hers accusingly. 'Why would you be angry? It wasn't my fault.'

'Of course it wasn't, I didn't mean that. What I mean is, if you were drinking, or messing about, I won't be cross.'

'We weren't drunk. We had a bit of champagne, that was all.'

'So, what made you go down to the lake so late at night?'

Bethany hesitated for a fraction of a second. 'We were in the boathouse and we heard some loud bangs. We went outside to see what it was and it was fireworks, you know, for New Year's Eve. Anyway, we wanted to see them properly so we walked down to the water.'

'Okay,' Avril said, nodding encouragingly.

'The next thing I know there's this splash and Poppy's in the water. I assumed she'd just pull herself out and that would be that. But then she went under.'

'But she can swim, can't she? What happened?'

Bethany's eyes filled with tears. 'I don't know, Mum!'

'Okay, sorry. What happened next?'

'I started screaming for help and Micky ran off. I think he went up to the clubhouse to get you guys. I didn't know what to do, Mum, I was so scared.'

'Shh.' Avril put her hand over her daughter's. 'It wasn't your fault.'

'I should have gone in after her, Mum. But it was like I was frozen, I couldn't move.'

'That's a completely natural reaction, love.'

'I feel terrible about it.'

'I know you do, but it wasn't your fault.'

'Anyway, then Steve got her out and she wasn't moving. I was so scared.'

'Was Steve there?'

Bethany looked away. 'No. He came when he heard me screaming.'

'Well, look, love,' she told her daughter, 'it was an accident. The important thing is that Poppy is going to be fine. So please don't worry, okay?'

Bethany nodded and her face relaxed. Avril realised then that she'd been just as anxious about this conversation as Bethany had been. She had probably been afraid that Avril would accuse her of being involved and bring up the past allegations again.

Avril sagged with relief. They'd had the conversation she'd been dreading all night and it had ended even better than expected. If anything, it might have brought them closer together. She had shown Bethany that she trusted her version of events.

The doorbell interrupted Avril's thoughts and she went to answer it. It was early for visitors but after the previous night's ordeal, normal rules were out of the window and she wasn't surprised to see Sandy at the door. She let her in and gave her a hug.

'Poppy's fine,' she told Sandy.

'I know, I've just heard from Lily too. Is Bethany okay?'

'A bit shaken, but she'll be fine. Apparently, they went to watch some fireworks down by the lake and Poppy just slipped and fell into the water.'

'That's what Micky said too.'

This reinforced Avril's belief that Bethany was telling the truth, not that she needed reassurance, she reminded herself. Now she only had to hope that Lily believed it too. She wondered what Poppy had told her mother and felt a nagging fear in the pit of her stomach.

'How's Micky?' she asked Sandy.

'He's fine. A bit shaken but much better this morning. I wanted to talk to you about something, though.'

Sandy looked worried and instinctively Avril went outside and pulled the front door to, rather than inviting her into the house. Something told her that this conversation needed to be private and the nagging fear surged. The cold January air seeped in through her dressing gown and made her shiver, and she folded her arms across her chest, involuntarily defensive.

'What is it?'

'This Steve guy. Don't you think it's odd that he was there?'

'Apparently, he heard Bethany screaming and came running.'

'But where was he, then? He was supposed to be at the party.'

Why was Sandy so interested in Steve? Was she right that he had been there with them all along? If she was, then it meant that Bethany – and Micky – were lying and there must be a reason why.

Why would a man in his thirties hang out with a bunch of teenagers, though? And they'd not been far from the boathouse, so it was just as likely that he was in there when he heard the commotion and came to help. In her mind, Steve was a hero and she didn't want to rewrite the narrative. She didn't want to doubt her daughter's version of events.

'Bethany says he wasn't there and I believe her,' Avril said firmly 'He probably went for a walk or to check on the boathouse. Maybe he left the party to have a smoke.'

'Maybe.' Sandy looked towards the direction of the lake.

'What is it, Sandy?' Avril was cold and growing impatient.

'I don't trust him.'

'Why not?'

'I don't know.'

'You think he had something to do with this?'

'I'm not sure.'

'But Micky and Bethany have both said he wasn't even there.'

'I know.'

Avril mulled it over. 'What are you getting at? Are you suggesting he was spying on them?'

Sandy shook her head. 'I really don't know. Forget I said anything, I'm just rambling.'

Avril looked at her friend and her expression softened. It was no wonder that Sandy was suspicious of men. But Steve was a kind, amenable man. He had been brilliant at teaching Tom how to kayak and Avril didn't suspect anything dodgy about him. She was good at sizing people up. Anyway, just a few weeks ago Sandy was worrying about her ex. Now it seemed her suspicions had turned to Steve and Avril was starting to see a pattern.

'I think we're all tired and emotional,' she said diplomatically. 'But it sounds to me like it was just an accident and I'm sure Poppy will tell her parents the same thing.'

'Mum?'

Avril turned around with a start to see Bethany standing in the front doorway. 'Hi, love.'

'What are you both doing out here in the cold?'

Sandy's expression transformed in an instant and she plastered on a smile. 'I just popped by to say hello and see how you were doing this morning.'

'Fine.' Bethany's eyes narrowed and Avril knew she was sizing them up, trying to work out why they were having a hushed conversation outside in the cold. *She thinks we're talking about her.*

She thinks I don't believe her and we're debating whether she had anything to do with this.

In a desperate attempt to deflect the attention away from Bethany, she blurted out, 'We were just talking about Steve, actually. Did you see him at any other point during the evening?'

Bethany was still watching them closely. 'At the New Year's party.'

'And after that? Did you bump into him near the lake at all? Before Poppy fell in?'

'No.'

Avril nodded, satisfied. 'Okay, love, thanks.'

Bethany looked from Avril to Sandy and then headed back inside.

'There we go,' Avril said to Sandy. 'It was nothing to do with Steve. Just teenagers being teenagers. There'll need to be a punishment, but I don't think we should go too far, I'm sure they've learned their lesson. What do you think?'

'Sure.'

'Listen, why don't you all pop over for lunch later? I've got loads of pizzas in the freezer.'

Sandy smiled. 'That sounds lovely, thank you.'

'See you in a few hours, then.' Avril touched her friend lightly on the arm and went inside. In the living room, Tom and Bethany were watching TV and Stuart was reading and sipping his coffee. It all seemed so regular, like the previous night's events hadn't happened.

But they *had* happened, and Avril still feared the consequences. Lily's texts had been brief, not enough to deduce whether she was angry, but then she had more important things on her mind than sending long messages with lots of kisses at the end. And why would she be angry anyway? Bethany and Micky's stories matched up and no one was to blame.

Last night she had been afraid, for Poppy of course but also for herself and Bethany. The memory of all her friends turning against her, the sting of their cold shoulder, was still raw and so was the way her daughter had closed in on herself, shutting everyone out, making it impossible for Avril to take her pain away. After Poppy's accident, she had feared it was going to happen again, that everyone would blame Bethany and they would become the pariahs of Westford Park. Bethany would fade away again, Tom would be unfairly targeted and she and Stuart would fall apart when they were only just coming back together.

It had been irrational. She looked at her children, snuggled up on the sofa in their PJs and at Stuart, half reading, half watching TV. Then she glanced out of the patio doors and saw a robin perched on the fence, its red breast vibrant against the frosty backdrop.

She exhaled slowly. Everything was going to be okay. But as she went upstairs to get dressed, visions of Poppy's soaking, lifeless body continued to flash on repeat in her mind.

18

The anonymous calls had started again. Clare had said that everyone, even the scammers, were back to work after the Christmas break, revived and ready to steal money from unsuspecting victims. But there was a flaw in her argument. No one was trying to steal anything, no one was asking Sandy if she'd been in a car accident that wasn't her fault or offering her an exciting new job if she'd simply be kind enough to pass on her bank details.

Every time she answered the phone there was nothing but silence.

'You're overthinking it,' Clare told her. 'You need to get back to work.'

But Sandy had worked non-stop in the run-up to Christmas, making seasonal cards, diaries and calendars to sell online and she was exhausted and struggling to concentrate. She was distracted too, increasingly by her growing obsession with Steve. She was using it as an outlet to distract herself from Grant, and she was clinging on to it with dear life.

The image of Bethany's picture of the girl trapped in the boathouse kept coming back to her too. She had almost told Avril about it a dozen times, but she never seemed to be able to get the words out.

There was something going on at Westford Park, something strange, and it was getting to Sandy. But it was a mess, a tangle of thoughts that she couldn't unravel. She sensed that all the incidents that had happened – the noises, the vandalism, Bethany's painting and Poppy's accident – were linked but she didn't know how. She had talked to Clare about it and while she had listened and empathised, and put her arm around Sandy, she had also said that all these incidents could be explained. That often the obvious explanation was the right one.

Around her, it was business as usual. Poppy had recovered, the kids had gone back to school, Clare had returned to work, and the tennis lessons had resumed. Avril and Lily were singing Steve's praises, calling him a lifesaver, and Sandy nodded her agreement, while inside she doubted him. She'd made some casual enquiries, asking Juan and some of the staff at the clubhouse if they knew much about his past, but she didn't want to push too much in case they became suspicious. She was watching him, though. She took her easel down to the lake whenever the weather was dry on the pretence of doing some work, one eye set permanently in the direction of the boathouse, the other on her perpetually blank canvas so she at least looked like she was painting. But it was too cold to stay for long and on the odd occasion she had seen him, he'd waved cheerily at her, headed inside and closed the door behind him, leaving Sandy deflated and confused.

Micky was sulking too. Poppy was grounded and the forced separation was making him moody and agitated. Sandy could add that to the list of things to worry about. She liked Poppy but she couldn't help but wonder if she was leading Micky on, enjoying his attention with no intention of reciprocating it. He was going to get his heart broken at some point and Sandy didn't trust Poppy to do it kindly.

To top it all off, Isla had cried at the beginning of term because she didn't want to go back to school and was having to be physically pulled away from her by the teacher every morning. Sandy fretted that Isla wasn't making friends or, worse, that she was being bullied, despite the teacher's reassurance that Isla was perfectly happy once she was in the classroom.

There was so much on her mind, so much to keep her up at night. So it was no wonder that she was checking the doors and windows constantly again, her relief at knowing they were secure rapidly being replaced by the fear that she'd missed something, which set her off on the routine again. And again. And she was just so tired. So very tired.

She stifled a yawn as she glanced over at Bethany. They got together most Saturday mornings now and today they had decided to paint inside because the weather was atrocious. Sandy had set their easels up in the living room so they could do some still-life work. Clare had taken Isla to the cinema and Micky was seeing a schoolfriend, so they had the place to themselves. Bethany was already hard at work, but Sandy was yet to make a single mark on the canvas.

'Poppy's recovered well,' she remarked, as she picked up a pencil.

'I haven't really seen her.'

Sandy looked sideways at Bethany. 'Oh? Why is that?'

'She's grounded.'

'Oh yes, of course.'

'Although her mum said she can start having friends over soon.'

'I bet you can't wait to see her again.'

'Yeah. Maybe.'

Sandy started sketching, keeping her voice casual. 'Everything okay between you?'

Bethany hesitated. 'Yeah.'

'And how are things at school.'

At this, Bethany's face lit up. 'Good. I've made some new friends. They're cool.'

'That's wonderful, Bethany. Your mum must be thrilled.'

'I haven't told her.'

'Why not?'

Bethany scrunched up her nose. 'It's complicated.'

Sandy smiled wryly. 'Life often is.'

'I guess I don't want her to make a fuss.'

'I understand that. Us parents can be a bit embarrassing some-times, right?'

Bethany smiled. 'Right.'

They worked in companionable silence for a while. Sandy knew better than to push Bethany; it was better to let her instigate the conversation. Instead, she tried to concentrate on her own drawing, but she couldn't seem to find the motivation. She rubbed out the outline she'd sketched and started over, wondering why a simple vase of flowers, which she'd painted a hundred times before, was causing her such a problem today.

'Why were you and Mum talking about Steve the other week?'

Sandy was thrown by the unexpected question. 'We weren't,' she replied hesitantly. But Bethany shot her a look, and she decided to be honest. 'I just wondered why Steve was by the lake the night that Poppy fell in. I thought he was at the party with the rest of us.'

'He's often around,' Bethany said.

Alarm bells rang but Sandy tried to keep her tone nonchalant. What do you mean?'

'Nothing. I just mean that sometimes when we're at the boathouse, he pops in.'

'Okay,' Sandy said slowly. 'And how long does he stay?'

'Not long.'

'Does he ever give you anything?'

Bethany raised her eyebrows. 'Like what?'

'Alcohol? Cigarettes?'

Bethany laughed. ''Course not. Why don't you like him?'

Sandy considered her answer. 'It's not that I don't like him. It's hard to explain. Tell me, Bethany, do any of you kids ever spend time with him? Other when you're all together, I mean.'

'No.'

Something on the teenager's face told Sandy she was fibbing. 'Anything you tell me will be in confidence, Bethany.'

Bethany shrugged. 'Poppy sees him sometimes. But it's not a big deal or anything.'

Sandy's heart began to race. She knew it. She *knew* it.

'Do you think they're having a relationship?'

Bethany snorted. 'No way.'

'What makes you so sure?'

'Have you seen Poppy? She's a goddess. She'd never go for a boring old guy like Steve.'

But Sandy knew better. Men could be manipulative, especially when it came to impressionable young women. And Bethany's revelation that Poppy spent time alone with Steve had added fuel to her fire. The problem was that she'd promised Bethany she wouldn't tell anyone and if she betrayed Bethany's trust, she'd never get it back.

There wasn't much to tell though, she consoled herself. Poppy and Steve had the occasional conversation on their own. It was hardly evidence of a tryst and Bethany said it was nothing romantic. Poppy was probably trying to keep him sweet, so he'd let the kids use the boathouse. If she even had an iota of suspicion that anything seedy was going on, she wouldn't hesitate to tell Lily. And by keeping Bethany's trust for now, she might learn more.

'Why do you think Poppy spends time with Steve?' she asked tentatively.

Bethany shrugged. 'She doesn't spend *that* much time with him. Like I said, it's not a big deal, forget I said anything.'

It was clear that Bethany was done with this conversation and Sandy let it go. She had to tread carefully otherwise the teenager would close herself off again. But Sandy thought of Lily and felt guilty that she knew something about Poppy that her own mother didn't.

Speaking of Lily, they were meant to be going out for dinner together that evening and it was good to have some normality back in their lives. Sandy was looking forward to catching up with Avril too. Conversely, while Sandy had felt increasingly troubled since New Year, Avril seemed to have gone the other way. There was a lightness to her step that hadn't been there before, a smile that went all the way to her eyes. Sandy sensed that something significant had happened between her and Bethany, and while she didn't know what it was, she was pleased for them both. Hopefully, Bethany was finally putting her troubles behind her.

It made her think about Bethany's painting of the boathouse, with the girl trapped inside, and instinctively she moved across the room to look over the teenager's shoulder at her work in progress. Her eyes widened in shocked horror.

Bethany, sensing her gaze looked at her. 'What is it? You don't like it?'

'I... uh... No, I do. It's excellent, Bethany.'

Sandy couldn't tear her eyes away. The painting was undoubtedly tremendous. But that wasn't what had captivated her. The vase in front of them held red roses and that's exactly what Bethany had painted. But the flowers that stood benignly in the gold vase on the table looked nothing like the ones on Bethany's paper. She had magnified the sharp thorns on the stems, almost grotesquely, and on each one, drops of blood spilled down onto the table, creating a puddle of red. The vase had a deep crack zigzagging from the top to the bottom and water spilled out of it, mingling with the blood. It was the most beautiful and horrific thing Sandy had ever seen. And it had been painted by a fifteen-year-old girl.

'I'd better go,' Bethany said, starting to pack up her things. 'It'll be lunchtime soon. Is it okay if I leave this here to dry?'

'Of course.' Sandy was still staring at the painting. She wanted to ask Bethany about it, to discover what had inspired her version of the flowers, but she couldn't find the words, and she remained silent as Bethany threw her bag over her shoulder and waved goodbye.

She continued staring at the painting long after Bethany had left.

* * *

Secrets. Sandy had somehow managed to gain two in a day. First, the revelations about Poppy and Steve and then Bethany's disturbing painting, which Sandy had not been able to stop thinking about. She hadn't told anyone about it and she wasn't sure she wanted to.

She liked Bethany. She believed that she was a good kid and she didn't want to get her into any trouble. Lots of teenagers went through dark or gothic phases, and it didn't have to *mean* anything. Except that Sandy had the nagging feeling that it did.

But, she told herself as she made her way to the clubhouse, perhaps she was putting too much weight on the painting. All the other things going on in her life had set her on edge, making her read too much into things. It was only art, it wasn't real. Except Sandy knew more than most that art imitated life. And that, fundamentally, was what worried her.

And now she had to go to dinner with Lily and Avril and pretend that everything was okay. She had to smile, and drink wine, and not tell Lily that her daughter was hanging out with a man more than twice her age or admit to Avril that Bethany might possibly be a lot more troubled than she thought. And she was still living in a state of near-constant fear that Grant was trying to scare her. If he was, it was certainly working.

She pushed open the clubhouse door and took a deep breath. It would all be fine, she told herself, she'd relax after a glass of wine. The familiarity of the clubhouse comforted her. It was one of the many things she had grown to love about Westford Park. The friendly staff, the tasty food and the fact that she could stumble home in minutes, knowing she was safe.

'Sandy!' Lily stood up to greet her.

'Lily! How are you?'

'Furious,' Lily spat. 'Someone's slashed the tyres on our Range Rover.'

Sandy was sympathetic. 'Oh no, that's awful.'

'I just don't understand what's going on. First the tennis courts and now this. How are these nasty people getting into Westford Park undetected? Or are they living here, among us?'

'Was anything spotted on CCTV?'

'No. Just like the vandalism. Whoever it is doing this knows how to evade the cameras, and the security patrols.'

Grant. Sandy's thoughts immediately turned to her ex-partner. He was cunning and he was a master at hiding undetected. Already her heart was racing and her palms were becoming clammy. Where was Micky? she thought frantically. But he was home that evening, watching a film with Clare. He was safe, she thought, as she exhaled. The windows and doors were locked; she'd checked them before she went out.

Anyway, why would Grant slash the tyres of Lily's car? If it was Sandy he wanted to frighten, what would be the benefit of going after a stranger? Unless he knew they were friends. Was it a warning that no one in Sandy's life was safe?

'Are you okay, Sandy?'

Sandy started as she was pulled from her spiralling thoughts. 'Yes.'

'You've gone as white as a sheet.'

Sandy forced a smile. 'I was just wondering who would do such a thing.'

'Well,' Lily began. 'A few months ago, I saw this man—'

She was interrupted by Avril bustling in. 'Hi, ladies,' she said, as she embraced them both and sat down. 'What are we talking about?'

'I was just telling Sandy about the tyres. Eric's apoplectic.'

'It's just awful. It almost feels like someone's targeting us, doesn't it.'

Avril's comment made Sandy choke on her wine. 'Sorry,' she spluttered.

Lily, shrewd as ever, narrowed her eyes. 'You think this is your ex again, don't you?'

'I don't know,' she admitted. 'The anonymous calls have started again. And Micky mentioned that a strange noise woke him up the other night. Oh God, I'm so sorry I've brought all this on you ladies. I feel awful.'

'You have nothing to apologise for,' Lily said firmly. 'You've done nothing wrong. Anyway, I really don't see why your ex would come after Eric and me. No, I think that it's someone else doing this. Actually, I have a theory.'

Avril leaned forward. 'Go on.'

'Well, when the planning application went in to convert the golf club into a residential development, there were a lot of objections, mainly from eco-warriors who said that the council was destroying the green belt and it was all about profit. Apparently, there were protests outside the council offices. What if it's them, trying to make a point?'

Avril nodded thoughtfully. 'You might be on to something.'

'I mean, they resent us, right? With our posh houses, tennis courts and Range Rovers.'

'But I still don't understand how they're getting away with it. What about Westford Park being the safest place in England?'

'I agree and apparently so does the site manager. He's getting more fencing installed to enclose the development. Hopefully, in a few months, our troubles will be over.'

Sandy listened to the exchange. She wanted to believe it. What a weight off her shoulders it would be to put this all down to activists. To know that it was nothing to do with her and Micky.

'I wonder if that man I saw had something to do with it,' Lily added.

Sandy's heart stopped. 'What man?'

'A few months ago, I saw a man outside Avril's house, allegedly delivering flyers. But I never got one. Perhaps he was actually doing a recce, getting the lay of the land?'

'All right, Miss Marple,' Avril joked.

But Sandy's humour was long gone. 'What did he look like?'

'He had a hood on,' Lily said, looking curiously at Sandy. 'So, I didn't get a good look. But he was tall and stocky. He was definitely older, not a teenager.'

'He could have been an innocent car cleaner,' Avril interjected.

Lily was still gazing at Sandy. 'You know my offer still stands.'

'What offer?'

Lily leaned forward and whispered, 'The private detective.'

It had slipped Sandy's mind until then. She'd dismissed the idea at the time but now she was beginning to wonder if it wasn't such a bad idea. 'I don't know,' she said.

'Look, you're clearly getting worked up about all this and I don't blame you. A lot of strange things are happening. You need some peace of mind, more than we can give you.'

'What information would they need?'

'As much as you can give them, darling. Full name, date of birth, last known address. Any photos if you have them.'

Sandy shook her head vehemently. 'I don't have any.'

'Of course you don't, I'm sorry. But really, anything you have. He's very experienced, this man. He can work with scant information, believe me.'

'How did you say you knew him again?'

'Eric's used him before.'

Sandy reached for her glass again. She needed to slow down. 'Okay, I'm in.'

Lily nodded. 'Email me some info and I'll make the call.'

Was this a terrible idea? Sandy wasn't sure but the frisson of anticipation that she felt suggested otherwise. She had been in the dark for too long and it was time to find out the truth, even if it wasn't what she wanted to hear.

'Is Micky okay?' Lily asked.

'He's fine,' she said, still thinking about the private detective.

'Has he picked up on how you're feeling?'

Sandy looked at Lily, confused. 'No, why do you ask?'

'Oh, you know what children are like. They're sponges, they absorb everything.'

Sandy was instantly on alert. 'Has he said something to Poppy?'

'No, forget I said anything.' Lily looked alarmed. 'I didn't mean to upset you.'

'Sorry,' Sandy exhaled. 'I'm a bit tetchy at the moment.'

'Of course, I understand.'

'And I know that Micky and Poppy have grown close.'

'He's been texting her constantly. It's very sweet. I've told Poppy that she can start having friends over again, but she's still banned from going out. And to be honest, with all this vandalism going on, I think they're safer at home for the time being.'

'Micky really misses her,' Sandy admitted. 'I think he's fallen for her.'

'Poppy doesn't date schoolboys,' Lily said apologetically. 'Apparently, they're too immature.'

This did nothing to alleviate Sandy's concerns about Micky's heart or Poppy's love interests.

'So, she prefers older boys, does she?' Avril asked, oblivious to Sandy's discomfort.

'Well, she claims to, but to be honest, she's not really had any boyfriends.'

That you know of, Sandy thought. Oh, God. Was she doing the right thing by keeping quiet? Or was she being irresponsible? Bethany had been sure that nothing was going on between Poppy and Steve, but if she was wrong, it didn't bear thinking about.

Suddenly she had an idea. 'This private detective. Could you put him on another job?'

'Ooh, intriguing.' Lily clasped her hands together. 'Who's the lucky person?'

'Steve, the guy from the boathouse.'

Lily frowned. 'Why do you want to know about him?'

Sandy thought on her feet. 'Do you remember I told you that I recognised him from somewhere? I just want to check it doesn't have anything to do with Grant.'

Lily nodded, satisfied. 'Good call. I'll see what I can do. Anyway, what are we eating?'

As the conversation moved on to easier topics, Sandy felt her tension begin to seep away. It was temporary relief, the effect of red wine and good company, but she'd take that for now. Even a few hours' escape was better than nothing.

When Sandy got home, it was dark and quiet. The house was asleep. She switched on a couple of lights, crept up to Micky's room and pushed the door open gently, smiling when she saw him sprawled on the bed, one leg peeking out from under the duvet. Next, she checked on Isla and Clare, before going back downstairs to double-check the windows and doors and get a glass of water. She stopped short when she saw Bethany's painting on the coffee table. Sandy had hidden it away as soon as it dried, not wanting Isla to see it and get upset. But someone had clearly found it. Micky? Clare? Or maybe even Isla.

Sandy stared at the painting in the gloom, looking at the sharp thorns on the roses and the large crack in the vase with a growing sense of foreboding. It felt like a warning to her, some sort of sign, and she was desperate to figure it out. Suddenly, she knew with absolute clarity what she had to do. It was time to talk to Avril, even if it upset Bethany.

It was time to work out what the hell was going on in Bethany's head.

19

Poppy's sweet sixteenth was fast approaching, and Lily was in full party-planning mode. Not that there was anything sweet about Poppy these days. She had been sulking pretty much constantly for the past five weeks, ever since the incident at the lake. She was furious because she wasn't allowed to go out, except for school and accompanied trips to friends' houses, but Lily had needed to keep her close. She had needed to know that Poppy was safe.

The events of New Year's Eve had terrified Lily, as she realised how close she had come to losing Poppy. There was no way that she was letting that happen again, especially with trouble-makers on the loose. But Poppy was about to turn sixteen and Lily couldn't keep her under lock and key forever. She hadn't been much older herself when she had left home and gone out into the world to fend for herself. The time was fast approaching when she would have to loosen the reins. She knew it, and she feared it.

Lily had spent her own sixteenth birthday alone in her bedroom, counting the money she'd saved up and working out when she would have enough to leave. She was determined to make sure that Poppy's experience was nothing like her own. She'd hired out the clubhouse for the evening, booked a popular DJ and ordered a beautiful cake. The guest list was seventy-two.

Today she was taking Poppy shopping for a new dress and she was looking forward to it. They hadn't been shopping together in ages. They hadn't been talking much either, but she hoped that would change when Poppy realised how much effort Lily had put into her party.

'Are you ready, Poppy?' she called from the hallway. When there was no answer, she trotted up the stairs impatiently. Pausing outside Poppy's bedroom door, her hand poised to knock, she heard Poppy giggling and talking quietly on the phone.

'Of course she doesn't know,' she heard Poppy say and then, a moment later, 'As if.'

Her curiosity piqued, Lily strained to listen to the conversation but then the floorboard creaked and she cursed silently as she heard Poppy say, 'I've got to go.'

Lily dashed downstairs before Poppy caught her earwigging. A few moments later her daughter appeared with a scowl on her face.

'Are we going then, or what?'

'Watch your attitude, Poppy. I'm about to take you shopping for a new dress, in case you've forgotten. Unless you'd rather stay here and feel sorry for yourself.'

'No, I'll come. It's the only time I'm allowed out of the house anyway.'

'About that.' Lily hesitated, then forced herself to say, 'I think you've had enough time at home. If you want to start going out again, that's fine. Just stay away from the lake, okay?'

Poppy threw herself at Lily in an uncharacteristic show of affection. 'Thanks, Mum!'

Lily smiled to herself. *Mum.* 'Now, shall we go and shop till we drop?'

Poppy pulled her phone out and started typing furiously, no doubt already telling her friends about her new-found freedom. 'Let's go.'

They set off for the shopping centre and a wave of contentment washed over Lily as she drove. She was back on good terms with Poppy, they were about to spend a lovely afternoon together and there was a party to look forward to. Life could definitely be worse.

'Daddy's coming home early from his business trip for your party,' she told Poppy.

'Tell him not to bother.'

'Poppy, that's not nice. It's your sixteenth birthday.'

'Yeah, so I get to choose who comes.'

Poppy didn't want her father watching her every move and scaring off any potential suitors who dared to get close to her, Lily thought. Not that there were any potential suitors she knew of. She thought about Poppy's hushed phone conversation earlier and decided to broach the subject, even though she was voluntarily throwing herself into the lion's den.

'Is there anyone coming to the party who you've got your eye on?'

Poppy rolled her eyes. '*Cringe*, Mother.'

'I'm just curious. Can't a mother be curious about her daughter?'

'No.'

Christ, she was impossible. 'Fine. But you know Micky's sweet on you, don't you?'

'Me and Micky are just friends.'

'Does he know that?'

'Yes.'

'And you're sure there's nothing there on your side? No feelings?'

'No.'

'What about Bethany?'

Poppy snorted. 'No, I don't fancy her either, Mother.'

'That's not what I meant. Does Bethany like Micky?'

'You know it's possible for boys and girls to be friends without fancying each other, right?'

Lily sighed with exasperation. 'Of course I know that. I'm just making small talk.'

'They're just friends too.'

'So will there be any romances at the party, that you know of?'

'Dunno.' Poppy started texting again, smiling to herself, and Lily wondered who it was that was making her daughter happy in a way that she was unable to do.

'By the way,' Poppy said, not looking up from her phone, 'I've invited Steve and Juan to my party. Can you add them to the guest list?'

Lily frowned. 'Steve and Juan? Aren't they a little old?'

'You're coming, aren't you? And you're old.'

'Fine, I'll add them. But if it's Juan you fancy, and I wouldn't blame you, I'm afraid you're too young for him and he's got a girl-friend back in Spain anyway.'

'Mother, you're obsessed with sex.'

'I am *not* obsessed with sex.'

The mention of Steve reminded Lily that she hadn't done any digging around about him yet. She'd given the private detective details of Sandy's ex, but she'd completely forgotten to ask about Steve. She'd do it after the party, she decided, when she had more time. The detective had said that he'd be in touch when he had any news about Grant, and Lily hoped he wouldn't keep them waiting too long. Sandy was increasingly anxious, and Lily wanted to help. And, although she was loath to admit it, it was a helpful distraction from her own life.

Just like an ugly weed, her resentment towards Eric was growing. In the past, when she had compared her relationship to those of her so-called friends at the golf or tennis club, it hadn't seemed that dysfunctional. Those women were always moaning about their husbands, constantly accusing them of some misdemeanour, as if it came with the territory of marrying a rich, powerful man. But at Westford Park, Lily had different comparisons. Sandy and Clare were so much in love and Avril kept talking about how she and Stuart were finding each other again. It laid her own marriage bare in a way that she hadn't allowed herself to analyse before.

What choice did she have, though? After everything that had happened with Poppy at New Year, a united front was more important than ever.

'You know you just went through a red light, right?'

Lily blinked. 'Gosh, I was miles away.'

'If possible, could you try not to kill me before my sixteenth birthday?'

'I'll do my best, although you seem to be doing a rather good job of that yourself anyway.'

'Touché, Mother.'

They pulled into the car park and found a space, walking towards the shopping centre together, Poppy still on her phone.

'Can you put that away now, Poppy? I'm sure an hour of screen-free time won't kill you.'

'Fine.' Poppy put her phone in her bag. 'Where shall we start?'

'Wherever you want.'

They headed into a department store and started looking through the clothes. Lily admired some beautiful floor-length gowns and Poppy pulled out a minidress.

'What about this one?' she asked, holding up the raunchy red number.

'Daddy will have kittens.'

'He won't if he doesn't come to the party.'

'He's already changed his flight.'

'Tell him to change it back.'

Lily could feel irritation rising. 'Poppy, don't be so rude. Your father wants to come to your birthday party, what's wrong with that?'

'I don't want him there.'

'Why not?'

'Because I hate him.'

Lily stared at her daughter, shocked. It was no secret that Poppy and Eric clashed from time to time, but she had never heard her talking like this before. 'Don't say that, Poppy.'

'Why not? It's true.'

'No, it's not.'

'Yes, it is.'

Lily was stunned. As a child, Poppy had doted on her father. Admittedly, once she'd reached adolescence, she'd increasingly distanced herself from him, but this was a natural part of growing up and anyway Poppy had done the same thing to her too. Lily hadn't been aware of any rows between them, not recently anyway. So why the sudden vitriol?

'What's going on, Poppy? What's all this about?'

Poppy turned away from her. 'Nothing, forget it.'

Lily was conflicted. Did she push it and risk a blow-up with Poppy in the middle of the department store or brush it to the side and try to make the most of the afternoon? It was teenage hormones, she decided, and Poppy was ratty given her recent house arrest. Once she had a bit more freedom, she'd mellow out again, even if it would have the opposite effect on Lily. She was certain that Poppy didn't really mean what she said about Eric.

She pulled out a stunning blue ankle-length dress and showed it to Poppy. 'What do you think?'

'Manky.'

'Well, what did you have in mind? Other than the red belt?'

Poppy held up another dress. This one was black and it was short, but not heart attack short. It would flatter Poppy's figure and the neckline wasn't too low. 'That's lovely, darling.'

'I'll go and try it on.'

Lily followed her daughter to the fitting room and sat down on the sofa outside to wait. When Poppy emerged a couple of minutes later, Lily gasped.

'Oh, Poppy, you look beautiful.'

Poppy grinned. 'Thanks.'

'That's the one, I'm sure of it.'

'I think so too.'

'What about shoes?'

Poppy frowned. 'I have those black heels.'

Enthused by their mother-daughter bonding moment, Lily said, 'Let's buy the dress and go and get you some proper designer shoes. Christian Louboutin?'

Poppy's eyes lit up. 'Wow, thanks, Mum.'

Two 'mums' in one day. Lily was on cloud nine.

She was waiting for Poppy to change back into her jeans when her phone rang, and she felt a rush of excitement when she saw it was the private detective. 'Hello, Lily speaking.'

She listened in silence, trying to absorb everything that she was hearing. 'And you're absolutely sure? Okay, I understand. Yes. Yes, I'll pass that on. Thank you.'

Lily hung up and dropped her arm limply by her side. Her heart thudded in her chest and her breathing became shallow. Suddenly, she wasn't excited about going shoe shopping with Poppy any more.

The department store was closing in on her and she was claustrophobic in the windowless, artificially lit room. She stood up, and as the blood rushed to her head, she felt light-headed. She needed to leave but she didn't know where she wanted to go.

The detective had tracked down Grant and it was bad. It was really bad. And she wasn't sure how she was going to tell Sandy about it.

20

Avril gazed in the mirror with contentment. She and Sandy were at the hairdresser, getting glammed up ahead of Poppy's party. Avril wasn't sure that Poppy had signed off on grown-ups attending, and she was certain that Bethany didn't approve, but Lily had insisted.

'I'm paying for it, so I can bring my friends,' she had said.

'But won't we cramp the kids' style?' Avril had asked.

'We'll maintain a respectful distance and turn away if there's any sign of snogging.'

Avril really didn't want to see her daughter snogging anyone. She wasn't even sure if Bethany had experienced her first kiss. She assumed that she must have done at some point, but her daughter had not divulged, and Avril hadn't pried. She no longer felt like she was treading on eggshells around Bethany, and it was a blessed relief, but she also wanted to respect her daughter's need for privacy. Bethany now knew that Avril was there for her if she needed to talk, and that was the most important thing. She also suspected that Bethany had been confiding in Sandy during their painting sessions and although their bond made her envious, she knew that she should be pleased about it. Bethany had found a safe space to be herself and for that, Avril was grateful to Sandy, even if it meant shaking off her occasional pangs of jealousy.

'Bethany loves spending time with you,' she shouted at Sandy over the hairdryer.

'She's an extremely talented girl,' Sandy shouted back.

'You really think so?'

'I do. She has a bright career ahead of her.'

'That's so wonderful to hear, thank you. I think she really needed *something*, you know? Something she could focus on, to boost her confidence and self-esteem.'

Sandy opened her mouth in response and then closed it again, as though she'd changed her mind. Avril looked at her quizzically. 'Are you okay?'

'Fine. Let's talk later when it's not so loud.'

Avril nodded and returned her gaze to the mirror. The blow-dry wasn't finished yet but she already loved it. She'd had her long brown hair cut a few months ago and the shorter style suited her round face. She'd picked out a lovely dress for the party and even Stuart had got his best suit dry-cleaned.

'I know you'll look beautiful because you always do, so I'd better make an effort too,' he'd said, and Avril had felt a glorious rush of affection for him.

As soon as the hairdresser had finished, she took a selfie and sent it to Stuart, along with a message asking how his day was going. When she looked up, Sandy was standing up to leave. 'You look gorgeous, Sandy.'

'Thanks. So do you.'

'Have you got time for a coffee?'

Sandy looked at her watch. 'A quick one but I have to pick Isla up from school soon.'

'How's she getting on?'

'Oh, she's as happy as a clam now. The back-to-school nerve

were all a fuss about nothing in the end and she runs into the class-room without a backward glance.'

'That's a relief. And how are *you*?'

'I'm okay,' Sandy said. 'The calls have stopped again.'

'Thank goodness. Do you feel better?'

'I think so.'

They paid and then walked along the high street to a coffee shop, sitting down at a table overlooking the window.

'Avril, there's something I've been meaning to talk to you about,' Sandy began, and something about her tone set Avril on edge.

'What is it?'

'It's Bethany.'

Anxiety rushed in. 'What's happened?'

'Nothing, really.' Sandy looked uncomfortable. 'But I think it's important that you know.'

Deep breaths, deep breaths, Avril told herself. 'Go on.'

'It's her art,' Sandy began slowly. 'It's quite, well, it's a little *dark*.'

Avril frowned, confused. 'Dark? As in colour-wise?'

'No. As in the mood of the paintings. They're quite sinister.'

Avril felt an unexpected surge of irritation towards her friend, even though she knew that this wasn't Sandy's fault. Why did she have to bring this up now?

'It's just art, Sandy. It's not real.'

'I know,' Sandy said quickly. 'But it's happened more than once, and one of her recent pieces has been playing on my mind ever since.'

Avril leaned forward, dreading the answer to her next question but knowing that she had to ask it. 'What was wrong with it?'

As Sandy began to describe the broken vase, the weaponised red roses and the pool of blood, the colour drained from Avril's face. Why would a fifteen-year-old girl paint something like that, unless she was deeply and profoundly troubled? Avril thought they had turned a corner but now she wondered if she'd been hopelessly naive.

Sensing her angst, Sandy put a hand over Avril's. 'You don't need to tell me what happened at Bethany's old school,' she said quietly. 'But it might help me to understand the inspiration behind the painting. I want to help.'

Should she tell Sandy? She had planned to months ago but had chickened out at the last minute. Sandy was a good friend and she had Bethany's best interests at heart. She wasn't a judgemental person. Instinct told Avril to trust Sandy.

She steeled herself. 'Do you remember I told you that Bethany got in with a new crowd at school, these popular girls, and she changed?'

'Yes.'

'So, what I didn't tell you, or not in any great detail at least, is that a few months later, a number of the girls made a serious allegation about Bethany.'

'What was it?'

Avril's hands were shaking as she picked up her cup, craving the warm, bitter coffee. She took a sip and closed her eyes for a moment before continuing.

'The girl said that Bethany had hurt her. She claimed that Bethany tied her up and cut her, saying it was some sort of occult ritual and this was the girl's sacrifice to her. And there were witnesses, other girls, who corroborated the story. The girl had marks on her arms.'

'Did the other girls say Bethany had hurt them too?'

'They said Bethany told them that they would be next. And they were scared, so they told their parents about it. Of course, their parents immediately called the school.'

'And what did Bethany say?'

'Nothing.' Avril looked down, fear, hurt and shame coming back to her. 'It was as though she didn't even want to defend herself.'

'Why?'

Avril let out a sob. 'At first, I thought it was because it was all true. It wasn't until later that I realised it was because she knew no one believed her, not even me.'

'Oh, Avril.'

Avril flinched as Sandy squeezed her hand. She didn't deserve sympathy. 'I wanted to believe it was lies, of course I did. But there was evidence! Injuries, witnesses. I didn't know what to think and Bethany's silence fuelled my paranoia. And there's more.'

'Go on,' Sandy urged.

Avril looked away. 'A few weeks before it happened, I was tidying Bethany's room and I found a notebook with lots of odd symbols and words written in it. I thought it was some sort of code, maybe homework, but later I realised it was to do with this occult stuff.'

'Teenagers love that witchcraft nonsense,' Sandy said diplomatically. 'It doesn't mean anything.'

'I appreciate you saying that, but it did nothing to ease my mind.'

'Do you think that Bethany would hurt another person?'

'No,' Avril said vehemently. 'But at the time, I couldn't come up with any other explanation. And everyone turned against me. Poor Tom lost all his friends too.'

'What about Stuart?'

'Stuart said it was all lies from the start. He refused to believe it. But he couldn't come up with any other explanation either, so he buried his head in the sand and I was angry with him too, for not talking about it, not supporting me. Oh, Sandy, it was just so horrible.'

'Is that why you moved?'

'Yes. We'd become pariahs. And I hoped that if I got Bethany away from those girls then everything would be okay. But, deep down, I couldn't help but worry that it wasn't the girls who were the problem... it was Bethany.'

'And now?'

'I don't think that any more. At least I didn't, until you told me about her painting.'

Sandy sat back in her chair, thoughtful. 'Bethany's been in a lot of pain and maybe this is her way of letting it out. Maybe she's the broken vase.'

This made Avril want to sob even harder. 'That's the saddest thing I've ever heard.'

'No, Avril, don't look at it that way. Broken vases can be mended. And I really think Bethany is mending. If she needs an outlet for her feelings, then art is a good place for it.'

Avril clung on to Sandy's words as though they were a life raft. 'And you think this is what this painting is? Just an outlet? Nothing more sinister or meaningful?'

Sandy was deep in thought. 'There was another painting too. I wasn't sure at the time, but...'

'What?' Avril demanded. 'What is it?'

'It's starting to make sense to me. These girls she was hanging out with, they were popular, right? They were beautiful on the outside, cruel inside. They're the roses. And they hurt Bethany. She felt trapped. Yes, the more I think about it, the surer I am. She's trying to tell us how she felt, but it doesn't mean that she feels that way any more.'

Avril had never been so grateful to anyone in her life. 'Thank you, Sandy.'

'Look,' Sandy continued. 'I've known dangerous people.

Bethany is not dangerous. She's fragile and she's a deep thinker. But she's a kind-hearted girl.'

Avril wanted to hug her. 'I think so too. But I have to regain her trust again.'

'And you will. You're already well on the way. She's a different girl to the one who arrived at Westford Park in the summer. And in a few months, she'll be different again.'

'So, you think she'll get over all this?'

Sandy smiled. 'I think she already has, in her own way.'

Buoyed by the conversation, and Sandy's incredible response, Avril pressed on. 'Why do you think those girls lied, though? Why would they do something so awful to Bethany?'

'Girls can be mean, especially as a collective. They sound like bullies to me. They knew Bethany was vulnerable and they preyed on that. They wanted to destroy her life.'

'But *why*?'

Sandy shook her head. 'I don't know. For their own, horrible amusement probably.'

'I never liked them,' Avril admitted. 'I never trusted them.'

'There you go, then.' Sandy looked at her watch. 'Oh gosh, I'm so sorry to leave it like this but I really must go and pick up Isla. I haven't got time to drop you home first.'

Avril stood up. 'No problem, I'll come with you.'

They paid for their drinks and made their way outside. Avril linked her arm through Sandy's as they walked towards the car. Hearing Sandy's words of reassurance had been exactly what she needed. But she also knew that not everyone would be as understanding.

'Please don't tell anyone about this, Sandy.'

'I wouldn't dream of it.'

'And don't tell Bethany I told you, either.'

'Of course I won't.'

They got into Sandy's car and drove to the school, arriving just in time as the children started piling out. Avril was wistful as she watched Isla run into her mother's arms, smiling and excited as she showed Sandy a picture she'd drawn that day. Avril had loved the children's primary school days, when life seemed innocent and uncomplicated, when it'd felt like all Tom and Bethany had needed was a cuddle and some potato waffles for tea. It seemed like another lifetime ago.

Sandy strapped Isla into her car seat and they set off again. Down the road, the secondary school was beginning to spill out and Avril craned her neck, looking for Bethany.

'Should we pick up the kids?' she asked.

'Oh, let them get the bus, you know how they like their independence. They'll be mortified if their mummies turn up to pick them up in front of their friends.'

Avril laughed. 'True. They'll be buzzing when they get home though, getting ready for the party. I wonder why Lily's doing it on a Friday and not a Saturday?'

'She couldn't get the clubhouse on Saturday night.'

'Ah, I see.' Avril scanned the crowds of teenagers, recognising plenty of faces from her teaching job, but not the one she most wanted to see. 'No sign of Bethany or Micky.'

'I see Micky!' Isla called from the back and Avril followed the girl's gaze. There he was, walking and chatting with some of his friends.

'Everyone duck,' Sandy joked, and Isla giggled.

'And there's Bethany!'

Avril looked and felt a rush of excitement as she spotted Bethany with two other girls. They were in a huddle and were laughing about something. Bethany was grinning, without a care in the world, and it was so wonderful to witness that Avril almost started crying again.

The car slowed as they hit a traffic jam and Avril hunched down low in her seat to avoid detection, peeking out of the window to catch another glimpse of Bethany. But she needn't have worried; her daughter was oblivious to the passing cars, and to her. She was distracted by one of the girls handing her something, which she snatched and slipped into her bag.

Avril squinted, trying to see what it was. But Bethany had been too quick, too furtive.

'You okay there, Avril?' Sandy glanced at her from the driver's seat.

'Yes, fine,' she said, still staring at Bethany as the car inched forward.

It had been nothing. A lip gloss or mascara. Innocent teenage stuff. And yet something had triggered a feeling in the pit of Avril's stomach. And she didn't know if it was the legacy of paranoia that had followed her for so long, whether the conversation with Sandy had brought raw emotions back again, or if it was simply parental instinct.

But she did know one thing. She wanted to know what it was that Bethany had slipped into her bag. She needed to know. And if that meant betraying her daughter's trust by going snooping, she'd do it anyway. It was nothing to do with Bethany's past, or what she'd told Sandy. It was what any mother of a teenager would do. Any normal mother.

21

Patio doors? Check. Windows? Check. Everything was secure. Sandy exhaled and turned to Clare. Her wife looked stunning and Sandy was looking forward to the evening ahead, but she was anxious about leaving Isla at home with the babysitter.

Clare took her hand. 'Isla will be fine. And we're five minutes away.'

Sandy nodded. 'I know. Now where's Micky?'

As if on cue, Micky emerged, fidgety in his suit.

'Micky, you look so handsome.'

'Cheers, Mum.'

'The girls will be fighting over you.'

Micky rolled his eyes. Sandy knew who he'd made an effort for, and she hoped that her son's evening wouldn't end in disappointment. Poppy was going to be the belle of the ball and poor Micky probably wouldn't get a look in. At least Bethany would be there.

Sandy was feeling much better about the Bethany situation since her conversation with Avril. She was pleased that she had decided to bring it up. Learning about what had happened in Bethany's past had helped Sandy to understand and decipher her work. It was all so clear to her now; Bethany did not want to hurt anyone. She was the one who had felt hurt and trapped by those horrible bullies. She was the broken vase, the girl in the boathouse.

Sandy knew what it felt like to feel trapped and, more than ever, she wanted to help Bethany. What the girl needed was love and understanding, and to know that she was trusted too. That's why Sandy had asked her if she'd babysit Isla a few days ago, when Micky was out and she and Clare had to go to a meeting at the primary school. They had come home to find Isla and Bethany making cupcakes in the kitchen, giggling as they licked the spoon. When Sandy had tried to give Bethany some money for her time, the teenager had refused it.

'It was my pleasure,' she'd said. 'Any time.'

The calls and vandalism had stopped too, and Sandy was starting to see the world for what it was again. There was nothing to fear. Everything was exactly as it should be.

But she still checked the doors and windows.

'Come on, Sandy, we'd better go.' Clare was shrugging on her coat.

The three of them left, Sandy and Clare holding hands, Micky walking beside them. Sandy smiled as soon as the clubhouse came into view. Lily had gone all out with the balloons and decorations, as Sandy had known she would. She saw glamorous-looking teenagers emerging from their parents' expensive cars. They all looked older than she knew they were and Micky was watching them too, wide-eyed.

Clare leaned into her. 'The private school crew, I'm guessing.'

'I assume so.'

'It feels more like a prom or a wedding reception than a birthday party.'

'Well, you know Lily, she doesn't do things by halves.'

Speaking of Lily, there she was, looking resplendent as she

greeted the arrivals. She rushed over to Sandy as soon as she spotted them. 'Lovely to see you, thanks for coming.'

'We wouldn't miss it. Where's the birthday girl?'

'Oh, inside somewhere.'

'And Eric?'

'His flight was delayed but he's on the way.'

Sandy peered inside. 'It looks beautiful, Lily, you've done a tremendous job.'

Lily beamed. 'Thank you. Listen.' She looked around and then leaned into Sandy. 'Can we have a chat later? There's something I need to talk to you about.'

'Of course, come and find me as soon as you're free.'

Lily was distracted by other arrivals and Sandy followed Micky and Clare into the clubhouse and politely declined a mocktail from a waitress.

'I need the real thing,' she said to Clare. 'Bar?'

'Absolutely.'

They ordered some wine and then stood, sipping it and observing the scene. Micky was standing to the left of Poppy, trying to join in the conversation. Poppy looked radiant in a black dress and heels, her glossy dark hair shining under the lights.

'Sandy!'

Sandy turned to see Avril making a beeline for her. 'Hey, you.'

'Well, isn't this glam!' Avril was grinning as she looked around. 'Although I feel about three decades too old to be here.'

'A glass of wine will help with that.'

They lurked at the bar, not sure what to do with themselves as the teenagers huddled together in groups, chatting and drinking mocktails. The DJ finished setting up and soon the room was filled with loud, throbbing music and the first brave youngsters took to the dance floor. Sandy spotted Micky and Bethany in the corner of the room, talking together. Then she noticed Steve, from the boathouse, and she frowned.

'What's Steve doing here?'

Avril followed her gaze. 'No idea. Maybe Lily invited him.'

'To a sixteenth birthday party?'

'Well, we're here.' Avril looked at her. 'Are you still funny about Steve?'

Sandy watched him carefully as he shook hands with a few people and then went over to give Poppy a chaste kiss on the cheek. 'I don't know.'

'Did Lily's private detective unearth anything?'

Sandy winced as Clare, who was listening to the conversation, looked at her quizzically. She hadn't mentioned anything to Clare about the detective. She had never withheld information from her wife before and she wasn't sure why she had chosen to do so.

'Lily hasn't said anything about it.'

'Well, perhaps that's because there's nothing to say.'

'Maybe.' Sandy quickly changed the subject. 'Bethany looks lovely.'

'She does.'

Sandy thought Avril looked agitated as she watched Bethany. She'd been quiet in the car on the way back from the hairdresser and Sandy wondered if something was worrying her again. She was about to ask Avril if everything was okay when she saw Steve making his way over to them and she couldn't hide her disapproval.

'Steve, what are you doing here?'

Sandy ignored the frowns from Clare and Avril at her rudeness. But Steve didn't seem to notice. 'The family invited me. Great gig, isn't it?'

'It sure is,' Avril piped in. 'Have you met my husband, Stuart?'

The two men started chatting and Clare turned to Sandy.

'What's going on?' she hissed.

'Nothing.'

'What's all this talk about a private detective?'

'I'll tell you later.'

'No, you'll tell me now.'

Sandy nodded, resigned. 'Let's go outside, where we can hear properly.'

The February air was biting, and they slipped their coats on as they sat down at a table. They were the only people outside except for a couple of teenagers vaping around the side of the building, who kept stealing glances in their direction to see if they were going to be told off.

'What's going on, Sandy?'

Sandy reluctantly told Clare about Lily's offer to hire a private detective to track down Grant, and her idea of getting him to look into Steve's past too.

When she was finished, Clare looked at her incredulously. 'When did all this happen?'

'A few weeks ago.'

'And you're only telling me now?'

'I'm sorry, I should have told you. I was just worried that you wouldn't understand.'

'Sandy, we've been together for years and you still don' trust me?'

'It's not that I don't trust you, Clare. I don't trust myself.'

'What do you mean?'

'I pivot constantly from thinking I'm fine to being on edge, waiting for something bad to happen. Sometimes I feel like I'm losing my mind.'

Clare looked into the distance, where the lights from the residential streets glowed warmly. 'You said things would be different at Westford Park.'

'I know, and I want them to be different. But I can't help how I feel, Clare.'

Clare turned and looked at her. 'I know. I'm sorry. What can I do?'

'Nothing. I think I have to figure this one out for myself.'

'With the help of a private detective.'

Sandy looked at her guiltily. 'Yes.'

'So, who is this dude? Some sort of Sherlock? Are we talking about a Benedict Cumberbatch type? Should I be worried that you're going to run off with him, Watson?'

Sandy laughed. 'I've never met him or spoken to him. Lily arranged it all.'

'How does *she* know a private detective?'

'Eric's used him for work before, to vet potential clients, I think she said. You know, check their criminal or financial records.'

'Well, that's not true.'

Sandy frowned. 'How do you mean?'

'That would be illegal and unethical, and Eric would know that.'

'You're right, I didn't even think about that. Maybe Lily got it wrong.'

'Or maybe it's Lily who's used the detective before, not Eric.'

Sandy looked at Clare in surprise. 'Why would she do that?'

'Because she wants, or wanted at some point, to find out what her husband is up to.'

Sandy considered this. 'No, I don't think so.'

Clare shrugged. 'Whatever. It doesn't matter. What has he found out about Grant?'

'Nothing yet, but I guess these things take time.'

'Do you promise you'll tell me as soon as you hear anything?'

Sandy meant it when she said, 'Yes, of course I will. I should have told you, I'm sorry.'

'And what about this Steve business? Why are you so convinced he's up to something?'

'I don't know,' Sandy admitted. 'I just worry that he's getting too close to Poppy.'

'What's your evidence?'

'Well, he was there on New Year's Eve, when Poppy fell in the lake. And Bethany told me that they sometimes hang out together.'

Clare considered this. 'Have you told Lily?'

'No. Bethany was adamant that there was nothing going on between them and I didn't want to cause a problem that's not there. You know what Lily's like, she'd go mad.'

'Oh, Sandy, how have you got yourself into this mess?'

Sandy frowned. 'I really don't know.'

Clare stood up. 'Look, it's freezing out here. Let's go inside and we can talk about this tomorrow, okay?'

'Good idea,' Sandy agreed gratefully.

She followed Clare back towards the clubhouse, gripping her hand and feeling the weight of hiding something from her amazing wife lifting from her shoulders. She was about to step inside when Lily appeared and put a hand on her arm.

'Can I have a word?'

'Sure, okay.'

Lily gestured outside, and Clare looked back at them. 'Everything okay?'

'You go in,' Sandy said. 'I'll catch up in a minute.'

As she followed Lily back outside, Sandy wondered what this was about. Did Lily want to talk about Micky and Poppy? Or had she found out about Steve? Sandy immediately felt guilty for keeping the secret, as she tried to work out how she would defend herself.

'I've been battling with how to tell you this.' Lily looked left and right, anywhere but into Sandy's eyes. 'And I've been waiting for the right moment, but is there ever a right moment?'

Sandy's heart began to pound. 'What is it?'

'It's Grant.'

Sandy felt the first trickle of dread. 'Go on.'

'The detective came through for us and managed to track him down.'

'And?' She didn't want to know but she'd come too far to back out now.

'He's alive. He works as a lorry driver and he spends a lot of time on the continent.'

So far so good. The further away, the better. 'Okay.'

'He doesn't have a family.'

Thank God. Sandy closed her eyes. One of her worst fears was that he would go on to hurt another woman or have more children. She had done all she could to stop him but she couldn't control what happened after he was released from prison.

Relief coursed through her and she smiled at Lily. 'Thank you for telling me. You were right, hiring the detective was a good idea. I feel so much better now.'

'Sandy, that's not all.'

Sandy frowned. 'What is it?'

'The haulage company he works for. It's based a few miles away from Westford Park.'

Sandy's blood ran cold. 'It's what?'

Lily looked uncomfortable. 'He started there a few months ago. And he was back in the country when you were getting those anonymous calls.'

This had to be a nightmare. Sandy wanted to wake up in her bed, safe and warm, and realise that this conversation had never happened. Except that it was real and there was no way of escaping it. She looked in through the clubhouse window, her eyes searching for Micky. Her throat constricted until she was gasping for breath.

'If there's *anything* I can do to help,' Lily was saying, but Sandy barely heard her. *You can run but you can't hide.* How many times had he called out those words to her as he prowled around the flat? She'd tried to run, and she'd tried to hide. But he had found her.

Which meant that he had also found Micky.

22

The last of the partygoers had left and Lily slumped in a chair, exhausted. It had been a successful evening, but she was upset about her conversation with Sandy, and the expression on her friend's face when Lily told her what the detective had discovered.

Perhaps she shouldn't have done it on the night of Poppy's party, but she hadn't wanted to keep it from Sandy any longer. If she was in danger, she needed to know about it. The private detective had assured her that if Grant came anywhere near Sandy he'd be arrested, but that hadn't reassured Lily, and she knew it hadn't reassured Sandy either. This was a man who had come into her home and stolen their child. The rules did not apply to him.

It was different now, though. Micky was tall and strong, maybe even bigger than his father. He could stand up for himself. And so much time had passed. Why would Grant decide to come back into their lives now and risk his freedom? Still, the evidence against him was mounting. Had Sandy been right all along to blame Grant for the noises and vandalism too? And what did that mean for Poppy, who spent most weekends with Micky?

'Lily?'

She looked up at Eric.

'Hi. Party's over.'

'I'm so sorry I missed it. I was stuck on the tarmac for three hours.'

Lily didn't answer. She was too exhausted for Eric's excuses, too tired to smile and feign sympathy for his plane delay. If there even was a plane delay.

'How was the party?'

'Fine,' she said, aware that her one-word answer made her sound just like her daughter.

'Where's Poppy?'

It was a good question. She hadn't seen her daughter for a while. 'I don't know, probably saying goodbye to her friends.'

'I didn't see her outside.'

Lily stood up. 'Are you sure?'

'I'm positive.'

'Maybe she's in the loo. I'll check.'

Lily hurried into the Ladies' but the cubicles were empty. Trying to stem the rising panic inside her, a product of what had happened on New Year's Eve, she rushed outside. 'Poppy?'

Eric followed her out. 'You don't think she's gone to the lake again, do you?'

'She'd better bloody not have done. Poppy!' Lily was spiralling now. Some kids waiting for taxis or parents stared at her. 'Have you seen Poppy?' Lily demanded but they shook their heads.

Where was she? Lily pulled out her phone and opened her Find My app, waiting for her daughter's location to appear. 'It says she's here,' she told Eric.

'She'll be around somewhere, darling. Stop panicking.'

Ignoring him, Lily headed back inside again. 'Poppy?'

But there was no answer. Lily ran across the room, throwing

open one of the back doors that led out onto the terrace. She spotted two figures in the gloom. 'Poppy?'

Her daughter turned to her. 'What is it, Mother?'

With a rush of relief, Lily said, 'I just wanted to know where you were, Poppy. We were looking for you. Calling you. Didn't you hear? Daddy's here.'

Lily's eyes homed in on the other figure, trying to make out who it was in the darkness. She relaxed when she saw it was just Steve. 'Hi, Steve.'

'Hi, Lily. I was just heading off. Great party.'

'Thanks.' Lily looked at Poppy. 'Come inside, darling, it's freezing out here.'

She went back in and found Eric. 'She's out the back.'

Eric took her in his arms. 'Told you. I've missed you,' He nuzzled into her neck.

Lily pulled away, still on edge.

'Everything okay, darling?'

'Fine, I'm just tired.'

The back door opened, and Poppy stormed in, scowling at her father.

'Here's the birthday girl!' Eric rushed over and hugged her. Lily noticed that Poppy didn't return his embrace either. 'How was the party?'

'Fine.'

'I've brought you something.' Eric pulled out a small, square package from his pocket and handed it to Poppy who took it and pulled the lid off. Inside was a Tiffany & Co. watch. It must have cost him an absolute fortune and yet Lily knew that Poppy probably wouldn't even wear it. It wasn't her style. Anyway, she'd wanted an Apple Watch.

'Thanks,' Poppy said, closing the box again and looking around the room, bored.

What a mess we've got ourselves into, Lily thought, depressed. A teenage girl who didn't appreciate a beautiful, expensive gift and a husband who tried to buy her affection. And where did that leave her? Should she tell Poppy off for being ungrateful or chastise her husband for spending too much money on a present that his daughter didn't even want?

So much for the party of the year. They should be as high as kites, giggling as they walked home, reliving the events of the evening. Instead, Lily wanted to cry. The evening did not feel like a celebration; it felt like the slow, painful death of Lily's fantasy life. Like the glass of a snow globe shattering to pieces and destroying the picture-perfect scene inside.

How much longer could they live like this? How much longer could she ignore the truth? She looked at her husband and opened her mouth, itching to say something, but then she changed her mind. Instead, with faux brightness, she said, 'Let's go home, then, shall we?'

* * *

When Lily woke up the following morning, Eric had already gone out to play golf. She headed downstairs to make a coffee, surprised to see Poppy already up.

'Hello, darling, I thought you'd be having a lie-in after last night.'

'I woke up early and couldn't get back to sleep.'

'Did you enjoy the party?'

Poppy smiled. 'Yeah, it was great. Thanks.'

'Oh, it was my pleasure, darling.'

Lily made her coffee and went to sit down on the sofa next to her daughter. Poppy had put on a reality TV show and Lily watched it absent-mindedly, her mind on overdrive, still reeling from the events of the previous night. She thought about poor Sandy and about Eric and Poppy. She thought about what she was doing with her life.

It had crept up on her, this feeling, a combination of discontent and shame. And she didn't like it one bit. Ignorance had been bliss, or at least that's what she had told herself. Not that she really was that ignorant. But she had enjoyed pretending that she was.

Now she couldn't stop wondering why she had put up with it for so long, or even how it had all started. Had she known when she married Eric that it was going to be like this? No, she hadn't. She had been head over heels in love with him and he had felt the same way.

It had happened gradually, maybe long before she even knew about it. He travelled a lot, so it wasn't difficult to hide his secret. She couldn't remember now what had first alerted her to it, although at first she had pushed her doubts away. Her darling Eric would never do that. He worshipped her. He worshipped Poppy. Over time, she had become better tuned to his behaviour and she had become equally skilled at tuning it out again because she hadn't wanted to know. She hadn't wanted to face up to it.

Anyway, Lily enjoyed her life. Eric made her feel like a queen. He treated his daughter like a princess. It was nothing like her own childhood and she was forever grateful for that.

She thought of Sandy then and felt a pang of guilt. Here she was feeling sorry for herself when her friend had much worse to contend with. It was time to stop wallowing in self-pity and be useful, for her own sake as much as Sandy's. She needed something to do.

With a renewed sense of purpose, Lily drained her coffee and stood up.

'I'm going to get dressed and pop round to Sandy's. Do you want to come?'

'No, I'm meeting a friend. Can I go out tonight?'

'Go out where?'

'With Micky and Bethany.'

Lily hesitated. 'I'm not sure, darling.'

'Mother! You said I was off the leash again.'

'I know, but there's a lot going on at the moment and...' Lily looked at her daughter's mutinous face and relented. 'To the clubhouse, then. Just the clubhouse.'

Poppy grinned and reached for her phone. 'Thanks.'

Lily headed upstairs for a shower. By the time she was dressed and back downstairs, Poppy still hadn't moved from the sofa, her eyes glued to her phone and the reality show still blaring in the background. A half-eaten banana lay on the table in front of her.

'I'll be back soon, okay?'

'Yeah, see you.'

Lily went outside, shivering in the cold, and looked at the Range Rover. She'd had the tyres fixed within a couple of days, paid for with cash because Eric didn't want to go through the insurance. That was one thing she'd never felt guilty about, spending Eric's cash.

She stopped dead in the street. *That's it*, she thought triumphantly. She was too reliant on Eric, she always had been. She needed a job, something to give her a bit of purpose. She was tired of being a housewife, constantly at Eric's beck and call, and Poppy hardly needed her any more either. That was the reason why she was feeling so lost at sea. It happened to lots of women in their forties, she was normal. Yes!

With a renewed spring in her step at the prospect of Operation Job, she reached Sandy's door and rapped three times.

Clare answered, looking like she hadn't slept a wink.

'Hi, Lily.'

'Hi, Clare.' Lily leaned forward and kissed Clare on the cheek. 'Is Sandy up?'

'She's still in bed.' Clare ushered Lily in and closed the front door softly. 'She's not in a good way.'

Lily panicked, wondering if Clare was angry with her for hiring the private detective and setting the wheels in motion.

'I'm sorry,' she began, but Clare interrupted her.

'It's not your fault, Lily. It's *his* fault.'

'Perhaps it's just a coincidence that he works so close by?'

'I know it could be, but what if it's not? I've dismissed all of Sandy's concerns up until now but I'm starting to wonder if she was right all along.'

'So, what do we do?'

Clare shrugged. 'I don't know if there's anything we *can* do. Unless he contacts her or Micky, I doubt the police will be able to help. We just have to be vigilant. But after all she's been through, it's so unfair. She's worried sick about Micky.'

'You don't think he'll try and take him again, do you?'

Both women started when they heard a noise on the landing and looked up to see Micky standing at the top of the stairs, rubbing his eyes.

'What are you talking about?' he asked.

'Nothing,' they both said guiltily.

Micky came down the stairs, brushing past them as he headed into the kitchen.

'Do you think he heard us?' Lily hissed.

'I don't think so, he looked half asleep.'

'Thank God.' Lily looked up the stairs. 'Can I go up and see her?'

'Sure.'

Clare squeezed her arm and Lily walked up the stairs, her anxiety growing. She'd been trying to help by suggesting the detective but now she was worried that she'd made things worse. She wanted to ask him to keep watching Grant but she had a feeling that Sandy wouldn't be able to afford it and would refuse to let Lily pay for it on her behalf.

She reached the bedroom and pushed the door open tentatively. It was dark inside, the curtains pulled tightly closed. Lily immediately threw them open.

'Rise and shine. Time to get up,' she said in a sing-song voice.

Sandy winced. 'What are you doing?'

Lily opened a window, letting a cold blast of air in. 'Sandy Delahaye, I may have only known you for a short time, but I know a fighter when I see one. And you're a fighter. So, you're going to get up, get dressed and get on with your day.'

'You don't understand.'

Lily sat down on the edge of the bed. 'You're right, I don't. But I do understand this. If you're too afraid to live your life, then he's won. And he's not allowed to win.'

'He's already won, hasn't he?'

'No, Sandy, he hasn't. Look at you, darling. You've got a beautiful family, an amazing wife, two wonderful children. You're an incredible artist. You're happy and successful, and you're strong. And, of course, you're fortunate enough to have me as a neighbour.'

The last comment brought a slight smile to Sandy's face. 'I suppose you're not bad.'

'And you get to play tennis every Friday with the handsomest coach in England and quite possibly the entire world.'

At this, Sandy laughed faintly. 'That's true.'

'So really, apart from a potentially dangerous ex, you have nothing to worry about.'

This time when Sandy laughed, it was from deep within her. 'Oh, Lily, I do love you.'

'So, get dressed. I'm taking you out for brunch.'

Sandy's smile disappeared immediately. 'I don't want to go out.'

'Well, you are,' Lily declared. 'And we're picking up Avril on the way. Come on.'

'Lily, I don't want to.'

Lily took in Sandy's stricken expression. 'I won't leave your side, the whole time. And Micky will be here, with Clare.'

'Can we just go to the clubhouse, then?'

Lily relented. Getting her out of the house was the priority. 'Of course we can. Tell you what, why don't I leave you to get dressed? I'll go fetch Avril and be back in half an hour.'

'Okay.'

Lily watched with satisfaction as Sandy reluctantly climbed out of bed and then she went back downstairs, popping her head around the kitchen door to tell Clare the plan.

'Lily, you're a genius. How on earth did you manage that?'

Lily winked. 'I can be rather persuasive when I want to be.'

She hurried out of the front door, still haunted by the look on Sandy's face. It had affected her far more than she'd let on to Sandy. As soon as she was out of earshot, she pulled out her phone and found the number she was looking for. Screw Lily 2.0, this was the right thing to do.

'Hi, it's Lily Sanderson again. Listen, I've got another job for you.'

23

What was it about sunshine that made the whole world seem brighter? Avril turned her face towards the sun and felt the warm rays soothe her exhausted soul.

Spring had come to Westford Park. The flowers bloomed in the beautifully manicured beds, the cover had been taken off the swimming pool to reveal the crystal-clear blue water underneath once more, and tables and chairs had been placed back out on the terrace.

The warmer days and lighter evenings also meant that the kids disappeared off together as soon as they had finished their school-work. With no more vandalism incidents, the mums had agreed that, as long as the teenagers stayed together, and as long as they stayed on the grounds, then they had their freedom. After all, Poppy and Bethany were sixteen now, Micky was seventeen. But they all had their reasons for finding it hard to let their children go.

Sandy, of course, was worried about Grant. Lily was worried about everything. And Avril couldn't stop thinking about what Bethany had slipped so covertly into her bag.

Ever since that day, Avril had been waiting for the right time to search her things. But Tom had been ill and was off school for a few days, and then Bethany had caught the bug, followed by Stuart. She had wanted the house to be empty because she was terrified of getting caught. Deep down, she knew she was doing a bad thing.

Finally, with everyone back at school and work, she had seized her opportunity. She had gone into Bethany's room and looked through her belongings, opening her dresser drawers, and sifting through the items on her messy desk. After several minutes of fruitless searching, she had lifted Bethany's mattress and that's when she had found her journal.

Avril had sat down on the floor, holding the leatherbound journal in her hands, battling with her indecision. If she did this, if she opened Bethany's private diary, there was no going back. All the trust that had slowly been building between them would be shattered in one move. She wanted to put it back. She wanted to read it.

Eventually, she had slipped it back under Bethany's mattress and crept out of the room. But she hadn't been able to stop thinking about the journal since.

The thing was, Bethany was thriving. Everyone said it. Even the teachers at school had taken Avril aside and told her what a joy she was to teach, how she was participating in class more. Now, when Avril saw Bethany in the corridors, she was always with a friend. Her grades were excellent and she had aced her mock exams. She was already looking forward to starting her A levels in September, which would allow her to work at a greater depth in art. For Avril's birthday, she had given her the most beautiful hand-painted card of a bird swooping down over the lake. The image had been happy and innocent, with no hint of the darkness that Sandy had described in Bethany's work. There was nothing to suggest trouble brewing.

Tom was thriving too, playing in football tournaments most

weekends and going to hang out with his friends. He was no longer glued to the screen of his iPad because he had a social life again and his cheeks were flushed from being outdoors. And he was growing up, transforming from a boy into a man, and had started wanting to go out on his own more. It was less of a wrench, letting him go. Perhaps it was because he was the younger sibling and she had been through it all before. But the truth was that she didn't worry about Tom so much. He was blissfully uncomplicated. Easy to read. The exact opposite of Bethany.

Sandy had become a recluse. She had stopped coming to tennis lessons and cancelled their dinners out, feigning a headache or tiredness. Avril and Lily had talked endlessly about what they could do but, short of visiting her regularly they were stumped. The worst thing was that Sandy had stopped her art sessions with Bethany, who had been distraught. Avril had tried to explain that Sandy was going through a difficult time, but she hadn't wanted to tell Bethany too much about the situation. She didn't want to frighten her daughter and, anyway, she had no idea how much Micky knew.

But today, with the sun on her face, she tried to forget about it all and enjoy a few moments of peace and quiet. It was so tranquil by the poolside that she could feel herself dozing off, and she started when she heard someone approach.

Clare was jogging towards her, in running gear.

'Clare! I thought you'd be at work today.'

'I'm working from home,' Clare said as she pulled up by Avril and sat down on the vacant sun lounger next to her. 'You're brave, sunbathing in April.'

'Well, I wouldn't exactly call it sunbathing. More lying in the general direction of the sun. And I'm certainly not going in the pool. How's Sandy?'

The look on Clare's face told Avril everything she needed to know. 'I don't know what to do,' she confessed. 'I'm all out of ideas.'

'Perhaps she just needs some time.'

'Maybe, but I feel helpless, Avril.'

'Lily and I said the same thing,' Avril admitted. 'We're desperate to help but we don't know what to do. And we want to reassure her that there's nothing to worry about, but we can't promise her that. I wish the police could do something.'

'I did call them,' Clare confessed. 'And I spoke to a solicitor too. But it's really complicated. There's no evidence that he has breached the restraining order against Sandy. And the no-contact order for Micky expired when his prison sentence finished. The police gave me a contact number to call at any time, but it didn't do much to alleviate Sandy's concerns. And I'm worried, Avril. I think she might want to move house again.'

Avril was horrified. 'But you've only just got here.'

'I know, but she doesn't feel safe any more. And the twenty-four-hour security we were promised doesn't seem to be up to scratch, does it? There have been all sorts of odd things going on.'

This made Avril think of Bethany again, but she forced it away. 'That bastard. Driving her away from her home.' Avril grimaced. Then she had a thought. 'Sandy's always said that she feels most at peace when she's painting. We need to get her working again.'

'I've tried but even getting her out of the house is a struggle. And Micky and Isla know something's wrong, and they're confused too. I don't know what to tell them.'

Avril mulled this over. 'Perhaps Bethany can help. They seem to have formed a bond. I told Bethany to give Sandy some space but maybe I'm going about it the wrong way. If Bethany tries to persuade Sandy to have a painting session, she might agree.'

'It's worth trying. Thanks, Avril.'

Avril smiled. 'Leave it with me. And if there's anything else I can do, let me know.'

Clare stood up. 'I'd better get back, I've got a Zoom meeting in fifteen minutes.'

'Look after yourself, Clare.'

Avril watched Clare jog away and then lay back down on the sun lounger and closed her eyes. Her hopes of dozing were out of the window; she was wide awake after her conversation with Clare. But perhaps a few minutes more in the sun would soothe her nerves again and give her an opportunity to plan what to say to Bethany about Sandy.

The sound of an incoming call cut through the silence and she cursed as she reached down for her bag and fished her phone out her heart sinking when she saw it was the school calling. Already her mind was whirring, coming up with possibilities for the call Bethany or Tom were ill again. They needed her to come into work to cover an absent teacher. Or? *No, don't think of it.*

'Hello, Avril speaking.'

'Avril, it's Mark.'

Avril's heart plummeted at the sound of the headteacher's voice. If one of the kids was ill, the call would have come from the school office. 'Hi, Mark, is everything okay?'

'It's Bethany. Can you come in now?'

* * *

By the time Avril skidded into the school car park, she'd narrowly avoided two car accidents. Her nerves were in tatters and her pulse was racing, although not as fast as her mind, which had gone into overdrive.

Worst-case scenarios were dominating her every thought. The headteacher had given her little information on the phone except to confirm that Bethany wasn't hurt or sick. Which meant that she was in trouble and Avril wasn't sure she had the strength to go through it again. She waved and smiled nervously at the receptionist, getting even more anxious when she saw the stern look on the woman's face. Oh, God.

Bethany would be expelled. And then what? Move again? Keep insisting there was nothing to worry about? Or, even worse, accept that there *was* something to worry about.

She felt sick as she knocked on the headteacher's door and pushed it open. Bethany was waiting for her inside and her daughter's vacant expression said a million words.

'Avril.' Mark stood up and strode over, extending an arm.

Avril couldn't even muster a smile as she shook his hand limply. 'What's this about?'

The headteacher glanced at Bethany and then back at Avril. Avril held her breath and waited for the world to come crashing down around her again.

'Every year we work closely with a nearby private school, Weston Abbey, to identify young people who have a talent for art,' he began. 'This year we told them about Bethany and they came to meet her and see her work. Well, I'm delighted to tell you that they called this morning and, subject to your consent, have offered her a full art scholarship for sixth form.'

Avril stared at him, agog, trying to recalibrate her brain. It wasn't bad news?

'Now, obviously we would love it if Bethany chose to stay here to do her A levels,' the headteacher continued. 'We never want to lose a pupil. But we recognise the world-class facilities offered in the art department at Weston Abbey and we're not too proud to admit that for a student like Bethany, being able to access those facilities would be of tremendous benefit.'

Avril was still speechless. She tried to collect her thoughts, to morph her expression into one of joy rather than gormlessness, but she was too shocked. She looked at Bethany who was now smiling shyly, proud in the modest, understated way Avril had always admired.

With relief coursing through her shaking body, Avril finally managed to smile. 'Bethany, darling, congratulations! This is such wonderful news!'

'Thanks, Mum.'

'I'm so, so proud of you. But why didn't you tell me about it before?'

'I didn't want to get your hopes up, in case they didn't pick me.'

'Oh, darling, of course they'd pick you.'

The headteacher was grinning at them both. 'I'm sure you have a lot to talk about and Bethany has a free period this afternoon. Why don't you go home early, Bethany?'

Once she'd started smiling, Avril couldn't stop. She was thrilled about Weston Abbey but she was even more happy that her daughter wasn't in trouble. 'Thank you, Mark.'

'It's my pleasure, Avril. As I said, we're extremely sad to lose Bethany but we're all absolutely delighted for her too. She has a bright future ahead of her.'

As they made their way out of the school, Avril saw the receptionist again. The woman smiled as she gave them a thumbs up, already privy to the news about Bethany's scholarship. She hadn't been scowling before, Avril realised, it had been her own insecurities reading something different into the woman's expression. She would never do it again, she vowed. She would never, ever doubt her daughter ever again. She would never read that journal.

As they drove away, she said, 'I really am so incredibly proud of you, darling, but I do have one question which I didn't want to ask you in front of the headteacher.'

'What's that?'

'Do you actually want to go to Weston Abbey?'

Bethany didn't hesitate. 'Yes.'

'And why is that?'

'I've been looking at their website. Their art department is amazing, Mum, and some of their students have got into the best art colleges in the world.'

Her daughter's excitement was infectious. 'Wow, that's amazing.'

'Plus, I won't have to worry about bumping into my mum in the corridor.'

'Oh, Bethany, does that annoy you?'

'Chill, Mum, I'm joking.'

Avril laughed, high on relief and happiness. 'Fair enough.'

'And I'll be with Poppy too.'

'But not Micky.'

'I don't spend much time with him at school, anyway. He's in the year above.'

'And what about your other friends at school? Won't you miss them?'

'Yeah, but this is too good an opportunity, Mum. It could change my life.'

'It could. And it'll be lovely for you and Poppy to go to school together every day.'

'Yeah.'

Avril stole a sideways glance at Bethany. She had a dreamy expression on her face, probably imagining the fancy art studio at Weston Abbey. And they wouldn't have to pay a penny to access the amazing facilities. It all sounded too good to be true.

But it was true and Avril couldn't wait to tell Stuart, and Lily and Sandy. There were just so many people she wanted to share the joyful news with. Perhaps it would perk Sandy up, to know that her input had helped Bethany secure the scholarship. It might even inspire her to start working with Bethany again and, in turn, benefit her too.

How lucky they were to have so many friends. In less than a year all of their lives had changed, and she couldn't believe how fortunate they had been. It was time to enjoy the present and look forward to the future too. And what a future it would be. Avril grinned as she thought about spending summer by the pool and having barbecues with friends.

Yes, she could breathe again. Because their troubles were finally over.

24

He was close. Sandy could feel him, his presence looming in dark corners, reminding her that no matter how hard she tried to escape him, she would never be free.

It didn't matter what anyone told her, how much they tried to convince her that he wasn't coming for her. She could hear him, she could smell him, his stench lingering in her nose. It had been more than a decade since she'd last seen him and yet his image was vivid.

But here she was, gathering up her art materials and going about her day as though nothing was amiss. It took every ounce of strength to do it, but she had to, not just for herself but for her family and friends. They were worried about her, they wanted to help. But no one could help. No one could free her from the darkness.

It had been a mistake to hire the private detective. Sandy wished that she could turn back the clock and be blissfully unaware of Grant's location. Well, maybe not blissful, but at least not this. Not this constant, acute fear that had wrapped its hands around her throat.

It was affecting Micky too. He wasn't himself, he was moody and withdrawn. Clare said he was bored because Bethany and Poppy had started their exams and had hunkered down for the next few weeks. But Sandy blamed herself. Micky was feeding off her anxiety because he knew something was wrong, which meant that she had, yet again, let him down.

Clare had been urging her to tell Micky about Grant again. She felt it was more important now than ever. But Sandy still couldn't do it. The idea of telling him was worse than seeing the look of disapproval on her wife's face every time she shook her head. It was the only thing Clare had never understood, and Sandy was running out of ways to explain it. She knew Clare was worried and it was one of the reasons why she was trying to pick herself back up again. But she was strapped so tightly into the rollercoaster, she couldn't get off.

In a few weeks' time, Bethany and Poppy would have finished their GCSEs and would be free again. She probably wouldn't see Micky for weeks and she hated the idea of not knowing where he was at every waking moment. But he was seventeen and in just over a year he would be going away to university. She had to let him go. She dreaded it.

Today she was meeting Bethany for a painting session by the lake. It was the first time they had got together in weeks, and she felt guilty about that too. News of Bethany's scholarship had lifted her heart, and her mood, and she had forced herself to resume their art sessions, especially given that Bethany needed a breather from revising. And Sandy needed to get back to work too, she had done nothing for weeks and it wasn't good for her.

She closed the front door and squinted in the bright sunshine, a stark reminder that she hadn't left the house for ages. She walked tentatively at first but the sun warmed her skin and she inhaled the sweet smell of freshly cut grass. She could hear children playing in the background, their voices carrying over the distant whir of a lawnmower. By the time she reached the path that led down to the lake, an unexpected calmness had spread over her, and her mood was already shifting, like a heavy blanket being lifted from her shoulders.

'Sandy!'

She turned to see Lily at the top of the path, waving.

'Hi,' she called back, retracing her steps until they were face to face.

'Darling, it's lovely to see you out and about. And is that your art stuff?'

'Yes, I'm meeting Bethany by the lake.'

'How wonderful. And what a glorious day for it!'

On closer inspection, Lily looked different. The changes were subtle; a pair of glasses that Sandy had never seen her wear before, some smart trousers. She was clutching on to a laptop bag in one hand and her car keys in the other.

'You look smart. Where are you off to?'

'I've got a meeting,' Lily said proudly. 'I've started my own events planning business.'

Sandy was perplexed. 'What? When did that happen?'

'Well, I decided a few weeks ago that it was time for me to start working again and I thought, what am I good at? And the thing that topped the list was planning things. So, I spread the word and I'm now organising a bar mitzvah for some friends of friends.'

'Lily, that's amazing.'

Lily shrugged modestly. 'It's a start. I need to build up my portfolio. Anyway, must dash, lovely to see you.'

With a flurry of kisses, Lily hurried off towards her car and Sandy resumed her walk. News of her friend's budding career venture should have pleased her, but it had made her feel excluded. She should have known about it, they should have discussed it over coffee or dinner, but she was out of the loop. She'd been hiding away from everyone, cancelling plans. And in the meantime, her friends had been living their lives, even transforming themselves.

She felt at once happiness and regret. She was glad to be out, and she was pleased to have seen Lily. But she felt as though she had been locked away from the world, isolated from everyday life, in her self-imposed house arrest. She was like that girl that Bethany had painted in the boathouse. Trapped and afraid. And more than anything she wanted to engage again, to be part of the life that she had built at Westford Park.

I wish he was dead. The thought came to her, suddenly and violently. She had thought it before, but this time it shocked her with its intensity. She couldn't see any other way out though, any escape other than Grant's permanent removal, not just from her life but the world. Only then would she truly be at peace. But that, like everything else, was out of her hands.

They would need to move again, she thought sadly, as she spotted Bethany setting up by the lake. She would have to uproot her family and this one would hurt the most. Of all the places they had lived in over the years, Westford Park had felt most like home.

She'd let them have the summer. Let them enjoy a couple more months here and then she would tentatively broach the subject, suggesting it casually even though she knew her mind was already made up. She would bring it up again a few days later, and then again. She had a formula, she'd been here before. Within a month, the house would be on the market.

She tried not to think about how she would feel when she saw the For Sale sign outside their beautiful home. She tried not to imagine the tears on Isla's face when she learned that she would be leaving Westford Park and moving school, or the resentment on Micky's. And most of all, she tried to put the image of Clare's bright, forced smile as she pretended it was a great idea to the back of her mind. She'd take them being angry, or bitter, as long as they were safe. All she wanted was to keep them safe.

Bethany looked up when she heard Sandy approach and smiled, her face open and happy. Sandy marvelled again at the change in Bethany and pushed down yet another pang of guilt. Another person she was going to disappoint when she left. Another person she was letting down.

'Bethany, hi! How are the exams going?'

Bethany shrugged. 'Fine. Bit boring.'

'They'll be over before you know it. Do you have any plans for the summer?'

Bethany started helping Sandy unpack the art materials. 'We're going to Spain for a week and I'm thinking of asking for a summer job at the clubhouse.'

'Oh, that's a good idea.'

'But mainly I'll be drawing and painting. I don't want to be bottom of the class when I start at Weston Abbey.'

'Speaking of which.' Sandy put her hand into her bag and pulled out a set of paints. 'These are for you.'

Bethany looked at them wide-eyed. 'For me?'

'Yes, to say congratulations.' The paints were one of the best brands available and Sandy could see the delight on Bethany's face. She felt a rush of pleasure and pride. 'I'm so proud of you, Bethany. Well done for a remarkable achievement.'

'Thank you, Sandy. These are amazing.'

'Shall we test-drive them, then, or what?'

'Yes, please.' Bethany carefully unwrapped the paints. 'I'm going to paint the old willow tree today, with the boathouse in the distance.'

Instinctively, Sandy gazed at the boathouse and thought of Steve. She'd been so hung up about Grant that she'd forgotten about Steve. It seemed insignificant and futile to her now, a silly distraction from the real threat. Still, she couldn't resist asking Bethany about him.

'Have you seen much of Steve lately?'

'I haven't seen much of anyone. It's been study, study, study.'

'What about Poppy?'

Bethany glanced at her. 'Same for Poppy. We're not allowed out until the exams are over.'

There we go, then, Sandy thought. The girls were at home studying. But now that she was out of the house, staring directly at the boathouse, the nagging feeling was returning.

'Has Poppy mentioned him at all?'

Bethany looked at Sandy suspiciously. 'You still think they're at it?'

'I didn't say that. I just want to make sure that Poppy's okay.'

'I swear, there's nothing going on between them. I would know if there was.'

'Okay.' Sandy nodded. 'Fair enough. By the way, you never told me which pieces you showed to the people from Weston Abbey when they came to see you.'

'Oh, some paintings I did at school.'

'I'd love to see them.'

'I've got some photos somewhere. I'll send them to you.'

'Great, thank you. And I'm sorry that I haven't been around much recently. I've not been feeling well, but I'm doing much better now.'

'That's okay, don't worry.'

'How are things at school?'

'Fine.' Bethany was sketching out the lines of the tree, her brow furrowed in concentration and Sandy let her be, knowing that she needed to absorb herself in her work. She turned to her own, blank canvas. She had been planning to paint some birds today, flying over the water, but she wasn't in the mood. Instead, she closed her eyes, shutting out her surroundings, and when she opened them again, she began to paint without thinking. She started with small brushstrokes and felt the stress of the last few weeks begin to transfer from her body to the paper. Her movements became larger, and more frantic until soon she was painting like she was possessed, covering the canvas with huge, angry brushstrokes, oblivious to everyone and everything around her. It was thrilling, and terrifying and liberating and she couldn't, and didn't want to, stop. She didn't know how long she painted like that for but when she finally came to, when the surroundings came back into focus again, Bethany was watching her.

'I've never seen you paint like that before,' she said quietly.

Sandy exhaled, exhausted. 'It's been a while. But I think I needed it.' She looked at the painting, cocking her head to the side. 'I'm not sure I'll be able to sell this one, though.'

'I like it.' Bethany was studying it intently and then, suddenly, she reached out a hand and gripped on to Sandy's tightly. Sandy looked down at their entwined hands, surprised by the teenager's uncharacteristic show of affection.

'I know what it feels like to hurt,' Bethany said. 'But it will get better. I promise.'

Sandy felt the first tears begin to fall and soon they were flowing freely, down her face, over her clothes. Bethany clasped her hand but remained quiet, letting her cry. It took a few minutes for Sandy to regain her composure and she gave an embarrassed laugh.

'Gosh, I'm so sorry, Bethany,' she said, wiping her eyes. 'I'm supposed to be the adult here and you're the one looking after me.'

'It's about him, isn't it? The man you told me about. The one who hurt you.'

Tears threatened again. 'Yes.'

'You're afraid of him.' It was a statement, not a question.

'Yes.'

Bethany nodded. Her maturity, and intuition, at such a young age amazed Sandy. 'I was afraid too. Of the girls who hurt me. But I'm not any more.'

'That's wonderful, Bethany. It's really wonderful.'

'I realised that people can only hurt me if I let them. And I'm not going to let them.'

'You're right. Oh, gosh, you're so right.'

'Don't let him hurt you any more, Sandy.'

Sandy looked at Bethany and thought that she had never met anyone like her before. 'Thank you.'

Bethany squeezed her hand and then released it, turning her attention back to her own painting. The willow tree was taking shape and Bethany had started adding some colour to it, beautiful bright shades of green. There was no hint of darkness, no fear or pain in her work.

Sandy watched her for a while and then looked at her watch. 'Oh, crikey, I'd better go. I have to pick Isla up from school soon and take her for her swimming lesson. Clare normally does it, but she can't leave work early today.'

'I hated swimming lessons,' Bethany said. 'Mum used to take us every week, and I would cry and refuse to go in. But she kept making me go back, again and again.'

Sandy smiled, remembering Isla's tears by the poolside when she was a baby. Now, though, she loved the water. 'Did you ever learn to enjoy them?'

'No. I hated the instructor. He was horrible.'

Sandy felt a jolt as an old memory resurfaced. It was one she hadn't thought about in years. She had been on maternity leave and Isla could only have been a few months old. Grappling with baby blues and feeling isolated, Sandy had decided to sign up for baby swimming lessons and she had been distraught as she stood by the water's edge, clutching on to a wailing Isla and watching all the other babies smile and gurgle as they splashed about. She had felt like the odd one out, the only struggling mother among a sea of happy faces.

Then an instructor had come up to her, a friendly looking man with a warm smile, and he had gently guided her down the steps, cooing at Isla and waving a toy at her to distract her as she entered the water. He had kept a close eye on them throughout the session, encouraging Sandy, telling her that she was doing great. Sandy had been so grateful to that man. The following week she had looked for him but he wasn't there. When she had asked about him, the instructor had scowled and said that he was gone and good riddance. Sandy had asked what she meant but the instructor had pursed her lips and changed the subject.

She could picture him again now, in his T-shirt and shorts, his hair cropped, smiling at all the mothers and babies and it hit her like a train, the full impact of recognition.

Because she realised now who the man was and she wondered why she hadn't worked it out before. But he looked different now and it had been one meeting, years ago, when she was a new, exhausted and overwhelmed parent. The memory had become lodged at the back of her mind, covered over with all the other events that had passed since.

It had come back to her now, though, along with confusion and trepidation as she tried to piece the past and present together. Because she finally knew why she recognised Steve. He was the swimming instructor who had disappeared from her life as abruptly as he had appeared. The one who had caused his former colleague to say *good riddance*.

Now he was back. And a shiver ran up her spine as she tried to work out why.

25

The bar mitzvah had been a roaring success and now Lily had been handed the crème de la crème of event planning – a wedding.

She couldn't believe how busy she was, or what she had done with her days before she started working again. It had only been a couple of months but already she felt like a different person and she was intoxicated by this new sense of purpose and responsibility.

Eric didn't get it. 'You know you don't have to work, darling,' he'd said.

'I know that,' she'd snapped, something she found herself doing more these days. 'I'm doing it because I want to, not because I need to.'

And he had nodded and chuckled to himself, as though she was an entrepreneurial schoolgirl offering to wash cars in the street for a few quid. He didn't take it seriously because he didn't consider Lily's work to be a proper job, but merely a hobby. She was going to prove him wrong. She'd done plenty of research into the business, she knew her worth, and she wasn't afraid to charge the going rate. Fortunately, most of the people she mixed with, or used to mix with, could afford her fees without so much as a second thought, and years of networking had proven to be a valuable tool, generating more business than any advert.

It did mean that she was around less to keep a motherly eye on Poppy, however. The exams had finally finished, and Poppy and Bethany were living the life of luxury, spending their days by the pool, ordering an endless trail of smoothies and snacks throughout the day. Their monthly clubhouse bill was going to be horrific. But let them enjoy themselves, Lily thought, they'd worked hard and deserved a break. And in September, Bethany would be joining Poppy at Weston Abbey and Lily couldn't believe how well it had all turned out.

She looked up from her laptop as Poppy appeared, bleary-eyed, in her pyjamas.

'Hello, darling, did you sleep well?'

Poppy grunted in response and went to the fridge. She'd been so moody lately, which Lily had put down to GCSE stress, even though, if she was being honest, it had started long before the exams had. And now that she had her freedom again, she was rarely at home.

'What are you up to today?' she asked, typing an email at the same time.

'Not much. I'm going out this evening.'

'Anywhere exciting?'

'The usual.'

Lily sent the email and observed Poppy as she reached up into a cupboard for a cereal bowl, the sleeves of her dressing gown riding up her arms.

'Poppy, what are those marks on your arms?' Lily jumped up in fright and rushed over to her daughter, grabbing her by the wrists.

'Mother!' Poppy tried to get away.

But Lily was stronger. 'Let me see,' she insisted, and Poppy reluctantly acquiesced.

'They're scratches,' she explained. 'From the woods.'

Lily scrutinised Poppy's arms, running a finger gently over the wounds. She was horrified and afraid at what it might mean. But on closer inspection, she began to calm down again. The cuts were superficial, narrow snaking lines which corroborated what Poppy had said about them being scratches from branches. There was nothing to suggest anything more serious and the relief was palpable. Still, her daughter had some serious explaining to do. Lily narrowed her eyes, her pulse slowing down again.

'What are you doing in the woods?'

'Just hanging out, getting some fresh air, you know.'

'Have you been frolicking with a boy behind a tree?'

Poppy rolled her eyes. 'Mother, you are so embarrassing.'

'Well, how do you explain these marks?'

'We go off-road sometimes, me, Bethany and Micky, walking through the woods.'

Lily frowned. 'At night?'

'Sometimes.'

'But Poppy, I thought you were at the boathouse or clubhouse. Is that safe?'

'You said yourself that Westford Park is the safest place there is.'

It was true, she had said that, but she was no longer sure if she still meant it. Too much had happened, too many unexplained incidents that had put them all on edge. And she certainly didn't like the idea of the teenagers roaming around the woods at all hours.

'It all sounds very *Blair Witch Project* to me.'

'Blair who?'

'Oh, never mind.' Satisfied that Poppy hadn't come to any

serious harm, Lily returned to her seat. 'Be careful, okay? I know you teenagers need to get your kicks somehow, but I really don't like the idea of you being in the woods late at night. It's creepy.'

'Why, are you scared of ghosts?'

It wasn't ghosts Lily was scared of. 'Don't be silly.'

'Anyway, it's fun.'

'And what if you can't see where you're going and you get lost or fall in the lake again?'

'We use our iPhone torches.'

'The Scout movement would be proud, darling.'

Fear was mounting in the pit of Lily's stomach and she wondered how she could stop Poppy from going out late without causing a full-on row.

She had an idea. 'I've been thinking, darling. Why don't we get a summer house built at the end of the garden? Then you can hang out in there with your friends, nice and cosy.'

'So you can spy on us, you mean?'

'No, I don't mean that. It would be your space, to do as you please. We could get some nice, comfy sofas. A TV too.'

'No thanks, Mother.'

Defeated, Lily decided to give up, for now at least. She had too much work to do. 'Well, listen, Dad's coming home from the States this afternoon and I thought we could have a nice family dinner, so you can go out after that.'

Poppy slammed the cereal bowl down hard on the kitchen surface. 'No.'

Accustomed to her daughter's teenage temper tantrums, Lily didn't even flinch. 'Come on, Poppy, it's only an hour. You can go out when we're finished.'

'No. I promised Micky and Bethany I'd meet them at six. It's important.'

'Why is it so important? You said you had nothing special planned.'

Poppy hesitated. 'We don't. But you told me I should never let people down, Mum. That friends are important.'

She had said that, hadn't she? And why was she so insistent that Poppy join them for dinner? Was it because she still wanted to maintain the veneer of the happy family or because, increasingly, she was finding it harder to be alone with Eric?

'Okay,' she relented. 'But we're having Sunday lunch together tomorrow.'

Poppy rolled her eyes. 'Fine.'

'Right, then. I'd best get back to work. I've washed and dried your favourite bikini if you're going to the pool today. It's hanging up in the utility room.'

'Thanks.'

Poppy took her cereal bowl, and her bikini, up the stairs and Lily returned to her laptop. Her daughter was a hurricane of emotions, but she was sixteen. She didn't want to spend her Saturday nights with her parents. Anyway, there would be plenty more dinners. Plenty more opportunities for her to play the doting mother and wife, cooking a beautiful meal, opening Eric's favourite bottle of red wine and pretending that their life was as picture perfect as a family television show. But, she realised with a sinking heart, that thought distressed her almost as much as the idea of her teenage daughter spending her evenings in a deep, dark wood.

* * *

As it happened, Eric's flight was delayed, again, and Lily's family dinner turned into a hastily made salad for one in front of her laptop. At least she had her work to keep her occupied. She'd been making spreadsheets and calling caterers and DJs all day. She was exhausted, but in a good way, relishing the feeling of having done a hard day's work.

It wasn't until she'd finished the bottle of wine on the table beside her that she realised it was gone midnight and Poppy wasn't home yet. It was the first time her daughter had stayed out beyond her curfew and the first trickle of worry began to seep in. She reached for her phone and opened the Find My app, frowning when Poppy's location didn't appear. Had she run out of battery? But Poppy never went anywhere without a fully charged phone. She tried to call her, but it went straight to voicemail, so she sent her a text.

> Where are you? Call me ASAP xx

Lily walked out onto the driveway and looked left and right to see if Poppy was on her way home, but the street was deserted. She glanced at Avril's house opposite and all the lights were off, including in Bethany's room. The trickle became a stream.

She went back inside and paced the house for a couple of minutes, trying to decide what to do. Then she called Eric, but his phone was switched off too. Next, she dialled Avril's number, praying that she would pick up. With each ring, Lily became more desperate.

'Hello?' Avril finally answered sleepily.

'Avril, I'm so sorry to wake you. Is Poppy with you? She didn't come home.'

She heard Avril shuffling around. When she spoke again, her voice was more alert. 'No. Bethany came home just over an hour ago and went straight to bed.'

'Can you check her room in case they decided to have a last-minute sleepover?'

'Hold on.'

Lily waited, agitated, praying for Avril to come back and say yes, Poppy was there, sleeping like a princess. She'd have it out with her daughter tomorrow, make it clear that this behaviour was not acceptable, but tonight she just needed to know that Poppy was okay.

But when Avril came back to the phone, she sounded worried. 'She's not here, Lily.'

'Shit. Okay, I'll call Sandy.'

Lily hung up and dialled Sandy's number, the stream now a river, drenching her entire body. This was not happening. This couldn't be happening.

'Lily?' Sandy sounded more awake.

'Sandy, sorry to bother you so late. Is Poppy with you?'

'No, she's not here. Is everything okay?'

'Is Micky home?'

'Yes, he's here with me. We're watching a late-night film.'

'Can you ask him when he last saw Poppy?'

Lily heard Sandy and Micky talking quietly. 'He says they were out together until about eleven and then he came home.'

'Was Poppy with him?'

More muffled talking. 'Yes. He said goodbye to Bethany and Poppy at the end of your road.'

'She didn't come home, Sandy!' Lily was getting hysterical.

'Stay there, I'm coming over.'

While she waited, Lily called Poppy's phone three more times, but it was still off. She could no longer control her spiralling fear. All her earlier anxieties came rushing back to her. Sandy's ex on the loose, the mysterious scratches on Poppy's arms. The vandalism. The late-night roaming around the woods. What had she been thinking, letting Poppy do that?

Sandy appeared, panting, minutes later. 'When did you last see her?'

'She went out just before six and said she was meeting Bethany and Micky. I haven't heard from her since.'

'Micky says they went to the clubhouse first for some dinner, then to the boathouse. After that, they walked in the woods and then parted ways at eleven.'

'That was an hour and a half ago, Sandy!'

'Stay calm,' Sandy said, even though she looked far from it herself.

'Did they meet up with anyone else?'

'No, not according to Micky.'

'Should I call the police?'

'Not yet. Let's go and look for her first and then if we can't find her, we'll call.'

Lily's hopes soared as she heard a knock on the front door and she hurried to open it, but it was Avril on the doorstep, wearing some hastily thrown-on clothes.

'What can I do?' she asked.

'We're going to look for her,' Sandy explained. 'Do you have a torch?'

Avril nodded and dashed back across the road, reappearing moments later.

'Okay, let's go,' Sandy said, and Lily followed, grateful that someone was taking control because she didn't know what to do, what to think, or even where to start.

They walked together to the lake path, and as soon as they were away from the glare of the streetlights, Avril turned her torch on, waving it from side to side.

'Poppy?' Lily called, and soon they were all shouting her name over and over again. Lily squinted in the dim light, looking for a lone figure, desperate for a glimpse of her daughter.

'What if she's fallen in the lake again?' she said, her voice shrill.

'Don't think like that, Lily. She'll be fine.' Avril was trying to reassure her, but her words were not enough to prevent Lily from escalating into terror.

They reached the boathouse and barged their way inside, looking around the empty room. But the lights were off and there was no sign of anyone.

'She's gone.' Lily was frantic. 'I need to call the police.'

Sandy took her hand. 'She's only been gone an hour or so, they probably won't come out yet. Let's keep looking.'

They circled the lake, calling Poppy's name, but the only reply was from animals, rustling through the bushes as they scuttled away from them.

'Why do they come here at night? It's terrifying,' Lily said, afraid of the silence and the darkness that enveloped them, where evil could hide, ready to pounce. She thought of the strange noises. 'We shouldn't have let them come. We shouldn't have been so damn relaxed.'

'Let's try the fishing platform,' Sandy suggested. 'The one we found Bethany and Poppy sitting on last summer. Can anyone remember where it was?'

'I think I remember. Follow me.' Avril led the way around the lake and down a narrow, overgrown path that took them to the abandoned platform. 'She's not here.'

'The woods are huge,' Lily said despairingly, her hopes of finding Poppy there fading fast. 'Did Micky or Bethany say where exactly they went on their walks?'

'No, but I'll wake Bethany and ask her as soon as we get back to the house.'

Sandy was gazing at the still, dark water. 'Could she have met someone, Lily?'

'Met someone? Who?'

'A friend? A boyfriend?'

'Poppy doesn't have a boyfriend,' Lily cried.

'Perhaps she does, and she hasn't told you about him?'

'Sandy.' Avril shot Sandy a warning glance and Lily seized on this.

'What is it? What aren't you telling me?'

'It's nothing,' Avril began, glaring at Sandy.

'It's probably nothing,' Sandy said haltingly. 'But I heard that she hangs out with Steve.'

Lily looked at her incredulously. 'Steve's more than twice her age! Why would he...?' She didn't need to finish her question because she suddenly understood what Sandy was implying. 'If you knew about this already, why didn't you tell me before?'

'There was nothing to tell. Bethany said...'

'Bethany?' Lily looked at Avril. 'Bethany knew about this too?'

'Bethany didn't say anything to me,' Avril insisted. 'This is the first I'm hearing of it.'

'Bethany said there was nothing going on,' Sandy said quietly. 'She said they were just friends. That's why I didn't tell you about it.'

'You should have told me, Sandy. What if she's with him? Oh my God.'

Avril pulled out her phone. 'Does anyone have his number?'

'No.' Sandy looked downcast. 'But I'm sure they'll have it at the clubhouse. Let's go there. You never know, Poppy might be there anyway, hanging out with the waiting staff. Weren't the girls talking about getting a summer job?'

'It'll be closed at this hour.' Lily was furious. 'Why the hell didn't you tell me, Sandy?'

Avril stepped in. 'We're jumping to conclusions here. I've spent some time with Steve because of Tom's kayaking. He's a nice guy. And he saved Poppy on New Year's Eve too. There's nothing to suggest he has anything to do with this. Let's not get ahead of ourselves.'

But Lily's terror was out of control. 'What about Grant?'

Sandy visibly recoiled. 'What does he have to do with this?'

'What if he's taken her?'

'Stop!' Avril's voice was uncharacteristically harsh. 'This isn't helping. Let's go to the clubhouse and take it from there.'

They hurried back to the main square, but the clubhouse was locked, its windows dark. Lily stood in the street, too horrified to cry, as the most painful realisation stabbed her through the heart. Poppy was not okay. Something had happened to her.

'Why did Micky and Bethany leave her on her own?' It was unfair but she needed an outlet for her fear, her anger, and her desperation.

'They didn't,' Avril said. 'They said goodbye on the street. She was metres from home.'

'Let's head back to yours, Lily,' Sandy suggested. 'For all we know, she's already home and safely tucked up in bed.'

Lily clung on to the prospect, a last chink of hope. Wordlessly she sprinted back to the house, throwing open the front door and calling Poppy's name into the darkness. She raced up the stairs and flung the bedroom door open, wondering whether she could make something happen through sheer will and determination. And then she sat down on Poppy's empty bed and finally began to sob with despair. It was nearly one thirty in the morning.

'I'm calling the police,' she said through her tears.

'Yes.' Sandy appeared in the doorway, her expression grave. 'Yes, I think it's time.'

* * *

How was it possible to be exhausted and wide awake at the same time? Lily's hands were trembling, her body shivering despite the summer's heat.

It had been twelve hours since Poppy disappeared and no one had heard from her.

The police had been questioning Lily and Eric for over an hour. Was Poppy upset? Was she depressed? Had there been a row? Did she have a boyfriend? Lily answered all their questions, her patience slowly unravelling. She knew they were just doing their job but she wanted to scream at them to stop asking inane questions and get out there and find Poppy.

She had told them about Steve. About the petty crime and Sandy's ex-partner. About the so-called security team who were meant to be keeping the development safe. She had given them every little thing she could think of that might explain Poppy's disappearance. At one point Eric had mentioned that Lily was working again and hadn't been around as much as usual and Lily had wanted to throttle him with her bare hands, furious that he was suggesting, even for a moment, that she was responsible. But he was just doing what she, herself had done, minutes earlier. Give the police everything and anything that might help in their investigations. Do whatever it took, throw whoever under the bus, to find Poppy.

When the police finally stood up to leave, though, she almost didn't want them to go. She didn't want to be alone with her dark, horrific thoughts. She craved their presence, their officialness, their reassurance. But they couldn't give her any. No one could.

'Talk to security,' she demanded, her voice hoarse. 'Ask them how the hell they've allowed this to happen.'

As she let them out, she glanced across the road at Avril's house and felt a strong surge of envy towards her friend. Avril's daughter was safe at home. Whereas her own daughter was somewhere out there, possibly afraid, possibly hurt. Possibly dead.

She retched and gripped on to Eric who was standing beside her.

'What's happened to her?' she gasped.

'We'll find her,' he said. 'Don't worry, we'll find her.'

But Eric's usually confident, booming voice seemed smaller and less self-assured. He was afraid too. They wanted to think the best, yet they were both thinking the worst.

Lily's phone rang and she almost tripped over in her haste to answer it.

'Poppy?' she said, without even glancing at the screen to see who the caller was.

'Lily, darling, it's Amanda, I've just heard the awful news.'

Amanda. Her so-called friend and the admissions manager at Weston Abbey. How had she found out already? Bad news, it seemed, travelled even faster than good.

'Can I do anything to help?' Amanda asked.

'I don't think so, Amanda, but thank you. We've already contacted all of Poppy's schoolfriends and no one has heard from her.'

'Could she be with a boyfriend?'

Lily thought of Steve and felt nauseous. 'She's never mentioned a boyfriend.'

'Have you spoken to the other children at Westford Park?'

'Of course we have,' Lily said impatiently. She didn't have time for this.

'Listen, I wasn't sure whether to say anything,' Amanda began, in a tone that implied that she was dying to say something. 'But I heard that Poppy is friends with Bethany Jones?'

'Yes, that's right.' Lily wanted to hang up the phone. She had no interest in talking to smug Amanda, or anyone else, unless they had information about Poppy.

'It's just that I heard something alarming about Bethany and I wondered if it was pertinent.'

'What is it?' Lily demanded.

'I was asked to follow up with her old school for references as she is due to start at Weston Abbey in September. And the head-teacher was terribly cagy at first. I sensed something was amiss and I used my best persuasion skills to coax it out of him.'

'She was expelled,' Lily said bluntly. 'I already know.'

'Do you know why?'

'Some false allegations about bullying.'

Amanda was silent on the other end of the line. Then she said quietly, 'They weren't false, Lily. And they were extremely worrying.'

Now she had Lily's full attention. 'Tell me.'

'Bethany tied up one of the other girls and tortured her. It went on for hours and she had knife wounds all over her arms. The poor girl thought she was going to die.'

Lily almost dropped her phone. How did she not know this? How could Avril, her so-called friend, have kept this from her? She looked at Eric, wide-eyed, her mouth hanging open and he stared back, sensing that something important was occurring.

'And you're sure the other girl didn't make it up?'

'No, the headteacher was adamant. There were other girls there who witnessed it. And he said that Bethany didn't deny it, not once. The girl had to have counselling. The entire school community was traumatised over it.'

'Amanda, I've got to go.'

Lily ended the call, her fear over Poppy's disappearance turning into blind rage as she looked at Eric. 'We have to find Bethany. Right now.'

'What's going on?' he asked, already looking for his keys.

The tiger mum inside Lily wasn't just growling now, it was preparing for attack. 'She's hurt Poppy,' Lily said as she rushed for the door. 'She's hurt our baby.'

26

The police were crawling all over Westford Park, knocking on doors, searching the woods. There were rumours of the lake being trawled. A local news reporter was hanging around, taking photos and stopping residents in the street. So much for twenty-four-hour security.

Avril stared out of the window at the house opposite. She could no longer stop herself from fearing the worst. A young, beautiful girl was missing. It wasn't difficult to add two and two together and come to a terrifying, unthinkable conclusion.

It didn't make sense, though. It was as if Poppy had vanished into thin air. The security team had apparently confirmed that no one had left Westford Park after 10 p.m. and the only people arriving back had been residents, returning from evening engagements. No visitors had signed in all evening. This suggested that Poppy was probably still somewhere in the grounds of Westford Park and it both reassured and scared Avril. Because if she was on-site then maybe she was safe. But, then again, wouldn't she be home by now? And she kept coming back to the same thing. Poppy was hurt.

The illusion of Westford Park being a safe bubble was now completely shattered. The lake where Avril had kayaked with Tom and fed the ducks with Sandy and Isla was a possible crime scene. So were the woods where Avril had walked for hours, breathing in the fresh air, and thanking her lucky stars that she lived somewhere so special. The woods didn't seem special any more, they seemed like a place where bad things happened. Evil things.

Evil. There it was again. Evil had infiltrated Westford Park and Avril didn't know what to think or who to trust. Was Sandy's ex somehow involved? Or the same people responsible for the crime and vandalism? If so why, and how? Did they live here, among them?

Perhaps Sandy had been right to be suspicious of Steve. Maybe he'd taken advantage of Poppy and then persuaded her to run away with him. Avril hadn't seen him since Poppy disappeared and the boathouse was closed. So, where was he?

There was something else too. Something she was desperately trying to ignore. But it was there, stubbornly prodding and poking at her. Bethany.

Her hands twitched as she thought about her daughter's journal. She had promised herself that she wouldn't look but the temptation was becoming stronger and more urgent. Just a quick peek, to reassure herself, that was all she needed. And then she could relax. Well, not relax because Poppy was still missing, but at least she could be one hundred per cent sure it had nothing to do with Bethany. Because of course it had nothing to do with Bethany. She would never do anything to hurt her best friend.

Her intrusive thoughts wouldn't go away. She wanted them to, she needed them to, but they were persistent, overriding her rationale, tormenting her with their presence.

She jumped at a sound behind her and turned to see Bethany

shuffling in. She tried to smile at her daughter, to hide her internal battle.

'Hi, love, how are you doing?'

Bethany came to stand beside her and gazed out of the window. 'Any news?'

'I'm afraid not.'

Bethany had been quiet ever since Poppy went missing. The police had spoken to her and she had answered all their questions in hushed tones, describing their evening and the moment when she parted ways with Poppy. Sandy said that Micky had told the officers the same thing.

Were they lying? Even if Bethany was, and Avril didn't want to think about that, Micky was the sweetest boy she'd ever met. His corroboration of Bethany's story reassured her more than she wanted to admit. And Bethany hadn't closed herself off either. She had cooperated with the police, quietly but confidently. She wanted to help. She wanted them to find Poppy.

'Some of the residents are getting together in an hour to help search the woods for Poppy,' she told her daughter now. 'Would you like to come?'

'Yes. Okay.'

Avril put her arm around Bethany. 'She'll be okay, love. They'll find her.'

But her words sounded empty. She turned her gaze back to the house opposite.

Her phone rang and she fumbled urgently for it. 'Sandy. Any news?'

'No. Have you heard anything?' Sandy sounded distant, her voice echoey.

'Nothing. Where are you?'

'I'll tell you later. Listen, I'm not going to be able to join the search party, I have something to do and Clare is away at a wor conference. Isla's at a friend's house but Micky wants to go. Can you and Bethany take him with you?'

'Of course, we'll pick him up on the way. Sandy, are you okay?'

'I'm fine. Talk later.'

Sandy hung up and Avril stared down at her phone.

'What is it, Mum?'

'Oh, nothing, it was just Sandy. She wants us to pick Micky up on the way to the search.'

'Mum. I didn't hurt Poppy.'

The statement came from nowhere, and Avril's heart broke that her daughter even needed to say those words. She forced herself to look Bethany in the eye. 'I know you didn't.'

'I wouldn't blame you for thinking it. After what happened.'

Fighting back tears, Avril took in her daughter's determined stance, the fear underneath her steely expression. This was it. This was the moment that could change everything.

'I didn't believe it then and I don't believe it now.'

'You could barely even look at me, back then. You hated me.'

'No.' Avril's voice was quivering. 'No, I never hated you. I love you. I just didn't know what to do, what to say. You shut me out and I was afraid.'

'I was afraid too.'

'I know. Oh, I'm so sorry, Bethany.' Avril was crying freely now, months of suppressed hurt and pain pouring from her body. 'I'm so sorry.'

Bethany moved towards her and rested her head on her shoulders. 'Me too.'

'All I ever wanted was for you to talk to me, to trust me.'

'I wanted to, but I couldn't.'

'I know. But we have to stick together, you and me. Promise me.'

'I promise.' Bethany gazed out of the window. 'She'll be home soon.'

Avril pulled away and looked at Bethany in surprise. How did she know that? But when she saw the look on Bethany's face, she understood her daughter's words. It wasn't insider knowledge that had made her say it, it was childish hope. Because Bethany, for all her teenage hormones, was still a child and she still wanted to believe the best in life, even after what she had been through. And in that moment, Avril knew what she had to say to her little girl.

'Yes,' she replied, her voice unwavering. 'Yes, she will.'

* * *

Even in the daylight, the woods now seemed menacing. The tall trees extinguished the summer sun, casting a permanent shadow over the ground beneath them. Avril felt, at once, hope and fear. Hope that they'd find something. Fear that they'd find something.

She was beginning to question the decision to bring Bethany and Micky to the search. They wanted to help, and they needed something to do, but she was dreading the prospect of them discovering something distressing. They walked closely together, their arms almost touching, calling Poppy's name and scouring the ground beneath them. But so far all they had found was a couple of empty crisp packets and a discarded can of Coke.

In the distance, Avril could see other groups trawling the woods, all calling out Poppy's name, all hoping for the best. So far there had been no calls or shouts cutting through the silence of the woods, nothing to suggest a discovery, and the light was beginning to fade. Soon they would have to return home and then another day would be over, another day gone with Poppy still out there somewhere. Avril had watched enough police dramas to know that with each day that passed, the chances of finding the victim were reduced.

Victim. Was Poppy a victim? It was such a horrible word. She thought of Lily, who hadn't joined them on the search, and felt sick.

One of the other residents walked over to them. 'We're stopping for the day,' he said. 'We'll start up again at first light tomorrow. Thanks for your support.'

'Of course. We'll see you tomorrow. Come on, Bethany, Micky, let's go home.'

The teenagers followed obediently as they made their way back around the lake and up the path. Avril was contemplating suggesting ordering some pizzas, wondering if it would cheer them up while fretting that it might be insensitive, when she saw Lily striding towards them, her face contorted with grief.

A ball of dread formed in the pit of Avril's stomach. 'Lily, what is it?'

Lily stood in front of her, with her hands on her hips, glaring at her with such venom that Avril took a step backwards. She realised then that it was fury on Lily's face, not grief.

'What has your daughter done to my daughter?' Lily demanded.

The ball of dread expanded. 'Excuse me?'

Lily turned her furious gaze to Bethany, her eyes narrowing with suspicion. 'I know all about you, Bethany, and what you did to that poor girl at your old school. You're evil and now you've hurt Poppy. Admit it now and tell us where she is before it's too late.'

Avril's entire body began to shake. How had Lily found out? Had Sandy told her? She looked helplessly at Bethany, who was staring at the floor, red blotches creeping up her neck and into her face. Across the square, some people had stopped and were watching the scene. Avril felt confusion, shame, fear, and anger. She needed to do something, anything, but she was frozen to the spot, a rabbit caught in the headlights.

Help came from an unexpected source. 'Bethany had nothing

to do with this,' Micky said firmly, standing next to Bethany, a united front. 'Bethany wouldn't hurt anyone.'

'Tell that to the girl she tied up and tortured,' Lily hissed.

'She didn't do those things.'

Avril was still immobile, knowing that she was the one who should be defending her daughter, not Micky. What was wrong with her? She remembered the conversation she'd had with Bethany just hours earlier and she rallied. It was time to be the mum Bethany deserved.

'Those allegations were false,' she told Lily. 'They were lies.'

Lily turned her glare to Avril. 'You lied to me. You deliberately withheld the reason why Bethany was expelled from her old school because you knew I wouldn't let her be friends with Poppy if you told me. And now look what's happened.'

'I didn't lie to you.' Avril's voice was steady now. 'I didn't tell you because it's not true.'

'Did you push her in the lake too?' Lily was snarling at Bethany.

Bethany looked up, her young face flushed with shame. But her expression was determined. 'Poppy is my best friend and I'd never do anything to hurt her.'

'You're a monster.' Lily poked Bethany in the chest. 'A vile bully.'

Lily was her closest friend and her daughter was missing. But Avril still saw red.

'Get off her.' Avril lunged forward and pushed Lily away. Lily stumbled on the kerb and fell backwards onto the pavement. Avril knew she should help her up, but she was too enraged, anger seeping from every pore. 'Bethany is not involved in this and how dare you confront a young girl in the street like this? Who do you think you are?'

'Who do you think *you* are?' Lily screamed back, scrabbling to her feet. 'You're living in cloud cuckoo land, Avril, convincing your-self that your daughter's an angel when she's the devil.'

'*My* daughter? My daughter's not the one who goes out wearing skirts so short you can almost see her underwear and who teases older men because she enjoys attention.'

'Mum,' Bethany said quietly. Both women ignored her.

Lily squared up to Avril, deliberately invading her space. 'How dare you?'

Avril stood firm. 'How dare you?'

It was a stand-off, both women refusing to back down. From the corner of her eye, Avril could see Bethany and Micky watching them, horrified.

'Go home, Bethany,' she said.

'But Mum...'

'Home. Now.'

Micky started gently pulling Bethany away. Eventually, she followed him, glancing anxiously over her shoulder. The momentary pause in her confrontation with Lily had given Avril a chance to calm down a fraction, and when she looked at Lily's distraught face she felt a stab of sympathy, quickly followed by guilt for her own harsh words.

'I know you're upset, Lily,' she said, in what she hoped was a more conciliatory tone. 'And I'm sorry. But accusing my daughter in the street like this isn't fair. She's just a child, and an innocent one at that. Why don't we go home and talk about this properly, okay?'

'Poppy had marks on her arm.'

Avril froze. 'Excuse me?'

'Just like that girl that Bethany hurt.'

'How do you know about that?'

'I know everything.' Lily was fighting back tears. 'My friend is the admissions manager at Weston Abbey. She told me that she'd been following up with Bethany's old school for a reference. The headteacher said there was an incident and she managed to persuade him to tell her exactly what happened.'

Avril was appalled. 'He shouldn't have done that. That's not fair, and your friend shouldn't have told you, that's a complete breach of privacy...'

'Oh, fuck privacy, Avril. My daughter is missing, for God's sake. Surely that's more important than protecting your psychotic child?'

'Shut up.' Avril was biting back tears as her anger returned, mingling with shame. All around her she could see people watching, whispering, judging. 'Take that back.'

'I've told the police and they'll be knocking on your door any minute now.'

'Lily, how could you...'

'What the hell is going on here?' Sandy appeared, breathless, and stood between them, placing a hand on each of their chests. 'Lily? Avril?'

'Ask Avril and her sick daughter what she's done to Poppy,' Lily spat.

'What are you talking about, Lily? Bethany hasn't done anything to Poppy.'

'Oh, of course you'd stick up for her, your little protégée.'

'Enough!' Sandy said it with such force that she even managed to silence Lily. 'We haven't got time for this. I've got something important to tell you.'

'What is it?' Lily demanded, still glaring at Avril.

Sandy took her hands off their chests. 'I think I know what happened to Poppy.'

The minute she had stepped inside the pool complex, with its pungent smell of chlorine, Sandy felt like she'd gone back in time. She'd looked down and half expected to see a pram, with Isla inside, wriggling and fussing. If only all she had to worry about was a crying baby.

Poppy's disappearance consolidated the theory she'd been building in her mind for months. At first, she'd wondered if Grant was somehow involved, but she'd quickly dismissed it. He was a violent partner, but she didn't think he'd abduct a random teenage girl. No, she felt that the person involved in Poppy's disappearance was much closer to home.

But she had to know for sure first. She didn't want to accuse Steve until she had more proof. All she had on him was that he had spent a short amount of time with Poppy and had once given her and Isla a swimming lesson. It wasn't enough, she needed more.

She smiled at the girl on reception. 'Hi there, I'd like to enquire about swimming lessons. Would it be possible to speak to the manager?'

The girl picked up the phone and spoke a few words before hanging up. 'She'll be down in a few minutes.'

While she waited, Sandy peered through the glass windows at the pool. There was a toddler session going on and mums and dads were lifting their little ones out of the water and gently dipping them back in again. The children were squealing and laughing with delight. It seemed like only yesterday that Isla was that old, but forever since Micky was a toddler.

Maybe it was the oppressive heat inside the pool complex, the purpose of her visit, or her state of high alert, but she suddenly felt like she was floating above her body and looking down at her life. If someone had told her when Micky was a baby that she would escape, that she would learn to love and trust again and even have another child, she wouldn't have believed them. And yet here she was. And although she was terrified for Poppy, and although the circumstances of her being here were truly awful, in that moment she felt emancipated. *Screw you, Grant*, she thought. *You can try, but you can't hurt me any more.*

'Can I help you?'

A woman was approaching with an impatient look on her face, as though she was outraged at being disturbed. This was not a good start. Sandy extended a hand and smiled brightly. 'Hi there, I'm terribly sorry to bother you. I wonder, can we talk in private?'

The woman looked suspicious. 'What about?'

'I'll explain everything, I promise.' Sandy looked pointedly at the receptionist.

'Follow me.'

The woman led them into a small office. Sitting down, Sandy began her rehearsed speech. 'I used to come here with my daughter, a few years ago. There was a man who taught here, his name was Steve, and I wondered if you had any more information about him?'

'Why do you want to know?'

'I live over at Westford Park.' The manager raised her eyebrows at this. 'And I'm organising swimming lessons for some of the children. Steve has applied and I just want to make sure that he's, you know, okay, before I hire him.'

The woman barely stifled a yawn. 'So email me for a reference.'

'Yes, I could do that,' Sandy admitted, 'but I was passing and I just thought it might be easier to pop in.'

The woman sighed and turned to her computer. 'What's his surname?'

Sandy grimaced. 'I can't remember.'

If the woman was wary of Sandy before, she was deeply suspicious now. 'You want a reference, but you don't even know what his surname is?'

'I'm so sorry, my head's all over the place. My daughter's not well, you see, and it's quite serious.' Sandy loathed herself for lying, but she had to find a way to get the information she needed. She pulled out her driver's licence. 'Here's my ID, and as you can see my address is Westford Park. I'm organising all this on a voluntary basis, so I don't have the correct systems in place and I've seen so many CVs, they've all blurred into one. My daughter loves swimming and I just want to give her something to look forward to.'

The woman softened. 'I'm sorry to hear that.'

Sandy smiled gratefully, hating herself even more.

'When did you say he worked here?'

'Just over four years ago.'

The woman started tapping on her keyboard and peered at the screen. 'Yes, here he is. Steve Bradfield. He worked here for a few months, but it was before my time.'

Sandy groaned. This visit was proving to be a complete waste of time. 'Do you have any instructors who worked here at that time and might remember him? I just want a quick chat, nothing formal. Like I said, this is all voluntary.'

'Rita's been here for donkey's years. She's on the poolside, you could ask her.'

With a rush of anticipation, Sandy stood up. 'Wonderful, thank you for your help.'

She made her way through the changing rooms to the poolside, looking around until she saw a woman in her fifties standing by the side. Hedging her bets, she ambled over to her.

'Rita?'

'Who's asking?'

Sandy introduced herself and began her spiel again. Rita's face immediately changed when she mentioned Steve and Sandy had to hide her eagerness. 'So, you remember him?'

'Hard not to, love, after what happened.'

Sandy's heart began to pound. 'What happened?'

Rita narrowed her eyes. 'What is this? Am I on record?'

'No, nothing like that,' Sandy reassured her. 'This is all very informal and no one will ever know that we've spoken, I promise.'

'Well, I certainly wouldn't hire him to work with children, I'll tell you that for one.'

Sandy could no longer conceal her impatience. 'Why?'

Rita looked around and then leaned in conspiratorially. 'He took up with some young lass who was training to be a swimming instructor. The shame of it, he was twice her age. When the manager found out, he was fired and we never heard from him again.'

Sandy listened, wide-eyed, as the pieces of the puzzle finally fell into place. The fact that Steve always seemed to be hanging around near the teenagers, Bethany's confession that Poppy was spending time with him. Had Steve been grooming Poppy all this time?

'This girl, how old was she?' she asked Rita.

'Seventeen. A sweet little lass, she was. I often wondered what became of her. I told people there was something off about Steve, but no one listened to me until it was too late.'

'Did Steve try to defend his actions at the time?'

'No idea, love. We never spoke to him about it. One day he was here and the next he was gone. I just hope he never gets another teaching job.'

But he had done, teaching kayaking at Westford Park, and Sandy needed to get back immediately. She had been right all along. Steve wasn't an innocent man, he was a predator, and if he had anything to do with Poppy's disappearance, Sandy would never forgive herself.

'Do you remember what this girl's name was, by any chance?'

'Kerry something.'

'Thank you, Rita, you've been very helpful. I'll leave you to it now.'

She almost ran out of the swimming pool, throwing herself into her car and fumbling in her bag for the card that the police officers had given her when they questioned Micky. She dialled immediately, explaining to the officer on the phone what she had just discovered and then started the car engine. It was time to tell Lily everything, even if her friend would never forgive her for keeping quiet for so long. She just hoped that she wasn't too late.

* * *

'So, let me get this straight. You knew Steve was a creep and you knew he was sniffing around Poppy and you didn't think it was important to tell me?'

They were sitting in Lily's living room. Sandy had persuaded Lily to continue the conversation at home, away from the curious gazes of the other residents, and Eric was hovering behind the sofa, listening to the conversation intently.

'I didn't know anything about him,' she said truthfully. 'Just that I recognised him from somewhere. I had no reason to suspect him, other than my own paranoia, and Bethany was convinced there was nothing going on between him and Poppy.'

'Where is Bethany?' Lily said. 'I want to speak to her right now.'

'I'm not sure that's a good idea. Not after what just happened.'

Lily's face crumpled. 'I was just so angry,' she said. 'When I heard what Bethany had done to that other girl, I couldn't help myself.'

'It's not true, Lily.'

'But how can you be so sure?'

'Because I know Bethany. And we both know Avril. I'm certain she has nothing to do with what's happened to Poppy.'

Lily's face switched in an instant. 'Of course you're sure because you knew who was responsible all along. And if you'd told me about this when you should have done, none of this would have happened. Poppy would still be here, safe and well. Get out of my house.'

'Lily, I...'

'Get out of my house!' she screamed.

Sandy stood up, her legs shaking. She understood what Lily was going through and she didn't blame her for being angry, but she still felt the full force of her friend's rage which was now aimed directly at her. It filled her with guilt, remorse and fear. She should have trusted her gut all those months ago and not left it too late.

But she clung on to the fact that there was still no evidence Poppy was hurt. If she'd run off with Steve, then maybe she was safe. Perhaps he genuinely thought he was in love with her. It was wrong, but it meant that Poppy could be found and brought home

All she wanted was for Lily to feel the relief she had felt when the police brought Micky home.

Eric followed her out. 'She's very upset,' he began.

'You don't need to explain. I understand.'

He nodded sadly and closed the door, leaving Sandy on the doorstep, evicted from the place she had come to think of as a second home. She wanted to force her way back inside to Lily, to hold her and to comfort her, but she was the last person that Lily wanted to see and it broke her heart. She glanced across at Avril's house and felt a strong urge to see her.

Avril answered the door with red-rimmed eyes and ushered her into the living room. Bethany was sitting on the sofa, her slim legs tucked underneath her, nibbling her nails.

'How are you, Bethany?' Sandy asked.

Bethany shrugged and Sandy immediately saw it in the teenager's eyes. The defensive wall that had surrounded Bethany from the world when she first arrived was starting to come up again. And if they didn't break it down, Bethany would retreat back into herself.

'Lily didn't mean what she said, Bethany.'

'She bloody did,' Avril interjected, her voice quivering.

'She's upset and she's scared. She hasn't slept for days. She's not thinking straight.'

Bethany looked up, her grey eyes boring into Sandy's soul.

'I know that you would never do anything to hurt Poppy and Lily knows that too. Anyway, we know what's happened to Poppy and I hope the police will find her soon.'

Bethany's eyes darted between her mother and Sandy, as Avril said, 'What do you mean?'

'She's with Steve. I think she's been with him all along.'

Sandy explained what she'd learned at the pool about Steve's history of running off with younger girls, choosing her words carefully in the presence of Bethany. But Avril understood exactly what

she was implying and, it appeared, so did Bethany. The more
Sandy spoke, the more distressed and fidgety the teenager became,
until finally she couldn't stay quiet any longer.

'No. You've got this completely wrong.'

'Bethany, I know this is hard to understand,' Avril began gently.

'It's not hard to understand, and I'm telling you, you're wrong
about Steve.'

Sandy looked at Bethany's young, innocent face. He'd pulled
the wool over her eyes too, perhaps even made her keep his secret.
He'd given them free rein of the boathouse, maybe plied them with
food, or alcohol, and gained their trust so that they would be loyal
to him. Sometimes it was easy to forget how naive they were, how
much they still had to learn about life.

Avril took Bethany's hand. 'They'll find him, love. They'll find
Poppy.'

'No!' Bethany was furious. 'No, this is completely wrong.'

Sandy and Avril looked at each other, frowning. Something
about Bethany's vehemence, her refusal to accept this version of
events, had placed doubt in both their minds.

'Bethany,' Avril began cautiously. 'If you know something, you
must tell us.'

'I know that Steve has nothing to do with this.'

'What makes you so sure?'

Bethany looked away. 'He's not interested in Poppy.'

Avril smiled sadly. 'Sometimes people aren't what they seem,
darling.'

'I know that, Mum, I'm not stupid!'

'Did you not think it was strange that he was hanging about
with you guys? You're so much younger than him.'

'But he likes hanging out with younger people.'

Her words hit Sandy hard. Here it was, the irrefutable proof
that Steve was the culprit in Poppy's disappearance. And they'd let

him get away with it for months. She had let him get away with it. Lily would never forgive her, and she wasn't sure she'd forgive herself either.

'Just ask Kerry.'

Sandy's heart stopped and she looked hard at Bethany. 'What did you just say?'

'Ask Kerry.'

Avril was confused. 'Who's Kerry?'

'His girlfriend.'

A deeply unsettling feeling began to develop inside Sandy. 'How do you know Kerry?'

'She works in the kitchen at the clubhouse. She's nice.'

Avril's eyes were moving from Sandy's to Bethany's. 'And you say she's his girlfriend?'

'Yeah, they've been together for years. They're engaged.'

The world was spinning, making Sandy nauseous. Pieces of the puzzle were being ripped apart and re-forming again, completely changing her perception of the situation.

'Do you know where Steve is right now, Bethany?'

The teenager shrugged. 'I think they said they were going to stay with Kerry's family for a few days. Her mum's not well and Steve's really good with her, apparently.'

Sandy sunk down onto the sofa. She thought of Steve again, the monstrous image of him she'd formed in her head morphing once more. The idea of a man in his thirties getting together with a seventeen-year-old girl didn't sit well with her at all. But if Bethany was right and the two of them were still together and getting married, then perhaps they really had fallen in love. It happened sometimes, even if it was unconventional. It didn't necessarily make him a predator, which was exactly what she'd just accused him of being.

Had she got this wrong? Had she let her own paranoia, her

suspicion of men, cloud her judgement? Somewhere along the way the lines between her own life, her own fears, had become intertwined with the rest of the world, making her suspicious of everyone.

'But, Bethany,' she said, still struggling to accept the new version of events, 'why was Steve spending time alone with Poppy if he wasn't interested in her romantically?'

Bethany visibly withdrew into herself, her long hair covering her eyes as she looked down at her hands, her nails blunt and bitten.

'Bethany.' Avril's voice was firm.

'Please, Mum.'

'No, I'm sorry, Bethany. You need to tell us the truth.'

Bethany picked at a nail. 'He was showing her how to navigate the woods.'

'*Navigate* them?'

Bethany nodded, still refusing to meet their eyes. 'Where all the secret paths are. The best places to hang out. And where you can get in and out without being detected.'

'What?' Avril's face turned ashen. 'Did Poppy use it?'

Bethany hesitated. 'Once or twice but she never went far.'

'Did you or Micky use it?'

This time Bethany looked up. 'No. Never.'

'Does anyone else know about this?'

'I don't know.'

Avril was pacing the room. 'Why the hell didn't you tell us this earlier?'

'I'm sorry. I didn't want to get Poppy into trouble.'

'Do you know where she is, Bethany?'

'No.'

'Has she run away?'

'No.'

'Bethany, if you know *anything...*'

'I don't know anything else, I promise.'

Sandy put her head in her hands. 'I need to call the police again.'

The world was still spinning, and Sandy didn't know how to make it stop. This revelation opened the possibility that Poppy had left of her own accord. Perhaps she was with schoolfriends right now, scoffing popcorn and watching a film, blissfully unaware of the drama she had caused at home. But as much as Sandy wanted that version of events to be true, she knew it wasn't possible. The police had contacted all of her friends and no one had heard from her. Anyway, Poppy had never missed curfew and she wouldn't disappear for so long without telling anyone. Bethany was convinced that she hadn't run away. And, apart from foolishly and irresponsibly showing a teenage girl how to sneak out, she now had to accept that Steve probably had nothing to do with this either.

There was something though, something which chilled her to the bone. If Poppy had found a way out then it meant that someone, anyone, might have found a way in. It also meant that the search for Poppy was no longer contained to Westford Park. She could be anywhere by now. And that threw this investigation wide open in ways she didn't even dare to think about.

28

Lily hadn't slept for days. She was fuelled by adrenaline and fear, both of which were gripping her mind and body in a permanent state of terror. She had experienced purgatory in the hospital waiting room after Poppy fell into the lake, but now she was in hell.

She watched out of the window as a police car pulled up and two officers climbed out. One was the family liaison officer they'd been assigned. Her name was Karen and she was lovely. But Lily hated her because she knew that it was this woman who would deliver the news that she feared more than any other, and every time she saw Karen walking up the driveway, she wondered if the moment had finally come.

She heard Eric opening the door and greeting the officers. She didn't move from the window because she didn't want to see Karen and she didn't want to speak to her. Until that woman came back with Poppy walking beside her, the news would not be good. But already her heart was pounding, her pulse racing, her body shaking.

She didn't turn when the officers walked into the room.

'Lily?' Karen said in that soft, lilting voice that she had perfected over years of comforting distraught families.

'What is it?' Lily replied, sharper than she had intended.

'We've found the exit point Bethany told us about. We also found something else.'

Lily forced herself to face the officers and it was only then that she noticed that Karen was holding something she recognised immediately.

'It's her bag,' she confirmed, her terror rising again.

Karen reached in and pulled out a phone. 'Is it Poppy's?'

Lily looked at the phone, shaking. 'Yes.'

'Thank you for confirming that, Lily. Shall we sit down?'

'I don't want to sit down.'

'I understand. Lily, I'm sorry to ask you again. Is it possible that Poppy has run away?'

Why did everyone keep asking her? Why would Poppy run away? She came from a good home, she had plenty of friends, she had parents who loved her. She had no reason to run away. No reason at all.

'No,' she growled. 'No, she hasn't run away. You're wasting time. Just go and find the person who has taken my daughter from me before it's too late.'

'I know this is difficult,' Karen said. 'But if there's anything you haven't told us, even if you think it's really small and insignificant...'

'She hasn't run away.' Lily was shouting now. 'Why does no one believe me?'

'Okay,' Karen said in a soothing tone. 'Would you like me to make you a cup of tea, Lily?'

'No, I don't want a fucking cup of tea, I want my daughter!' Lily looked at Karen's kind face and felt immediately guilty. 'I'm sorry.'

'No need to apologise, Lily.'

Eric was asking questions. Had they checked the CCTV in the local area? Had Poppy's bank card been used? Had they interviewed Steve? Were they pursuing Bethany for withholding information? Had they spoken to Bethany's old school? His manner was business-like, not devoid of emotion, but contained. She knew it was his coping mechanism, just as hers was to rant and rave. But she still loathed him for it.

She loathed everyone. Karen. Eric. Bethany. Avril. Sandy. But most of all she loathed herself. Because this was her fault. She could blame everyone else around her, but she was Poppy's mother. It was her job to protect her daughter and she had failed. It was what everyone was thinking, all the officers who came and went, and made her cups of tea. Underneath their kindness and professionalism, they were thinking, *What kind of a mother are you?*

Everyone was talking about them. Poppy's disappearance was all over the local press and they'd started getting calls from national newspapers too. Someone, perhaps a friend from Poppy's school, had started a social media campaign to find Poppy. Lily, who never went on social media, had created accounts so she could scroll obsessively, searching for the #findpoppy hashtag, devouring the comments. But it made her feel worse, especially when she read the vile messages from trolls. It sickened her and yet she couldn't stop reading.

Karen had asked her and Eric to do a televised press conference, appealing to the public for information. She did not want to go on television. She did not want to cry in front of millions of people and beg strangers to help find her daughter. She did not want everyone to know that she was the mother who had lost her child.

But she had agreed to it because it might help find Poppy. Let the world watch and judge. It didn't matter what people thought any more; she didn't care as long as they found Poppy.

She tried to tune in to what Karen was telling Eric. Steve was in the clear. They had tracked him down at his girlfriend's parents' house, fifty miles away, where he had been for four days. Bethany, it seemed, was not under investigation either.

Everything had been thrown wide open since Bethany's revelations. It had changed the whole investigation and Lily couldn't help feeling that people's opinion of Poppy had changed too. The narrative had adjusted, the storyline now about a wayward teenage girl who had run away. And Lily hated that more than anything. Because her daughter was the innocent victim here and yet she increasingly felt like the only person who believed it.

Anyway, if Poppy had snuck out, where would she have gone? They lived in the middle of nowhere, so it wasn't like she could sneak off to a pub or club. Unless someone had given her a lift. There were plenty of men who would happily pick up a beautiful, young girl and drive her wherever she wanted to go. But then why would she have left her bag behind, and her phone too? Poppy would never do that. But she could have dropped it, if she was being dragged away.

Lily rushed towards the kitchen, just making it to the sink in time before she threw up.

Eric hurried in after her.

'Lily, are you okay?' he asked, rubbing her back.

But she didn't want him to touch her. She couldn't bear the feeling of his hands on her. She pushed him away, wiping her mouth and going to the fridge to get some cold water.

Yes. This was hell. And the more time that passed, the more she felt that she would be trapped there forever, alone, afraid and bleeding. For all of eternity.

* * *

Later that morning she lay on the bed, listening to the sound of a helicopter flying over the house. She needed to get up, to do her hair and make-up for the press conference, but she had finally succumbed to exhaustion and her limbs were heavy, weighing her down.

She looked up at the ceiling and imagined sitting in front of a room of journalists, reading out the script that the police press officer had drafted for her. She had watched press conferences before and clucked sympathetically at the people making desperate pleas for information about their loved ones. And then she had turned the television off and gone about her day, as though nothing had happened because those people were so far removed from her life and her world. Now she felt guilty for not caring enough. She had been living in a blissful state of ignorance and denial, immune to life's cruelties, certain that tragedy wouldn't touch her family. But it had reached out now, wrapping its tentacles around her.

She heard a car pulling up and immediately her energy returned. She leaped off the bed and ran to the window in time to watch Karen emerge. For a brief, glorious second, she imagined Poppy appearing behind her. But Karen was alone and so the heavy blanket of despair settled over Lily again. She walked heavily as she went downstairs to open the door.

'Any news?' she asked.

'Let's go and sit down.' Karen's words gave nothing – and everything – away.

'Tell me,' Lily urged. 'Tell me now.'

Karen gently guided Lily into the living room. 'Is Eric here?'

'He's gone for a walk, he'll be back soon.'

'Shall we wait?'

'No. Tell me.'

Karen nodded. 'Forensic officers have found traces of blood in the woods.'

No. *No.* Lily's hand shot to her mouth. This couldn't be happening. 'Is it Poppy's?'

'We don't know yet. I'll let you know as soon as we do. Lily, we also found a knife.'

'Oh, Jesus.'

Lily leaned forward, clutching her stomach, as if she had been punched in the gut. She could no longer pretend that Poppy was going to walk through the door any moment now. The nightmare was only getting worse, and she didn't know how much more she could take.

'Oh, Jesus,' she said again, rocking back and forth.

Karen rushed over to put an arm around her. 'We're checking it for fingerprints as we speak. We're doing everything we can to find out who is behind this.'

The narrative had changed again. Lily knew it from Karen's words and the grave expression on her face. The police no longer believed that Poppy had run away. But as bile rose in her throat again, she didn't feel victorious, she wished that she had been wrong. If Poppy had run away, and if it was all Lily's fault, she'd hold her hands up and accept full responsibility. She'd tell the world she was a terrible parent. She'd do whatever it took.

But it was out of her control. She was helpless and it was unbearable. When the doorbell rang, she made no move to answer it because her hope was fading, darkness dragging her under. It would not be Poppy at the door so what was the point in going to it?

After a few moments' silence, Karen stood up to answer it and Lily heard her exchange quiet words with someone before closing the door softly and returning to the living room.

'It was your friend, Sandy,' she said. 'She just popped by to see how you are.'

Friend. Sandy was not a friend. Nor was Avril. For a while, Lily had thought they were the closest friends she'd ever had but it was all a lie, a façade to hide the truth. Because in the end, they had both lied to her. She had lied to them too but that was different. She had lied about her marriage and that hadn't put anyone in danger. Sandy and Avril's lies had harmed Poppy.

But they haven't harmed her. The voice of reasoning echoed around her head. Steve had nothing to do with Poppy's disappearance, so Sandy was not responsible. And Bethany? Everyone kept telling her that Bethany was innocent, that she would never hurt anyone. But what about this knife? Bethany had a history of hurting people with a knife.

'You need to speak to Bethany again,' she said.

'We will,' Karen reassured her.

'What about this Grant? Have you found him?'

'He's overseas, Lily. He's due back today, according to his employer.'

'Could it be activists? The same people who caused all the trouble a few months ago?'

'We're looking at every angle, Lily.'

Lily knew she was clutching at straws, trying to find an anchor to stop her from drifting further away into the depths of hell. Because already her mindset was shifting, against all her wishes and desires. Her brain was speeding ahead even though she was trying to slam on the brakes. It was shouting, screaming to be heard over the noise. *She's dead.*

'We need to leave for the press conference in an hour,' Karen said softly.

'I'll go and get dressed.'

Lily went into the bathroom and switched the shower on.

turning the water up so hot that it almost burned her. She wanted to feel pain. She made herself go through the motions, washing her hair and shaving her legs, as though she was getting ready for a pleasant lunch date, while hot steam gathered around her and forced itself down her airways.

And suddenly she couldn't take it any more. She slid down the wall, sinking onto the floor and she cried; loud, distraught wails. And even when Eric rushed in and turned off the shower, even when he wrapped her in a towel and gently helped her to stand up, she didn't stop.

'I can't do it,' she said, her voice thick with tears. 'I can't do the press conference.'

'I'll do it,' he said. 'You just need to sit there. I'll do all the talking.'

'I can't do it.'

'Lily,' he said, and his voice was firm. 'We must do it. For Poppy.'

'Is it our fault? Is it my fault?'

'No. It's not your fault, it's someone else's and we won't rest until they are caught and punished. I'll do whatever it takes, I'll pay for the best lawyers...'

And that's when she finally realised the truth of it. Her soul had been exposed by Poppy's disappearance, the layers of self-protection she had gathered over the years stripped away. She didn't love Eric. She didn't even like him. In fact, he made her sick. For years she had told herself that Eric was a good man, a kind man, and that was what mattered.

But Eric was not a good man.

'Why do you do it, Eric?'

'Why do I do what, honey?' Eric was stroking her back soothingly.

'You know what I'm talking about.'

The stroking stopped, his hand stiffened. 'No, I don't.'

'Is it an addiction? Or am I just not enough for you? Am I too boring?'

He removed his hand from her back. 'You're tired, you're upset.'

'You think I don't know? I've always known.'

'Lily, it's the grief, you don't know what you're saying.'

'I know exactly what I'm saying.'

He looked like he was going to argue, but then his face crumpled and she knew that he wouldn't deny it. He, too, was exhausted. He was too vulnerable to keep up the pretence any longer. Perhaps it was a relief to finally admit it. 'How did you know?'

'I suspected for a long time. And then a few years ago I hired a private detective.'

'Why didn't you say anything?'

She sobbed, half laugh, half cry. 'I don't know. I didn't want to break up our family. I didn't want to give up the pretence that our marriage was perfect.'

'It *is* perfect, Lily.'

'Oh, come off it, Eric,' she scoffed, her temper flaring, and it felt good. 'You know that's not true, and I know it too. I guess that's why I hired the private detective. I used him again recently when your business trips increased again. I think I knew, deep down, that I might need proof at some point in the future. Once Poppy had left home and it was just the two of us, I wasn't sure I'd be able to pretend any more. I didn't think you'd admit it so easily.'

'You should have talked to me, Lily. I can't believe you hired someone to follow me.'

'Oh, I'm the one who's in the wrong here, am I?'

'What I do...' He looked away, embarrassed. 'It's not love. It's physical. It means nothing. I always come home to you and Poppy; you two are what's important to me.'

'Can you hear yourself, Eric? Can you hear what you're saying?'

'You have to believe me, it means nothing.'

'So that makes it okay, does it?'

'No.' He looked away. 'I'll stop. I'll never do it again.'

'I don't believe you.'

'I promise.'

But Eric's promises were empty and meaningless. Because she didn't love him and she didn't want to hear it. He would never touch her again, she decided then.

'I'll stay,' she said quietly. 'I'll stay for Poppy. Because when she comes home, she'll need her mum and dad more than ever. But that's it, that's all there will ever be between us.'

'I'll stop,' he said again, quietly.

'No, you won't. You can't. It's not a one-off, Eric, it's not a midlife crisis, it's an obsession. I'll keep your secret but I'm not doing it for you, I'm doing it for Poppy.'

'Lily, please.'

She stood up, oddly calm now. 'I need to finish getting ready.'

'Can we talk about this later?'

'There's nothing left to say.' She turned her back to him.

She could feel him lingering as she went to the wardrobe to fetch her clothes. She could smell him, but his scent no longer aroused her, it disgusted her. She closed her eyes for a few seconds, steadying herself, and then she opened them again and pulled out a dress. She understood what she had to do now. She had to get dressed, put her make-up on, dry her hair and go to the press conference. She would be okay, she realised, she would get through it because all she had to do was play a role and she could do that well enough.

She'd been doing it for almost her entire life.

29

'Tom, have you seen Bethany?'

Tom was on the sofa, watching TV. 'She went out for a walk with Micky. She left you a note on the kitchen counter.'

'Thanks, love.'

At first, Avril was pleased that Bethany had gone out. She had barely left the house since Poppy disappeared, and she needed some normality back in her life. But then another thought came rushing to her. A teenage girl was missing, possibly snatched from the development, and Bethany was out in the grounds without an adult.

She turned back to Tom. 'Do you know where they went?'

'The usual place, probably.'

'The boathouse?'

Still not looking up from the screen, Tom said, 'No, the other one.'

'What other one, Tom?'

Tom's eyes widened as he realised he'd said the wrong thing and was trying to work out how to take it back.

'What other place, Tom?' Avril demanded.

Her son looked as guilty as hell.

'Tom!' Avril shouted, making him flinch.

He looked up, a hangdog expression on his face. 'They made me promise.'

Adrenaline started to course through Avril's body. 'Who made you promise? Bethany?'

Tom nodded, his mouth downturned.

'Tom, this is really, really important. You have to tell me where it is.'

'I don't want to get into trouble.'

Tom was thirteen now but, in that moment, he looked like a little boy again. And Avril was so desperate to make him talk that she decided to play a cruel hand. 'If you don't tell me, you'll be in huge trouble with the police.'

This had the desired effect. Tom looked at her, panicked, and the words came rushing out. 'They made a den in the woods. They have a fire and benches made of logs and stuff.'

'How do you know about this?'

'They took me once. They made me promise not to tell.'

'This den, where in the woods is it?'

He scrunched up his nose. 'I can't describe it, exactly.'

'Can you take me there, Tom?' When Tom squirmed uncomfortably, she added, 'I promise you won't get into trouble.'

'Fine.' He stood up. 'Okay.'

'Let's go. We'll pick Sandy up on the way.'

Avril found her bag and darted out of the door, with Tom following reluctantly behind her, and called Sandy as she walked, explaining what she'd learned.

'I'll meet you in five minutes,' Sandy said.

They met at the top of the lake path. Avril's mind was frantic. Could Poppy be at the hideout? But the police had combed the woods, they would have found her by now if she was there. So, what was it that was compelling her to go? She had an inkling, something was telling her that this was important, she just didn't know why yet.

The summer sun was strong, and beads of perspiration began to form on Avril's temples, despite the shade of the trees. Tom had his shoulders hunched as he ambled along in his shorts and T-shirt, his long, lanky legs making the walk look easy.

Finally, after twenty minutes, he pointed into the distance. 'It's there,' he said.

Avril looked and saw a mass of trees ahead. They were deep in the woods, in a place that no one was likely to find except for a police search party or an enthusiastic dog walker.

'Thank you, Tom. Why don't you go home now? I'll see you back at the house.'

Tom didn't need telling twice. He turned and left before she'd even said goodbye.

Avril looked at Sandy and put her finger to her lips. Sandy nodded and slowly they began to creep towards the trees. Avril peered in through a gap and saw the den. It was made of sticks and shaped like a tepee. Under different circumstances, she would have been impressed with the teenagers' construction skills. She took in the area around it and saw the pile of twigs which must be the fireplace that Tom had told her about. Fallen logs had been placed around it to make a seating area and she noticed some discarded crisp packets.

She started when she heard a twig snap and Bethany and Micky emerged from the den and sat down side by side on one of the fallen logs. Avril moved behind the nearest tree, not sure why she wanted to stay hidden. On the other side, Sandy did the same.

The two teenagers were talking quietly, and Avril strained to listen.

'I can't do it any more,' she heard Bethany say.

'You have to,' Micky replied.

'It's too hard, Micky.'

'It's not for much longer.'

'We should never have done this. It was a mistake.'

Avril risked peeping around the tree and saw Micky pick up a stick and start prodding the ground with it. 'It's too late to turn back now.'

'I feel sick.'

Micky was drawing something in the ground, but Avril couldn't see what it was. When he spoke again, his voice was clearer. 'Remember the pact.'

Bethany stared at the ground and then looked away. 'I remember.'

Desperate to hear every word, Avril leaned forward and lost her balance. She cried out as she tripped on a tree root, and instantly the teenagers' heads shot up.

'Come on,' Sandy said. 'They know someone's here.'

Sandy stormed through the clearing and Avril followed, trying to decipher what she had just heard. What was this pact and what did it have to do with Poppy going missing? And was Bethany still lying to her even when she had promised to be honest from now on?

'What's going on?' Sandy demanded.

'Nothing,' Bethany and Micky said in unison.

But Sandy was in no mood for games. 'Enough,' she said in a harsh voice. 'Your friend is missing. Everyone is beside themselves. If you know something, tell us now. I mean it.'

Bethany and Micky exchanged a look. They seemed to be communicating silently, almost an entire conversation happening between them, unspoken.

Finally, Micky said, 'We haven't done anything to Poppy, if that's what you think.'

'I don't think that,' Sandy said. 'But you know something.'

Micky nodded, looking at the ground.

Avril glared at Bethany. 'You know what the right thing to do is. You *know* it.'

Bethany's eyes filled with tears. 'I don't know where she is, she's not answering her phone.'

'She doesn't have her phone.'

Wordlessly, Bethany put her hand into her bag and pulled out her own phone. Scrolling through a list of numbers, she passed it to Avril.

'What's this?' Avril asked, looking down at the screen.

'Poppy's number.'

'But they found her phone in the woods.'

'Not that one. The other one.'

Avril's jumbled thoughts were beginning to take shape, a picture becoming clearer. Bethany and Micky were covering for Poppy. That was the pact they had been talking about. It was a promise that they had made to Poppy to keep her secret. Because what Avril was now beginning to suspect, with immense relief, was that Poppy had left of her own accord. The question now was why? And where the hell was she? There was only one person who could answer that question. Avril looked down at the number on the screen and pressed dial.

There was no answer, but Avril wasn't giving up. She immediately pressed redial, then again and again. On the sixth attempt, Poppy answered, sounding annoyed.

'What is it, Bethany?'

'Poppy, it's Avril.'

There was silence on the other end of the line and Avril feared that Poppy would hang up. Quickly, she said, 'Poppy, darling, you're not in any trouble but your mum and dad are so worried about you. They don't know where you are. You need to let them know you're okay.'

More silence. Avril tried again. 'Poppy, the police are looking for you. Your parents are about to go on television and give a press conference.'

'Tell them not to do that.'

Avril closed her eyes, reassured by the familiar sound of Poppy's confident and slightly petulant voice. 'They will do it, Poppy, unless you call them and tell them you're okay.'

'I'm fine. Just tell them I'm fine. I'm perfectly safe. No need to stress.'

'I'll do that Poppy, I will, but they need to hear it from you. Where are you, darling?'

The phone clicked as Poppy hung up. Avril dialled the number again but it went to voicemail. This time, Poppy had clearly turned it off.

She looked at Bethany. 'Where is she?'

'I don't know, Mum.'

'Who is she with?'

'No one.'

'Is she with a boy? It's okay to say.'

'She's not with a boy.'

'Why did she run away?'

'I don't know.'

Avril turned to Sandy, waiting for her to interrogate Micky. But instead, Sandy said, 'We need to go and tell Lily and Eric now.'

Avril looked at her and then back at Micky, who was staring at the ground.

'Come on,' Sandy urged. 'We have to go.'

Avril nodded, still clutching Bethany's phone. She turned to her daughter. 'Come home now, Bethany. And don't think for a second that this conversation is over.'

She looked down at the ground where Micky was still prodding with his stick. He'd written a word, in capital letters, in the dirt. L.I.V.E.

'What does that mean?' she demanded, pointing at the ground.

Micky hurriedly rubbed it out. 'Nothing.'

'Come *on*, Avril.' Sandy was calling to her impatiently.

Avril turned. 'Home, Bethany. Now.'

And with that she took off after Sandy, her legs carrying her as fast as they could, to deliver the news to Lily and Eric that their daughter was, thank God, safe.

* * *

Lily looked exhausted and frail when she opened the door, but her expression immediately hardened when she saw Avril and Sandy.

'I don't want to talk to you.' She began to close the door again.

'I've just spoken to Poppy,' Avril said, and Lily froze.

'What did you say?'

'I've just spoken to Poppy. She's okay.'

'Where is she?' Lily yanked the door open and looked frantically behind Avril and Sandy, as though expecting Poppy to be right behind them.

'I don't know. I spoke to her on the phone.'

'But she doesn't have her phone.'

'She has a different one, it must be a pay-as-you-go. Listen, Poppy is fine. She's okay.'

Lily seemed disorientated. 'Where is she?' she asked again.

'She wouldn't tell me, but she was fine, that's the main thing. And she told me to tell you not to do the press conference.'

'Give that to me.' Lily snatched Bethany's phone out of Avril's hand.

'It's that number,' Avril said, pointing to the screen and Lily immediately dialled it.

'It's gone to voicemail.'

'I think she switched it off after we spoke.'

'What did she say to you? Tell me everything. Eric!'

Lily was hysterical, and Avril put a calming hand on her arm. 'We've found her.'

Eric appeared behind his wife. 'What's going on?'

'They've spoken to Poppy.' Lily's voice was shaking. 'She's okay.'

'Oh, thank God.' Eric fell against the door-frame. 'Where is she?'

'We don't know,' Avril explained. 'But she said she's fine. I think she ran away.'

Avril expected Lily to deny it and to say that Poppy wouldn't do that, that it was somehow Bethany's fault, or Micky's, or Steve's.

But instead, she said, 'What about the knife? And the blood?'

Avril's eyes widened. 'What knife? What blood?'

'They found it in the woods. Forensics are examining it.'

Avril frowned, trying to work it out. 'I don't know, Lily. Maybe it's unrelated.'

Lily's body began to sag and she staggered backwards. The truth finally seemed to be sinking in. 'She's okay,' she said quietly, and then louder, 'She's okay.'

And for the first time in three days, Avril's face broke out into a smile. For a brief, glorious moment, it didn't matter that Bethany and Micky had lied to them. It didn't matter that she and Lily were barely speaking to each other, or that they still had no idea where Poppy was and what had caused her to flee. And it didn't matter that the police had found a knife in the woods. All that mattered was that Poppy was alive.

'Yes, Lily,' Avril said. 'She's okay.'

30

Sandy could still feel her own relief as though it was yesterday. The tsunami of joy that flooded her when she learned that the police had found Micky. The world coming together again. Clare had just got home from the conference, and as Sandy hurriedly filled her in on what had happened, she was almost falling over her words.

Clare was rapt. 'So where is she?'

'We don't know. But she says she's okay and Avril says she sounded fine.'

'So, she ran away? No one took her?'

'It seems that way.'

'Do we know why yet?'

'No.'

'Or when she's coming home?'

'No to that too. But the main thing is that it's over, Clare, she's okay.'

'Well, yes, it's a huge relief, but it's not over. There are a lot of questions. A child doesn't run away for no reason. Something must have happened to make her leave.'

'Teenagers run away for all sorts of reasons. Sometimes it's just a cry for attention.'

'Attention? Poppy gets enough attention for an army. I've always thought she was rather spoiled, to be honest. Not a bad kid, but you must admit, she's quite precocious.'

'Maybe she was just rebelling.'

'No, there's more to it. It could be trouble at home.'

'But she comes from the perfect home.'

'Does she, though? I mean, I have no doubt that she's very much loved. But there's something that's always bugged me about Lily and Eric. They're beautiful and they're wonderful hosts, and they gaze into each other's eyes at all the right moments. But do you ever get the feeling that they're acting?'

Sandy thought about it. 'I suppose I know what you mean.'

'It's like that film, *The Truman Show*. I sometimes wonder if it's real.'

'You think they're hiding something?'

'Occasionally, I do, yes.'

'But what?'

'I don't know. It could be as simple as cracks in their marriage. Perhaps I'm reading too much into it. Poppy could just have easily run off with a boy.'

'Bethany says there's no boy involved.'

'Well, no disrespect to Bethany, or Micky, but they both lied to us. They could have saved us all, not to mention Lily and Eric, so much anguish.'

'I know, and I'm furious too. There will be severe consequences for both of them, not to mention the possibility of police charges. But Poppy put them in a difficult position. They made some sort of pact where they promised not to tell. You know how persuasive she can be and they both adore her. Let's face it, they worship her a bit. They'd do anything for her.'

'What about the knife they found, though? How does that fit in?'

'I don't know. It could belong to hunters, sneaking in at night. There are deer in the woods and it might explain the strange noises we kept hearing. Or it might have been dropped by the same gang of youths who were responsible for the vandalism.'

'And the blood?'

'I have no idea, Clare, but I don't think it's related to Poppy.'

Clare gazed at Isla, who was watching a film on full blast, oblivious to her parents' quiet discussion. She was wearing a princess dress and was wielding a lightsaber.

'I just don't know what I'd do if it were Isla who went missing,' she whispered, before throwing her hand to her mouth. 'Oh, Sandy, I'm so sorry, I shouldn't have said that.'

'It's fine,' Sandy said. 'That all happened a long time ago.'

'But still, this whole thing must have brought back some awful memories.'

'Yes, it did. But it's also made me see how far we've come. How lucky we are. It could have been so different, Clare. If I'd stayed, I mean.'

Clare took her hand. 'You could have been so different.'

'I know.'

'You're not the same person you were back then.'

'I know that too. But it's hard to let go. I've spent years looking over my shoulder, wondering if Grant is watching us. It's habitual now. So when all these strange things kept happening I convinced myself it was him and it nearly tipped me over the edge.'

'Maybe it *was* him.'

Sandy shook her head. 'No. Lily and Avril were right all along. Vandalism isn't really his style. Nor is leaving a knife lying about in the woods. I think it was kids.'

Clare grimaced. 'That doesn't make me feel any better, to be honest.'

'I know what you mean. But at least it's nothing to do with me, or Micky. I've been a wreck these past few months and I'm sorry. I was just so afraid, Clare.'

Clare's eyes filled with tears. 'You know I'd do anything for you, right?'

'I know and I love you for it. But I want to stop running.'

'Actually, I think we should move.'

Sandy looked at her wife in shock. 'You do?'

'Yes. Westford Park was a mistake. It's too isolated, too remote. I miss the city.'

Sandy was flummoxed. 'But you said you love it here.'

'I thought I did but now I'm not sure. Too much has happened. Crime. A knife and blood in the woods. A near drowning at the lake. A missing girl. Do we really want our children growing up here? Westford Park isn't as safe as we thought it was, and let's face it, the security team is useless. And even if you don't think Grant is responsible for any of it, I still don't think we'll ever be at ease knowing that he's so close by.'

Sandy didn't know what to say. Clare had never once suggested that they move house; Sandy had always been the instigator. 'I don't understand,' she began but then she stopped. Because she *did* understand and Clare was right. Westford Park. The glossy brochure had promised a dream, but it had become a nightmare, and despite its beauty and luxury, it was also where Sandy had almost sunk to her lowest. They had moved to feel safer, but the opposite had become true, and they had never felt more in danger. City life seemed like a fairy tale compared to this. It would be so easy just to sell up and start again.

But Westford Park was also the place where Sandy had finally confronted her demons and decided that Grant could no longer scare her. Where she had made the best friends she'd ever had, even if one of them was barely speaking to her. And what about Micky and Isla? They loved it here and they were happy and settled.

'Can we take some time to think about it?' she asked. 'I don't want to rush anything. Perhaps we could wait until Micky finishes school, there's only a year left.'

'I can't watch you fall apart again, Sandy.'

'I won't,' she replied, her voice determined. 'I'm different now. I'm not afraid. Anyway, Lily and Avril need me. The fallout from all of this is going to be huge. I have to help them repair their friendship and I have to support Lily too. She's going to need it.'

'They're grown women, Sandy, they're not your responsibility.'

Sandy looked at Clare curiously. Normally she was the first one to offer help to someone in need. 'I know that, but they were there for me when I needed them. It's time for me to pay that back. They're good people, Clare.'

Clare sighed heavily. 'And what about Grant?'

'Wherever we go, and whatever we do, if he wants to find us, he will. But now it's time for me to take back control.' Sandy thought of what Bethany had said to her months ago when they were painting. 'He can't hurt me if I don't let him.'

As she said the words aloud, she realised that she meant it. Westford Park could feel safe again because it was a community where everyone looked out for each other. There could be a real future for them here. She imagined Micky graduating and going off to university. Coming home in the holidays and meeting up with Poppy and Bethany again. And Isla, swimming in the pool in the summer months. Finishing primary school and starting at the local secondary school. Maybe she could even go to Weston Abbey if they could afford it. Somewhere along the way, a bit of Lily must have rubbed off on her, she thought wryly. She pictured herself having tennis lessons with Lily and Avril, their friendship repaired, the Westford Park Ladies Club back in action. She would get some counselling to help with her obsessive checking of the windows and doors, she decided. The plans to build fencing around the development had been accelerated due to Poppy's disappearance which would help everyone feel a little safer. And Sandy had no doubt that Lily would be demanding a review of the security team and would whip them up into a frenzy of competence in no time.

She looked at Clare, waiting for her to smile and tell Sandy how proud she was. To agree that they should stay on at Westford Park after all.

But instead, she said, 'I've moved for you, Sandy. I've moved time and time again and I've never once complained. Now it's my turn.'

Sandy stared at her wife, her mouth hanging open in shock. 'I didn't realise that you felt so strongly about it.'

'I do.'

'Can we even afford it?'

Clare pulled out her phone, her face animated. 'I've found this beautiful house in Manchester. It's fully refurbished and it's still cheaper than here so the mortgage payments and stamp duty will be less. And work has an office there, so I could easily transfer. There's a fantastic primary school within walking distance and a great college for Micky.'

Manchester? Sandy could hardly believe what she was hearing. How long had Clare been thinking about this? How long had she been planning? As Clare started scrolling through photos of the house, looking at Sandy with anticipation, she tried to gather her thoughts. She didn't want to leave. She was ready to stand up to Grant, once and for all. To finally put down the roots she'd promised herself she would do time and time again. But Clare's words kept coming back to her. *I've moved time and time again and*

I've never once complained. Now it's my turn. Clare wasn't happy at Westford Park. She'd tried to be and for a while, she even had been, but the bubble had burst and there was no way to repair it.

Sandy looked at her amazing wife, the one person who had been by her side throughout everything, and she knew in the pit of her stomach what she had to do.

So, even as tears pricked at her eyes and her heart fractured, she smiled and said as enthusiastically as she could, 'Wow, Clare, that looks perfect!'

31

Lily was doing laundry. It seemed such a pointless, menial task in the grand scheme of things, but she was restless and agitated and she needed something to do. The police were trying to trace Poppy's location through her pay-as-you-go phone, but now that they knew she was safe and had seemingly left of her own accord, Lily had sensed a deacceleration in their efforts. It infuriated her because her daughter was a child and she was still missing, and until Poppy walked through that door, Lily could not even think of letting her guard down.

She oscillated between relief and fear. It was a never-ending rollercoaster. What if they were wrong? What if Poppy wasn't okay? What if she was injured and bleeding out somewhere? Or what if she was okay after all but she refused to come home?

Would she ever see her daughter again?

Lily had agonised over finding a reason for Poppy to run away. Was she too overbearing? Had she not realised that Poppy was depressed? Was Poppy in some sort of trouble? But the only person who could tell her was her daughter.

Until Poppy came home, if she came home, all Lily could do

was torment herself while she waited. And the only distraction from torment was chores. Which was why she was hanging up bras when the call finally came.

Lily looked at the unknown number on the screen and her heart stopped. She couldn't answer it quickly enough. 'Poppy?' she said, her voice urgent and shrill.

'Mum?'

Lily's entire body sagged with relief. 'Yes, darling, it's Mum. Poppy, where are you?'

'I need to talk to you.'

'Tell me where you are and I'll be there as soon as I can.'

Poppy hesitated and for a moment Lily was terrified that she had hung up. But then she said, 'Come alone. And don't tell Dad.'

'Darling, Dad is so worried about you. The police are looking for you. I...'

'Come alone or don't come at all.'

Poppy's voice was firmer now, the hint of petulance back in her tone. 'Of course, of course I won't tell anyone. Just tell me where you are.'

'The picnic area off the main road. The one near the river.'

'I know it. I'll be there in ten minutes.'

Lily grabbed her car keys and ran for the door, refusing to think about what she was doing, her deception at keeping this from Eric and the police. The only thing that mattered right now was getting her daughter back. Everything else could wait.

She reached the picnic area in seven minutes, her mind on overdrive for the entire journey as she considered possibilities. Poppy was pregnant. She'd got into a fight and hurt someone. She'd tried to hurt herself and those marks on her arm had been a cry for help. Lily skidded to a halt in the car park, leaped out and ran towards the river, looking around frantically until she saw a lone figure, hunched over a bench. Her heart exploded.

'Poppy!' she called, running towards her.

Poppy turned and looked at her and for a second her face lit up. But it was quickly replaced with something else Lily couldn't read. Fear? Caution? Anger?

Lily stopped short in front of her daughter, drinking in the sight of her. And then she threw her arms around her and breathed in the unfamiliar musty, unwashed smell.

'Thank God you're okay.'

'All right, no need to crush me to death.'

Lily released Poppy and stood back to look at her, her body pulsating with joy and her mind swimming with a million unanswered questions. She looked fine, she looked just like Poppy. Unwashed and stinky, but still Poppy. Lily reached out a hand to touch her daughter's face, still struggling to believe that this was real. Was it really over?

'Are you okay?' she asked her.

'Yes.'

'Do you want something to drink?' Lily reached into her bag and pulled out her water bottle, but Poppy waved it away.

'I'm not thirsty.'

Lily paused, still holding out the bottle, feeling uncertain. There was just too much to say and do that she didn't know where to start. But she had to tread carefully, in case any sudden movement or rash words made her daughter run again.

She sat down on the bench next to Poppy and for a while, neither of them spoke. But eventually, Lily couldn't take it any longer. 'Poppy, where have you been?'

'In an old, unused stable I found, just down the road.'

Lily gasped at the idea of her daughter sleeping rough. 'On your own?'

'Yes.'

'Why?'

'I needed a few days to myself.'

'But why, Poppy?'

'It got too much.'

'*What* did?'

Poppy refused to meet her eye. 'I'm scared to tell you.'

Poppy's voice was unusually small and afraid, and Lily was suddenly yanked back in time, to her daughter's first day at school. Poppy had stood behind Lily's legs, terrified, silently pleading with her mother not to make her go in. Unlike other children, she hadn't cried or made a scene. Her fear had been quiet, understated. And as the teacher took Poppy's hand and gently pulled her away, Lily had thought her heart was going to shatter. That was how she felt now.

'You can tell me anything, Poppy. *Anything.*'

Poppy started crying and Lily put her arm around her, holding her close. Poppy rested her head on Lily's shoulder as she sobbed, burrowing into her neck. It was the most intimate moment they'd shared in a long time.

'Whatever it is, Poppy, I can't fix it unless I know. And I want to fix it.'

'It's Dad.'

Of all the words Lily expected to hear, these were not it. She had been bracing herself for accusations of her own failings, a blow-by-blow account of how she had unwittingly ruined Poppy's life. Or perhaps a confession that Poppy had done something bad. Maybe disclosure of anxiety or depression, revelations that she'd been secretly bullied for months. For a moment Lily was bewildered and disorientated.

'Dad?'

'I hate him.'

She had heard those words from Poppy before but she hadn't attached much meaning to them. Now, though, it was different.

Now, the same words were loaded. Dread washed over Lily, as she tried to work out what Poppy was trying to tell her. What had she missed?

The tiger mum inside her started to growl again.

'What has he done?' she asked, and her voice was cold and hard.

Poppy sniffed. 'He made me promise not to say anything.'

'It doesn't matter what he made you promise.'

'You won't believe me.'

'I will believe anything you tell me.'

'It'll kill you if I tell you.'

'I can take it.'

Poppy's face crumpled. 'I don't want to be the one to tell you Mum.'

Lily was scared. Very scared. 'Tell me, Poppy. I won't be angry.'

Poppy looked away. 'I caught him with someone. Another woman.'

Lily closed her eyes. Two worlds had collided, her family life and Eric's secret one, and she was not prepared. She had never considered this possibility, in all the years that she had been living a lie. Now she feared what she was going to hear next. Because this was not a simple case of a married man having an affair. Eric's indiscretions were darker and seedier. They were sordid. And she felt sick as she imagined what her daughter might have witnessed.

'When did you see this?' she asked Poppy.

'The first time was last year, in his office. And it was horrible Mum. She was tied to his chair and he was doing things... I can't even talk about it.'

Lily almost retched. The idea that her innocent daughter had witnessed such a scene disgusted her. The fact that Eric had let happen, that he had been stupid and selfish enough to engage in that behaviour in his workplace, filled her with an uncontrollable rage. But what upset her the most were three simple words. *The first time.*

'There was another time?'

'A few weeks ago when you were at that wedding conference. I was supposed to be sleeping over at Bethany's, but I forgot my toothbrush, so I came back to get it.'

'They were in the house?'

Poppy's lip trembled. 'Yes.'

It was a red rag to a bull. All these years Lily had told herself that she could turn a blind eye to Eric's indiscretions if it didn't intrude on their family life. If he kept them out of it. However weak or pathetic that was, she had agreed to it, an unacknowledged rule of play. Because this was a game to Eric, but he had just committed an unforgivable foul.

'She was young,' Poppy said. 'And I think she was, you know, a *hooker*.'

He had brought a sex worker to their home. A young one. It was like rubbing salt in the wound, even though it didn't even surprise Lily. Eric liked them young. Not too young, never under-age, but fresh-faced and perky, like Lily had been when they first met. Lily couldn't prevent herself from ageing. She had tried. She'd bought all the expensive face creams, she'd worked out regularly, eaten healthily. She'd had Botox a few times. But it had not been enough for Eric. She had not been enough because she couldn't stay twenty-three forever.

He had never asked her to play his games, even at the start. It was like he wanted to preserve her innocence, to keep their marriage pure, and so he had taken his inclinations underground. When she first learned of his *hobby* from the private detective she had tried to entice him back to her, buying handcuffs and whips online and lying on the bed in leather gear, waiting for him to get home. She had been willing to do what it took to stop her husband from straying. She wanted to give him what he needed. But he had taken one look at her and his face had contorted with horror.

'I'm sorry,' he'd said, looking away. 'I don't want that.'

And then he had left the room, leaving Lily wondering why she was the one who felt dirty and ashamed. Why he could do it with other women but not her? She later understood that Eric needed to keep his two lives separate, so he did what he always did. He threw money at it, hiring escorts to satisfy his sexual desires. And afterwards, he took a shower and came home to his beautiful wife and child, where he could still be the perfect husband.

Except that his daughter had caught him at it. Twice. And Lily was going to kill him.

She fought back tears as she stroked Poppy's hair. 'I'm so sorry you saw that, darling.'

'The first time,' Poppy continued, 'he tried to tell me I'd got it wrong, that I was too young to understand. But I understood enough and when he finally realised that he couldn't fob me off with a bag of sweets and a Barbie doll, he begged. He said it was a mistake and that it would never happen again. He said he loved you and he didn't want to hurt you. And then he gave me a load of money to go shopping.'

'Oh, Poppy.'

'I should have told you, but I didn't know how to. I was scared.'

Lily's world was being blown apart. She had built a fortress to protect Poppy but it had been infiltrated in her own home. By her own father. And Lily had let it happen.

'After that, he was always buying me things – a new phone, a voucher to go shopping. He said it was because he loved me, but I knew what he was doing. He was buying my silence.'

'He should never have put you in that position.'

'When I caught him the second time, I couldn't even look at him. I couldn't be around him, but I didn't know how to tell you.

Every time I tried, I couldn't get the words out. And I was just sick of it, I was sick of the lies. I was sick of him. Running away felt like the only option. But after I spoke to Avril, I realised I'd made a mistake. I'm so sorry, Mum.'

'You have nothing to be sorry for, darling.'

'And please don't be angry with Bethany or Micky. I made them promise not to tell. They were just trying to protect me. It was all my doing, not theirs.'

Lily had a sudden thought. 'Do they know? About your father?'

Poppy's guilty look told Lily the answer to that. So, that was that. Soon everyone at Westford Park would know about it. But, oddly, she found that she didn't care. Screw what everyone else thought, screw the whispers and the gossip. The only thing that mattered to her now was Poppy.

'Let's get you home,' she said. 'You can have a hot shower and something to eat, and then we can talk more about this.'

'I'm not going home.'

Lily's heart broke all over again. 'Poppy, come on, you don't mean that.'

'I don't want to see him. I never want to see him again.'

'Dad loves you, darling. No matter what he does with those women, he loves you.'

Poppy's head shot up and she looked at Lily suspiciously. 'Did you know?'

'What do you mean?'

'I don't know. It's weird. You don't seem surprised. I thought you'd be in pieces.'

The only way to move forward now was to be honest with each other. Poppy had shared her secret and now it was time to reciprocate. Poppy's innocence was long gone anyway, there was no point in protecting her any more. Lily's lies had not worked and her secrecy had not shielded Poppy.

'I know,' she said. 'I've known for a long time.'

Poppy's eyes widened. 'What the hell, Mum?'

'He still loves us, Poppy.'

'And that makes it okay?'

'No.' Lily shook her head. 'No, it doesn't.'

'I can't believe this.' Poppy was getting agitated, her temper flaring. 'I can't believe you knew all about it and you let him get away with it. Why would you do that? It's disgusting.'

'Yes, it is,' Lily admitted. 'But I made a decision because I wanted to keep our family together. I wanted you to have a different life to the one I had growing up. A happy, normal one with parents who love you and money to give you opportunities I never had.'

'But it's not normal!'

Lily began to cry, guilt and regret spilling out of her. 'I know.'

Poppy stood up and began pacing around. 'I can't believe you knew,' she repeated. 'How could you be around him? How could you pretend everything was fine?'

'It got easier, over time. I perfected the art of turning a blind eye. And I told myself that one day I would confront him, one day, when you were grown up, I would leave him.'

'I hate him,' Poppy snarled. 'And I hate you too right now.'

Poppy's words stung. But Lily deserved them. She thought about her own parents, how much she had hated her father and resented her mother for doing nothing about his behaviour. She could no longer pretend that she was any better. If anything, she was worse. Because she could have left Eric, he wouldn't have stopped her. He would have begged and pleaded for her to stay, he would have hired expensive lawyers to protect his interests, but he would never have forced her, and he would have made sure that they were provided for.

'I'm going to fix this,' she told Poppy. 'Things will be different from now on.'

Her phone rang and she looked down to see it was Eric calling.

'Don't answer it,' Poppy said, staring at the screen.

'He'll be wondering where I am. He'll be worried.'

'Don't answer it, Mum.'

Lily did as she was told and let the call ring out. But her phone immediately started ringing again. She looked at Poppy. 'Do you trust me?' she asked.

Poppy met her gaze and for a moment she said nothing.

'Poppy, do you trust me?'

Poppy nodded, almost imperceptibly, and Lily answered the phone.

'Hi, Eric. I've found her. Where are you? Okay, come home and I'll meet you there.'

She hung up and turned to Poppy. 'We don't have much time, I need you to come with me now.'

'Where are we going?'

'Home.'

Poppy scowled. 'I've already said I'm not coming home.'

Lily didn't waver. 'Poppy, trust me. I'll explain everything in the car. I know what to do.'

* * *

When Eric's car pulled into the driveway, Lily was waiting outside, with a suitcase in each hand. He climbed out of the car, frowning in confusion.

'Are those Poppy's?'

'No, they're yours.'

'I don't understand.'

'You're leaving.'

Eric's face paled. 'What are you talking about?'

'You know what I'm talking about.'

Realisation dawned on Eric's face, and he leaned back against his car. 'She told you.'

'Yes, she told me.'

He began to cry now, holding his face in his hands. 'Is that why she ran away?'

'Yes. And she doesn't want to see you. Neither do I.'

'Lily, let me explain, let me talk to her.'

'No Eric, it's too late for that.'

He looked at her, his eyes pleading, but he didn't argue. He had gone too far this time and he knew it. There was nothing he could say to justify what had happened, no expensive lawyers who could prove him to be the innocent party. He was as guilty as charged.

'I'm sorry,' he said.

'I know you are. But it's not enough.'

'Can I see Poppy first?'

'She doesn't want to see you, Eric.'

'I love you both so much.'

Lily shook her head in disgust. 'All this time that Poppy was missing, you knew that she'd seen you with those women, but you didn't say anything. Why?'

He buried his head in his hands again. 'I was ashamed.'

'Good. You deserve to be ashamed. I thought she'd been kidnapped. Murdered. You should have told me, Eric, and you definitely should have told the police.'

He nodded, a broken man.

'And to think you tried to buy her silence with expensive gifts. She's a *child*, Eric.'

He had no comeback, and he knew it. He looked at her, resigned. 'I'll go.'

'I want a divorce.'

He nodded. How simple it was, two decades of marriage ended in a brief conversation on the driveway. No hysterics, no tears, at least not for now. They'd probably come later.

He fingered his keys. 'I don't want to lose Poppy.'

'Give her time. She just needs some time.'

'Can you tell her that I love her and that I'm sorry?'

'I'll tell her.'

Eric stared at the house. 'So, this is it, then?'

'This is it.'

'I never meant to hurt you. Either of you.'

'But you did.'

There was nothing left to say. Eric stepped forward as if to hug her and then stopped himself. Instead, he picked up the suitcases and put them into the boot of the car. With a final nod at Lily, he climbed back in and began to reverse out of the driveway. Lily watched him leave. Her eyes were dry, her heart, although bruised, still beating. She wondered where – or who – he would go to and felt a familiar twist of pain inside her, and then she remembered that it wasn't her problem any more. This time, she would not be waiting for him to come home.

She was shaking as she turned around and began to make her way back to the house. Her sole focus now was Poppy. She would fight every day to earn Poppy's trust again, she would do whatever it took to heal her pain and make her happy. She just hoped that it wasn't too late.

Something caught her eye, and she looked up at Poppy's bedroom window and saw her daughter watching her. They stared at each other and Lily held her breath, waiting for Poppy to cry, or scowl, or simply turn and walk away. Then, slowly, Poppy began to smile. And Lily smiled back. One shared moment between mother and daughter. A million words spoken.

She went inside and closed the door behind her.

32

Butterflies – and not the good ones – danced in Avril's stomach as she made her way nervously across the road. It had been five days since Poppy came home. The police cars were gone and so were the journalists. The newspapers had moved on to the next story. And Westford Park was back to normal again.

Well, not quite normal. Avril and Lily still weren't speaking. Bethany hadn't heard from Poppy. Steve was gone and apparently Kerry no longer worked in the kitchen. Bethany's scholarship offer to Weston Abbey had been rescinded and Avril had been furious and ready to kick up a fuss about it. Bethany, however, had taken it in her stride.

'I just need to get my A levels, Mum,' she'd said. 'Then I can go to art college. And I'm happy where I am. I've got friends, I like the art teacher. Who needs Weston Abbey?'

Her daughter's reaction showed just how far Bethany had come. She was not the same girl who had arrived a year ago, silent and mistrustful of everyone. Thankfully, although the police had given her a stern talking to about withholding information, they had not pursued the matter further, leaving the teenagers' parents to dish out an appropriate punishment.

At first, Avril had been incandescent, unable to control her fury at Bethany for lying to her about Poppy's disappearance. But Stuart had sat her down and taken her hand.

'Let's talk about it,' he'd said.

'How could she do this? How could she lie about something so serious?'

'She's a teenage girl who made a promise to her friend. She knew it was wrong, but she felt a sense of loyalty to Poppy. And she did the right thing in the end, didn't she?'

'Three days too late, Stuart! Can you imagine what Lily and Eric went through? And Bethany could have prevented that heartache and pain, but she said nothing. She did *nothing*.'

'Can you imagine how scared she was? She had made this pact with Poppy, promised to keep her secret, even though it put her in a terrible situation. But, ultimately, she realised that telling the truth was more important than protecting her friend. I'm proud of her.'

Avril considered his words. And slowly, she began to see it from his perspective. This was not Stuart burying his head in the sand; this was Stuart seeing the best in their daughter. And this was the man whose steadiness had held their family together the first time, when Avril had descended into chaos, a nervous wreck unable to cope.

She loved him, she realised. She always had, it was just that somewhere along the way that love had got buried under layers of other emotions, temporarily suffocating it.

'She still needs to be punished, though,' she told him.

'Yes, but nothing drastic. Grounded for two weeks and an apology to Lily and Eric?'

'Agreed.'

They had made the decision together and Stuart's willingness to talk to her about what had happened meant that she no longer felt alone. Despite Poppy's disappearance and the damage that it had caused, a warmth had spread over her then. She had repaired her relationship with Bethany, and Stuart too. They were a family and that had enabled them to withstand the hurricane of the past few days. They had held firm, together. And she had made a promise to herself then that she would never think of reading her daughter's journal again.

But she couldn't stop thinking about Lily. She had to try and speak to her, even if it was for the last time. If Lily wanted nothing to do with her then so be it. Avril would, eventually, make peace with that. But she couldn't do that until she had at least tried.

She knocked on the door, nerves churning her stomach. And she waited.

But it was Poppy who answered the door, not her mother.

'Hi, Avril.'

'Poppy, it's so good to see you. How are you?'

'Good. How's Bethany?'

'She's fine, thanks, love.' Avril hesitated. 'She misses you.'

'I'll text her soon. I've been busy, looking after Mum.'

Avril frowned. Why would Poppy be looking after Lily? Shouldn't it be the other way around?

'Is your mum in?'

'She's upstairs. Mum!'

Avril stood awkwardly in the hallway, afraid to go any further in case Lily ordered her to leave. When Lily finally emerged, her face was guarded but not hostile.

'Avril, darling.' Lily leaned forward to kiss Avril on both cheeks. When she pulled away Avril noticed how thin she looked, even thinner than usual. And her usually immaculate face was stripped of make-up. She was still beautiful though. She would always be beautiful.

'Lily, I...'

'Coffee?'

'Um, okay, yes, please.'

Avril followed Lily into the kitchen and saw detritus all over the countertop, mixing bowls, spoons, whisks and broken eggs.

'Poppy and I were baking a cake,' Lily said, placing some bowls in the sink.

Avril couldn't imagine Poppy baking with her mother. Everything about this scene felt off but she couldn't put her finger on what it was, what she was missing.

'How are you, Lily? How's Poppy?'

'We're good,' Lily replied, flicking on the coffee machine.

'Lily, I don't know where to start.'

Lily turned then and looked at her, her expression remorseful. 'I'm so sorry, Avril.'

Avril frowned. She hadn't been expecting that. 'You are?'

'Yes. For all those awful things I said about Bethany.'

'I'm sorry too. For the things I said back.'

The two women smiled at each other, and Avril felt the tension seep out of the room.

'Poppy and I have talked a lot over the past few days. Not only do I know that Bethany had nothing to do with her running away, but I also know that she didn't do anything wrong at her old school. Poppy's explained everything. Poor, poor Bethany.'

'Weston Abbey has rescinded the scholarship offer.'

Lily's nostrils flared with indignation, a sign that the old Lily was still there somewhere. 'That's outrageous. I'll smooth this over, I'll call them first thing on Monday.'

'Thanks, Lily but it's okay. Bethany's fine with it. She wants to stay put.'

'But all those art facilities...'

'I know, but she's happy where she is. She has friends and she's settled.'

Lily looked like she was about to argue, but then she said, 'I'm divorcing Eric.'

Avril stared at her, stunned. 'Excuse me?'

'I'm divorcing Eric.'

'Lily, I'm so sorry.'

'Don't be, I'm not.'

'What happened?'

Lily waved a hand dismissively. 'Oh, you know, the usual story. Affairs, lies, deceit. Poppy caught him in flagrante and that was the final straw.'

'Oh my God. I can't believe it. You two always seemed so happy.'

'Yes, well, appearances can be deceptive, can't they.'

'Is that why Poppy ran away?'

'Yes. He was trying to bribe her with expensive gifts, the bastard, but it all got too much for her. So, you see, I tried to blame everyone else, but the problem lay at home all along.'

'None of this is your fault, Lily.'

'Well, I don't know about that, but things are going to be very different from now on.'

Avril's heart broke for Lily. She was putting on a brave face, but Avril knew how much she must be hurting. This was a woman in pain, a woman who had been humiliated. A woman who cared acutely what other people thought and would now have to ignore the gossip and rebuild her life. But Avril also knew that if anyone could do it, it was Lily.

Lily looked at her then, her face creased with concern. 'Are we okay, Avril?'

'We're more than okay. And if there's anything I can do, anything at all, let me know.'

Avril took a sip of her coffee, enjoying the familiarity of being in Lily's kitchen again. There was a way back for them after all, a way to restore their friendship and the life they had built at Westford Park. She would be there for Lily, she could be the support that her friend needed as she navigated the rocky path ahead. Then she had a horrible thought.

'You *are* staying, aren't you? You're not selling the house because of the divorce?'

'Of course I'm staying. Eric will sign the house over to me, don't you worry. He won't give me any trouble with the divorce, and if he does, I have my little dossier.'

Avril frowned. 'What dossier?'

'I've been keeping tabs on him for a while now, just in case. I think I knew, deep down, that I was going to need it at some point, when I was ready. I just wish I'd done something sooner so that Poppy didn't have to go through what she did.'

Avril was aghast. 'How long have you known about this?'

'Years,' Lily admitted. 'Feel free to judge me, I judge myself.'

'I don't judge you, but it must have been so difficult for you to accept.'

'It wasn't, strangely enough. It was easier to brush it all under the carpet and pretend it wasn't happening. But I see now that I handled it all wrong. Never again.' Lily tapped her back pocket. 'And I have my ammunition, if he puts one foot wrong.'

'You wouldn't use it though, would you?'

'Only if he makes me. It's always good to have a little something in your back pocket, darling. For a rainy day.'

'Are you going to be okay, Lily?'

'I'll be fine. I'll get plenty of money in the divorce and I'm going to keep growing my events business. I plan to stand on my own two feet eventually.'

'I'm sure you will sooner than you think. How's Poppy?'

'She's good. We're talking a lot and being honest with each

other. And,' Lily leaned forward conspiratorially, 'she hasn't called me "Mother" once.'

'Wow, you've really turned a corner.'

'I hope so. There's a lot of hurt, a lot of anger. A lot of guilt on my part. But we're working through it. I've nearly lost her twice, I won't lose her again.'

Lily's voice shook and Avril reached out and put a hand over hers.

'Poppy came home. Remember that she came home to you.'

Lily smiled as a single tear dropped. 'She did.' And then she quickly wiped it away and started fussing with the coffee machine. 'Another?'

'Sure, why not. By the way, have you spoken to Sandy?'

'No, not for a while.'

'So, you haven't heard?'

'Heard what?'

'Grant was in a crash. He was driving too fast down a country road and his lorry jackknifed on a bend. He died at the scene.'

Lily spun around to face her. 'Are you serious?'

'Yes. It's been all over the local news.'

'My God. How is she?'

'In shock. I mean, it's awful, of course, but she's free, Lily. She's finally free.'

'Yes, but it also means that Micky's father is dead.'

Avril looked down, guiltily. 'I know. But he wasn't a good man.'

Lily abandoned the coffee and slumped on a bar stool opposite Avril. 'I don't know what to think. Should I be happy? Sad?'

'It's okay to be confused. That's how Sandy feels, I think. But when the dust settles, I hope that it will finally give her the closure she's always craved.'

Avril looked up as Poppy appeared. 'I'm starving, Mum. What's for lunch?'

'I'll make a salad. Avril, will you join us?'

'No thanks, I need to get back.'

Poppy sat down next to Avril. 'Tell Bethany I'll pop over this afternoon.'

Avril saw the tiny pause in Lily's actions, an almost imperceptible hesitation, before she turned with a broad smile. 'What a lovely idea! Send her my love.'

'She's grounded,' Avril warned. 'But you're welcome to go and see her.'

Poppy considered this. 'How long for?'

'She has just over a week left.'

'And after that?'

Avril and Lily looked at each other. 'No going to the woods at night,' Avril said, and Lily nodded her agreement. 'And no boathouse or dens.'

Poppy shrugged. 'It was getting boring anyway. Mum was on about getting a summer house built at the end of the garden for us.'

Lily was already reaching for her phone. 'I'll do some research.'

It all felt so normal, but it was far from it, no matter how hard they tried to pretend it was. Too much had happened and there would be shock waves for a long time to come. Eric was gone. Steve too. Sandy and Micky had to come to terms with what had happened to Grant. The teenagers would have to earn the adults' trust again and that wouldn't happen overnight.

But still, Avril felt hopeful. They had been through the worst and now they were emerging on the other side. They would rebuild together, she decided. Because while Westford Park had brought each of them pain, while it had pushed them to their limits, it had also given them friendship. The Westford Park Ladies Club. No more secrets, no more accusations. Just loyalty and support. Perhaps they could learn a lesson or two from their children on that, she thought with a smile.

Speaking of the children, she needed to get back. She had promised to take Tom shopping for a new football kit and she might see if Bethany wanted to come along because she was bored of being stuck at home. Soon the kids would be back to school and clubs, and Bethany would be un-grounded, so she wanted to spend as much time with them while she could. They may not be the perfect family, but it was everything Avril had ever wanted. The life and the home that they had created here was more than enough.

She stood up, watching Poppy and Lily together in the kitchen, two peas in a pod. Lily sliced a cucumber and gave a stick to her daughter. For a moment she imagined herself walking across the road and finding Stuart waiting for her. Looking at her husband with affection and saying, 'You know, Stuart, moving to Westford Park was the best decision we ever made.'

And him smiling, and replying, 'Bloody right it was.'

33

They walked side by side, the three teenagers, not children any more, not yet adults either. Poppy was in the middle, her long, glossy hair tied back, her make-up perfect despite the rain. To her left was Micky, tall and gangly, his long hair wet against his forehead. On the right was Bethany, huddled under the hood of her raincoat, her wellies squelching in the mud.

Winter had come to Westford Park and the bleak woods mirrored their mood, for the occasion was sombre. As they weaved through the trees, they didn't need to ask each other where they were going because they all knew. It would end where it began.

They reached the den that they had managed to conceal for months, while their unsuspecting parents thought they were cosy in the boathouse. They had ditched the boathouse because it had got too popular with the other teenagers at Westford Park and they wanted to be alone. Anyway, as friendly as Steve was, he was a bit of a creep. He was always hanging around them, trying to impress them with his knowledge of the woods, inviting Poppy over when Jerry was working. So, they had created their own, private hideaway. They rarely came now, but today was ceremonious and they all wanted to go for one last time.

Micky crouched down and fished out a lighter, trying to start a fire on the pile of twigs they'd collected. But they were too damp.

'Dammit,' he said.

'Micky.' Bethany put a hand on his arm. 'Leave it. It's not going to work.'

Instead, they went into the makeshift tepee, sitting down on the logs they'd placed inside to sit on. They huddled together, shivering, but at least it was dry.

Micky reached into his coat and pulled out the bottle of wine he'd swiped from home and Bethany handed out some crisps and chocolate.

'The last supper,' Micky said as he took a deep drink, before passing the bottle on.

'This is so shit,' said Poppy, taking the wine and putting it to her mouth.

'Agreed,' said Bethany, licking salt from her fingers.

Sandy and Clare had sold the house in record time. Apparently properties in Westford Park were in demand, particularly when they were priced sensibly. A family with young children had bought it and they were moving the following day. Micky would finish his A levels at a college in Manchester where he didn't know anyone. After that, he was leaving home for good. He would finally make his own decisions, no longer a slave to other people's.

The three of them had discussed it in great depth. Why Sandy and Clare would want to move house again when the threat of Micky's father was finally gone. When they had sat Micky down to tell him they were selling, they had said it was because they wanted to live in a city again. It was too isolated at Westford Park, they explained. They missed the buzz of city life. They had found a wonderful school for Isla and a great college for Micky. There w a good university too, so Micky could even apply to study there and live at home, if he wanted to. The new house was perfect. This was the final time. Blah, blah, blah.

It was all bullshit.

Micky knew about his father. He'd known for years. His grandmother had told him, sitting next to him on the bench in their garden one sunny afternoon when Sandy was in the hospital having Isla. She had shown him the press cuttings, pointing at a sentence that referred to a boy being abducted.

'That was you,' she'd said.

She had wanted him to know so that he didn't ever try and find his father. So that he knew to raise the alarm if Grant ever tried to contact him. She was afraid for him, and Sandy too, she'd admitted. Then she'd made him promise not to tell his mother.

'She wants to protect you,' she'd told him. 'But you're old enough to know the truth.'

He'd been thirteen at the time.

He was glad that she had told him, though. It explained a lot of things, like why they had moved house every few years. Why his mum always seemed like she was on edge, checking windows and doors over again and pretending that she wasn't. And it had killed any burning desire to find out more about his father. But with it, it had also killed his youth and his innocence. Because he finally knew that he was the son of a monster.

He didn't speak about it to anyone. He kept it all locked away inside and it ate away at him, making him question his family, his mother, himself. And then, when he met Bethany and Poppy at Westford Park, he finally felt safe enough to tell them.

'He's a bastard,' Poppy had spat.

'You're nothing like him,' Bethany had said, her eyes filled with tears.

But, increasingly, Micky had begun to fear that Bethany was

wrong. Dark thoughts consumed him more and more and he worried that one day they would spill out of him. He started getting flashbacks, of being with his dad, eating chips by the sea. A police officer approaching him and taking his hand. Crying because he didn't want to leave his father.

It made him feel guilty, and sad, and disgusting.

When Bethany had heard Micky's story, a few months after they met, she had wanted to throw her arms around him and never let go. She understood him better than anyone because she knew what it was like to feel fear and shame. To believe that you were a bad person, that you had done wrong, even when you hadn't. And by then, she had fallen so deeply in love with Micky that she felt his pain as though it was happening to her. She wanted him to know that she understood. That they were kindred spirits.

So, she told him about what had happened at her old school. About how she had been bullied relentlessly for months by a group of girls but had been too afraid and ashamed to tell anyone. And when they had made up those lies about her to get her into trouble, she had refused to deny it because she didn't think anyone would believe her. The girls had chipped away at her self-esteem and her mother had obliterated it when she had refused to defend her.

'Do you hate your mum?' Micky had asked her curiously.

'I did, but not any more. Do you hate your mum?'

'Sometimes, when she tells me we're moving again. But most of the time, no.'

And then the two of them had looked at Poppy, who had been listening quietly. 'I hate my dad,' she'd said.

Everyone thought Poppy lived a charmed life. Her friends dreamed of a mother like Lily and a father like Eric. They cooed over her new handbag or phone, and said she was so lucky.

But Poppy hadn't felt very lucky when she'd walked in on her father whipping a naked woman tied to a chair in his office, her legs splayed and her face covered by a mask. No, she hadn't felt very lucky at all. She'd felt disgusted and very, very angry.

'How dare he?' she'd raged to Bethany and Micky. 'He makes me sick. And the worst thing about it is that he's getting away with it.'

'Why don't you just tell your mum?' Micky had suggested.

But Poppy couldn't do it. She couldn't break her mother's heart. It had come to her then, an unexpected but compelling thought. She'd take the matter into her own hands.

'I have an idea,' she'd said.

It was hard to believe that a year had passed since that conversation. Poppy still remembered it like it was yesterday. The curiosity on Micky's face and the look of horror on Bethany's. Bethany had been against it from the start. It had caused a huge row between them at Christmas the previous year, when Poppy had accused her of being a wimp. Poppy had hit a nerve and she had felt guilty about it afterwards – until Bethany had proven that she wasn't a wimp by pushing her into the lake on New Year's Eve.

Poppy hadn't hesitated to cover for her friend, insisting she fell in by accident. Part of her wanted to protect Bethany and the other part was too afraid to explain what they had been arguing about and what had made Bethany so furious that she would do such a thing.

In the end, it was Micky who had talked Bethany into it. Micky fancied Poppy, Bethany fancied Micky. It was quite the love triangle. But Poppy had used this to her advantage, knowing that if she got Micky on board, Bethany would follow.

It hadn't been easy. It had taken weeks of persuasion and then even more weeks of careful planning. But Poppy always got what she wanted, in the end.

'We're sticking to the pact, right?' she asked Bethany and Micky now.

'No! Not after what happened.' Bethany was appalled.

'Bethany,' Micky said quietly. 'We have to.'

'But you're leaving.'

'We can still stick to the pact.'

'Micky, how can you say that?'

'We promised, Bethany.'

Poppy smiled with satisfaction.

Bethany wanted to cry.

Micky wondered if there was something fundamentally wrong with him.

But the truth was that they couldn't back out now. Not after what they'd done.

The pact. It was the best-kept secret of all, the one which they'd vowed to keep for the rest of their lives. Till death did they part. It had been simple. Get revenge on the people who had wronged them. One by one, like dominoes, until they all fell.

But part one hadn't gone according to plan. The idea had been to scare Micky's father, to make him think that he was being haunted by his ghosts. Karma for all his previous sins. They'd got the idea from the boathouse when the lights kept flickering on and off.

'Being haunted makes you feel like you're going mad,' Poppy had said. 'You don't know what's real or what's not. It'll totally mess with his head.'

After overhearing that her mother had hired a private detective to investigate Grant, Poppy had logged into Lily's laptop and found the information she needed in an email. Grant worked at a haulage company down the road. She had snuck out and gone there, flirting with the boys on-site, until one of them invited her to wait in the office for him until he finished his shift. And then she had riffled through documents and diaries and discovered what routes Grant drove. She had learned his itinerary for the next month.

It had seemed so easy, a bit of flirting and she had all-hours access to the site where Grant worked. At first, she had left typed notes in his cab. *I know what you've done.* And *I'm watching you.* She knew he'd be too scared to say anything to his colleagues and she always made sure she was out of sight if he was there. Then it was time for phase two and she had practised her route, working out how long it would take to get there. Her arms had been scratched and bloody from pushing her way through the overgrown trees and hedges, but it had been worth it. When the time came, she had snuck out again and waited.

But he hadn't come when expected and it had dragged on, while she hid in some trees by the roadside, hungry and bored. The police had looked all over the country for her, she had gone viral on social media, and the whole time she was hiding a few miles away.

When she realised that she had been gone for too long and that everyone would be worried, she concocted a plan to explain her protracted absence. She would blame it on her father, claiming that she ran away because of him. It meant telling her mother, and Poppy dreaded seeing the look on her face, but it was her best option now. The lesser of two evils.

When the lorry eventually came, she was ready. It was dark and raining, which made the atmosphere even spookier than she had hoped for. And when she had stepped out in front of the lorry, a ghostly figure in the road, she had counted the seconds before she had to jump away.

Except that she didn't need to get out of the way. The lorry had skidded, jackknifed and tipped onto its side. And Poppy had watched, rapt and horrified, before running back into the cover of the trees and crouching down, her breath catching in her throat.

She still thought about it. At night, when she was lying in bed, she pictured the lorry hurtling towards her, then crashing off the road. And it scared her, but it also excited her. To know what she'd done. To know that she, Poppy Sanderson, had rid the world of a bad person who could never hurt anyone again. And no one would ever know it was her.

The thrill of getting away with something like that was addictive and it had made Poppy want to set the next stage of the pact in action as soon as possible. But she had been patient, giving Micky time to come to terms with it. He had been quiet, even angry with her.

'It was an accident,' she had told him. 'I didn't mean for it to happen.'

'I know,' he'd said. 'But it *did* happen. And it was our fault.'

She had been afraid then. She had thought that Micky would crumble and tell someone what had happened. Or that Bethany would lose her nerve. Poppy had meticulously planned her excuses, her denial. But time passed and they remained silent. And Poppy began to relax again.

A thrill ran through her now, as she realised that Micky was still on board with the pact.

And whatever Micky said, Bethany would agree to.

'Micky, you're up next,' she said.

Micky nodded. He had been tasked with getting revenge on the girls from Bethany's old school. He'd already set the wheels in motion, setting up fake social media accounts and following them, waiting for the right moment to engage them in conversation and to trick them into revealing their darkest secrets. As soon as he had them, he'd be exposing them to the world. Soon everyone would know how cruel they really were.

'I'll keep you posted,' he said. 'It'll be harder, with me not being here though.'

'There can be no paper trail,' Poppy warned.

'Agreed.'

Bethany listened in, nauseous. 'I don't want to carry on,' she said, her eyes wide, terrified.

'We have to,' Poppy insisted.

'We *killed* someone, Poppy.'

'No, we didn't. That was an accident.'

'I don't want to,' Bethany insisted.

'Those girls tried to ruin your life, Bethany. They deserve what's coming to them.'

'We've gone too far, can't you see that? We have to stop.'

'*They* didn't stop, Bethany. They kept going until they had destroyed your life.'

Afraid and conflicted, Bethany thought about her mum. She had been trying so hard to show Bethany that she loved and trusted her. That she believed in her. Bethany didn't want to let her down. And she didn't want to be a bully either. If they did this, then she was no better than those girls, was she? But then she looked at Poppy, her best friend, and Micky, the boy she loved. Perhaps if she was brave, like Poppy, Micky would see her differently and realise that she was the one he wanted after all. She couldn't compete with Poppy's beauty, so she had to find another route to Micky's heart. Another way to prove to him that they were soulmates. Then she thought about the girls who had ruined her life for their own, vile pleasure. And as anger began to grow inside her again, so did the need for vengeance.

She looked at Micky. 'Okay. But make sure no one gets hurt. Do you promise?'

He nodded. 'I promise, Bethany.'

After this, it would be her turn next. Poppy had set the wheels in motion for her revenge on her father, but she wasn't done yet.

She had other plans. And Bethany would be in charge of carrying them out. An eye for an eye, a tooth for a tooth.

Micky reached out and took her hand, and Bethany felt a thrill run through her. One day soon she would tell him how she felt. And then she just had to pray that he finally saw her for who she was and forgot all about his silly crush on Poppy. Poppy and Micky were not well suited, anyone could see that. But her and Micky? They would be perfect together.

'Remember, Bethany, we only go after people who deserve it,' he said.

Bethany smiled weakly. 'Like Robin Hood, you mean?'

Micky nodded encouragingly. 'Kind of, yeah. It's for the greater good.'

Bethany nodded. Then she picked up a stick and started writing a word in the ground.

'LIVE'.

The motto had been her idea and she had flushed with pride when Micky had understood and told her how clever it was. And so it had become a symbol of their pact and of their friendship. They had brought each other back to life, helped one another to heal. But they hadn't forgotten their past and now they were serving their own justice on the bullies and the liars who thought they had got away with it. They were destroying evil, one by one.

The three teenagers looked at the ground now and clasped their hands together. Life as they had once known it would never be the same again. Their innocence was long gone. Micky was leaving and the dynamic between Poppy and Bethany would be different without him there. But the bond, and the pact, that they had made at Westford Park would remain. They were soulmates now, bound together by what they'd done. What they still had left to do.

'Remember, we're going to apply to the same university,' Poppy said. 'We'll be together again, just like the three musketeers. And God help anyone who gets in our way.'

They were quiet then, lost in their own worlds. Poppy thought about all the things they would get up to when they were reunited at university. Bethany thought about being with Micky again and imagined them finally getting together. And Micky's lips moved silently as he read the motto backwards over and over again in his head until it no longer made sense, it was just a jumble of letters and sounds all merged into one. *Evil, Evil, Evil.*

EPILOGUE

Clare wrapped her arms around her shivering body as she looked at the fallen leaves floating on the surface of the swimming pool. She had stood in the same spot on the day that they first moved to Westford Park, when the sun's rays had reflected off the glistening water. It had felt like they were bouncing directly into her heart, filling her with hope and happiness.

With a final glance, she turned and walked away.

That first summer at Westford Park felt like another lifetime ago. How innocent she'd been. How blissfully naive. She had known all along that Westford Park was selling them a fantasy, but she had gone along with it because she, like everyone else, had been seduced by the idea of the perfect home. The ideal community. But such a concept didn't exist because the reality was that bad things could happen anywhere.

What Clare hadn't understood then was the scale of just how bad things could get.

Perhaps it would never have come to this if Lily hadn't discovered where Grant worked. Maybe they could have brushed every thing else that happened under the carpet. Or maybe not. Clare would never know so there was little point in dwelling on it.

But she did know one thing. Watching Sandy fall apart was one of the worst things she had ever been through. Lying awake at night wondering if Grant really was messing with them was hell. And the more Sandy withdrew into herself, the angrier Clare got. Her rage became attached to Westford Park, wrapping itself tightly around the foundations of their home and the trees in the woods, until it was tightly intertwined. Until all Clare felt when she went jogging or took Isla for a swim was fear, fury and resentment.

Clare had not liked feeling this way. It was new to her and it had unsettled her deeply. She wanted to see the joy in life, she wanted the sun to shine again. But the darkness had succeeded in one thing. It had finally helped her to understand what it was like for Sandy.

It was a punch in the gut, to get a small taste of the burden that Sandy had carried around with her for all these years. That's when Clare had realised that if she was going to find her way back to the light, then she had to work out how to bring Sandy with her.

Oddly enough, it was Lily who had given Clare the idea. If Lily could find a private detective, Clare had thought, then so could she. And if Sandy could keep a secret like that from her, even if only for a short while, then Clare could do the same. It was for the greater good, after all. So, Clare had done some research and found a woman who, when she heard Clare's story and the reason why she wanted to track Grant's movements, told her she'd not only take the case but that she'd do it for a reduced fee.

She had turned out to be extremely efficient. Within a few weeks, she had sent Clare photographs of Grant entering the grounds of Westford Park on two occasions, via the woods. He was wearing a hoodie and in one photo, his gloved hand could be seen clutching a knife. Clare had looked at the photographs, her heart racing and her blood boiling, and she had never known such hatred.

And so, Clare found herself descending further into the bleak darkness. How dare this man terrorise her beautiful, fragile wife after all that he had already done to her? And what were his intentions? Did he mean only to frighten her or was he planning to go further? What if he tried to harm her or take Micky? What if he tried to hurt Isla?

He had to be stopped. Clare had never been so certain of anything in her life. The easiest thing would be to contact the police and present her evidence. It was irrefutable proof that Grant had breached his restraining order. But what then? He'd be arrested and maybe he'd go back to prison, but he'd be released again at some point. It would never stop.

No, Clare had decided. She would have to take matters into her own hands.

The detective had told her something else too. It seemed that Grant was a creature of habit. He liked to go to the same motorway services and truckers' cafés on every lorry journey he took, one of which was only a few miles away from Westford Park on a quiet country road. He always stopped by for a flirt with the waitress on the way home.

Clare had considered her options and had come up with a plan. Once she had decided, there was no going back. That was what love did to you, it made you a tiger, fiercely protective of your family. And Clare was willing to do whatever it took to keep her safe. Sandy needed her, she relied on her. Clare would not let her down.

She told Sandy she was going to a work conference. But instead, she went to the truckers' café and waited for Grant. She knew what to do. Her father had been a mechanic and he had taught her a few things over the years, promising her that they come in handy when she was older. She hadn't believed him; she'd wanted to be out with her friends rather than hanging around in his cold, stinky garage. But it turned out that her old dad was right after all. Because when Grant eventually pulled into the car park, Clare had immediately taken advantage of him being distracted by the waitress so that she could tamper with his brakes.

And that's why Grant's lorry had failed to stop on the wet, deserted road.

She didn't regret her actions. She had done what she needed to do. Sandy was safe, she never had to worry again. When Clare had seen the relief on Sandy's face after she learned that Grant was dead, she knew that, whatever happened next, it was worth it.

For days she had waited for the police to come. Her alibi was flimsy; she could have been seen, or the private detective might watch the news and put two and two together. Clare had mentally prepared herself for the knock on the door. She would admit to it straight away, there was no point in lying. She was willing to go to prison to free Sandy from the burden that had weighed her down for most of her adult life. She had planted the seed in Sandy's mind about moving to Manchester so that she could take Micky and Isla away from all the trouble and go to a new place, where no one knew their story. Knowing that they were safe, and happy, far away from here, would keep Clare strong while she was in a prison cell.

But the police didn't come. The accident was put down to a speeding lorry driver with traces of alcohol in his system and a wet, slippery road. Possibly a deer trapped in the headlights that caused him to swerve. A lorry with a sketchy service history.

And, slowly, Clare began to hope.

But they still had to leave. Westford Park was tainted and although Clare would never forget what she had done, she hoped the distance would blur her memories until, eventually, they became lost in the darkness as she moved back into the light. This time was for good. There would be no more looking over their shoulders, no more worrying. They would finally put roots down and they would rebuild, better and stronger. They would be happy.

Clare knew she should go back to the house to help Sandy finish packing, but instead, she turned down the lake path, walking past the locked boathouse and into the woods. She needed a few moments alone, to say goodbye to Westford Park. To tell the ghosts that they couldn't haunt her any more and they couldn't haunt Sandy either.

The driving rain was sneaking in through the trees, soaking her hat and her coat, and she shivered but she kept walking, on and on. A noise startled her, and she stopped dead, listening keenly as her eyes scanned the trees. She spotted three figures in the distance and relaxed. It was just Micky and his friends. They were walking with their heads down. They were probably saying goodbye, Clare thought, with a pang of regret. Micky was furious that they were leaving but he'd get over it. Eventually. When he got to Manchester and realised how fabulous it was, he'd forget all about Bethany and Poppy and Westford Park. Micky had his whole life ahead of him, he'd make new friends, find a girlfriend, finish his A levels.

Then he'd go off to university and Sandy would be upset to see him go but she could wave him off without being consumed by dread, because she didn't have to worry about his safety any more. Grant was gone and so, too, was the threat to Micky.

He must have sensed her presence because suddenly Micky stopped and looked directly at her. His head was covered by a hoodie and his face was unreadable but for a moment Clare's breath caught in her throat because she'd seen that look before. She'd seen it in the photographs the private detective had shown her, and it sent chills up her spine.

'Grant,' she whispered.

But then the moment passed and Clare found herself looking

into the kind, good-natured eyes of her stepson again. It had been a trick of the mind, nothing more. She lifted a hand to wave at him and he waved back. And then he hurried off to catch up with the girls.

Clare felt a thrill run through her as the realisation settled in that they were finally free. This time tomorrow they would be on their way to Manchester, heading towards a new and better life. In a moment of childish excitement, she stretched her arms out wide and started turning around in circles, her face angled up towards the rain, laughing in exhilaration about it all. What she had done. How she had, against all the odds, got away with it. What exciting things their future held. She turned and turned until she was dizzy.

'Goodbye, Westford Park,' she shouted. 'And good-bloody-riddance.'

And then, with a light head and an even lighter heart, she walked away.

ACKNOWLEDGEMENTS

I've walked alongside Avril, Sandy and Lily for so long now that sometimes I forget that they're not my actual friends. What always helps me to remember is the unwavering support of my 'real-life' friends, who have been by my side throughout my journey. Whether it's helping with the children so I can get some writing done, getting excited about my books, or assisting me with plot conundrums over a glass of wine, I'm incredibly grateful to you all.

I'm also grateful to my publisher, Boldwood Books, and the amazing team who are just brimming with enthusiasm, ideas and support. Thank you to my editor, Isobel Akenhead, for loving Avril, Sandy and Lily as much as I do, and for all your input which helped to make this book what it is. I cherish our meet-ups and I'm looking forward to overdosing on coffee with you again soon. Huge thanks also to the marketing, editing and production teams for the immense amount of work you put into every single book as it goes out into the world. It is an honour to be part of Team Boldwood and I am so excited to be working with you.

As always, a big shout-out to my family, Jon, Rose and Alice. Girls, I know you wanted me to include a magic cat in my next book, but I just felt that it might be pushing the boundaries of a psychological thriller that bit too far. I did put in a couple of tigers for you, though.

And finally, thank *you*, my readers. I hope you enjoyed visiting Westford Park as much as I did. Your support, as always, means the world.

ABOUT THE AUTHOR

Natasha Boydell writes internationally bestselling psychologica suspense stories. Her debut, The Missing Husband, was ar Amazon Kindle UK top 100 bestseller in 2021. She previously worked as a journalist and in communications in the charity and education sectors before pursuing her lifelong dream of writing novels. She lives in North London, with her husband, two daugh ters and two rescue cats.

Sign up to Natasha Boydell's mailing list for news, competition and updates on future books.

Follow Natasha on social media:

facebook.com/NatashaBoydellAuthor

x.com/tashboydell

bookbub.com/authors/natasha-boydell

instagram.com/tashy_boydell

tiktok.com/@natasha_boydell

ALSO BY NATASHA BOYDELL

The Fortune Teller

The Perfect Home

THE

Murder

LIST

THE MURDER LIST IS A NEWSLETTER DEDICATED TO SPINE-CHILLING FICTION AND GRIPPING PAGE-TURNERS!

SIGN UP TO MAKE SURE YOU'RE ON OUR HIT LIST FOR EXCLUSIVE DEALS, AUTHOR CONTENT, AND COMPETITIONS.

SIGN UP TO OUR NEWSLETTER

BIT.LY/THEMURDERLISTNEWS

Boldwœd

Boldwood Books is an award-winning fiction publishing company seeking out the best stories from around the world.

Find out more at www.boldwoodbooks.com

Join our reader community for brilliant books, competitions and offers!

Follow us

@BoldwoodBooks

@TheBoldBookClub

Sign up to our weekly deals newsletter

https://bit.ly/BoldwoodBNewsletter

Printed in Great Britain
by Amazon

46106967R00195